Knight of Rome Part II

By

Malcolm Davies

Following events described in "Knight of Rome Part I" friends and comrades, the Suevi warrior Otto, now called Otto Longius, and Tribune Lucius Taurius Longius, (nicknamed "Boxer") have been summoned from their legion camp on the Rhine to an audience with Emperor Augustus. Impressed by Otto's act of courage in saving his commander's life in battle, the Emperor grants Otto Roman Citizenship and promotes him to the Equestrian Order. At the same time, recognising the personal loyalty shown by Lucius, Augustus politically rehabilitates his family and makes him a generous gift of gold. The Emperor ends the audience and they are escorted from his presence leaving them still in Rome under the care of Praetorian Tribune Cassius Plancus.

Chapter 1

It was two in the afternoon when they stood in the street with the doors of Augustus' palace closed behind them. Lucius and Otto wrapped their arms around each other and danced on the spot. When they stood apart, gasping, Cassius said it had looked like a blond bear was crushing Lucius to death and that he for one, was glad the spectacle was over. There was an awkward pause. Neither Lucius nor Otto quite knew what to do next. Cassius took control; he stepped in between them and linked both their arms.

"Banks. Merchants. No time for idleness! Sound just like Augustus, don't I?" he said, guiding them down the Palatine Hill. "Congratulations by the way. No idea how you managed it but you seem to have really impressed him. Bit of advice, Boxer, in general, it doesn't do to tell an emperor he's got the wrong end of the stick. And Otto, never say death before dishonour because on another day, he would have taken you at your word. First thing, let's get you to a public bank and deposit your money."

"I have no money," Otto told him. "They gave Boxer a purse of gold, they just handed me a piece of paper."

"That is your money, Otto old boy; it's a draft on the Imperial Treasury for what the Emperor promised. We pay it into the bank, the banker gives you his draft and you can use that to pay for your new estate." Otto looked at the small sheet of best Egyptian paper with its wax seals. "Think about it. Could you walk around with one hundred and five thousand denarii in your purse? You'd need a couple of mules with saddle bags to hold it all. And how long do you think you'd last before someone stole the lot? No, the paper system works well; provided you use a public bank, not a private one."

Otto's "money" was paid in and he received a banker's draft for the amount less one thousand denarii he took in cash. The banker suggested he keep the draft in his strongbox.

"If you were robbed and it was taken, all your money would be gone exactly as if it had been in gold. I will give you a receipt. If you show it to me or my senior clerk, you can retrieve your draft at any time," he advised.

Otto looked at Cassius who nodded and so the business was completed.

"Congratulations, sir, on winning such favour of the Emperor," the banker told him as they left.

It was still only mid-afternoon.

"Let's go back to the tailors and get you your tunics," Lucius suggested to Otto who looked at him blankly. "You are a member of the Equites, a knight. You must now wear a narrow-striped tunic. It is expected."

Otto looked again at Cassius who had become his accepted expert on all matters pertaining to wealth and rank. Cassius nodded. Otto handed him his purse bulging with silver.

"Can you arrange a banquet?" he asked. "I must feast the officers to celebrate my good fortune...and wine for the soldiers, all the soldiers!"

"I most certainly shall, Otto. I'll do you proud," he said feeling the weight of the purse.

They went to the same tailor again but before Lucius could say anything, Otto spoke.

"Good man, we are not Praetorians although our friend who was with us the other day is. He advised us to wear their white togas for our protection in the city. I want two narrow-striped tunics in the pattern worn by Roman Knights," he gestured to Lucius, "my other friend here will pay the correct price for them and for the clothes we have already bought from you. Do not cheat us."

Lucius glared at Otto. The tailor went pale and then beamed with delight.

"Sir, I thank you from the bottom of my heart. I have your measurements, one hour is all I need but, sir there may be a problem.... "

Lucius anticipated him. "The Emperor has just enrolled the noble Otto Longius who stands before you, in the Order of Equites. You may proceed."

Otto then insisted they paid the bootmaker who still looked terrified and looked at the coins Lucius had placed in his hands as if it they represented some sort of entrapment. Next, the jewellers that

Cassius had recommended A swarthy, black bearded man wearing robes and a skullcap from which two curled strands of hair tumbled on either side of his face, led them into his workshop and showroom past two guards with cudgels thrust through their thick leather belts.

"Cassius Plancus gave us your name," Lucius said.

The jeweller's face fell.

"We will pay a fair price," Otto told him

"Ah, who is to say what is fair?"

"What we agree." Otto replied simply. "I want to buy a gold ring, for me."

"Let me see your hand," the jeweller said and took Otto's massive left paw in his own. "For a ring is no problem. It must be tight enough to stay on but not so tight you can't take it off. Here try this one."

"Too tight," Otto told him.

He was fitted at the next attempt and gazed down complacently at the thick gold band.

"What is your name, sir?

"Otto Longius."

"I'll have it inscribed O and L on the inside, no extra charge."

Lucius showed him the marble finger. "Can you put a mounting on this so it can be worn around the neck on a thong?"

"When did you take that, Boxer?" Otto asked.

"When you weren't looking."

"What is it? Religious?" the jeweller asked with a hint of distaste.

"No," Otto told him," it's just a beautiful thing, look at the tiny details and the nail. It is a wonder."

"Come back tomorrow. We'll settle up when everything's finished."

"How do you know we'll pay up?" Lucius laughed.

"Look at your friend. This little piece of stone is a treasure worth more to him than anything else in my shop. He trusts me with it tonight so I trust him. About you, I'm not so sure."

At eight-thirty Cassius escorted Otto into the officers' mess. He was self-consciously wearing the formal tunic of his new rank for the first time. The guests thumped rhythmically on the long wooden table with their dagger hilts as he was led to the place of honour. The table had been laid with plates and trenchers of bread. Wine flasks and cups were ready and waiting. But before he could sit down, Cassius clapped his hands. The doors to the kitchen were flung back and six stewards marched in, carrying an enormous tray on their shoulders. They processed once around the cheering table. On the tray was a full-grown sow, roasted and glazed, supported on a rack. Space was made so the stewards could put their burden down in the middle. A sword as pushed into Otto's hand.

"Go and slice its belly, open," Cassius instructed.

"Trojan Pig! Trojan Pig!" everyone chanted.

The bemused Otto took a firm grip on the sword and made a long cut beneath the sow's flank. Once the crisp skin had been sliced through, it burst open; coils of steaming sausage, slithered out like entrails followed by roasted vegetables and birds. Otto was astonished then his face clouded over as the sight recalled Quadratus' disembowelled horse screaming as its rider was thrown.

"Enough sausage for you?" Lucius shouted.

That brought Otto back to the present. He forced a smile and waved his sword in acknowledgement. The serious business of feasting began. At ten-thirty, Otto requested that the substantial remains of the Trojan Pig be sent over to the men's canteen, which was greeted by more cheers. Desserts and cheeses took its place and the serious drinking began.

The next morning, Otto lounged beside Cassius in the hot room of the bathhouse. He had felt better. Cassius seemed as fresh as if he had gone to bed early the night before after a frugal supper washed down with fruit juice.

"Remind me to return what's left of your money, old thing," Cassius said.

"Didn't you spend it all?"

"Actually no, not a lot."

"You did pay properly?" Otto accused.

Cassius sighed. "This is the Praetorian Barracks; we have a staff of excellent cooks and a well-stocked kitchen. Most of us would all have been dining in the mess last night, feast or no feast so all you've had to pay for is the pig, more sausages and extra wine. So, please don't expose me to your conscience yet again; the world will still be unjust. Because you're now a knight, you get a seat in the front row at the circus; is that fair on the paying public? Anyway, look at poor old Boxer."

He was lying flat on the bench with his mouth open, dead to the world.

"People who fall asleep in the hot room don't always wake up. Come on.…"

They half-carried Lucius, who was complaining about his headache. Cassius tipped him into the cold plunge. He went right under and came up thrashing and shouting vile threats. He was a different man after drinking several cups of cold water and a massage.

As the jeweller had predicted, they did return to his shop. The end of the marble finger was covered by a gold dome from which a ring projected. Otto turned it over in his hands.

"It's perfect, such skill, thank you. Now we must pay."

Lucius handed over the price demanded without haggling; a thing outside of the jeweller's experience. Otto insisted on buying gifts for Lucius' family.

"Something for the sister, mother and grandmother of my friend," he said.

"Is the sister married?"

"No."

"Is the grandmother a widow?"

"Yes."

"In that case, I've got just the thing for each of them. And I'll throw in presentation boxes, can't say fairer than that."

The next morning, they left Rome. Cassius Plancus was a little depressed to see them go.

As he told his parents, "They were originals, the pair of them. They achieved more with their simple decency than most courtiers will ever do, no matter how they deviously they plot and plan. Ah, well, good luck to you Otto and Boxer."

Their welcome in Luca was ecstatic; not least because it was unexpected. The family had not known of their summons to Rome. Otto gave his presents to the ladies, repeating in his own words the jeweller's comments as they opened the small boxes.

"As you are unmarried, Poppaea, moonstones are a symbol of your purity," he told her, blushing scarlet as she held up the pendant earrings he had bought for her. Sabina had a delicate bracelet studded with cornelians, "To bring colour to the lady of the house." Finally, Aelia had a necklace with a large amber pendant. "To warm your heart, most noble lady Aelia,".

"And I have a gift for you, father," Lucius said and handed him the letter exonerating their family, signed and sealed by the Emperor.

Vitius took it and read it. "You will excuse me," he said and walked into his study. He returned half an hour later, his eyes red with the tears of joy he had been ashamed to shed in front of his family. "What honour the Emperor does us. But how did this come about?"

When Lucius explained, it was Aelia's turn to weep.

"What a man your father was to bear the burden of that catastrophe and tell no-one, not even me," she said.

"But surely, he should have explained, you were his wife after all…" Sabina suggested.

Aelia shook her head. "You know nothing of those times. A wrong word carelessly spoken could result in far worse than exile to a modestly prosperous life in a pleasant city. His silence protected me and your husband when he was a little boy."

For most of the two days of their stay, they ate, slept and talked; going over every detail of their time in Rome. The last afternoon was spent in discussing what Otto should do with his new wealth.

"Noble, sir," Otto told Vitius, "I know nothing of buying an estate nor how to run one. Will you act for me?"

"This is a grave responsibility, Otto but I will guide you as best I can."

They went into every last detail of what was practical, Vitius making notes. Finally, Pinerus was called in to write out three copies of a simple contract dictated by Vitius.

"The Equestrian Otto Longius appoints Vitius Lucius Longius to act as his agent in obtaining a land holding on his behalf. Vitius Lucius Longius will give Otto Longius the fullest description of the proposed estate before the purchase becomes legally binding. Otto Longius entrusts the sum of one hundred and four thousand denarii to Vitius Lucius Longius to be expended solely on said purchase. If an acceptable property is available at a lower price, the balance of the one hundred and four thousand denarii reverts to the account of Otto Longius. No commissions will be charged."

Both signed each document and Pinerus, as a freed man witnessed the agreement.

"I shall deposit your draft in the public bank tomorrow and leave a copy of our contract at the temple of Ceres; She will approve and bless this business."

Otto had some time alone with Aelia. She came into his room in the early evening, graceful as ever.

"Well, sir, you are enrolled in the Order of Equites and a great man now," she began with a smile.

"Oh, my lady Aelia, how can you call me "sir"? You taught me to read and opened a wider world to me. I owe you more than I can repay."

"But you had the intelligence and desire to take the opportunity I offered. The credit is yours, my dear Otto. What next for you, I wonder?"

"Owning land I suppose but it troubles me and that is your fault."

"Why is that?"

"To work it, I must have slaves. I think of Zeno's words and I do not want to "look down into the pit".

She sighed. "Philosophers describe the world and people as they should be but we have to live with things as they are. Be aware of how we should all ideally behave and act justly. That is all you can do."

Otto smiled. "Always so wise, my lady."

"I do not think so," she replied.

"That is because Romans do not value women's intelligence, especially older and experienced women. My people listen to and appreciate them."

"Your people Otto?" Aelia queried. "Are you not a Roman now? Read widely, think deeply and perhaps you will be able to answer that question in time."

Day after day they rode north, first along paved roads and then over dusty tracks. They did not cover the ground at the furious rate they had ridden on their way to Rome but neither did they dawdle. They trotted through the gate of their legion camp in the last week of August.

Standing to attention in front of their legate's desk, Otto handed over the documents he had received from the hands of the Emperor.

Quadratus read them with increasing delight breaking out over his usually austere face. He stood up and shook hands with Otto.

"I welcome you as one of my officers with all my heart. Our Emperor has been gracious to you but no more than you deserve. Boxer, did the audience with Augustus go well for you?"

"Beyond my greatest hopes, sir. Tribune Fuscus used his connections in Rome to discover that my family were never directly allied to Marcus Antonius. The Emperor accepted that he had been misinformed and issued this letter to me. Only a copy sir, my father has the original, but it is to be made public in Rome."

Quadratus read it and looked at Lucius with a shrewd expression.

"This letter changes everything for you, Boxer; perhaps as great a prize as our Otto has won. It seems we have much to digest and discuss. For now, go bathe and refresh yourselves. Officers' conference in three hours." As they turned to leave, he called after them. "Otto, if you have a striped tunic wear it; let the men see your new status."

At the appointed time, Otto and Lucius marched up the Via Praetoria and stopped dead when they saw the legate standing outside the Praetorium beside Titus Attius and an aquilifer holding aloft the legion eagle.

"Otto Longius," Titus called out, loud enough for half the camp to hear him, "I call on you to take the sacred military oath under the eagle and in the presence of your legate. Stand forward and swear before the gods."

Once the oath was administered, Attius handed Otto his identification disc inscribed with his name and legion number.

Quadratus lead them inside the office. The clerks had been told to go elsewhere and a table had been set with the best food the legion could come up with at short notice and flagons of the legate's own wine.

"Otto, you have frequently stood by the door listening to discussions when you had no business to be in the room. Now I invite you to sit at table with your brother officers as is your right.

Tertius Fuscus, Aldermar, Rufus Soranus and Cestus Valens, for once in a spotless uniform, were already seated. They raised their wine cups and said "Hear! Hear!" in unison.

"Firstly, let us get our business out of the way," Quadratus began. "Otto is appointed a decurion of cavalry by our Emperor himself. He holds that rank as of the minute he took his soldier's oath under the eagle. The pay is fifteen hundred denarii per annum less deductions. However," he paused, "although far be it from me to deny the will of the Emperor, there has to be a process of training and induction to be supervised by Prefect Aldermar before the new decurion is ready for command. Otto, is that acceptable to you?"

"Yes, sir."

"Good; now, Aldermar, everyone present knows in what high esteem I hold our cavalry but there is a problem. It is one of language. I tell you frankly that those of your men who believe they speak Latin are largely deluded. We rely on you, our prefect, to relay any complex operational commands and interpret vital intelligence the cavalry may have discovered. Therefore, I propose to appoint Otto Longius as Principal Decurion. His Latin is now fluent and that may be of tactical importance. Effectively he will act as your second in command once you can confirm that he is fully trained. Your thoughts would be appreciated."

They all looked at Aldermar who sat in silence for while, considering the legate's words.

"Sir, it would be of great assistance to me to have a reliable deputy and I take your point in respect of the language but a lot depends on how Otto responds to the demands that will be made on him. May I tell you on the first day of September of next year at the latest whether or not I believe your suggestion is in the best interests of the legion?"

"Eminently reasonable; now you two, tell us what you got up to in Rome."

Lucius thanked Tertius profusely for the family information he had given him.

"I repeated it to the Emperor," he said, noticing a sudden shadow fall over Tertius face, "but I made no mention of your name or any hint of how I came by it."

Tertius smiled and said that thanks were unnecessary.

Otto was cajoled into standing up and performing his formal address to Augustus. They laughed until the tears filled their eyes.

"It wasn't that funny," Otto complained as he sat down.

"Friend Otto, it truly was," Titus told him.

"I paid a tutor good money to learn that off him."

"You should have asked him for your money back before you left Rome."

"That's what the Emperor said," Otto replied to a further burst of guffaws.

"I was given a purse out of which I am charged to pay for Otto's equipment and a horse," Lucius told everyone.

"But Boxer, I have a horse," Otto said.

"Yes, and a good horse too," Aldermar responded. "But you need a warhorse; a stallion strong enough to carry your armoured weight all day long and trained to use his teeth and hooves to defend himself and his rider. We'll look for one together and have a word with Uncle Martellus as well…"

The party went on for three hours in good spirits and comradeship. As they were all leaving, Quadratus looked at Otto and Lucius with a sigh.

"Do not think, you two, that Augustus will say to himself, "Well, they were a couple of fine young fellows," and then forget you. He will not. You have been favoured by the Emperor's regard; he knows your ranks, your legion and where you serve. Be aware of this for the rest of your careers and make sure you are worthy of the interest he has shown in you."

The next morning, they returned to garrison duty.

Otto reported to Aldermar to begin his training.

"You'll have to do something with your hair," Aldermar told him. "Your head is shaven on one side and long on the other. No helmet is going to sit straight and stay on that. Your choice, decurion, either cut it short like a Roman or grow it long on both sides.

The cavalrymen preferred mail shirts to the new armour. They needed flexibility in the saddle and arm protection. However, Lucius was honour-bound to equip Otto, so they settled on a parade set of lorica segmentata fabricated in mild steel chased in silver with a helmet to match. Felix was overjoyed at having something new to polish to perfection, especially since the armour was for dress purposes and unlikely to be dented or scratched. The horse proved more problematical. Aldermar and Martellus put the word about and soon every day brought a hopeful trader to the gate with yet another possible mount that was invariably rejected. The horses were too old, too young, too small, too heavy and sometimes ridiculously unsuitable.

Aldermar had harsh words for one of the hopeful sellers of horse flesh when he appeared with a mare.

"What do you not understand?" Aldermar shouted one day, annoyed at being called away to inspect the animal. "Is that a stallion?"

"No sir, but I assure you she has a very bad temper; she kicks and bites all the time…"

One morning he was called to the gate to look over yet another possibility. A slender, dark-haired man wearing a full-length, hooded robe stood with his arms folded in in front of two grooms each of them holding one rein attached to the headstall of a black horse. The man unfolded his arms and bowed.

"I am Rashid," he said and then gestured to one of his men who flicked the blanket off the horse's back.

What was revealed nearly took Aldermar's breath away. The stallion was tall and deep-chested with a long body. Its muscular hindquarters tapered to firm thighs and strong legs. The arched neck thickened as it flowed down into the chest. The head was well-proportioned with generous, alert ears and large, liquid eyes which gazed back at Aldermar with an expression of curiosity, its mane and tail were full and long. Aldermar walked around him searching for some flaw but there was none.

"Please wait," he said and sent for Otto and Martellus.

Martellus took a long time to survey the animal. When he had done, he said nothing but simply nodded at Aldermar. Otto put one hand under the horse's muzzle and spoke to it softly letting his breath blow into its nostrils which opened and closed as it snuffed his scent. He nodded his handsome head and pricked his ears forward as if to hear this strange man's voice better.

"Let us see him move," Martellus demanded,

At a nod from Rashid, one of the grooms led the great horse into a walk and then a trot. The stallion stepped high and arched his neck, dancing over the packed earth.

"What do you think of him, Otto?"

"I think we should send for Lucius; he has the Emperor's purse."

"His price is five pieces of gold," Rashid told Lucius.

"Oh, no, far too much; I can buy a good horse in Luca for one gold piece, a racehorse for two…"

Rashid smiled and bowed. "He is almost four years old and of the race of the heavy, tall horses of these northern lands but mixed with the blood of Spain and Africa to give him fire. We are a long way from Luca, young sir and he is more than a mere racehorse, a rich man's toy. You have heard his price."

Lucius looked at Aldermar for guidance but his face was deliberately expressionless. Martellus seemed to be silently urging him on. Otto was looking at the horse as if he had found a long-lost friend.

Lucius counted out the five coins. Rashid tested each of them before they vanished into one of his pockets.

"Who will be his rider?" he asked. Otto indicated that he would. "If he loves you, he will carry you until his heart bursts. Treat him like the noble creature God has made him."

"Does he have a name?" Otto said.

"He is called "Djinn". It means a spirit of the wild places."

Djinn's back and girth were measured and a fine saddle made for him. Lucius regarded the commission given him by Augustus as completed. He deposited the remainder of the gold coins in the legion bank.

At the end of September, the lucky few legionaries chosen for leave and some of the officers left in a body. Quadratus reduced the number of soldiers permitted to return to their homes by half as compared with last year. Titus Attius said going anywhere was pointless in his case as he had no family and nowhere to stay. Cestus Valens now had sufficient faith in Lucius to leave his precious artillery pieces in his care. Rufus Soranus rode out but Quadratus elected to stay over winter. Tertius Fuscus also took leave, on the legate's insistence. The reduced garrison settled down to the hard labour of preparing for the cold and snow soon to come.

In the middle of October, Otto and Lucius were called into the legate's outer office.

"A package for each of you, from Rome," he told them and pointed at two wrapped boxes on one of the clerk's desks.

He was far too well-mannered to show any curiosity but it was obvious he wanted to know what they contained.

"May I open it here, sir?" Lucius asked innocently.

Quadratus waved a hand airily as if to say it made no difference to him. Lucius tore the cloth cover away. Inside was a polished box in which twenty scrolls in individual tubes were lined up. There was also a letter.

"*To the Noble Tribune Lucius Taurius Longius, Greetings,*

I am instructed to send you the enclosed books. We are advised that they are the best works available on the subject of military engineering.

The Emperor requires you to study them assiduously. When you are confident that you have thoroughly grasped the knowledge they have to impart, you are to write to me so that I may inform the Emperor that you have carried out his wishes.

Menities."

Lucius passed the letter to Quadratus who read it and whistled.

"It appears Augustus has plans for you, Boxer. I told you he forgets nothing and no-one, did I not?"

"You did, sir. I wonder what he has in mind?"

"No point worrying about it. Time will reveal all. You now have something to occupy your mind on these long, dark evenings to come. Might be best to send a brief note to Menities to acknowledge receipt."

Otto opened his package. It was also a polished wooden box but filled with straw. He lifted off the top layer. Forty perfect figs nestled in the remaining packaging like eggs in a nest. There was a note.

"To My Loyal Equestrian Otto Longius who had never seen a fig, Greetings.

Fruits from my orchard. Share them with your comrades. Eat too many at your peril.

Augustus Imp."

Lucius and Quadratus read the note while Otto picked up one of the purple fruits and sniffed it. It smelled a little like honey. Lucius showed him how to peel the skin back with his fingernails and suck up the rich pulp inside.

"It's good," he said. "Here, take one Boxer, and you sir," he offered.

Two figs each later, Quadratus suggested that was enough for one day.

"Augustus wasn't joking when he warned you to go steadily with them. If you overindulge, you'll spend the night in the latrines."

Otto thought he should write a thankyou letter but hesitated to take anyone's advice. Paying for public speaking lessons before his audience in Rome had resulted in farce. No, he would write respectfully in his own words.

"To Emperor Augustus, Greetings.

Thank you for the box of figs. They are very sweet and good. I am eating only two every other day on the advice of Legate Quadratus. I have shared some of them, as you told me.

Tribune Lucius Taurius Longius has bought me a warhorse, a saddle and bridle with the money you gave him for the purpose.

Prefect Aldermar and Farrier Martellus both say they have never seen a finer stallion. He is black and called "Djinn" which means something like "wild spirit" in an Eastern language unknown to me.

I have now taken the soldier's oath and am being trained in the duties of a cavalry decurion.

I am very grateful for the goodness you have shown me sir. I shall do my best to serve you as one of your loyal soldiers and I am always ready at your command.

Otto Longius."

Augustus read it with a smile. "File it under "Personal Correspondence - Friends"; it reads like a letter from a country cousin," he told Menities.

Chapter 2

Felix took charge of the boxes in which the Emperor's gifts had arrived and added them to his collection of objects to be brought to a daily shine. He treated them as almost religious artefacts. Had they not been touched by the hands of Augustus?

"You can use them to keep small, valuable objects in."

"We don't have any," Otto objected

"Yes, you do. There's the letter from the Emperor to start with," Felix told him.

"And there's my letter from Menities," Lucius added.

"Yes, well, he's very important I dare say but he's still only a secretary…." Felix replied, sniffily.

Otto now occupied the billet next door to Lucius. He had been summoned to the legate's office and given a dressing down.

"I will not have one of my officer's sleeping out on a porch all winter long. Gods, you are living like a wild animal and even they have the sense to find a cave or hole to crawl into. Enough of it; it's a bad example to the men. Get your own quarters and begin to behave in accordance with your rank. If it's too warm for you indoors, leave the shutters wide-open for all I care but no more of this behaviour, Decurion Longius. Dismissed!"

Not that Otto spent much time in his rooms. His training had begun in earnest. He had thought he was a fair horseman but Aldermar soon destroyed that illusion. Otto had to learn to ride with a spear in one hand, an oval shield in the other, and guide Djinn by the pressure of his knees. He had to gallop at a straw dummy on a pole, thrust at it and recover his spear as he rode past. More than once he crashed to the ground when the spear-blade jammed in the strawman and yanked him from the saddle. But the bruises and saddle-skinned buttocks did not deter him and he began to make progress.

Then he had to learn the bugle calls; a separate group of notes for all commands, advance, fall-back, wheel-left, wheel-right and the infinite variations to keep a body of horsemen acting as one on the field of battle. The day arrived when he was allowed to lead out his own command; a "turma" of thirty-two cavalrymen. They lined up on the open ground leading down to the Rhine. Aldermar watched as the bugler by his side blew his first notes. At the head of his men, Otto used his spear as a pointer and they began to follow him, moving in complex patterns in response to the calls. When the exercise was over. Otto trotted up and saluted. He was very pleased with himself.

"That was pretty to watch, Decurion Longius. As a parade-ground exhibition, it was near perfect. Well done," The prefect told him then grinned. "Same place, same time tomorrow, that's all."

The grin had made Otto uneasy.

When he rode out the next day, two centuries of infantry were deployed on the training ground, facing each other one hundred paces apart. Aldermar took up his position, the cavalry calls were blown.

Otto and his men began. That is when the legionary ranks erupted in a cacophony of noise. The men thumped on their shields with sticks, they shouted and yelled. Their centurions and optios blew their whistles and yelled orders. Otto faltered. It was difficult to pick out the sound of his own commands over the din. Then, to make it worse, the infantry buglers began to blow their calls. The turma disintegrated from two lines of well-spaced horsemen into a mob but Otto did not give up. He shouted at his men, signalled with his spear and bullied them back onto formation before raggedly completing the exercise.

He was crestfallen as he made his way over to Aldermar, expecting some sort of sarcasm at the least but he was pleasantly surprised.

"Well, done, Decurion," the prefect told him.

"It was a shambles," Otto replied.

"Yes, pretty shambolic but you completed the manoeuvres and that's the main thing. Imagine a whole legion in battle and the noise of the enemy screaming war cries, ten times, a hundred times worse, but you still have to pick out the sound of your buglers. Not a bad day's work all the same. Get your men in, see to the horses and we'll talk in my office. Oh, by the way, you owe those two centuries a big drink each for coming out in the cold to assist in the training. It's traditional."

Aldermar was sitting in the booth partitioned off one of the stables that he grandly called his "office" when the crestfallen Otto entered.

"Sit down Otto and don't look so glum You did well; no-one has ever finished the course with all that racket in their ears the first time of trying until today. Have a cup of wine and cheer up."

Otto managed a half-smile and took the proffered cup. Aldermar ginned. Otto recognised it and inwardly groaned.

"Here's a question for you. How many bales of hay and what weight of corn will one hundred horses go through in a month?"

"I don't know," Otto replied.

"Neither do I but your answer should have been better than a straight, "don't know". You might have asked what the season of the year was; if it's summer, will they have grazing to supplement their rations? What quality of hay, how old? Is the grain mixed or all one variety, are there any beans in it? Are the horses on active service in the field? You are improving as a cavalry-officer much quicker that I'd thought you would but there's more to it than riding and fighting. You must study the administration involved in keeping men and horses in peak condition with minimum wastage. Starting tomorrow, you're going to spend a lot of your time with Uncle Martellus, the blacksmiths, the saddlers and most of all, the quartermaster. Good luck with him; he's not a friendly man. Conniving, lying soldiers have soured his attitude to his fellow men."

Lucius was not idle during this period. He and Titus Attius had been summoned by Quadratus. They sat in his inner office; no snacks or wine this time. The legate was grim. He launched into his speech without any pleasant preliminaries.

"My information from the general staff is that there is no doubt that our new acquaintances the Marcomanni are preparing to launch a concerted campaign against the Roman military presence on the German border. We are situated just within Belgic lands with Raetia to the east of us. We are isolated. It would take ten days march to join the bulk of our army group, eight days without heavy transport and four by cavalry alone. The Marcomanni have tried to destroy this legion with a combination of subterfuge and violence. They did not succeed but they will try again. I believe an attack in force against us is probable. We need to prepare, gentlemen, and I need your support. Ideas, please."

"Just the usual, sir," Attius said. "Disguised pits with spikes in the bottom, more sharpened stakes in the ditch. I already have all those chests of stones on the parapets…."

"If we're attacked, you're going to throw stones?" Lucius asked with amused disbelief.

"Oh yes, Boxer, I certainly am, with the legate's permission. A one-pound stone dropping twenty feet or more onto a man stops him in his tracks at the least. Also, they cost us nothing."

"The Germans have no war machines not are they inclined to undermine our walls. What they will do is launch attack after attack to wear us down. In a siege, you run out of food, then ammunition and finally men. The stones Titus has collected are a valuable defensive resource," Quadratus told Lucius.

"I stand corrected, sir. If the stones are so useful to us, why not gather a lot more? We could get them out of the stream this time. That would make it a little deeper and a better barrier."

"Simple but probably effective, tribune. Liaise with First Spear Centurion Attius and make a start," the legate ordered.

The stream rose in the south, took a curve parallel with one wall of the camp and then turned again to flow down the gentle slope to the Rhine on the western side. Lucius stood in the cold drizzle, showing willing, while the soaked legionaries waded into the water, heaved heavy, rounded pebbles out of the streambed and hauled them through the open gate. His mind wandered and he began to picture the whole area. To the east, the land rose sharply to the forest but the tree stumps had been deliberately left when the legion had cleared it. A mass charge down that slope was almost impossible. To the south and west, there was a degree of protection offered by the watercourse which they were labouring to improve. But there were no natural obstacles on the gentle slope leading northwards to the Rhine. The idea came to Lucius out of nowhere.

He went back into the camp and climbed up to the walkway over the Via Praetoria. To his right was the treacherous deforested slope, to his left, the farmlands cultivated by veterans with the silver line of the stream running through it down to the broad river. He studied the ground for a long while then came down and walked outside to the northwest corner of the camp. He proceeded to take long strides, counting each pace until he reached the foot of the deforested slope. He looked back. It seemed a very long way, still he knew every legionary was trained to dig his share of a marching-camp ditch each night when they were in the field. He asked for a meeting with Quadratus and Attius.

He had made a charcoal plan on a wide wooden board which he propped up. He stood to one side of it and looked at the two officers. All his confidence evaporated. He wanted nothing more than to rewind time to before he had requested that they hear him. But it was too late. Lucius took a deep breath and began in a faltering voice which grew stronger as he noticed Attius' eyes narrowing in concentration. They were not dismissing him out of hand.

"My idea is to dig a ditch three feet deep and six feet wide across the front of the camp beginning at the stream. At its nearest point it will be twenty paces from our walls and forty paces at the farthest where it finishes at the foot of the slope. It will naturally fill with stream water most of the year. If it runs dry, it is still a hindrance to an enemy force. The side nearest us will be sloped so no hostile warriors can hide in it unseen. The other side will be vertical and lined with stones to help hold the water level and prevent erosion."

"Why isn't it straight across?" Attius asked.

"Because water naturally flows downhill. We want it to flow along our ditch, not spill out at the highest point."

"The farmers won't like you interfering with their irrigation and we need the grain they supply," Quadratus told him.

"We build a simple sluice gate where the ditch joins the watercourse. In the event of an attacking force being sighted, a party goes out and destroys it. It will only take a few moments."

"What are you going to do with all the earth the men excavate?" Attius asked.

"Dump it, either in the river or spread it out on the slope up to the forest."

"What do you think, Titus," Quadratus enquired.

"It's practical. But why didn't we think of it before?"

"Because the best ideas are always staring us in the face, we just don't see them. Very well done, Boxer. But twelve feet wide and six feet deep, can we manage that, Titus? I want a timber bridge in line with the Porta Praetoria. Men naturally crowd round bridges; makes them a big target."

"Very well, sir. When the news of your grand scheme gets out, Boxer you're going to be the most hated officer in this camp, including me. I echo the legate, well done!"

But Lucius was not finished scheming; he had taken Quadratus' words about sieges to heart and began to worry about the ammunition supply. He spoke with Centurion Corvo.

"Is there anything wrong with using pebbles as sling ammunition if we run out of bullets?"

"Yes, sir, there is. Each bullet is cast using the same lead in the same mould. They are all of identical size and weight. Pebbles vary and accuracy is lost."

Thank you, Corvo," Lucius said and gave the problem some thought. There was nothing he could do to obtain a supply of suitable stones all of the same size but he could do something about the weight. With Corvo to advise, he collected fifty rounded pebbles from the stream, which was now substantially deeper and faster flowing, He then borrowed a pair of scales from the reluctant quartermaster, who made him sign for them. He and Corvo put ten lead bullets on one pan and then added stones to the other until they had the identical weight on each side. On average, twenty-five stones were needed to equal ten bullets. Corvo's century was set to bringing in even more. The weighing and sorting process went on until they had five-thousand stones of nearly similar size and weight. They set up a range and practised with them, gathering up all they could find at the end of the session.

Neither Lucius nor Corvo could do anything about the supply of arrows. They had to be made by experts and brought in.

The quartermaster refused to accept the scales when Lucius returned them.

"They're badly scratched and worn. It says, "To be returned in the same condition" on your chit, Tribune Longius. I'll have to charge you."

"Very well, quartermaster, let me know how much and I'll pay. I will, of course, be keeping the scales."

The quartermaster grudgingly took them back without charging Lucius anything.

"Suppose they could be repaired," he muttered.

Lucius turned his attention to his artillery. He had ordered as many scorpion bolts as the armourers could supply. He had stacked hundreds of rounded stones of between ten and fifteen pounds for his ballistas. But he had something else on his mind. Huddled with the artillerists discussing tactics, he asked a fundamental question.

"The ballista throws a single missile. If it strikes the effect is devastating but it if misses by a hairsbreadth, all the effort and wear on the torsion ropes has been for nothing. Is there any way we can fire multiple stones?"

One experienced soldier shook his head.

"Never been tried, sir. Probably a good reason why not."

"Let's have a go and see what happens," Lucius ordered.

A ballista was dragged out of its shelter and aimed approximately at half-way up the wall. Two operators cranked it into the ready position. Five smaller stones were placed in the slide that would normally hold just a single, larger one.

"Fire!" Lucius shouted.

The trigger was pulled. The tension on the string holding back the twin arms was realised. The block shot up the firing groove and hit the stones. Two fell off sideways. One went vertically up into the air and landed within a foot of Lucius as it plunged back to earth. One hit the base of the wall. They had no idea where the last one had gone until an outraged shout from a sentry on the walkway let them know.

"Is that you lot chucking stones up 'ere? Could've taken my head off...sorry, sir."

"Not a success," Lucius admitted.

"Shows you why we never do that, sir," said the soldier who had been against the experiment in the first place with as much satisfaction as he dared show to an officer.

"There's got to be a way," Lucius persisted. "What if we used a sort of sack?"

"Then it would be the same as now, sir. A sack full of stones instead of one big stone; no different, if you ask me."

"Yes, well no-one is asking you," Lucius snapped. "There has to be a way. Get that ballista back under cover for now."

He stood over his workbench with a wax tablet and stylus calculating and sketching. A ballista was a simple machine, nothing more than a giant crossbow on a movable stand. It should be possible to fire multiple missiles at a single discharge. It was only a matter of working out how…. He heard someone cough behind him. A legionary stood at attention.

"Legate wants to see you, sir."

A hard-faced centurion was standing beside the commanding officer when Lucius entered.

"Did I see you and Centurion Corvo weighing pebbles and sling bullets in a set of balance pans recently?" Quadratus asked, pleasantly.

"Yes, sir,"

"And would you tell me why?"

Lucius launched into a detailed explanation, including remarks on accuracy, range and the need to standardize the ammunition as much as possible.

Quadratus let him go on. "How are the trench-works progressing?" he asked once Lucius had finished.

"I've worked out that, at the current rate, if the weather does not …." Lucius gave a second lecture quoting figures and projections.

The legate listened patiently.

"And what were you attempting a short while ago when you bombarded the interior of my camp with random missiles?"

Lucius once again educated his legate into the mysteries of trajectory, angles of fire and the effect of the missile weight.

"I am pleased that you are taking your duties so seriously and studying as recommended. Tell me, Tribune Longius, are you a philosopher?"

"No sir."

"Perhaps you are a mathematician?"

"No, sir."

"Indeed not; you are a soldier. A soldier who spends all day making calculations. You have lost your sense of proportion, Boxer but I shall restore it to you. Do you know who this is?" Quadratus asked, gesturing to the centurion at his side.

"The legion training officer, sir."

"Yes, and very good at his job too. It is not part of a tribune's duties to take up a shield and sword and stand in the ranks with the men but the occasion can arise. The Divine Julius himself did so at the Battle of Alesia. Think of it, Boxer, a general in the front-rank exchanging blows with furious Gauls. He survived as we all know but he knew what he was doing. I do not think you do. You will report to the training officer every day for the foreseeable future for an hour's weapons drill. Perhaps you will fix it firmly in your head that the sword and shield are mightier than the stylus and wax tablet. Dismissed."

Quadratus turned to the training officer.

"Do not defer to his rank. He is to be treated exactly like any other soldier, that is all."

If Lucius was in trouble for falling in love with figures, Otto hated them. He had been raised in a culture where arithmetic was basic; fifty cattle, less ten sold equalled forty. Now he had to get his head around numerous variables to come to a workable solution. How to keep one hundred and fifty horses and men in the field for twenty-one days with only two transport carts in support. What quantity of grain for the men, for the horses and then taking into account the fodder required by the mules hauling the carts? It was a series of nightmares for him, more challenging than anything he had faced before. Some nights he laid himself down to sleep close to despair but he rose with the dawn and struggled on. Gradually, things began to make sense to him and he no longer needed to write down every single thing.

Quadratus wrote to Tertius Fuscus in Rome and requested that he doubled up on the supplies he had been requested to obtain on his return.

"Io Saturnalia! Io Saturnalia!" resounded from hundreds of throats and the festival of misrule began. Otto picked up his gear and walked over to the auxiliary cavalry billet where he stayed for a week.

Long after the revelry was over, a delegation of the veteran farmers asked to speak to the legate. They had watched the defensive works with growing concern. Quadratus explained that, as far as he knew, war was imminent.

"Will we be given the protection of the camp?" one of them asked.

"No," Quadratus told him, gravely. "Women and children will not be admitted if hostilities are breaking out."

"What are we supposed to do?" the famer angrily demanded.

"Pack up your families and your tools and head down into Gaul."

"What about our land, what about the crops we have sown?"

"Land is no use to you if you are dead. As for your crops, the choice is yours. If you take the risk and stay until harvest, we shall buy all you have. But I urge you to depart while you can."

It was the artillerist who had been so dismissive of Lucius' attempt to turn a ballista into a multi-shot weapon who solved the problem. He showed Lucius a simple basket woven in the shape of a tube with one end left open. Five stones were slipped into it and then it was placed on the slide. When it was fired, it hung in the air for an instant at the highest point of its flight like all missiles and then plunged back to earth. On the descent, the stones dropped out of the open end of the basket and smashed into the ground in a rough line several feet long. Lucius was impressed.

They dragged a ballista outside the gate and demonstrated for Quadratus and Titus Attius.

"Now that I call deadly," Attius said admiringly.

"Congratulations, Boxer, you worked it out," the legate enthused.

"No sir, it was one of the men who came up with the solution to the problem," Lucius informed him.

"Stand forward that man," Quadratus commanded. "You have made an important contribution to the defence of our camp. I appoint you Duplicarius; your pay is now doubled. Tribune Longius, ensure that this is recorded in the proper manner."

Tertius Fuscus arrived with his supply column in mid-March. He had not been able to obtain twice the original requirement of grain and equipment but the amount he had with him was impressive. It took four days for the last of the contracted wagons to be unloaded and begin the hurried journey south.

Spring came but brought no enemy on its heels. As the year wore on in relative tranquillity, the younger soldiers grumbled about the restrictions on their off-duty movements imposed by Quadratus' security measures. The old sweats looked at them, shook their heads and spat into the dirt. They had been here before and could sense the change in the atmosphere; like those breathless moments before the thunder growled and the lightning crashed.

A letter arrived for Otto from Vitius Longius in Luca.

"To Decurion Otto Longius, Greetings,

I trust that you are well and in good spirits. Our thoughts are as often with you as they are with our dear son, Lucius.

In the matter of the estate purchase which you have honoured me by trusting to my care, I have a proposal for your consideration.

A south-facing vineyard with a good house and wine presses has come up for sale. The present owner is too old to cultivate his vines

and has no sons or nephews to continue the enterprise on his behalf.
On enquiry, I have discovered that the surrounding land is also
available. It rises in a wide swathe from the banks of the River
Auserculus to a wooded hillside and beyond that, the Apuan Alps. It is
well-drained and suitable for growing wheat, spelt and for cattle-
grazing. The water-meadows along the river which flood each spring
are ideal for sheep-rearing. The harvesting of filberts and chestnuts in
the woodlands is another, considerable source of income.

Since you are with the army, it occurred to me that owning land
and renting it out would be more practical for you than trying to farm
it yourself at long distance.

My steward has been with me for many years and I have the
highest opinion of his expertise. He informs me that you could
reasonably expect between eight and ten thousand denarii per annum
in rents once fully tenanted. He has a son who has worked with him
and who would be happy to act on your behalf; selecting and
overseeing the tenants and making sure they keep your land in good
order. If he was allowed to live in the house mentioned above rent-free
during his employment, he would accept a salary of one thousand two
hundred denarii.

The land I have briefly described could be purchased for the
sum of eighty-seven thousand denarii. If you wish to proceed, a letter
to me, perhaps witnessed by an independent party, would be sufficient
for me to make the arrangements. I recommend that you open an

account with the public bank I have always used in Luca. This can be arranged by letters of authorization. If you do so, I shall pass the residue of your funds to this account.

If this proposal does not find favour with you, please let me know. I suggest that we then leave our business on hold until such times as you can make your own inspection of what is available.

Vitius Lucius Longius

"Oh yes and blessing on you noble Vitius; now I do not have to buy slaves!" Otto thought once he had read it. He consulted Lucius and Tertius who advised him on the form his replies should take, Tertius acted as his witness. The letters were sent by the next available courier.

"So, you're a Roman country gentleman now, are you?" Aldermar said. "You'll have to provide wine for everyone. It is the custom."

"It seems to me that the custom is I always have to pay for the wine if something good happens," Otto told him, drily.

"That's right," Aldermar laughed and slapped him on the back.

Summer came; a beautiful summer of blue skies and hot sun to ripen the grain the die-hard farmers had planted. On Aldermar's recommendation Otto was promoted to Principal Decurion in July. His rank was now equivalent to that of a senior centurion and his pay eight thousand denarii.

He bought wine. It was the custom.

In that same month, Lucius wrote to Menities in Rome informing him that he had now made a study of all the engineering books he had been sent and reached the fullest understanding of them that he could.

August came and with it the harvest. The farmers who had held their nerves took a rich yield from their own fields as well as those of their neighbours who had left immediately after the meeting with Quadratus. The legion quartermaster bought all they had to offer A few days later, a convoy of farm carts loaded with tools, wives and children lumbered past the camp heading towards Gaul and the hopes of a new start. Only three went back to their homesteads. The camp-followers' settlement shrank, day after day. Most of the hucksters, tavern-keepers and brothel-owners drifted away leaving squares of bare earth where their huts and tents had stood for years. No itinerant pedlars arrived at the camp gates anymore.

There had been no more skirmishes than usual, the scouts had not reported any suspicious activity and yet everyone felt war was creeping up on them like a beast ready to pounce. This belief was confirmed by a despatch from the general's aide-de-camp ordering all cavalry other than the minimum needed for scouting duties to report to army headquarters. The reason given was that increased enemy activity was threatening supply lines and protective measures were an urgent requirement. Quadratus called an officers' meeting and gave them the news.

"One turma under the command of Principal Decurion Otto Longius will remain," the legate said. He saw Otto mouth opening to protest and quickly silenced him. "Decurion, be quiet, my decision is made."

"Permission to take Decanus Martellus and his apprentice with us, sir. I trust no man more with the care of horses," Aldermar requested.

"His apprentice?" Quadratus said.

"The boy Passer, sir. Tribune Longius' freed man. Uncle Martellus says he's learning his trade well and is a considerable help."

"As you wish and gods with you until we meet again, Prefect Aldermar."

Titus Attius stood in the almost empty stables with a group of defaulters lined up behind him. He took a deep breath.

"Stinks of horse shit. But when you lads have scrubbed it out for me, it will be as sweet as a rose garden."

"But sir," one of them protested, "there's still going to be thirty odd horses in here."

"A faint aroma will be acceptable. Get on with it."

The week after Aldermar's horsemen had left, Lucius received an order to join to the Engineer General's staff at headquarters.

"It seems the General and our Emperor are determined to deplete my forces without me having any say in the matter," Quadratus commented on being shown the written command.

"The Emperor, sir?" Lucius asked.

"Oh, don't be dim, Boxer. You write to Menities confirming you have studied the manuals he sent you and a few weeks later, the Engineer General requires you on his staff. The timing tells you everything. Menities showed your letter to Augustus and he wrote to headquarters recommending you. A recommendation from the Emperor is a command. I wish you good fortune and have every confidence you will make a fine senior artillery and engineering officer to make The Second Lucan proud. When are you thinking of leaving?"

"The orders don't say, sir."

"In the army that means as soon as possible or yesterday. It's the first of September tomorrow, sort out what you have to with Cestus Valens and say your goodbyes. Start out the day after."

Although their duties had meant they spent less time in each other's company, neither Lucius not Otto had imagined that they would be separated. They were both in low spirits as Lucius began to pack up his belongings; even Felix had stopped whistling.

Cestus Valens had been thrilled. He felt that his young protégé deserved recognition and said so. His pleasure was genuine with no taint of jealousy. He was dyed-in the-wool Second Lucan and would have put in his papers and resigned rather than accept a transfer.

A gentle south-west breeze had blown all that day of the first of September. The Rhine was flowing cold as ever, fed by the last of the summer-melt of glaciers high in the mountains to the east. When the warm, moist air moved over the river, a dense fog bank rose high above it. As the afternoon wore on, it thickened. When the breeze dropped, it flowed outwards to cover most of the tilled farmlands in a dense white cloud. The sun sank early into the white mist and darkness came.

Chapter 3

The sentry over the Porta Praetoria squinted his eyes trying to make sense of what he had glimpsed when the fog had momentarily thinned. It might have been a faint yellow glow in the heart of the white wall over the river, solid-looking in the moonlight, but he could not be sure. Now, he could see nothing. "Trick of the light", he thought. It was easy to be deceived on night-watch. Tree-stumps resembled crouching men and shivering leaves, spear points. The fog shifted once more. The glow was orange now and he realised what he was seeing. His throat constricted in fear. All he could hear was the hammering of his heart. He stood, frozen, unable to drag his eyes away. At last he shook his head and roared out "Alarm! Alarm!"

Boots thudded up the steps.

"What is it soldier?" a voice demanded.

He pointed with his javelin.

"There, sir, the signal beacon."

The optio who had been first to respond stood beside him staring out. He could see nothing and was about to reprimand the sentry when an orange flower flared briefly before being hidden from view once more.

"Gods with us now," he muttered then took up the cry of "Alarm!".

Whistles blew, calls to arms blared out of the brass throats of horns. Men tumbled out onto the parade ground tightening buckles and freeing swords in their scabbards, javelins clattered, boots thudded. Everywhere was a tumult of noise and a mass of running men. It looked like panicked confusion but it was not. Each man had his place and his duties. They were well-drilled and knew exactly where to go and what to do. Within a few minutes relative calm was restored. The senior officers, helmeted and in full armour, stood where the sentry had hesitated such a short time ago, staring out at a band of white reaching hundreds of feet up into the starlit sky and from which occasional flashes of fire glared.

The optio commanding the forward position hated two things above all; ice and fog. It was always possible that they would be swamped by hundreds of thousands of Germans if the Rhine froze over. That had not happened yet. However, mist coming off the river was a regular occurrence but not usually as thick as this. He had the authority to remove the planks from the bridge if hostile forces were massing to cross but he could see none. He looked across the narrow compound at his men. They seemed as unnerved by the lack of visibility as he was. He walked over to them.

"Lads, I don't like this, so let's do what we can."

The stronghold had two gates, one facing the river, the other the camp. He ordered both opened. Then he and three others stamped some earthenware cups and bowls into small pieces under their hob-nailed boots. They used a cloak as a sack and carried them fifty paces out on the bridge where they spread the broken crocks on the footway over a distance of several feet. He returned and gave his orders.

"I'm going to stand outside the front gate and listen. If I hear something, I'll run back in. You and you; stand by the gate. As soon as I'm through, get it shut and fall in with the others. You two, get some fresh oil on the beacon now and find yourselves a good flint and steel. Light it as soon the gate closes, get down and form up. We shall then double-time it for the camp. I know we can't see fuck-all in this mist but there's a well-worn path, look down at your feet from time to time and we won't get lost. Now, does everyone understand? Say if you don't because if we have to do this, it'll be in total silence. Any questions? Right, to your places, boys. No talking, not even a whisper and try not to make a noise with your kit. Fortuna with us this night."

He removed his helmet to prevent the sidepieces muffling his hearing and stood listening in the gloom. He leaned forward supporting himself on his vine-staff and closed his eyes. At first there was nothing but silence then his ears attuned themselves. The gurgling of the river came to him, the splash as a small wave broke on one of the piles, the creaking of the timbers. A night-bird flew close overhead making him start. Time crawled and as it passed, achingly slowly, his sense of dread increased. He was certain a malevolent force was out there, creeping inexorably nearer with murder in its heart. Two hours went by, three and then he heard the smallest sound. It could have been the noise of someone breaking a biscuit. It was repeated, repeated again. Someone was crunching the pottery shards on the bridge as he approached. He caught what might have been a muffled curse and a whispered order urging someone onward.

He turned and strode quickly into the fort. It would not do for the men to see him run. Then another sound arose. The unmistakable thump of a paddle striking the side of a canoe. They were coming. The gate swung shut behind him and the locking bar dropped into place. Sparks crackled off flints and a fiery bloom grew out of the beacon. He walked swiftly to the head of his men standing ready in two files and doubled out into the fog. The lack of visibility that had allowed the enemy to come up on them unseen now came to the aid of the retreating Romans. The invaders, he still did not know if they were there in any numbers, could not see them retreating. They all heard banging and thumping behind them as the closed gate of their fortress was attacked. Then silence followed by howls of rage as the enemy saw the beacon flaring up.

They marched at their quickest pace enveloped above, in front and behind in a wet, white blanket. Drops of moisture glistened on their helmets and armour, their faces soaked as if with sweat. They were aware of sporadic movement around them; a wave of colder air as some unseen presence caused an eddy with their passing, the padding of running feet, the clack of a spear shaft against a stone but the all-encompassing fog also distorted sound. They were isolated in a blank nightmare. A spear point came from nowhere and smashed into a legionary's shield. He staggered but automatically thrust with his javelin. An anguished face loomed into sight and then was gone with a shrill cry.

The optio suddenly noticed that he was no longer on the path. It was difficult enough to keep up the pace without either slamming into the man in front or being left behind; to have lost the straight line between the signal beacon and the camp was a disaster. He veered slightly left for ten paces looking down at his feet but seeing only grass. He moved to his right for ten paces and felt harder ground under his right boot. Two paces more and they were back on the path.

Without any warning, they burst out into bright moonlight fifty yards from the bridge over Lucius' new ditch.

"Run!" the optio roared. The men responded without thinking.

Figures were sliding out of the fog like ghosts passing through a wall. Lightly armoured or wearing only skins, then loped towards the small group of Romans, converging on them like wolves on a flock of sheep. Some fell suddenly with a scream as they stumbled into one of the shallow traps and a foot was spiked through. But on they came. The first spears were thrown, one hitting a legionary in the thigh. He cursed and stumbled then pulled out the spear blade.

"Halt," the optio shouted when they reached the bridge. "About face. Close up, double rank and prepare to receive the enemy."

Ten men with an equal number of comrades behind them formed their line, crouched and waited. The soldier who had been hit was bleeding heavily but on his feet and ready to fight as best he could before the strength drained from him. Scores of warriors were now converging on them. They should have leaped the ditch and cut them off but, as Quadratus had predicted, the bridge drew them like a magnet.

"First Spear Centurion Attius, time to act I believe, the legate said calmly from his vantage point over the gate.

Attius turned his back to the parapet and roared down at the troops ready on the parade ground.

"First cohort, century one out of the gate to the left, century two to the right. At the double to the rescue. of our lads, and don't get out-flanked. Throw open the gate! Boxer! Take one century and smash down your sluice gate. Corvo, get your men up here in support!"

The men on the bridge were heavily engaged. In spite of their efforts to hold their ground, the sheer weight of the mass of yelling, blood-thirsty warriors thrusting and hacking at them was pushing them back. But their line held and their short swords struck out again and again, momentarily relieving the pressure. Then their optio heard the sweetest sound of his life. The gates behind him had been flung open and the jingle of armoured men on the move came to his ears.

"One two! One two!" the centurions of the first cohort shouted, keeping their men in step. They did not rush but kept to a fast jog from which they could quickly deploy. They did not have much ground to cover and soon the isolated group of men who had fled through the fog were supported on either side by a triple rank of comrades.

Lucius had planned in advance for the destruction of the sluice gate. Two of his strongest artillerymen ran with him and his century carrying crowbars and two lengths of thick rope with loops spliced into one end.. The sluice gate had been simply constructed by driving a wooden pile into the ground either side of the ditch and nailing horizontal boards across them. It was crude but effective. Protected by the shields of the legionaries, Lucius and his men looped a rope over each pile and, while as many soldiers as could be spared pulled on them, the two artillerymen prised the planks away. Nothing seemed to happen at first. Lucius saw that a straight pull would not do it.

"Haul and release lads, on my count, haul and release; and one and two, and one and two!"

As the boards were levered away, one of the supports canted sideways and broke free. The bottom of the ditch had been dug deeper than the stream bed. Water flowed in, pushing the last of the battered woodwork aside. It did not come in a roaring flood but steadily reached its level and began to fill the length of the ditch.

Whistles blew, centurions shouted and the Romans began an orderly withdrawal into the safety of their camp. The triple rank became a quadruple one as the legionaries shortened their line. They formed an almost solid phalanx as they began to filter back in. The two centurions of the first cohort made sure that they were the last men to step through the narrowing gap as the gates closed and the locking bar dropped. Hundreds of the enemy were now clustered where the fighting had been hottest, howling threats and curses. They had made a grave error. A hail of sling bullets and arrows smashed them down in their scores and soon they were sprinting back towards the river, desperate to get out of range.

The soldier who had been speared had somehow hobbled back to safety before fainting. He was carried to the infirmary where his wound was staunched and stitched. The medical officer ordered him to drink red-wine gruel and eat some sliced, raw liver to restore his blood.

"If you live through the night, you'll be fit for light duties in three days," he told the waxen-faced man on the palliasse to cheer him up.

Quadratus heard the report of the signal party's optio.

"You have shown ingenuity, initiative and courage. I award you an exemplary service silver medal to be attached to your armour. Well done, optio. Dismiss and get some food and rest."

The legate called Lucius to walk up to his position over the gate with him. They leaned on the parapet looking out over a plain starkly differentiated between light and dark in the moonlight. Another fire flared up, closer, then more.

"They are burning the farmhouses and barns," Quadratus said. "Stupid; why deny yourself shelter? It appears that you will not be leaving us quite yet, Boxer; can't be helped."

They went to their quarters. Lucius was woken out of a fitful sleep in the early hours by screaming and a stench of burning. The marauders had worked their way round to the remnants of the camp-followers' settlement, slaughtered the inhabitants and put it to the torch. When dawn came, the sentries on the southern wall could see groups of naked bodies spread out for miles; the final resting places of the few who had tried to flee at the last minute. The first ravens were already picking over the choicest morsels.

The fog had melted away overnight. The signal beacon and the charred wreckage of the homesteads joined their smoke with the cooking fires of the enemy now encamped along the river. The bank was thick with tents, rough shelters and high-wheeled wagons on both sides of the Rhine bridge as far as the eye could see. Men and some women and children wandered around the area casually beginning their daily tasks. The fort at the bridgehead had not been destroyed; there were warriors in helmets and armour passing in and out of the gate facing the camp. Quadratus and Attius had taken a look at first light.

"More than ten thousand would you say, Titus?" the legate asked.

"Yes, definitely."

"More than fifteen thousand"

"I should say not. I estimate nearer to fifteen than ten, but a serious number, alright."

"Indeed; it looks like they have established their headquarters in the fort. I do not like that; it shows some tactical awareness. I think we shall need to have our wits about us."

Titus Attius was cheerfully demolishing a huge breakfast when Lucius entered the praetorium. The outer office was now the officer's mess. The clerks had been armed and sent on active service as stretcher-bearers, cooks' helpers or wherever they may be useful. Only the legate's two personal scribes remained.

Titus was in a cheerful mood. He had placed his sentries, arranged rotas for eating and sleeping. For now, there was nothing more he could do.

"Got to keep your strength up Boxer, that's the main thing. Have you seen your ditch this morning? Plenty of water in it along its full length. Good idea of yours, that was."

"Shouldn't we be doing something?" Lucius asked.

"Like what? It's up to our uninvited guests to make the first move. Very boring, sieges; lots of waiting around and then bloody mayhem. That's why it's important to eat when you can. Care to join me?"

It had been less difficult for Helmund of the Marcomanni to assemble a new force than he had thought. Yes, the ambush of the

Romans at the edge of Treverii lands had failed. But their shield wall had been breached, if only briefly. Their proud commander had been flung from his horse and laid low at the mercy of one of Helmund's warriors. It was the unexpected arrival of the Romans' cavalry that had lost him the day. As the story of the battle was told and re-told, the number of warriors that had been lost faded in significance when compared with bringing a Roman "General" down into the dust. Hulderic, Helmund's adjutant and intelligence officer, had made sure the "near victory" was celebrated with ale and songs. So, when Helmund proposed a new attack, hundreds of warriors joined him. When the news came that the Roman cavalry had ridden away to the north, men flocked to his standard in their thousands.

He had been moving steadily down the German side of the Rhine, by-passing Raetia, with the aim of taking the camp of The Second Lucan. If this stronghold was eliminated, Roman forces to the east would be forced to fight on two fronts when he advanced back up through Raetia, but this time on the Roman bank. There had been spies and informers to deal with on the way; they had been neutralised in a very public and agonising way to discourage others. The Marcomanni Confederation were closely related to Otto's people, the Suevi. That was sufficient for them to obtain free passage through the territories of other tribes who, if they were not exactly friendly, did not want to provoke an open conflict.

He had planned to attack across the river at night with two hundred warriors in canoes. He had been patiently waiting for an overcast sky to launch them when the fog came like the blessing of Tiw, the War God he also made use of the bridge. His tactic had been to overwhelm the garrison of the forward fort with its signalling tower and take control of the bridgehead. This would allow him to bring his forces over in relative security. He had partially succeeded. He now commanded the fort and the Rhine crossing but he had wanted to be in position before the Romans had any warning of his coming. He had wanted them to wake in the morning with a whole army arrayed against them where the day before, there had been no-one. That would have jolted their morale. The garrison had escaped into the main camp and he had lost eighty of his warriors. They had disobeyed his orders to stay put and instead chose to blunder around in the fog in pursuit of the fleeing Romans. Their lack of discipline was troubling but the first objective had been achieved. His army were sitting down in front of his enemy's camp and with the bridge closed to them and no effective cavalry force, the Roman's options were limited.

Helmund looked up the slope to the enemy camp brooding like an alien presence on the landscape. He believed that it was his to take but he knew that he had two struggles on his hands. The first was the military one of destroying the enemy stronghold and its occupants, the second was political. The Marcomanni were not one people under one leader. They were a group of tribes and clans united by their hatred of the Romans. To defeat their mutual enemy, he had to persuade them to put aside age-old rivalries and blood-feuds. Chieftains had to submit to his orders and carry them out with precision. He walked into the fort and addressed the leaders assembled to hear his words.

"When the Romans first came, our forefathers asked who were these arrogant black-haired dwarves daring to behave as if they owned the world? They rushed upon them and died on their swords. So it has been ever since. The meanest of their soldiers, the ones they treat like dogs, whipping and beating them, the meanest of these wears on his back the armour of one of our kings. They all have swords; they all have many javelins. They burrow their greedy, gold-lusting way into everything like maggots gorging on what is not theirs. Are they better men than we?"

A great roar of "No!" burst from the sixty chieftains within the fortress walls.

"Are they nobler born?" Helmund continued, raising his voice.

"No!"

"Are they braver warriors?" he shouted

"No, never!"

"Then how is it that they defeat us time after time after time?" he asked in a quieter tone. No answer came to this question. "We lose because we fight as we have always fought, for glory. They have no warrior's pride. They never come out man to man if challenged. No, they make a plan and they all follow it. All of them; if any man does not, his general executes him. We are not like them, we are free men, but now we must act as one, following orders like they do. Then and only then, will they be defeated."

"And are we to be executed if we disobey?" yelled one chieftain with a greying beard.

"No, that is not our way. But if men disobey, they are stealing victory from all of us. Such men are no better than thieves."

"And who will give these orders?" another dissident voice shouted.

"I, Helmund, and no other. If you cannot not accept my leadership, you and your people may leave now in peace but remember, you will have no part in our victory."

"And what will be different this time, Helmund? It is not so long ago that your warriors were slaughtered by these same Romans?"

"Many brave men were lost, but their glory is undying. This time it will be different. This time, we will do things our people have never done before. We will play them at their own game and we shall win. Who is with me?"

They looked around at each other, unsure. "We are with you! The bravest are with you!" Hulderic shouted from behind the semi-circle of clan leaders. Like a wave building as it approaches the shore, they stood and acclaimed Helmund. Chanting and waving their fists in the air, they swore damnation to Rome and loyalty to him.

"What do you think?" he asked Hulderic when they were alone.

Hulderic sucked his teeth and spat. "You can hold them for seven days. If we haven't hit the Romans hard enough to hurt them in that time, you'll start to have problems."

Lucius went up on the walkway and wandered right around the walls several times that first day. He could see Marcomanni moving to and fro, apparently aimlessly, showing no signs of organising for an attack.

"Perhaps we could dig more spike pits around the outside of our walls," he suggested.

"No, Boxer, won't do at all. Suppose we had to make a sortie in force; we'd risk crippling our own men," Titus told him.

"I just wish something would happen…" he began but the centurion stopped him and touched his lucky amulet.

"Never say that. When it begins, then you'll really wish for something to happen alright; for it to stop! They are deliberately letting us stew to wear down our nerves. Don't fall for it."

The following day a large party left the enemy camp and crossed back over the bridge. They lined up their wagons with canvas screens in between to obscure their activities from the camp but the elevation gave the Romans a partial view. Another long, sunny day of inactivity was followed by a tranquil moonlit night. But the weather was changing. On the morning of the third day, dark clouds began to roll in from the south and west. By late afternoon, they had completely covered the sky and that night, neither a moonbeam nor a glimmer of starlight penetrated the thick blanket overhead.

Quadratus called Otto into his office.

"The night is as black as that horse of yours decurion. It may be dark enough for a messenger to slip through the enemy lines and carry a message to headquarters. What do you think?"

"I'm willing to try, sir…"

"No, no, no! Unthinkable; who will commend your turma in your absence? I need two volunteers from among your men. I cannot send legionaries; whoever goes has to be able to blend in with anyone whose path they may cross in the forest. There will be a substantial reward but don't mention that until after they've offered to go. Report to me in the next hour; hopefully, with your volunteers."

When Otto returned with two of his cavalrymen who had agreed to carry messages, a small-scale officers' conference had been set up. Rufus Soranus sat beside Lucius and Cestus Valens. Titus Attius paced the space behind them looking grim.. Tertius sat by Quadratus.

"Are these the men?" the legate asked Otto.

"They are, sir."

"Good; translate for me as I go along. I want them to have the fullest understanding of what is proposed before they commit themselves," he turned his attention to the assembled officers. "One hour before dawn the third cohort led by Tribune Soranus will leave by the Porta Decumana. Their ostensible mission is to scour the remains of the camp-followers' settlement for any of the enemy who may be concealed there. This, tribune, is what you will tell your men and all you will tell them." Soranus nodded, and the legate continued. "Our messengers will go out with you as inconspicuously as possible; when they judge the moment right, they will slip away into the forest and be on their way to headquarters, gods willing. I want the third cohort to be carrying torches and to make a great deal of noise. The recall will be sounded at dawn. That's the plan. gentlemen. Your First Spear Centurion is about to tell me he does not like deploying troops at night. Neither do I but we need to give Otto's lads the best chance we can. Cestus, can your artillery offer any support?"

"We have a limited number of fire-pots for the ballistas, sir. We can lob half a dozen into the ruins just as the gate is opened for Tribune Soranus. They'll blaze up on impact and add to the general effect."

"See to it," the legate said and turned once more to Otto. "Do your men completely understand what is required of them?"

Otto held a brief conversation in German and then replied that they did. Quadratus nodded his approval and gave each of them a small scroll wrapped in oiled cloth.

The two leaves of the gate parted. From up on the walkway, crouched over his ballista, Lucius watched Cestus beside his. When his arm dropped, both machines bucked and kicked simultaneously as the fire-pots arced into the night. They were clay jars filled with a mixture of oil, tar and naptha, covered in cloth with a wick which was lit as soon as they were placed on the slides. They landed among the charred wreckage and shattered with the sounds of small explosions and a rush of blue and bright yellow flame. The third cohort was by now half-way through the gate, whistles and horns sounding, one in four of them holding a pine-pitch torch. They spread out and began to advance in skirmish order, kicking over burned posts and plank walls throwing up clouds of ash and soot. They reached the far-end of what had once been a thriving commercial centre with three hundred permanent inhabitants and others who came and went. The first silver line appeared low in the eastern sky and the horns called them back in. With blackened faces and kit, all of which would have to be restored to its acceptable spotless state, they marched in.

"Did our Germans get away?" Tertius asked Soranus.

"Must have done, sir. They're gone but I never saw them leave."

"That's as it should be," Tertius commented.

"Well, Boxer," Quadratus said, "Titus has told me that you have been pestering him for some action and we have made our first move; sending messages begging for help. Not very glorious eh?"

Chapter 4

As the day wore on, the sound of hammering and sawing was borne on the breeze from the Marcomanni camp. A small group of officers stood on the walkway staring out but unable to see anything.

"Now what are they up to?" Tertius asked Attius.

He shrugged. "Some sort of woodwork; perhaps they're building a wooden horse for us to drag inside, then they'll all jump out and cut our throats."

Lucius and Soranus, who were both within earshot, laughed. Tertius flushed.

"If the enemy is constructing some sort of war-machine, that is hardly a subject for humour, First Spear Centurion Attius."

Titus snapped to attention. "Since we have no idea what they're doing and no possibility of finding out, expressing concern in the hearing of the men is fruitless and could damage morale, Senior Tribune Fuscus."

Tertius smiled. "I stand admonished Titus; apologies if I have offended you," he leaned closer and spoke in a quieter voice. "I am truly concerned, more than that, I'm worried. The accepted wisdom is that they have no skill in making siege engines but the more they are exposed to Roman military tactics and equipment, the greater the opportunity they have of learning from us."

"Possible, I suppose but I've yet to see any evidence of them learning much," Titus replied.

It came on to rain, raising the level of water in Lucius' ditch and making the bottom and sloped side softer and slicker. The rain faded away during the night and the moon broke through the clouds intermittently.

Dawn brought a new and unwelcome sight. During the night, a forked branch had been stuck into the ground three hundred paces from the camp gate. To a single shout from thousands of throats and blare of native horns, a tall warrior approached it at a casual saunter. His hair was the colour of autumn leaves where it flowed out under the rim of Roman officer's helmet he wore. His leggings were checked in squares of green and faded red and a bronze breast plate covered his broad chest. He held a human head dangling by the dirty braids in each hand. In plain view of the Romans behind the parapet, he threw them to his feet, opened his breeches and pissed on them. Gales of laughter rose from the assembled Marcomanni. By now, the parapet over the gate was packed.

Quadratus sighed. "Our messengers no doubt, I grieve for them. Cestus, Boxer, can you knock that barbarian down for me?"

"He's in ballista range sir but he'll be able to see a bolt coming and step aside," Cestus replied with a shake of the head.

"We need to distract him.," Lucius said. "Look at him swaggering; he loves that applause. Can I try something?"

"Make sure it does not make things any worse; if they could be. The men really won't like this."

"Corvo," Lucius shouted, "Get up here with your bow and the two best archers you've got. Cestus, please load a bolt on the ballista in the tower and sight it on that bastard. Loose when I call out."

Corvo came back at the run with his men.

"Can you hit that big German standing out there on his own?"

Corvo looked carefully, wet one finger in his mouth and held it up to test the wind. "No, he's out of range by a few paces."

"Good," said Lucius, "shoot at him anyway when I drop my arm."

Their arrogant target lifted the two heads and hooked them over the forks of the pole by their hair. He swung them so they knocked together and laughed. He turned again to the Roman spectators and flung his bent arms wide in a gesture of contempt. Lucius let his own arm fall.

Three arrows hurtled up into the air and dropped with increasing speed towards the enemy warrior. For a moment it looked as if they would find their mark but they plunged into the turf in a tight group ten paces short. Corvo looked crest-fallen; it had been magnificent shooting but they had missed; exactly what Lucius had wanted. The warrior strolled forward and plucked the arrows out of the ground. His silver arm-rings glinted as he raised them above his head and shook them, turning his back on the Romans to accept the praise of his own people. He took a stride towards the pole with its grisly trophies.

"Loose!" Lucius shouted and Cestus himself pulled the trigger.

The thirty-inch iron bolt sped in a high arc and began to descend, a dark blur against the lighter clouds above. It struck him in the spine below the shoulder blades, passed through his body, ripping his breast plate like paper before travelling on for another twenty feet and slanting into the ground. He toppled his full length, to drop on his face, dead; with the arrows still clutched in his hand. A stunned silence fell on the Marcomanni. Then their previous cheering and laughter was replaced by shrieks of rage. A confused turmoil of movement broke out among their packed ranks like an ant-heap being upturned. All the cheering now came from the Romans.

"Oh, well done, Boxer," Quadratus said and slapped him on the back.

"Corvo and his men put their arrows in the right place and Cestus fired the killing shot, sir."

"Quite right, well done Centurion Corvo and both of your archers." Then he called up to Cestus Valens. "Excellent, you took the shot yourself?"

"Couldn't ask one of the men to take the responsibility in case of a miss, sir," Cestus shouted back.

"Well, that's woken 'em up," Titus observed laconically.

Out of the churning, furious mass of the enemy, warriors were streaming away from their camp, at first there were only a hundred or so but more and more joined the stampede until over two thousand men ran with murder in their hearts towards the Roman walls. They carried spears, axes and knotted climbing ropes. They flourished shields, shrieking in berserk hatred as they sprinted up the slope. Titus shook his head and looked amused. They had begun their charge too far away, they needed to be saving their wind, not yelling.

"Man the walls to repulse a general assault," he shouted. Brass horns relayed the order throughout the camp. Legionaries rushed to their positions. "Tribune Longius, let's have half your archers and slingers over the Porta Praetoria. Artillery, fire at will according to the orders of your officers."

The ballistas were loaded with the new basket-tube ammunition. Four scorpions had a field of fire and were loaded and cocked.

Helmund stood with his arms folded, watching in a mixture of disgust and despair. Yet again his men acted without thought and without orders, giving in to their desire to wipe out the perceived insult they had received when their champion had been cut down. Helmund had not wanted him to make his provocation with the messengers' heads in the first place. It would have been better to let the uncertainty gnaw away at the Romans' nerves day after day while they watched and waited for their return with news or relief. Now they knew that no help was imminent and were about to massacre a substantial part of his force, among them many of the youngest and bravest.

The bridge over the ditch proved an irresistible attraction. The attacking force merged into a wedge with its narrow point heading straight for it. As they crowded together, the Roman artillery began to punish them. The basket-tubes spun at their apex dropping stones that broke collarbones, arms, feet or killed with a head-strike. The scorpions bowled men over, sometimes two at once. The uphill run was taking its toll on tired legs and they slowed making things even easier for the artillerists. Eventually, the survivors were so close to the walls that neither the ballistas nor the scorpions could depress their sights low enough to fire down on them. But now sling bullets buzzed around their ears like angry hornets and arrows tore through shields and armour.

But on they ran, or jogged now, fighting for breath, over the bridge, less than forty paces from their goal. Some had tried to leap the ditch and were clutched ankle-deep by the clinging mud of the bank where they floundered; soft targets. The javelins now fell on them like October rain. Not one of them lived to touch either the wall or the gate. The slow and the laggards looked into the abattoir the ground at the foot of the Roman walls had become and turned their backs to the jeers of their own people. They may as well have died under the arrows and javelins, for their lives were now over. Their places in the assembly of warriors were lost. They were forever shamed.

Titus Attius bellowed for a ceasefire and turned to Quadratus for further orders.

"It would seem that our enemies have enjoyed themselves enough for one day. Send some men out and carry the bodies to the far side of the ditch. Do not fling them about and put them down neatly. Retrieve every missile that is re-usable. Someone fetch me Decurion Otto Longius."

An hour later, six-hundred bodies lay on their backs along the far side of the ditch. Their arms were by their sides and their legs straight with the ankles together. Hundreds of others were scattered across the slope further down where they had died. The Porta Praetoria opened again and two figures rode out. Quadratus' armour had been polished and his red cloak fell from his shoulders and spread evenly over his horse's rump. Beside him rode Otto in his parade armour mounted on Djinn. He carried the legate's personal flag. The gate closed behind them and they walked as far as the end of the bridge over the ditch where they halted. Otto thrust the end of the flagpole firmly into the ground. There they waited. After five minutes during which they neither moved nor spoke, two horsemen cantered towards them from the enemy camp. Behind them others followed on foot but stayed a respectful two-hundred paces back. Helmund and Hulderic pulled up their horses on the far side of the bridge. The two pairs of mounted men looked at each other for a moment then Quadratus spoke.

"Decurion, tell them that they have until sunset to collect their dead. Our men will not hinder them provided they do not attempt to attack us,."

Otto began to translate the legate's words into his German dialect but Hulderic interrupted him. "Why do you waste words? You know I speak your language." Otto carried on as if he had heard nothing.

"I also speak your tongue," Helmund said when Otto had finished.

Quadratus nodded his head and began to turn his horse around. This seemed to irritate Hulderic. He felt as if he and Helmund had been summoned, in some manner given an order and were now being dismissed.

"Is that all you have to say?" Hulderic asked.

"The noble Legate Publius Quadratus has nothing to say to you, man. He knows you to be a liar and a bearer of false tokens," Otto replied, according to the instructions he had been given and pulled the flagpole out of the turf.

They trotted back into their camp as the two Marcomanni made their way back to their own lines.

A large troop of the Marcomanni including some women, all unarmed and carrying green branches as a sign of peace, removed the bodies. The soldiers on the parapet watched keenly for any sign of treachery but remained silent.

"I'm surprised the legate made that offer to the enemy; to let them retrieve the bodies of their dead," Soranus said as some of the officers sat enjoying a flask of wine.

"Why?" Titus asked.

"I would have thought they should be left there as a warning to the rest of them."

"Well, maybe, but after three days the stench wafting up to our lads on the walkway would be unbearable. This way, they get carted off and we don't have to dig any burial pits. But it's political as well. Tribune Fuscus can explain all that to you. He's noble you see, and understands these things; me, I'm just common. I don't know nothing about politics," Titus said.

Tertius Fuscus raised one eyebrow. "But First Spear Centurion Attius, your rank automatically makes eligible to become a member of the Equestrian Order. You are no longer entitled to call yourself a commoner."

"Only if I show sufficient wealth and formally request to be enrolled," Titus shot back.

"And there you have it, Soranus. He doesn't want to let us all know the staggering amount of money he has accumulated over the years."

"Not as much as you imagine."

"Titus, you have no idea how much money I can imagine!"

They laughed and clinked wine cups.

"Give us the benefit of your noble insight, if you please," Titus requested.

"Very well," Tertius began. "The potential Equestrian, First Spear Centurion Titus Attius, is correct when he says our legate has arranged hygienic disposal of the enemy corpses with minimal effort on our part but he has done far more. The Marcomanni mutilated the bodies of our scouts and made a game of their remains. We, the civilized Romans, allow the removal of the enemy dead with dignity, demonstrating our innate superiority. As previously arranged with Quadratus, Otto tells Hulderic that he is a liar, something he cannot deny, while at the same time we keep our word and respect the truce we have proposed. Finally, Otto, obviously a German by birth, appears beside the legate riding that magnificent horse of his and wearing his parade armour; living proof of the advantages of allying oneself to Rome. We end up with the moral upper hand. They have played with our minds for days by doing nothing and letting us fret, now our legate has turned the tables on them. It's all part of warfare and not the least important part."

"See?" said Titus. "All that out of a little chat with the Marcomanni chiefs, marvellous stuff, politics. I wonder exactly how many men they lost today?"

"All of them," remarked Otto who had just walked in. He sat down and reached for a wine cup.

"I don't think so," Soranus corrected him. "We estimated one thousand four hundred bodies but around two thousand charged at us."

"Yes," Otto replied. "Those warriors who ran away will have to leave their army now. They challenged us and then were too weak to see it through. They're disgraced and they won't fight us again."

"Have you told the legate this?" Titus asked.

"Yes, he was pleased to learn it."

"This the victory you promised us is it, Helmund? Hundreds of our young men fallen and nothing to show for it. Where is this great difference under your leadership?" one of the chieftains raged at Helmund, spittle flying out of his snarling mouth and hanging in his beard.

"I told you clearly that the only way to defeat the Romans is by being as disciplined as they are. I do not remember ordering an attack.

"Our warriors had to respond to the insult the Romans offered us. Honour demanded it!" another aggrieved clan loudly complained.

"What insult?" Helmund asked mildly. He was sitting on a bench leaning against the fort wall enjoying what was left of the afternoon's warmth.

"They cut down the great Neidhard, champion of many battles, with their arrow machine. They did it to challenge the valour of our army!"

"No, they killed Neidhard because he was taunting them. I told him it was unwise but he would not listen and now he is dead."

"They killed him in a cowardly way, using a sly trick."

Helmund sighed and looked at the angry faces half-surrounding him.

"Neidhard was a great warrior but he was conceited. He loved acclaim and battle-fame above all. The Romans saw that even though he was so far away and they used his desire for praise to bring him down. They knew he could not resist picking up the arrows and brandishing them and that is how they killed him. They used his weakness against him, we must discover theirs and use it against them."

"Neidhard was a better man than you!" a middle-aged, burly warrior growled and pushed forward.

"Neidhard was a fool who died for nothing and cost me two thousand men," Helmund replied with a hard edge to his voice.

"You say he was a fool. I say you are a coward. If you and our whole army had charged today we would have smashed those Romans beneath our axes and spears. But you, you did nothing; you let better men face our enemy while you stood and watched. You are a coward and unfit to lead."

Helmund stood up and drew his sword. Men pulled back and made a space between him and his challenger. He stood with his feet the width of his shoulders apart, knees flexed, and waited. The enraged warrior levelled his spear and flew at him. Helmund half-turned to his left and bent his body like a bullfighter. The tip of the spear blade clanked against the chainmail links of his armour and passed by without doing any damage. Helmund pivoted to his right and extended his sword arm. The spearman could not stop his forward momentum. He ran onto the blade which tore through the base of his Adam's apple. He fell, writhing, and died; coughing and hacking blood from his mouth and gashed throat. Helmund raised his sword above his head.

"Let this man's war-band take his body and leave now. I will not enter into the blood-feud with them over this so they must be gone. Anyone else who disputes my right to command, let them also return to their homes. I want nothing of hotheads who refuse to listen to reason."

By the next morning, the Marcomanni army was smaller by over four thousand.

"Light more fires and spread the people out," Helmund ordered.

But two of the wagons had been taken by the disenchanted clansmen who had left. The Romans could not see exactly how diminished the Marcomanni were but guessed their number had shrunk considerably.

"Quarrelling among themselves and deserting; they never learn," Titus remarked complacently.

Helmund looked up at the sky. Sheets of high cloud were drifting in out of the west.

"It will have to be tomorrow," Hulderic told him quietly. "If we lose as many men in the next day or so, we'll be so weak the Romans can attack us and pin us against the riverbank".

"I know," Helmund responded. "It looks like it will be overcast tonight and the moon is waning. Call the leaders in."

It was a very dark night but not a silent one. The men on the walkways heard thuds and sounds like the squealing of wheels but no-one could make sense of what was going on. The first glimmers of daylight showed them.

Baulks of timber had been thrown down to reinforce the bridge over the ditch and standing on it was what looked like a shed. It was forty feet long and ten wide, its peaked roof and sides were covered in rawhides, skin-side out, dark with the water that had been flung over them to prevent fire-arrows having any effect. Ranged on either side were fifty, eight feet square log shields, far to heavy for a man to carry in battle, they were propped up on posts leaning back at a slight angle.

"Well I'll be buggered, it's a ram!" Titus exclaimed.

Inside the shed-like structure, a thirty-foot pointed, pine trunk was suspended on crossbeams. The roof was solid timber for protection against stones being hurled down on it. The side panels were of woven beech hurdles under the hides to lessen the weight; they were not as strong as the roof but they would stop most arrows and sling bullets. Six low wheels were bolted to the interior of the chassis on either side.

Behind each propped shield, crouched ten men and there were eighty manning the ram under the shelter of the roof. They were too close for the ballistas to play on them and solid enough to withstand a volley of arrows. A mass of warriors was gathering down the hill well beyond the range of the Roman artillery. They were waiting only for the light to improve and a signal to begin the assault.

Horns sounded and whistles shrilled inside the camp as the legionaries ran to their positions. The officers' hearts sank although they all retained an impassive expression. If they lost the Porta Praetoria, they were in severe trouble and they knew it.

Titus saluted the legate, "Preparing to repel sir, all we can do."

"Sir, if I may," Tertius broke in. "I have a better idea. I need five centuries, all our archers and slingers and all the scorpions, if they can be deployed in time; looks like we have five minutes or less."

"Proceed, Tribune Fuscus," Quadratus told him.

"Right Titus, on me. Cestus! Boxer! I want every available scorpion placed on the parade ground ten feet back from the Ports Praetoria, lined up and aimed dead level. Get them as tight together you can. Corvo! Where is Corvo? Oh, there you are, all your men behind the artillery ready to loose on command. Titus, strong ropes and a century with siege spears, no shields. Other men standing by. You lot," he pointed at a group of twenty soldiers, "drop your shields and javelins and stand ready to fling the gates open on my signal then close them again."

But the ram did not trundle towards the gate. It stood menacing and silent while frantic activity went on only thirty or so paces away behind the camp walls. The defenders had longer than they thought. Helmund was going to attempt to advance in well-spread ranks the full width of the front, leaving a space of four paces between each. Initially, they would march and run only when in range of the Roman missiles. It took a great amount of shouting and pulling men back into place and until he was satisfied, he would not give the signal for the ram to engage.

It was a well-thought out strategy. The ram would smash the gate, the warriors heaving it would be supported by the others rushing in from behind their fixed protective shields. This elite would fight in the entrance to the camp until the bulk of the army joined them when the Romans would be overwhelmed by superior numbers. For it to work, everyone must be in his place and ready to take his part. The Marcomanni were not used to forming straight lines and keeping the correct distance between them and the next man. Helmund had explained that he could not prevent missiles being fired at them but if they were widely spaced, casualties would be less and each man had some chance of stepping out of the way of an incoming bolt or stone. In theory, they had agreed but now every warrior wanted to be in the front and centre, the place of glory. The minutes were ticking by.

"They seem to be organising in formation rather than rushing up in a body," Quadratus shouted down to Tertius on the Via Praetoria below him.

"Thank you sir. Please shout "Now", when the front of their ram-housing is one-foot from the gate," Tertius called back.

"One-foot away call, "Now". Understood," the legate confirmed.

"Right, explain," Titus demanded.

"You put the idea in my head," "Tertius told him. "You mentioned the Trojan Horse so we are going to reverse it. When they are ready to pound our gates, we fling them open and pour scorpion bolts and arrows the length of their ram killing everyone under the roof. The men with siege spears go in to finish them off and protect the open end while the rest of us throw ropes over the beams and drag it inside. Our spearmen retreat with it. We bang the gates shut and we're done."

"Gods, what a risky manoeuvre," Titus said.

"We have nothing to lose. If they force their way inside, we shall all be wading in blood in any case."

Titus said nothing in reply but roared out to the centurions and optios of the various groups. He issued a series of precise orders to them and watched them run back to their men and repeat what they had to do. He did not even shout at them for running instead of, "walking at a brisk pace to avoid panicking the men". His own heart was racing but he stood calmly holding his vine-staff in both hands behind his back and rocking on his heels, the model of the imperturbable First Spear Centurion.

Helmund finally got the bulk of his force moving. After only three paces their lines were already bowed and bent but he could expect no better. He signalled to his herald who blew repeated, long horn-blasts. It had taken two hundred men to position the ram overnight. The eighty men under its roof were fresh and the biggest and strongest in the army. They heard the call to engage and put their massive shoulders to the side supports and heaved. Nothing happened. During the time it had rested outside the camp, the wheels had sunk slightly into the ground. They pushed again and this time there was a tremor, a minute forward movement and a falling back. The third time the wheels began to turn, slowly at first and faster as the warriors found and stamped out a rhythm. Sling bullets began to hit the sides and bounce off. A few arrows penetrated a little but did no damage. It grew darker inside as they gate came nearer and cut off the light. The warriors began to chant in unison as they rolled towards fame. The adrenalin rush of coming battle flowed through their veins.

Up on the walkway, Quadratus yelled, "Now".

The darkness changed to a widening band of brightness as the two leaves of the gate folded back in front of them. In the growing rectangle they saw scorpion crews and archers just feet away. They began to loose their arrows as soon as they had a target. At point blank range, the scorpion bolts transfixed two or three men with one strike. There was nowhere to hide from the arrow-storm in that enclosed hell. Within seconds, Helmund's shock troops were sprawled, dead or dying, in a what had become a charnel house. A whistle blew, the artillery pieces were dragged out of the way and the archers fell back. The eighty proud warriors who had been destroyed were replaced by an equal number of legionaries who ran in with eight-foot broad-bladed spears. They thrust at the Marcomanni, irrespective of whether they were completely dead or not and formed a hedge of spear points at the open rear of the ram housing. A second whistle, ropes were flung over any convenient beam or projection. Three-hundred legionaries and officers jostled for a place on them, grabbed and hauled. The legionaries within retreated with it and, once it was fully inside the walls of the camp, the gates were slammed-to. The whole operation had taken less than three minutes. A great shout of triumph echoed off the walls of the camp.

The enemy concealed behind the fixed wooden shields below the Roman walls did not know what to do. They had been told to remain in place ready to charge to the attack when they heard the gates splinter and the victorious war-cry of their comrades manning the ram. There had been no sound of smashing timber and the roar they had heard was not their own men. One of them looked round the side of the logs and fell back with a star-shaped, bloody hole in his forehead where a sling bullet had smashed his skull. They looked back towards their own lines and saw a sight of total confusion. Some were running forward, others retreating. The chieftains were shouting and waving their arms about. Gradually, order was restored and the army retired. This left them in an impossible position. If they ran back, they would be brought down like hares by the archers but if they stayed, the legion might sally out in force and annihilate them. The logs they crouched behind gave them their only security and none of them was inclined to leave it.

"A good beginning to our day's work, gentlemen, but we are not yet finished. We have to do something about those men hiding at the foot of our walls," Quadratus said.

"The First Cohort marches through the Porta Praetoria, sir and wipes them out. Simple and effective," Attius suggested.

"I have no doubt that they could not resist you more than a few minutes, First Spear Centurion Attius but, so far, we have not lost a single Roman life although, sadly two of our scouts have been killed. Let me rephrase so no disrespect is shown to our auxiliary cavalry as none is intended. We have lost no-one in battle. I would like to maintain that happy state. It will depress the enemy's spirits to think that so many of them have fallen while we remain unharmed. Boxer, you have studied the books the Emperor sent you; Cestus, you have been at this game a long time. Come up with something between you," the legate responded.

They looked at each other with a resigned expression and wandered about staring at their artillery pieces, muttering together and occasionally scratching triangles and arcs in the dirt with a stick. Then they both stood with their backs to the gate and paced the length of the parade ground to the far end, twice. The artillerymen were ordered to drag a ballista to the cross they had marked on the ground just inside the Porta Decumana opposite the Porta Praetoria. Cestus had ammunition brought up while Lucius returned to the legate and saluted. He pointed to Cestus in the distance.

"We believe we have the range to lob a missile over the gate from there sir. I'll need the entire front wall cleared just in case of error. Oh, and Corvo's century standing by and the loan of a whistle…."

"Here," said Titus, "take this one."

Lucius stood alone on the walkway over the gate. He had removed the scarf he used to stop his armour chafing his neck and tied it to an arrow-shaft. This was his signalling flag. He raised it horizontally in both hands and brought it down sharply. Cestus fired. The twenty- pound stone with which it was loaded left the slide and hurtled up into the air to crash into the parapet three feet from Lucius. The whole wall vibrated with the shock and a burst of splinters flew off, one spiking Lucius in the forearm. He grunted at the pain but ignored it for the moment. He flapped his flag in one hand indicating that they must adjust for height. He waited patiently, picking at his splinter while the ballista was being tautened and reloaded. This time the missile screamed over his head and thudded into the turf two paces short and three to the left of one of the log refuges. Lucius signalled, Cestus fired and missed again, and the next time and the next. The sixth shot hit the top edge of a log shield shattering it. The shocked men who had been hiding behind it, extricated themselves and ran for their lives, leaving behind them one dead and two injured comrades. Cestus and his crew had their line now and every other shot hit its target. When nine had been toppled over or smashed into firewood, the

Germans ran out of all of them, damaged or not. Lucius blew his whistle. Corvo and his men jogged up onto the walkway and began to cut down the fleeing figures. Of the original five hundred warriors, one hundred and twenty reached safety.

Chapter 5

It was not yet noon. The Romans had completed their clean-up operation. The enemy bodies had been moved to the other side of the ditch but this time they were left in an ignominious heap of tangled and bloody torsos and limbs. The undamaged log squares they had attempted to use for the protection of their advance force were dragged into the camp so that nothing of any use was left. The soldiers were grinning. They admired Tertius even more now, in spite of him remaining a cold and remote figure. They loved a clever trick that deceived an enemy above everything and the business of stealing the Marcomanni battering-ram was the best they had ever heard of, let alone witnessed.

Around the table in the officers' mess, faces were jubilant at the midday meal. Quadratus was cautiously pleased.

"This Helmund is a formidable opponent. From his strategy so far, it is clear to me that he is attempting to use our own methods against us. However, he lacks both the technology and the disciplined troops to match his ambition. We must not fail to remain wary of him."

A legionary was admitted with news from the centurion commanding the guard on the north walkway. Quadratus read the wax tablet.

"It would appear that a considerable number of the enemy are passing back over the Rhine. Good news, but we do not know the precise number," he said.

Attius looked at him with an unvoiced question. The legate read his thoughts and smiled.

"Yes, Titus, I am considering engaging them on the riverbank. Let us prepare and stand by to attack tomorrow if they have lost enough men today and overnight. I am unwilling to commit to battle without cavalry support on our flanks if we are outnumbered by three to one. Below that, we should be able to handle them."

"But we have our secret weapon, sir," Titus replied, "the genius of Senior Tribune Tertius Fuscus. I salute you." He raised his wine cup to Tertius. The others followed suit.

Tertius smiled modestly. "Hardly genius; a simple application of logic. We could not destroy their ram. Their ram could not be allowed to destroy our gate. Therefore temporarily remove the gate and the ram cannot destroy it. Let us not forget the contribution of our artillery officers, practical mathematics to the rescue!"

"Indeed not," said Quadratus, "how is the arm today, Boxer?"

"Fine, sir" Lucius lied. It was throbbing under the linen bandage he wore on his forearm. The splinter had gone in too deep for it to be removed with forceps alone so the medical officer had cut with a scalpel while his orderly pulled at the exposed end. They had poured salt and vinegar into the wound to disinfect it. The nagging pain had kept him awake most of the night. "I've had an idea about protecting our flanks sir, if we go for them tomorrow…"

"Come on then, Boxer, what have you thought up now?" Titus asked.

"Well, Principal Decurion Longius has thirty cavalry. Suppose we divide our archers and slingers into two groups and mount eight scorpions on carts. We can have sixty missile troops, four scorpions and their crews on each wing of the legion. If the archers are pressed back by the enemy, the cavalry can protect the artillery."

"Well worth considering, Tribune Longius. No doubt First Spear Centurion Attius will give it more thought," Quadratus told him.

"It will be difficult to get the men into formation fast enough," Tertius commented. "We have only that one bridge over Boxer's Canal." As his ditch was now universally called by the men.

"But we've got lots of those log efforts they tried to hide behind. We could fasten them together in pairs. Should be alright and we'd get nearly a score of crossing points…." Titus told him.

Quadratus slightly raised his voice. "You are all speaking as if a general engagement is certain. Please remember, I will not make my decision until I have a clearer picture of the enemy's strength."

Helmund was not facing furious opposition this time. No-one hurled abuse at him or challenged him. They avoided making eye-contact and said nothing. It was as if he had become unclean, a pariah, to many of the chieftain. He retreated into the fortress and sat alone brooding. He knew as well as Quadratus did that this was becoming a numbers game. It always was when fighting the Romans. In the open, their superior arms and tactics made them favourites even if the odds were four to one against them. He knew they had no cavalry but if his army shrank much below ten thousand, they would come for him and with only one Rhine crossing at his back, his people would be massacred.

The attack for which he had so carefully prepared for days had ended not in failure but in humiliation. In a few minutes, all the work building his devices and the ideas behind them had been blown away like a dandelion clock on the softest breeze. He was coming to the painful conclusion that the Romans were too good at what they did for he and his men to best them playing to the same rules. Late in the afternoon, Hulderic entered with a platter of cold meat and bread. He left the door open behind him. In the shaft of light that streamed in, Helmund saw a stream of warriors, some with their womenfolk, crossing the bridge back they way they had come. Their heads hung low, their shoulders were slumped and they carried their weapons despondently. They were defeated; yet again.

"How many?" he asked Hulderic who squatted down beside him.

"Three, four thousand, more by morning. This time tomorrow you will no longer have an army and you will never raise another one."

"Bring me some ale then leave me. I need to think," Helmund said.

He ate and drank He stood up and stretched then walked out into the golden, afternoon light. He stood in an open space, drew his sword and holding it over his head, he addressed his people.

"No more of this. No more behaving like they do with their deceit and machines and twisted, southern minds. We are Marcomanni. If we are challenged, we rise up and face whoever dares oppose us. If we see an enemy in front of us, we rush on him and bring him low. Tonight I go to attack the Roman camp. Dawn will bring them spears and axes. I shall spill Roman blood or I die where I stand but I shall die like a warrior and songs will be sung about my ending in the ale-halls. Who is with me?"

Many had looked up while he spoke only to turn back to their packing or stare down at their feet when he was finished. But some got to their feet and went to him, only a few at first. As the group around Helmund swelled, others glanced hesitantly at their companions and walked over to the growing war-band. Close to a thousand warriors still had faith in him. Helmund surveyed them with grim satisfaction. They were enough. If they succeeded, waverers would follow.

"Eat, rest; we go at sunset," he told them and stepped over to the wagons with Hulderic to pick up the equipment they would need.

In the long gloaming as the sun sank over the abandoned farmsteads to the west, Helmund left his camp followed by his volunteers. Their shadows danced long in front of them as they made their way eastwards towards the forest edge.

No matter how forcibly Quadratus warned against complacency, the legionaries and the inexperienced among the junior officers believed they had already won. The men were thinking about what they were sure would be the decisive battle to come the next day. The sentries still looked out over the dark land but their minds were elsewhere and they stopped for quick, illicit talks with their comrades. Nothing was lax, no-one left their post but the legion had lost its sense of being in danger. The huge mass of Marcomanni that had appeared so threatening at first had been thrashed on the two occasions they had dared to attack. Tomorrow, would bring an end to them.

Twenty of Helmund's men crawled through the bracken from tree-stump to tree-stump down the steep incline towards the north-east corner of the camp. When the sentries on the walkway approached, they froze. When the soldiers turned their backs to patrol in the other direction, they advanced. Once at the bottom of the hill, one of the warriors cupped his hands and made the churring sound of a nightjar. At that signal, another forty men who had been waiting half-way up, began their cautious descent with others breaking out of the skirts of the forest behind them.

The sentry reached the end of his beat at the corner of the northern wall and turned. A loop of rope flipped up over one of the hundreds of wooden posts that together formed the walls. Where it caught was in the deeper shadow cast by the floor of the ballista tower ten feet above. A silent, naked man, his face and body blackened with charcoal-dust, swarmed up the knotted rope and crouched against the parapet. A second man flowed like ink over the wall and squatted beside him. The legionary on guard reached the far end of his designated length of walkway, turned and began to walk towards them. He was looking out into the distance and never saw the man who rose up like a dark wraith at his feet until crushing fingers grabbed his throat. He was unable to make a sound, staring into the white eyes of his killer as life faded from him and other hands gently lowered him to the wooden walkway. The nightjar called again. More ropes were thrown, more men scrambled up them, grabbing at spears and axes and shields passed from below. There were over a dozen of them now. The guard on the eastern wall saw movement and came nearer, unable to believe his eyes He fell dead to a thrown axe that smashed into his face. He dropped his shield which slid down the earth slope below the walkway onto the parade ground but it did not make enough noise to alert anyone. Twenty of the enemy were within the walls when the alarm sounded. They prepared to defend their comrades still climbing in. A grapnel attached to a stout cable was hooked over the parapet. Unseen hands hauled on it from below. The sound of digging was heard as mattocks cut into the earth at the base of the wall. As long as their fellows already inside could defend this corner of the rampart, they could work without having spears and stones thrown down on them.

The sun rose over the eastern, ridge suffusing the camp in a steely, grey light. The invaders were now clearly visible. Whistles and horns sounded, legionaries tumbled out of their barracks or ran up onto the walkways and rushed to the threatened corner. Viewed from the parade ground, two groups of men were locked in fatal struggles on both the east and north walls. The Romans still had the advantage of their superior arms but they were fighting man to man on a narrow platform. The Marcomanni spears held them at bay out of the reach of their short swords and as more men poured in over the corner of the walls, they were forced back.

Titus Attius took in the situation in one rapid glance. It was essential that the Germans did not fight their way to the gates. If they did, it was possible they could unlock them from the inside with catastrophic results. He called the nearest thirty men to him and ran closer to the base of the wall.

"Javelins, loose," he roared.

The heavy javelins smashed through the flimsy shields the warriors carried and several fell. Then things took a turn for the worse, as far as Titus and his men were concerned. The invaders noticed the chests of stones. One at first, and then a few more, began to shower them on the legionaries below. They clanged off helmets and dazed the men who lifted their shields high to protect their heads. This left their legs and feet exposed and very soon they were forced to withdraw out of range.

With a groan, the first post of the wall was wrenched out of position. It canted outwards at an angle like a half-pulled loose tooth. Axes played on the bindings holding it to its neighbours and it fell free into the external ditch with a shower of earth as its part of the rampart was destabilised and collapsed. The grapnel was transferred to the next and it fell with less effort, and another and another. There were now two hundred Marcomanni in the camp. They began to leap off the walkways and fight on the parade ground and Via Praetoria, inching towards the gate.

The Roman defence was faltering. Their strength lay in their ordered and mutually supportive ranks when facing an enemy but this battle was a disorganised melee. A century would try to form up and act together only to find that a warrior had hurled himself on them from behind. Some legionaries were forced to turn to deal with this threat, exposing their backs to others coming in from the front. One quarter of the camp interior was soon full of frantic men thrusting with spears and swords. Axes hooked over shield-rims to drag them aside exposing legionaries to spears, others split helmets and heads, lopped hands and arms. Screams, curses and war-cries blended together into a discordant pandemonium. The stink of sweat, blood and spilt bowels hung like an invisible miasma over the struggling combatants.

Titus stood back, panting. His sword and vine-staff were both dripping with blood. An axe stroke had carved away half his left-hand shoulder protection. The steel and leather hung against his chest, swinging as he moved. As he surveyed the battle, he recognised the pattern underlying the apparent chaos. Quadratus came over and stood beside him.

"What next, Titus?" he asked in a casual tone.

"I see our way through this now, sir. When we regain control of that corner, we can pinch this mob off and deal with them. Double pronged attack on the walkways and containment down here," he turned away and yelled for Corvo. The centurion doubled over to him and saluted.

"Are your men engaging the enemy?" Titus asked.

"Yes, sir."

"Withdraw them at once and get them to me with their slings and bows. Send one of them to bring me Boxer."

Lucius arrived red-faced and blood smeared.

"What are you doing?"

"Trying to organise our left to keep them back from the Porta Praetoria."

"Let Cestus take over and...."

"No more Cestus sir, spear," Lucius said blankly.

"Very well, leave it to me. Find Otto. Half his men on the east wall half on the north. Drive those bastards back and hold that corner."

At that moment, the artillery tower crashed down spilling the heavy ballista it had carried onto the struggling men, indiscriminately smashing limbs and skulls.

"Oh that's the cherry on top, that is," Titus muttered just as Corvo ran up. "Withdraw your men to the other side of the Via Praetoria and start shooting at those swine on the walkways. Be sure of your targets and don't hit our own."

The massive First Spear Centurion strode forward. A warrior leaped at him with his axe raised. Titus thrust his vine-staff into the snarling face. He heard the satisfying crunch of breaking teeth and hit him on the temple as he recoiled. Titus stepped over him as he fell at his feet and shouted at the top of his parade ground volume.

"Right lads. Sort yourselves out. Form up. Form up. Close 'em in. Stop fannying about and knock that big bugger down. That's it. Second rank into position…."

With shouts, shoves and encouragement he managed to deploy his soldiers in a treble rank, enclosing the enemy between it and the walls. The arrows and sling bullets began to fly. A few warriors fell and tumbled down onto their comrades below but it was impossible for Corvo's men to use volley fire with their own men so close..

Otto had given Lucius half his men and armed him with a cavalry lance, a long sword and an oval shield. Lucius took the northern wall while Otto moved his men up onto the eastern walkway. They pushed through the legionaries, still fighting although hard-pressed, and faced the Marcomanni. They had no advantage now. They faced lances as long as their spears and swords as good for a swinging cut as a stabbing thrust. The walkway was only wide enough for three men to stand shoulder to shoulder so their numerical superiority meant nothing. After a minute or two, the invaders were no longer advancing and after a further short time, they took their first backward steps.

All this while, the demolition works had continued out of sight. A total of fifty feet of wall was gone. The earth rampart had collapsed filling what had been the defensive ditch. The unsupported walkway sagged on top of the heap of sand and earth from which wall-posts protruded at all angles; many of them had been dragged yards away and hacked through with axes.

The unbroken arc of Roman shields began to move forward squeezing the warriors tighter into the corner. The psychological tipping point was reached and a few began to scramble through the gap with the intention of flight. A horn from outside the camp sounded the recall. They were compelled to fight on the retreat. Some knew that there was no hope for them so they flung themselves on the legionaries intent on taking as many of them with them as they could. The last few minutes of the engagement were the bloodiest, on both sides.

It was over; no more clashing of arms, just silence other than for the groans and screams of the wounded and dying but a sudden smell of smoke. Otto looked out over his side of the parapet. Men were loping up the hill into the forest but they had left a parting gift.

Brushwood soaked in pine-pitch had been piled up around the base of the broken wall and set alight. When the big timbers caught, they hissed and sizzled as the resin boiled out of them before flaring up and adding to the conflagration.

A weary band of legionaries was detailed to throw earth over the fire to starve it of air. After half an hour, they had managed to cover it but it was still smouldering underneath; whips of smoke and the odd flame broke through. An unfortune soldier climbed to the top of the heap to tip on another bucket of sand and was killed by a long, black hunting arrow. The enemy had left archers hidden behind the tree stumps ready to pick off any easy target.

The wounded intruders were sent to hell with a boot-heel to the throat or a sword strike. The bodies were sorted into two groups; the Marcomanni in a grotesque heap which was quickly thrown over the walls, the Romans laid out in rows for cremation. The infirmary was overflowing and added a trickle to the number of the dead for the rest of the day and overnight as men succumbed to their wounds or were given the mercy of a quick cut from the medical officer's scalpel.

How different was the officers' midday break than it had been the day before; no smiling faces now, no talk of marching out to give battle. They drank to the shade of Cestus Valens but his was not the only face missing. Soranus was sleeping in the infirmary under a draft of poppy juice. In the course of the fight, he had picked up a fallen shield to protect himself in the close-quarters butchery. Unfortunately it had already been weakened. A lance thrust went through and sheared off the thumb of his left hand. Had the injury been to his right hand, he would no longer have been able to hold a sword and his military career would probably have been over.

Quadratus was making an attempt to show his usual calm face to the world but the strain showed. He looked drawn, the lines around his mouth deeper since last evening.

"How many?" he asked Titus, bleakly.

The First Spear Centurion consulted a wax tablet.

"Four hundred and twenty legionaries and non-commissioned officers, ten centurions and eight optios, dead. Our valued artillerist and dear comrade Cestus Valens dead. One hundred and fifty wounded of whom one hundred are fit for duty or will be in a day or two. Of the others, the medical officer will make no comment, waiting for time to kill or cure. Tribune Rufus Vulso Soranus has a permanently damaged left hand. Of theirs, we have counted three hundred and seventy-five."

Tertius broke the long silence that followed Titus' reading of the "butcher's bill".

"We have lost a valuable senior officer and ten percent of our effective force in one engagement. We cannot sustain losses at this level for long."

"Indeed not," Quadratus responded. "It would seem that Helmund has given up trying to out-think us and reverted to the usual tactics of his people. It would further seem that he has succeeded, probably beyond his expectations. What of the physical damage to our camp?"

Titus looked at his notes and continued.

"A twenty-foot length of the northern wall and thirty feet of the eastern are down. The ditch in that area is filled with soil off the rampart and they have lit fires in the gap. The walkway is now incomplete. The corner artillery tower is destroyed as is one ballista. We are weakened, there's no denying it. We can't march out in force to give battle with our defences incomplete. If we were outflanked, we should lose the camp. If we hold enough men in reserve to defend it, we do not have the numbers to take them on down by the river."

"We shall need carefully to consider our next move. Abandoning our position is not an option, even if we did have our full compliment of cavalry to screen our withdrawal. My orders are to hold this camp at all costs. We need to reflect. Boxer, study the broken-down wall and report to me with your ideas of the best engineering solution to rectify that problem. You do not have long to come up with something. Now, Titus, awards for this action?" Quadratus asked..

"Principal Decurion Otto Longius and Tribune Lucius Longius for their spirited attack helping to clear the walkway. Tribune Rufus Soranus for fighting on with a wounded hand until he fainted due to loss of blood…" Titus began but the legate interrupted him.

"… And First Spear Centurion Titus Attius for rallying the men, forming ranks and tactical awareness when all might have been lost."

"Those are the duties of my rank, sir." Titus protested.

"Oh, shut up and take another decoration Titus, you know you deserve it. Gentlemen, we must look to ourselves and anticipate another attack of a similar nature."

"But not at dawn tomorrow, sir," Otto said. "Tonight there will be feasting and ale by the river and sore heads in the morning."

Accompanied by four legionaries to protect him against hidden archers and covered by Corvo's men up on the walls, Lucius scrambled around the ruined section of wall taking measurements. Two of his bodyguard soon had arrows embedded in their shields. It was a mess and a massive problem but he had the theoretical knowledge and manpower to solve it. He examined the battering ram that still stood in the centre of the Via Praetoria then went to his room and began his calculations.

Otto had been correct about the Marcomanni. By noon the fire pits had been dug and glowed white hot with charcoal. Pigs and two oxen were suspended over them on spits. Their sizzling fat sent a delicious aroma along the riverbank. Men salivated at the smell as the ale horns began to be filled and knocked back although it was not yet late afternoon. By nightfall, drunken men with a hunk of roast meat in one hand and an ale horn in the other danced around the fires. "Hail Helmund!" they shouted, "Hail Helmund the Victor!" "Hail King Helmund!" Some waved pugio daggers, swords or helmets seized as booty. Others had more grisly trophies: hands and ears which they hurled into the flames as an offering to Tiw.

Helmund sat on a high seat of honour raising his ale horn in acknowledgement of the praise being heaped on him with a fixed smile on his face. If he raised the horn, he drank little. His smile masked his contempt of the orgy of self-congratulation going on around him. As soon as most of his warriors were too drunk to notice his absence he slipped away and walked a little along the bank of the Rhine with Hulderic.

"What victory is being celebrated? We have wounded the beast but he remains in his lair. When we go again to try to drive him out, he will turn and rend us," Helmund said.

Hulderic chuckled. "You are too intense. Let them drink and celebrate, it will give them courage in the next attack. Those who were not with us today have seen the fine swords and daggers their comrades have looted. They are jealous and will want to be with you next time. We have drawn blood, that is our victory; be content with what has been gained however little it may be."

"We needed to hit them again at first light tomorrow..."

"That would have been better," Hulderic conceded, "But it is not in the nature of our people to let a reason for feasting pass us by."

"You're right but we must press them again and even harder..."

"I know, I know..."

The fast flying clouds let moonlight flood across the river. They pulled their cloaks tighter around them against the chill breeze. Helmund turned and saw a few torches flickering around the base of the corner of the Roman camp that his men had destroyed and laughed softly, imagining their panic.

Chapter 6

In spite of their orders to stay in position until nightfall, the Marcomanni archers drifted away during the hour that followed the end of the battle. They did not want to miss their share of glory and feasting. Lucius did not know that and began his exploratory repair works behind a screen of two heavy-infantry centuries overlapping their shields as a defence against in-coming arrows. The work party was set to clearing away the sand and earth half-covering the fallen wall-posts. Smoke began to rise as they dug down and fire broke out again when air reached the timbers which had been slowly smouldering since early morning under their blanket of soil. Water was thrown on the flames and the posts dragged clear for inspection. This was no easy task. Each of them was an eighteen-inch diameter tree-trunk striped of its branches. The wall had been built by dropping them upright side-by-side into a trench which was then back-filled with tamped-down gravel and sand. Each post was fixed to its neighbour with bindings and horizontal support timbers. They lasted longer if they were positioned upside down. Of the thirty-three that had been pulled free, twenty were reusable. The others were too hacked about by axes or severely charred. The useless ones were dragged away and flung into Boxer's Canal where they sank into the mud and made it even more treacherous underfoot. The remainder were carried inside the walls through the gap.

Lucius was busy making measurements using a knotted string and a wooden set square when Quadratus surged up behind him.

"Well?" the legate asked sharply, his anxiety evident in the tone of his voice.

"I cannot repair the wall…." Lucius began but then he was stopped short.

"And I cannot accept that. You are the nearest thing to a military engineer we have. It's up to you. Find a way…"

It was Lucius turn to interrupt. "If I could finish speaking, sir?"

Quadratus sighed. "Of course, my apologies, Boxer."

"I cannot repair the defences as they were because I do not have enough posts. Some are weakened by fire, others damaged by axes. I can, however, make a new wall straight across the gap in the existing one. We will no longer have a north- east corner. My wall will cross between the broken ends of the north and east walls diagonally."

"So I shall have a five-sided camp. Four long sides and your new, short side?"

"That's the best I can do sir."

"And not a bad best at that. What do you need?"

"All the men who are delegated to assist in laying out a marching-camp, all the carpenters we have, the blacksmiths and as many men with spades and mattocks as First Spear Centurion Attius can spare."

"You have them. Can it be done by dawn tomorrow, working by torch light?"

"Honestly, sir, I don't know. I have never done anything like it before. We shall try, for all our sakes."

He stretched a pair of strings two feet apart and told the first party of legionaries Titus sent over to dig a trench between them three feet deep.

"Get right up to the ends of the walls and keep the sides straight and unbroken," he ordered.

The second party were sent outside to dig a new ditch and rampart to meet up with the two undamaged ones. While the soldiers sweated in the warm afternoon and the earth from their spades was loaded into baskets and carried away, Lucius consulted the master carpenter.

"A couple of posts on each side of the breech are weakened. They will need extra support. I had an idea but I don't know if it's practical, come and look at this." He led him over to the battering-ram and slapped the massive log still suspended under the roof-beams. "Can we cut this to length and use it to reinforce the ends?"

"'Course we can sir. I'll get a couple of lads on it right away. Looks to me like we can get two lengths just short of fourteen feet. Got to cut the point off you see. While we're sawing it up, can I suggest some of my men take down what's left of the walkway and the artillery tower? Probably be able to re-use some of it…"

"Can we build a new tower?

"Not by tomorrow. Can make an artillery platform behind the parapet of the new wall if you like…"

Lucius stood watching, temporarily without employment while legionaries and immunes swarmed over the worksite to cries of "Watch your head! Out the bloody way! Oi, mind what you're doing!". He went over to the artillery store. All the specialists were engrossed in trying to repair the ballista which had been thrown off the tower when it was cut down.

"How's it going?" he asked.

"We're getting there sir, bit tricky, if you'd excuse me..."

Which was a polite way of saying, "Get lost, we're busy."

He went to the blacksmith's forges.

"I need some sort of ironwork to clench the uprights of the new wall that's going up."

"Can we have a look sir?" the master smith asked.

The ram was resting on the wedges on the ground now with two pairs of sweating men working on it with double-handed saws. Two other crews stood by to relieve them. The blacksmith asked the diameter of the timber.

"Three-foot," the chief sawyer told him.

"And you want this clenched to another post, is that it sir?

"Two other posts, actually, and they're both eighteen inches diameter," Lucius told him.

"How many attachments do you want?"

"Three each side."

"What you want is six-foot strips of iron pierced for spikes, and the spikes, of course. Easy enough to make. But they'll cool down too much in the time it takes to get them over from the smithy. Won't be soft enough to bend around tight. I'll get them made and set up a field-forge over here near the work and we can heat 'em up enough to bang 'em round the woodwork when you're ready."

Ropes to be used for bindings were soaking in saltwater. It was better to coil them around the posts wet so that they would tighten even more as they dried. A little pitch would waterproof them against sagging in the rain.

Felix hobbled over with bread and wine for Lucius "to keep his strength up" but really to take a look at the works. He approved. Titus kept hovering in the background asking if Lucius needed anymore men.

"Not at the moment, but we will when we are ready to start construction," Lucius told him.

Because he could not bear to be standing idly by, the First Spear Centurion went over to the men digging out the trench and new ditch. "Put your backs into it you idle sods. Boxer will be reporting any man who doesn't do his share to me. Gods help that man," he yelled and nodded to Lucius as he walked away as if to say, "No need to thank me.".

The trench was dug and cut out wider at each end to accommodate the timbers which had previously been the battering ram. It was now neatly sawed into two equal lengths and had been smoothed with adzes. An hour before sundown, they were lifted into place using only manpower and foul language. They dropped into position with satisfactory thuds. The leather-aproned blacksmiths bent the hot iron around the posts and hammered in the spikes. The timber hissed and smoked sending up a sweet aroma of pine. The ends of the north and east walls were now secured and stabilized.

Once the teams had established a rhythm, it took ten minutes for each intermediate post to be wrestled into place, bound and the trench backfilled with crushed stone and sand, well tamped down with heavy wooden mallets. Twenty posts took them past the natural light of the long northern evening and into working by torch-light but before midnight, the wall was complete. The new length of ditch and rampart had been completed before the last, low western rays of the sun had faded.

Now it was the rime for the carpenters to prove their expertise. After lengthy discussions, Lucius vetoed the construction of a new ballista platform on the walkway.

"The kick-back is too powerful," he said.

"Respectfully, sir, are you questioning our skill when it comes to woodwork?" the master carpenter asked.

"Respectfully, are you questioning my skill when it comes to artillery?" Lucius countered.

They both grinned and settled on a scorpion platform. The machine was lighter and so was its ammunition. The battering-ram housing was dismantled. The timbers were cannibalized to make the upright supports of the new length of walkway and artillery platform. A scorpion was hauled up into position and secured with a ring bolt. It could be swivelled through one-hundred degrees without risk of the recoil pushing it off backwards onto the parade ground. The blacksmith at the field-forge had obligingly stood by and was able to provide some extra angle-brackets and heavy nails to strengthen the new timberwork.

As the sky showed the first hint of dawn they were finished. A runner was sent for the legate to inspect the works. He arrived with Tertius and Attius in tow, all three wearing immaculate uniforms and looking like they had just stepped out of the baths.

The legate climbed up onto the repaired section of wall first followed by Tertius and Attius who jumped up and down a couple of times to see if it would splinter under his weight.

Red-eyed and aching with fatigue, Lucius stood to attention at the head of his party of exhausted craftsmen. Quadratus came back down the ladder and stood in front of them, beaming.

"I have always been proud to lead The Second Lucan but seldom as proud as I am this minute. Magnificent work men; the general would not approve of a five-sided camp, but I do. I most certainly do. We shall have to call it the pentagon. Go and have something to eat and rest, knowing you have earned the gratitude of your officers and the entire legion."

After their own breakfast, Hulderic and Helmund rode out of their lines to the east. They halted at a spot half-way up the slope where they would have a good view of the damage their raid had done yesterday. There was nothing to be seen, only a level and upright wall over a ditch where they had left fallen timbers and heaped earth. Hulderic threw up his hands.

"The bastards, the scum! They remade it!"

"They worked all night, we feasted, think on that," Helmund told him.

"All that blood and battle fury, those men lost for nothing," Hulderic said bitterly.

"No, not for nothing; look more closely. They could not rebuild it as it was. Their camp is smaller now., We have diminished them."

"Maybe, but at what price?"

Helmund smiled grimly. "The price we must pay to be rid of them. There are two lessons here. Firstly, we can damage them, secondly, when we have weakened these Romans, they must be given no time to restore the damage we have done them. If we lose five-thousand warriors we can fight on. If their numbers are reduced by half that, there will not be enough of them left to defend their walls. Victory to the last man standing, my friend. Come. Let's go back and think about our next move."

When the news that the Roman fortress had been repaired spread through the Marcomanni lines, a thousand warriors left the army. But this time, as they crossed over the Rhine, they did so to a barrage of cat-calls and displays of bare buttocks as the determined core of Helmund's force demonstrated their contempt. They took the heroic efforts the Romans had made overnight to repair the damage as a personal insult. Their commander cautioned them against a mad rush for revenge.

"The night is our friend. The demons and evil spirits that walk abroad in the darkness are our friends; they are of this land and the Romans are not. Surprise and craft are our friends, we shall use them. But our greatest friend is undaunted courage. We shall cut them to pieces bit by bit until they run south like women and then we shall fall on them and slaughter every last one."

Soranus appeared at midday, pale and walking very carefully. The jolt of his boots hitting the ground sent waves of pain up his left arm and made him feel sick but he gritted his teeth.

"Trying to show an example to the men," he told Attius who had asked him if he should be up and about.

"Fainting on the Via Praetoria won't be much of an example: take it easy for a day to two," the First Spear Centurion advised, not unkindly; the young tribune's determination had impressed him.

Soranus had left the infirmary on his feet, a score of others left wrapped in in blankets, dead. Their wounds had been too much for them. They had died crying for their mothers or begging the gods for life; neither of the parties responded.

"No, Titus, I say again, we cannot go down and engage them without cavalry. There are simply too many of them at the moment," Quadratus said.

The officers were sitting at the long table of their mess but Lucius was missing,; still sleeping although it was past noon.

"More were seen crossing back over the Rhine this morning," Titus persisted.

"A few hundred, a thousand at most, not enough. Come to me when the bridge has been full of Marcomanni heading across all day long."

"You are right, sir. I simply think we need let 'em see we have teeth of our own."

"I believe they know that. Still, so far we have not shown any aggression. We must do more than react to their initiatives but what?" the legate asked

Tertius had been calculating on a wax tablet during the conversation. He finished and nodded to himself.

"Tribune Longius had the idea of using scorpions mounted on carts to compensate for our lack of cavalry. Perhaps we could adapt this. Send out two carts with two scorpions on each. My figures show it will take five minutes for them to be within range of the enemy lines. If they slew round side on, it will take them a further minute to loose off between twelve and sixteen plunging bolts between them. The enemy will take a while to react to the appearance of the carts, especially if we disguise the artillery pieces with canvas. After firing, they will head back to the camp at top speed. I don't believe our bolts will do any major damage but we demonstrate we have little fear of them and it might provoke a them into another wild charge…"

"Do it now," Quadratus said.

Within an hour, two carts has been selected, their wheels checked and greased and four scorpions mounted in them. The horses were being brought up and harnessed when Attius said they should let Lucius know what was going on.

"He's the designated officer for the artillery, the only one now Cestus Valens is no longer with us…"

Lucius, still looking at little bleary-eyed although he had flung a basin of cold water over his head, strode up behind the legionary who had been sent to inform him. He started to climb up onto the nearest cart.

"Not a chance, Boxer," Titus told him. "Express orders of the legate, you stay here. He says we may all yet need your talents before this is over."

"Well, at least get Corvo's century up on the wall and some men who are good with a javelin," Lucius snapped. He was tired, irritable and disappointed. Everyone liked the thought of irritating the enemy.

"Right, then," Titus, gave his final instruction, "You drivers, you're are not charioteers and this is not the Circus Maximus. Take it steady on the way down and they won't think you're a threat. With a bit of luck they'll just stand and stare. Scorpion-crews, keep a look-out from under the canvas and let the drivers know when you think you're in range. One minute and one minute only, then head back and get a wriggle on because they'll be after you. However, have no fear, Senior Tribune Tertius Fuscus has made all the necessary calculations and assures me you will be fine. Let's hope he hasn't got his sums wrong, eh lads? Go on, bugger-off and we'll see you back through the gate in ten minutes."

The gate opened. The carts came through at a fast trot in tandem. They rattled over the bridges towards the enemy lines down the track that had once led to the signalling post. Marcomanni, heads went up at their appearance. As they came nearer, people called out to their friends and pointed at them. Some shouted witty or ribald remarks suggesting what the Roman could intend. Those within hearing laughed at the comments. There was no sense of a danger, as Titus

Attius had predicted, even as the horses hauling the carts broke into a gentle canter. The watching crowd increased as word of this strange sight spread. Men stood with folded arms or leaning on spear shafts trying to work out what was going on.

When the pair of oncoming vehicles slowed and peeled off, one to the left the other to the right and stopped sideways on, tension grew among the onlookers. It was only when the canvas was pushed back and the scorpions fired that they realised that they were under immediate threat and by then, it was too late. The bolts flew high up to hesitate before plunging down into the middle of the assembled enemy. The crowd eddied as men and women shoved each other aside, trying to get away from where they thought the missiles would land. Shouting and screaming rose up, punctuated by the crack of the scorpions firing again and again without aiming and without pause. Fourteen bolts smashed into the lines. Two men and an ox were killed but the greatest damage was done by a warhorse.

A chieftain had been leading his stallion to the river to drink when it was struck a glancing blow that ripped open its flank without penetrating. In pain and fear the horse bolted, lashing out with its hooves at anyone and anything within range. A dozen or more were kicked or trampled; bones were broken and a woman died. It charged through a fire throwing embers up in a spray of sparks, setting a tent ablaze. Someone managed to grab the horse's reins and halted its mad, destructive dance. The fire was beaten out with wet cloths. Panic and confusion turned to rage. The mass of people bulged forward like a dam about to break. The mobile artillery galloped towards the safety of their own camp as furious warriors broke into a run after them. Mounted men rode across the Marcomanni front shouting and gesticulating for them to stop but more joined in until five hundred young men were running towards the Roman stronghold.

The gate opened to allow the carts inside and closed behind them. Seconds later, the first of the onrushing warriors were in artillery range and the missiles began to fly off the top of the Roman walls. Men were transfixed or bowled over but none came on into range of Corvo's archers and slingers. Shaking their fists at and yelling curses, the survivors made their way back towards the river carrying or dragging the wounded and most of their dead with them. Between seventy and eighty had been hit.

"A modest success; we have hurt the enemy without ourselves sustaining any losses," Tertius said to the assembled officers. They raised their wine cups in a subdued toast; all except Otto.

"It shows us that without cavalry we may lose this fight," he commented.

His words were greeted by shock. Otto tended to be a silent observer at officer's meetings. His statement was the more powerful because he had said something the others knew in the back of their minds but suppressed.

"A sweeping conclusion to arrive at after a minor engagement," Quadratus told him in a disapproving tone.

"Your words, sir; it was minor because this time only a couple of hundred hotheads rushed at the camp and they fell back before they were in range of our archers. When that chieftain insulted our dead scouts and he was shot down, thousands of them poured up the slope. Today we went close to their lines and fired a dozen or more bolts into them but they did not charge. Am I the only one who saw their leaders riding up and down in front of the warriors urging them to holdfast?"

"Yes but even so…"

"Helmund has a grip on his people now. Our advantage is our discipline. If the enemy has become a controlled force acting under that man's orders, we are in grave danger. I have looked onto his eyes. He is shrewd and a good leader."

"Surprised you're still here if you admire him so much," Soranus snapped.

In the horrified silence that followed this outburst, Otto smiled coldly at him.

"I am a Roman officer, an Equestrian and a citizen until I say something that no-one wants to hear, then I am what, exactly? Another German? Do not attack me tribune, because you do not want to acknowledge the truth of what I am saying."

Soranus stood up and bowed his head briefly at Otto.

"Principal Decurion Longius, I humbly ask your pardon. The pain of my wound and sleeplessness makes me irritable."

"Graciously said," Quadratus told him. "There is not the slightest possibility of doubting the integrity of any officer present. We must not fall into the trap of disunity, that truly would be fatal to us at this point."

"Everyone agrees that no cavalry is the problem, Otto, but it doesn't do to say too much. We don't want the men to be uneasy," Titus reprimanded him.

Otto shook his head. "First Spear Centurion Attius, we all know that hostile German forces do not sit down in front of Roman fortresses, patiently probing for a weakness. Yet that is what they are doing. Do you think your junior officers and veteran troops haven't seen that as well as the rest of us?"

"What do you suggest, then?" Titus shouted and slapped his hand down on the table with a meaty thud.

Otto smiled and shrugged. "It is not for me to say. Senior Tribune Tertius Fuscus is the expert at mathematics, along with Boxer. But I know if you have ten-thousand men and lose two-thousand you have less of a problem than we do if we lose that number."

"We go around in circles, gentlemen. For the moment we have no choice but to defend out camp, our home, to the limit of our determination and ability," Quadratus told the meeting in general, with an air of finality.

Helmund sat a in circle of chieftains and clan leaders patiently trying to keep them in agreement with his strategy.

"How can you claim we won today when they fired on us and killed or wounded eighty of our warriors who ran to chastise them?" one of them was asking with an edge of disbelief in his voice.

"Because they wanted to provoke us into a general charge. Our victory is that we remained in our lines, apart from a small number of very young men hungry for reputation. Even they had the good sense to fall back when they saw there was nothing to be gained. I commend them. Let there be no talk of shame or cowardice; they were momentarily overcome by righteous anger but most came to their senses before it was too late," Helmund explained.

"They fire on us with their machines and drive away untouched, scores of us are brought down, yet you claim this as a victory. I tell you, Helmund, we cannot afford too many such victories…"

"If you will not accept what I say, think of it from the Roman point of view. They tried to encourage a mass assault on their heavily armed stronghold and failed. Mark my words, failed. It is a sign of their growing weakness and fear." He stood up and stretched out his right arm pointing in the direction of the Roman camp. "If they are so formidable, why do they skulk behind their walls? Why do they not join us in battle in the open? Because they know that they are not strong enough, that is why. The bracken on the hillside is yellowing but still too wet for them to burn and leave it exposed. We will use it to get near enough to launch another attack just before dawn tomorrow. I need two thousand spearmen, axemen and two hundred archers each with twenty good arrows; who is with me?" Enough of his listeners pledged their men for Helmund to proceed. "But pay heed," he told them sternly, "after we return tomorrow with yet more of their blood on our hands, we cannot feast the night away. They can expect no rest, no time to put right what we have destroyed. We must squeeze them in our fists until they are crushed."

While the force was being assembled, Helmund was alone with Hulderic.

"What luxury the enemy commander has. He says. "Let a thousand men do this or that," and they do it. I have to persuade them to give me warriors every time and then argue for my tactics to be employed," he complained.

"You lead free men. If they cease to be free, what difference between us and the Romans?" Hulderic replied.

The warriors under their war-leaders began to drift over to the assembly point. In the end there were two thousand four hundred of them including three hundred archers. Hulderic checked their ammunition and rejected those who could not show him twenty arrows, which left two hundred and sixty. While this was going on, Helmund requested that every able-bodied woman and children who were old enough to go up into the edge of the forest to collect and bundle all the brushwood they could find. They were to return by sunset leaving their harvest stacked.

"Why do we women have to labour for you "King" Helmund?" one broad-shouldered matron asked him sarcastically.

"Because the enemy are always watching and I do not want them to see your men going into the forest. That would warn them that something is planned for tonight," he replied.

This explanation was found to be satisfactory and shortly afterwards, a procession wound its way up the slope.

With Hulderic's assistance, and a fair amount of shoving, Helmund divided one quarter of the warriors and half the archers into a separate section. This took a long time. Individual clans refused to be split up; they always went into battle together. As many as fifty men at a time passed from one side to the other until everyone was reasonably content. At last things were settled enough for Helmund to be able to address them.

"Under Hulderic's command…." he began when voices shouted him down.

"Who is he to lead? Is he better than anyone else among us?" a tall chieftain with no beard but moustaches down to his chest demanded.

Helmund was reaching the end of his tolerance.

"Stand forward, you and your war-band" he barked.

The clan leader with the moustaches strutted to the front with forty men around him.

"You have no place in this attack tonight because you dispute who commands. How many times must I repeat how important it is for us to work together?" he said with bitterness.

"If we are denied the right to fight in this battle, we shall quit your camp," their leader said defiantly.

"Go!" Helmund snapped, turned his attention to the others and started his explanation again.

"Hulderic will lead you. You are to attack the part of the wall we destroyed before. You will continue with your attack until you hear the horns calling you back when you will break off and head for the river, keeping under cover…."

"We are a diversion. There is no glory in this…"

"Unless you do as ordered, there will be no glory for anyone. Are we fighting to destroy Romans or only to gain reputation? When the gates have been torn down and their camp is a graveyard, there will be glory enough for all."

After some grumbling, they agreed.

"Eat, rest, we move out as soon as darkness falls," Hulderic told them.

Just when all seemed to be settled, a delegation of archers objected.

"Our bows aren't as powerful as theirs, we don't have the range…"

"That doesn't matter. You'll be close up hidden in the bracken. They will be outlined against the sky but you will be invisible. Make sure you keep behind a tree-stump and loose only when you have clear shot."

The sun declined towards the west. The women and children began to filter back into the lines. Cooking fires were lit. Men sat beside them honing blades in the flickering light as their shadows lengthened and deepened in the dying daylight. Most would carry only their weapons but others were to transport equipment for all to use.

As was his custom, Helmund stood for a long time looking at the Roman camp and mentally reviewing his campaign. Today had been a good day. Tomorrow would be better. He had his pickets out to the south and in the forest covering the trails. He had a guard-post at either end of the bridge. He had an army that out-numbered his enemies. The faintest sense of coming triumph entered his consciousness. He pushed it down. To anticipate victory was aggravating to the gods. They punished such arrogance.

The first stars glimmered between the broken cloud cover. He called up his men and moved out to the east uphill into the gloom of the forest, followed by Hulderic with his party.

Chapter 7

The sentries were edgy. They started at the sound of every night-bird. They peered into the blackness so hard that strange colours and shapes appeared to their eyes. They threw flaming torches down into the ditches to flare brightly for a minute but none revealed an enemy creeping closer. With nerves strained to breaking point, they patrolled their few yards of walkway throughout an endless night. Tension is exhausting. In the half-hour before dawn they were worn-out and bone-weary. A sentry leaned over the parapet topping the new length of wall to look directly down into the ditch. An arrow struck him in the face below his right eye. He cried out, staggered back and tumbled down onto the Via Praetoria with a clash and clatter of weapons and armour. With shouts of, "Alarm! Alarm!" others ran up but already the first knotted ropes had snaked out of the gloomy pit below and looped around the posts. As more soldiers rushed to respond, other arrows flew. Some missed and glided harmlessly onwards, others hit helmets, limbs, shields causing men to fall, hindering their comrades. Heads and muscular arms appeared over the parapet. Within seconds, half a dozen warriors crouched on the walkway, spears and shields at the ready. There followed a series of dull thuds as crude ladders were flung against the wall and the half dozen quickly became twenty. The arrows still came over; not in volleys but seeking out individual targets and the legionaries still fell.

Horns sounded, whistles shrilled and the rattle and roar of hundreds of men hurrying out of their billets and running to their positions filled the camp with noise. More torches were lit to reveal the situation. Exactly as before, the enemy were flooding over the wall and the sentries fighting to prevent them moving out of the narrow point of entry they had established. Titus Attius had been expecting something but he had not believed they would be so stupid as to attack again at the same place. He noticed that this time, they seemed to be concentrating on fighting their way towards the Porta Praetoria, using their rear men to defend against the Romans coming at them from the eastern side.

Titus shouted for Corvo and gave him the same instructions as previously; to cut down the interlopers but avoid hitting his own men. He then sent a century up to defend the gate and another one behind the Germans to hold them in position while Corvo's men annihilated them. But some enemy archers had infiltrated and were now shooting back. The Romans lost two slingers and an archer. Titus quickly ordered up three more centuries to use their shields to protect his own missile troops.

At that moment, five of the men on guard over the Porta Principalis Dexter, the eastern gate, fell to arrows streaking at them out of the darkness. Scores of Marcomanni erupted out of the bracken and sprinted at the gate. They looked grotesquely misshapen until they flung down their burdens of dry brushwood at the base of the gate and ran back. Some were hit by Roman javelins but it was almost impossible to see the scurrying figures below. The enemy archers had no such problem. The defenders were silhouetted against the sky and many fell to long black arrows. There was a brief lull until more warriors ran forward and threw leather bags of raw turpentine on the brushwood and over the planks of the gate. The sharp, sweet smell of concentrated pine filled the soldiers' nostrils. A fire-arrow flared from the hillside. After a fractional silence, the turpentine exploded into blue-white flames. The kindling caught, red and yellow as the gate was engulfed in a cloak of fire. The heat and fumes drove the Roman sentries back along the walls on either side where yet more fell victim to the invisible archers.

A horn sounded from the forest. The warriors attacking the new wall flung themselves back over it and vanished. Within a few minutes all was calm. Only the dead and wounded were left to prove they had ever been there.

Quadratus, Fuscus and Attius looked at the eastern gate. Plumes of smoke were already spiralling upwards through the inside of planks. Legionaries had been detailed to crawl as near as they could, keeping their heads below the parapet to tip buckets of water down over the gateposts and the walls either side. There was no hope of saving the gate itself.

"Lesson learned," said Attius. "Next year I'll have that bracken mowed down."

Quadratus smiled. "So you think that we shall be here next year?"

"'Course we will, sir," Attius replied and then after a moment of reflection added, "At least, Rome will be. . ."

"What is to be done, First Spear Centurion?" asked Tertius Fuscus.

"Kill 'em when they come through the gate. Old fashioned infantry tactics. A front and two wings five ranks deep with no space between them. We form up in an open box, they advance into it and then it's down to steel and the men behind it. Their bows aren't as powerful as ours so we'll have two ranks of men on the walkway overlapping their shields protecting a couple of hundred lads with javelins they can throw at an angle. Not a lot of room to work in so the First Cohort should do. Better get ready, if you'll excuse me…"

Hulderic arrived back in the Marcomanni lines. His force had been diminished by seventy dead or too badly wounded to move. But he had no intention of taking time to recuperate. He shouted for the horns to call general assembly in the few minutes before the sun broke over the forested ridge. Already the stars were blinking out as morning crept over the land. He had the final part of Helmund's plan to execute and little time.

"Helmund is hard-pressed. He wants us to arm and advance on the Romans. We will not attack but when they see all of us on the move, they will pull soldiers back to man the wall and gate facing us. Every man they order to defend against our supposed assault is one less facing Helmund and our noble warriors."

Not even the most awkward of the leaders could find fault with this proposal. They hurried to arm and march out grouped in family and clan blocks of between forty and five hundred men. There were many mail shirts, helmets and broad-bladed spears among them to glitter in the first rays of the sun as they moved steadily up the slope.

The guard commander over the Porta Praetoria took one look at the distant host, said "Oh fuck it!" under his breath and shouted for his optio. "Find the legate and report the enemy are coming at us in full force," he ordered and turned to his men. "Busy day lads, stand firm. They'll reinforce us long before that mob arrive."

Quadratus heard the news the breathless optio gave him with his usual imperturbable air.

"Tertius, to the Porta Praetoria with the second and third cohorts if you will. Boxer, every artillery piece you can deploy against a frontal assault under Senior Tribune Fuscus' orders. Tribune Soranus, how are you?"

"Hand's still not good, sir," Soranus answered.

"Never will be again, sad to say. Are you mobile and can you write?"

"Yes, sir."

"Very well, find a wax-tablet and stylus then stay by me as my adjutant for today. Bring a dozen reliable men with you to act as runners. First job, get the fourth and fifth cohorts standing-by at the gates not yet under threat." He walked over to Attius. "Look for me at the Praetorium if you need me, Titus. Jupiter and Mars with you this day."

"And with you, sir," he replied as the first plank of the burning gate fell inwards.

Nothing could be seen through the gap. The last flames were leaping off the brushwood and super-heated air was shimmering above the gate.

"Get ready for the entertainment to begin boys, not long now and you've all got front row seats like senators!" Titus roared.

The men grinned; they had heard something similar a score of times before but somehow it was still reassuring. They tightened their grips on their shields and swords, not enough room for javelins, and squinted towards the fire under the rims of their helmets. Another plank fell and another; the whole gate sagged slightly as the frame into which the hinges were secured charred and weakened. A shower of arrows came over the wall. It did no damage but heralded an extraordinary event.

The gate exploded in a flying mass of burnt wood, sparks and flames as a giant warrior smashed through it in one leap. He crashed to the ground, rolled and came to his feet at a run. He carried a huge axe which he raised above his head, his singed beard and braids smoking and crackling. He ran a few more paces and leaped again, hurtling into the front rank. His speed and weight flattened the legionary who took his full force, as well as the man behind him. The third rank man received an axe blow which split his helmet and killed him instantly, spattering the men around him with blood and brains. The berserker died under half a dozen sword thrusts but others were jumping the remains of the fire and laying about them with axes and longswords. The Roman ranks reeled but held firm.

Helmund however, was not going to play according to Titus' rules. As the Marcomanni burst through in greater numbers, they turned sharp left and hacked and chopped at the end of the Roman line battering their way between it and the wall. The few legionaries taking the brunt of their ferocity could not hold out against twenty, thirty axes and spears on such a narrow front. The Germans were bigger, heavier and stronger and by concentrating their force on this one point, their physical advantage was unstoppable. Titus' right flank was being chewed up. The enemy were now through the gap they had made and beginning to attack his rear ranks while over two thirds of his men were standing at the ready but taking no part.

Orders were shouted above the thundering war-cries of the Germans and the screams of falling Romans. The rear rank peeled off the left flank and front, formed up to double over to support the weakening right flank and contain the enemy. Helmund had been waiting for this. Another wave of warriors came in but this time, they turned right and repeated the process on the other Roman flank with the same result. The men on the walkway were unable to loose their javelins as the action was too tight to the base of the walls and the risk of hitting their comrades too great.

Cavalrymen were not equipped to fight in the infantry ranks. Their designated task was to protect the stable buildings and horses; they hardly expected to be involved but small groups of the enemy were now rampaging around the interior of the camp. They had no plan; they simply hacked at anyone that came within reach of their weapons. Otto's men were better armed for this kind of fight than the legionaries and more used to actions which were confused by opponents coming at them from all sides. They fought as they rode, close together, defending with their oval shields and thrusting with their lances or slashing with the long horseman's sword each of them carried. They beat on their shields shouting insults and defiance, eager to avenge their comrades whose severed heads had been so shamefully abused. Their defiance brought more opponents to them and soon they were backed up against their stable walls with a harvest of bleeding or dead enemies at their feet. Their eagerness for the fight had inadvertently given Titus a small respite because they had engaged most of the warriors who had burst through the gap on his right flank, although more were making their way between it and the wall.

Titus Attius was an old hand at his trade of warfare. He saw that the Marcomanni could not be contained with his present force and it was time to act decisively. He sent his optio to the legate.

"First Spear Centurion Attius sends his compliments, sir, and requests that you order one cohort to his right flank and another to his left," the blood-splattered optio asked, after saluting Quadratus.

"Noted, optio. Soranus, send runners to the fourth and fifth. They are to report to First Spear Centurion Attius instantly."

The optio ran back to the fight and Soranus' men raced across the camp to call up the reinforcements so urgently needed.

The leading centurions of both cohorts stood to attention in front of Titus Attius awaiting his commands.

"Fifth, behind the rear rank on my right flank, fourth on my left. I'm falling back five paces to straighten the line. You are to fill in to form my new flanks once the first cohort has completed the manoeuvre. Got it?"

There was no possibility of even Titus' voice being heard above the raging battle. He nodded to the bugler standing next to him.

"You know what to do," he said.

The brass horn resonated clear above the clamour and clash. The legionaries and their officers understood the meaning of the repeated musical phrase. They stood by for the second call. As the last note was sounded, the first cohort marched five paces backwards to the timing of their centurions' whistle blasts. The mauled remnants of the flanks folded back like doors swinging. The front the Romans were presenting to the Marcomanni was now one straight line little short of twice its original length. The fourth and fifth cohorts rounded the ends and formed more powerful replacement wings. They now began to take advantage of their greater numbers and advanced one step at a time, squeezing the enemy back to the ruined gate.

Quadratus sent runners around the camp ordering every man not engaged on the northern walls to assist in eliminating all of the enemy who had broken past the ranks of Titus' men.

Horns blared again but they blew the strange wailing cadences of the Marcomanni musicians sounding the retreat. The warriors backed through the smouldering wreckage of the gate and fled uphill towards the forest. But Helmund had left a sting in the tail. Fifty of his archers remained behind, well hidden and each supplied with a flask of water and bread. They would stay until sunset, shooting whenever a target presented itself. Only if the Romans came out in force were they to make their escape. The recall had carried on the breeze to the Marcomanni lined up out of artillery range of the Ports Praetoria. As a man, they turned on their heels and made their way back to their own lines.

When the soldiers were directly in line with the gap where their gate had been relaxed and lowered their shields, a flurry of arrows flew in at them, wounding three. Two wagons with sacks of barley leaned against the wheels were pushed up to block it and hinder any repetition of the assault. While the legionaries piled up the dead and carried the wounded to the infirmary, the senior officers stood in a small knot on the parade ground looking at the result of the carnage and contemplating what to do next.

Felix hobbled up to them with a tray of wine cups and two flasks. When everyone had been served with neat wine he put his tray down and came to attention as best as he could.

"First Spear Centurion Attius, I ask you to request the Noble Legate Publius Quadratus to allow me to take the soldier's oath and enrol in The Second Lucan Legion.," he said.

They looked at him in surprise. Tertius and Soranus were having difficulty in not laughing at the crippled ex-soldier. He was aware of their supressed sniggers but continued to look directly at Attius.

"Former Decanus Felix, as we both know, anyone with an honourable discharge from his legion may request to serve again as an evocati, a returned veteran, but you are not fit to march and therefore I can't do what you want."

"I know that, sir but I can lean against the parapet and use a siege spear or throw down a javelin as well as anyone. So far they've pulled down part of our wall and burnt one of our gates. How many of us have been killed or wounded? A thousand…."

"Not so many as that…."

"But not far off. Soon enough you're going to need every man who is willing to fight, never mind his age or fitness. I'd rather take my chance as a soldier, sir."

"Aquilifer!" Quadratus shouted. A tall man with a leopard skin draped over his armour trotted over holding the staff bearing the gilded bronze eagle of his office. "Take the oath, Felix. You will be designated evocati and soldier-servant to Tribune Lucius Longius. If called upon, you will fight under his direct command."

Felix repeated the words with the eagle held over his head.

"Draw your kit and an identity disc, soldier. Dismissed. Officers' conference in one hour, include the senior centurions of each cohort, Titus" Quadratus ordered.

Helmund re-entered his lines to the men's shouts of triumph and the women's ululating songs of praise. They had seen the smoke rising into the sky as the gate blazed and heard the clamour of the battle. That not all of their warriors had returned was a matter of brief regret. If they had died well with their faces to the enemy, they had fulfilled their destiny. It was not the dying but the manner of it that was important. A few optimists began to dig out the roasting pits expecting another night of feasting but Helmund stopped them.

"After we pulled down their wall we feasted and they rebuilt it. Now we have destroyed one of their gates and we must march upon them again as soon as possible. I have left archers hidden on the slopes to hinder them but no doubt they will succeed in hanging a new gate by the morning. To do this, some of them will be forced to work all night. Tomorrow they will be tired. We shall fall on them again and again and again until they are so exhausted and weakened they can resist no more," he shouted.

Spears and axes were brandished overhead as men demanded to go with him to kill the hated Romans. Helmund raised his hands for silence.

"Let the chieftains and leaders drink ale and break bread with me and we shall decide what we shall do next."

When they were seated and the first ale horns had been emptied in honour of their dead, the process of cajoling those fiercely independent tribesmen to act together and in accordance with a fixed plan began once more.

"We have twice been successful by using darkness to approach and launching ourselves on them at first light…."

"How many of the swine have we sent to Hell?" someone called out.

"If I listened to the boasts I have heard, nearly all of them. In truth, between five hundred and a thousand…" Faces fell and unhappy looks were exchanged between the leaders. "This is more than one man in ten of them," Helmund continued. Again he was interrupted.

"That is still fewer than our own losses, much fewer."

"It is bound to be so. They have stout walls and better arms. Victory will be bought at a high price in blood but think of this. Their walls are long and they need soldiers to defend every yard of them. If we kill a few hundred more next time and the same after that, they will be too few to cover their walls; then we can overwhelm them. Think of the treasure in weapons and armour in their camp. That will be ours. We shall be rich. We shall be powerful..." He looked around and saw nods of approval and greedy eyes; he had them now. "We are going to storm them, all of us. No more creeping up in the dark. We will fight like our fathers; in the light of day where our enemies can see us and know we are not afraid. Listen now to Hulderic who is a crafty man, skilled in warfare..."

The Roman conference was the mirror image of the Marcomanni's. The legate spoke first, looking round at the senior officers seated at the table and others on stools or standing against the walls.

"The enemy have been able to surprise us on two separate occasions. This is not good enough. I appreciate that the cover afforded by the eastern hill allows them to approach unseen but even so, we must do better..."

"If I may, sir?" Titus Attius broke in. "It is not yet noon, with your permission, I intend to send a strong party out with sickles to cut down as much of that bracken and undergrowth as we can during the rest of today..."

"Give the order as soon as we are finished here, First Spear Centurion. Boxer, how are we with the Porta Principalis Dextra?"

"Nothing can be saved. Your choice is either a substantial breastwork with fighting platforms which will be stronger than any gate but not so high, or a new gate. In either case, we do not have sufficient timber in store. I shall need to demolish the bridge over the ditch outside the gate and part of the stables. We can re-use the planks, beams and roof supports…."

"The point of having a gate is so that we can sally out and take the fight to the enemy when we choose," Tertius Fuscus objected.

Lucius nodded. "Understood sir, but with no cavalry and reduced effectives, are we likely to do so?"

"Which brings me to the most painful question of our losses," Quadratus responded.

As acting adjutant Soranus had the figures. He cleared his throat and read off a wax-tablet.

"Three-hundred and eighty dead or gravely wounded and not expected to survive. Seventy-five walking or lightly wounded, mostly arrow wounds, sir. Of the dead and dying, fifteen centurions and optios. That is our most accurate assessment at this stage."

No-one spoke for a moment then Quadratus continued.

"Boxer, I favour a breastwork but I am unhappy that it will be lower than the walkways. If an enemy climbed over the wall they would have the advantage of height."

"If we make a double defensive wall filled with earth and rubble, we should have enough to build a walkway and parapet over it, sir."

"Very well, see to it immediately." Lucius stood, saluted and left. "Now, gentlemen, how are we to go about improving the way in which we are defending ourselves?" asked the legate.

Otto stood up. "I would like to speak freely, although what I have to say will not be pleasing to this assembly, yet again. We can die quickly by marching on the Marcomanni or we can die slowly while they whittle us down until we can no longer resist. We must drive them off and to do that we need cavalry. I propose to go and find us some."

"We have already lost two men on that mission," Tertius said.

"We have, but now we know better. They block the river. They undoubtedly have pickets in the eastern forest. Our only other route to assistance is to the south but they are watching this as well. They imagine we are in a box, with the only exit being to the west. Westward is nothing but miles of forest and riverbank for days on end. There is no help for us there. That is why I will take that direction."

"But you have already said there is no relief to be had in the west," Soranus blurted out.

Otto laughed. "Exactly, that is why it will be weakly guarded, if at all. I shall work my way round and ride upstream to seek reinforcements at headquarters. Aldermar is there and he can speak to the general for me."

"When do you propose to go?" Quadratus asked.

"This afternoon; Boxer will be working on his defences, the men will be out on the hillside under heavy guard, all enemy eyes will be on the north and east. I shall ride through the southern gate but I need a sacrifice from you. I have twenty-eight cavalry men and thirty-five mounts. I ask any officer who is willing to donate one of his own horses. We shall leave the camp at speed leading spare horses, saddled and bridled. It has been dry and the sun is bright today, when we gallop through what was the camp-followers' settlement, our hooves will throw up a lot of dust and ash. We ride until we contact the Marcomanni pickets. They will try to stop us with spears and arrows. At that point, we scatter then ride at full speed back the way we came. Most of the spare horses will be released. They will run wild and add to the general confusion. I will break off to the west, change mounts under cover and proceed alone."

"You have clearly given this a great deal of thought Principal Decanus Longius," the legate commented.

"Yes sir, there are other minor points but they are for me to organise."

"You have my consent."

"Thank you sir, oh, there is every hope that some of the loose horses will join in the hasty retreat and return to their owners. As Virgil says, "Be resolute, comrades and save yourselves for better times." I should like to begin make myself ready …."

Otto rummaged through the stores in the cavalry lines until he found a worn mail-shirt that had been discarded and a dented helmet. One of the smiths knocked the dents out but the repairs were obvious.

He scavenged a pair of chequered breeches and a non-descript shield out of the pile of Marcomanni corpses and their kit. He also found himself a decent grey cloak. Felix gave him a brightly coloured scarf instead of his red, military one. With his head shaved, dressed in his shabby kit and oldest pair of boots, he looked like any other impoverished Germanic warrior wandering the borderlands in search of war-glory. He tied his gold ring, marble finger pendant and a few coins into his belt purse. The final part of his transformation was easy. He took up the two spears he had made when he first entered the Roman camp. With his pugio dagger, they were the only weapons he carried.

His final preparation was a visit to the priests. He handed over a scrap of paper on which he had written that in the event of his death, all his property was to be left to Tribune Lucius Taurius Longius, known as Boxer, with the exception of ten-thousand denarii which were to go to the legion funds for the relief of soldiers discharged on medical grounds and an equal sum to Decanus Felix. The priest read the paper with surprise at the sums-involved but gave his solemn oath both to preserve and enforce this simple last will and testament without comment. Lucius had been engrossed in his building-works all day, a lot of the time just outside the camp, and had no idea what Otto was about to attempt.

Horses were saddled. Cavalrymen mounted-up and took lead reins into their hands. Felix handed up a leather satchel with some bread, smoked meat and a cup to Otto.

"Fortuna with you, Otto Longius," he said and turned away without waiting for a reply.

Quadratus came over to clasp hands in farewell.

"Look for me on the ninth day sir. When the reinforcements arrive, I shall ask for all the buglers to blow the call to mount-up at the same time. You should be able hear it and when you do, The Second Lucan can come out in force."

"Any message for Boxer?" the legate asked.

"No, sir. I've left hm all my money. The priest has my will."

The horses walked once around the interior of the camp, then trotted so that they were warm and moving easily when they were unexpectedly joined by Soranus. He was on the back of a showy bay with a white mane and tail and dressed in his parade armour, a long red cloak flowing from his shoulders. He glittered and glinted in the afternoon sun which was past its zenith and beginning to settle in the west.

"I'm going with you," he shouted. "They'll expect to see a Roman officer."

"Well, they won't overlook you!" Otto shouted back.

The Porta Decumana opened and they were gone, accelerating over the bridge and onto the road south. Forty horses in all, hooves shaking the ground in their wild gallop, flinging their heads about, manes tossing as they jostled each other to get to the front. The riderless mounts reared and tried to pull away from the restraint of their lead ropes adding to the confused motion of the mass of jolting men, flying tails, rolling eyes, dust and madness. When they hit the camp followers' settlement, a dense fog of black and grey ash flew up around them. They carried it with them for several hundred yards. In four minutes their headlong dash had covered a mile. A little beyond this distance, the ground began to rise steeply either side of the track and a fallen tree blocked their way forward.

The Marcomanni guarding the road saw what they were intended to see; a Roman officer in gleaming armour leading a desperate break-out heading towards Gaul for reinforcements, dragging spare mounts behind them. They had been sitting on the hillsides for days, bored and resentful that they had no share in the glory of the main army. Now was their chance but they took it a fraction prematurely. The leading Romans spurred as if they were going to jump the barrier. The guards rushed down and stood behind it, holding their spears at an angle ready to rip the belly out of any horse attempting the leap. They misjudged both horses and riders. The cavalrymen hauled on their reins and leaned back in the saddle. Their mounts straightened their front legs and bent their back ones, practically sitting as they slammed to a skidding halt in a shower of grit and dust. The led horses were flung around sideways-on, kicking and rearing. As a body, the Romans turned and sped back up the track dropping their lead ropes. Some of the "spares" ran with them, some broke off to the left and right in their panic. Yet others slowed to a bewildered halt before trotting after their vanishing companions once more. It was too great a temptation to resist. The guards abandoned their position and hurried forward to catch one of these valuable prizes. They had left their high vantage point so when the fleeing horses threw up a dense cloud of ash once more, none of them noticed one figure bent low in the saddle with a great black horse keeping pace alongside him, race off to the cover of the trees half a mile to the west.

Chapter 8

Otto slowed his wild flight under the tree canopy at the edge of the woodland. He dismounted and took the small sack of crushed grain off the saddle-horn of his cavalry mount. He removed the lead rope around its neck and turned its head back towards the camp before giving it a mighty slap across the rump. The horse snorted and ran out onto the neglected agricultural land, cavorting and huffing at the indignity. He looked up at the sky. Although it was gloomy under the thick foliage, there were three hours of full daylight left and then the long gloaming. He took Djinn's bridle and walked at his head deeper into the forest, heading roughly northwest. He would have been cheered to know that, of the forty horses that had left the camp, thirty-six had thundered back through the Porta Decumana.

Lucius was at a loose end. The legionaries had broken down the bridge over the ditch and taken down the roof of most of the stables. Both faces of the heavy timber breastwork were in position. Soldiers were digging the ditch deeper and wider, throwing the earth and sand in between to make a fire-proof core. Lucius noticed a flushed and excited Soranus climbing down off the back of his horse which was fretting at its bit and flecked with foamy sweat. Loose horses were running about the parade-ground being chased by soldiers who thought they were helping to catch them by shouting, whistling and waving their arms about. Gradually, the still mounted cavalrymen captured and quieted them.

Lucius walked up to Soranus and held his horse for him while the young tribune took several deep breaths.

"That was excellent," he said, "Completely forgot how much my hand hurts."

"What have you been up to?" Lucius asked.

"Helping Otto with a diversion."

Lucius looked around but could not see his friend.

"Where is he?" he asked.

"On the way to headquarters, with any luck," Soranus told him with a broad smile which faded when he saw the horrified expression on Lucius' face as his words sank in.

"He's gone, just like that on some suicide mission? Without even telling me about it?"

"Thought you knew, Boxer. You must have seen us setting out?"

"No, I did not. I was busy. So what is going on?"

"Otto is getting us some cavalry support. He had a plan to leave camp unseen and now he's off…."

Lucius turned his back and walked quickly away across the parade ground and up to the northern wall where he had seen Quadratus and Tertius gazing out over the parapet at the Marcomanni lines. He saluted abruptly.

"Why was I not told Otto was leaving the camp? I could have ridden with him… sir," he said to the legate without even a greeting, adding the "sir" as an obvious afterthought.

Tertius answered. "It is not customary to inform every officer of actions approved by our commander."

It was a deserved rebuke and Lucius knew it.

"My apologies. I have been discourteous. But I was shocked to discover that Otto had left on his mission without discussing it with me beforehand. I must admit, I feel wounded that he did not even say goodbye. Clearly, I was far from his thoughts…"

"On the contrary, Boxer; his last act before departing was to entrust his will to the priests. He has left you practically his entire fortune. Congratulations," Quadratus told him, drily.

Lucius reddened. "I've made a fool of myself, haven't I?" he said after a pause.

Quadratus shook his head. "No, not at all. It is natural that you are thrown out of equilibrium to discover your close companion gone without your prior knowledge."

"Indeed, sir but it is in my reaction that I am at fault. Otto often quotes Cicero, "People make too many emotional decisions and not enough by reason and law." That is one of his favourites. I should have thought before I approached you."

"He was reciting Virgil before he left," Tertius remarked. "From where does he get it all?"

"He studies the sayings of philosophers and poets. He is himself a philosopher in his way, since he seeks after truth and wisdom."

"Who would have thought it of a German?" Tertius laughed but it was his time to be corrected.

"The Principal Decurion Otto Longius is a Roman Citizen enrolled in the Equestrian Order by the Emperor Augustus in person. "German" no longer has any place when discussing our brother officer." Quadratus told him sharply.

Tertius had meant no harm. Until joining The Second Lucan, he had spent his military career in Italy where the word "German" stood for savagery and mindless violence. When had he arrived to begin his service on the border, he was amazed that the legion relied on these very same Germans for intelligence gathering and cavalry support. He had a mind that craved order; that is why he felt most secure when immersed in his administrative duties where everything could be categorized and written down. He simply did not know what to think of Aldermar and Otto. They did not fit into a category he could define; Men were noble or common, civilised or barbarians but where did they belong?

Otto had cut a leafy branch and was trying to sweep his tracks aside as he made his way towards the riverbank. After forty minutes, the trees thinned significantly and he could catch the odd glimpse of the shimmering surface of the Rhine. He tethered Djinn and crawled forward. Looking both up and downstream, he could see nothing but a peaceful grassy bank with a few saplings growing close to the water's edge. He then wriggled back into deeper cover and scouted the edge of the forest in either direction for several hundred paces. He found no watchers, no dead fires left by guards. It appeared he had been right; the Marcomanni had not considered their western flank needed protection.

He took Djinn to the river and let him drink a little, then mounted and walked him upstream. He rounded a bend and found he had blundered into the outskirts of the enemy lines. There was no defensive ditch, no palisade. One moment he was on the open bank, the next among tents and rude huts made of interlaced branches, some with canvas over them, others crudely thatched with long grass. Women walked down to the water to wash clothes or fill cooking pots. Barefoot children, mostly naked, ran shrieking, playing their games. Warriors squatted on logs by their fires, some alone where their families had settled, others in groups passing around an ale-jug. One to two looked up at him with mild curiosity, others called a greeting. Djinn took him further into the encampment where the crowd was thicker. Otto now had to control Djinn carefully to avoid pushing over a tent or stepping in someone's fire circle.

His heart was pounding so hard he was sure it could be seen. He was fighting to breathe normally and give the impression that he belonged among this host. He was sure that the looks cast his way by those he passed were becoming more and more suspicious. When he reached the end of the bridge, his hands were beginning to shake. He had not put a great deal of thought into how he was going to proceed once he was free of the Roman camp. That had been such a huge risk, he had not seen clearly beyond it but here he was and a decision was called for. He was now between the river and the walls of the signalling fort. The gate was open. Thirty or so clan-leaders and chieftains sat on a ring of logs listening to a warrior with green snakes tattooed on his face. With a sick lurch in the pit of his stomach, Otto saw it was Hulderic. He was sure that he too would be recognized and denounced; fifty yelling warriors dragging him down to be tortured to death and his mutilated body displayed to the Romans. Hulderic did not even glance his way.

Otto looked over at the bridgehead, as casually as his anxiety let him. A dozen warriors were grouped around it. They wore good armour, silver arm-rings and carried spears and axes. Most of the men he had seen had not been fully armed and he guessed that those hard-looking men were there to control the river-crossing. He thought of approaching them and asking for passageway but there was something about them that made hm hesitate. As he sat in the saddle undecided, Djinn kept walking slowly into the heart of the enemy. Now, he was in the area behind the line of carts which was hidden from the Roman camp. It was full of activity. Men and women were constructing large hurdles out of split birch-wood and making crude ladders. They were too busy to glance up at the undistinguished young warrior on the dusty horse. He found that Djinn had ambled past the last of the wagons where the settlement thinned out as he moved eastwards, upstream.

The last makeshift shelters were behind him and he now rode a pitted track towards the treeline. Up ahead, half a dozen men were sitting on the verge or leaning on their spear shafts. They were the same big, experienced warriors as those at the bridgehead. One came forward into the middle of the track. Otto pulled his mount to a halt. His terror had left him and he felt calm. The hand of fate had touched his shoulder; he could no longer control events. He sat patiently waiting for whatever was coming next.

"Why do you leave the camp of King Helmund?" the guard asked.

"I am not one of his people."

"No? Then who are you?"

"I am the son of Badurad who led a clan of Suevi."

"Take off your helmet."

Otto removed it and the leather skull cap he wore underneath as padding

"If you are who you say, why do you not wear the Suevian Knot like any honest tribesman?"

"I will grow my hair again when the war is won."

His questioner grunted. "What is your business?" he demanded.

"I have been sent to see if the bridge and King Helmund's army are still here. Now I know, I am going east to tell my people and will return with fifty or more horsemen to fight in this place."

"If you came out of the east, why did we not see you when you arrived?"

"I crossed the river further down. I was advised to be cautious. We have had only rumours of this army."

"That horse you ride is very fine underneath his dust and dirt. You should take better care of him, son of Badurad. I will exchange him for one of mine."

"No."

"I will buy him."

"No."

"Then I shall take him from you."

Otto whipped the spear in his right hand over in a blurring arc and without the man having time to move, the point was aimed at his throat.

"No." he said flatly.

There was a moment of crackling tension then the warrior burst into laughter.

"A fierce young man is the son of Badurad. Take your horse and go on your way. If any others stop you, tell them Audo of the Bright Axe gives you leave to pass."

"Thank you for your courtesy, my Lord Audo," Otto said, giving him a title of nobility to which he was probably not entitled.

Audo responded with a bow of the head and stepped aside.

Djinn walked on. The skin of Otto's back crawled, anticipating the pain of a stabbing blade but he forced himself to keep to his steady pace. He travelled a hundred yards or so and came to slight bend, once through it, he flicked the reins and clucked with his tongue. Djinn responded by breaking into a trot. Otto would like to have gone faster but there was a long way to go and there was no sense in tiring his mount early on.

Twenty minutes later, he heard the sound of approaching hoofbeats; two horses being ridden at an easy hand-gallop. He hung his shield on one of the horns of his saddle and dismounted, shooing Djinn forward down the track. Otto looked around him. It was half overgrown by a blackthorn tree a few yards further along. Directly opposite on the other side was the thick trunk of an oak. Otto stood waiting beside the oak, hidden from view of the oncoming riders. He was sure any horse seeing the blackthorn would instinctively move away, closer to his spears. He took several deep breaths and readied himself, listening carefully as the horsemen approached.

He judged the moment perfectly. The instant before the leading horse came level with this hiding place, he thrust the shaft of one of his spears through its front legs. It went in between them and snapped but brought the animal down, head over heels. He caught a glimpse of a man still on its back frantically windmilling his arms. Otto leapt out with his other spear. The second rider was concentrating on controlling his own horse which was throwing its head up and dancing on the spot, trying to avoid trampling its fallen companion. Otto's thrust caught him in the groin. The blade went in but he manged to stay in the saddle scrabbling for his axe. Otto leaned forward and pushed harder. The spear-shaft bent like a bow and finally the warrior was forced sideways, lost his balance and fell. He had recovered as far as his knees when Otto withdrew the blade and stuck again. The thrust took him in the throat. He died with bright-red blood cascading down his chest.

The horse that Audo of the Bright Axe had been riding had broken its neck in the fall and now he lay pinned under it by both his legs.

"I should have listened when you said you would not let me take your horse, son of Badurad," he gasped.

Using his elbows to raise his shoulders, he tipped his head back. Otto drove his pugio up through the soft flesh under his chin into his brain pan. He convulsed and died. He took two arm-rings off each of the fallen men, as was his right, and the spear of the second one, before mounting his victim's horse and riding after Djinn who was a little way down the track grazing on a clump of late grass. He took his shield back, untwisted the tether rope from his own horse's neck, took a firm hold of one end and rode on but this time at a dead gallop. It would be an hour at most before Audo and his friend were missed and a search party was sent out. He needed to cover as much ground as he could before it could catch up with him or night fell.

Lucius and his men finished their task as the last rays of the sun were slanting sideway, plunging half of the camp into darkness but giving a warm, kindly glow where they still shed their light. The legionaries had built a six- foot deep platform where the Porta Principalis Dexter had so recently stood. Eleven feet high on its outer side and seven feet inside, it gave the defenders a four-foot protective parapet. It was lower than the walkway but the ditch in front was nearly ten feet deep and had been dug out on either side. On Lucius' orders, the smiths had been busy all-day forging caltrops, the four-pointed iron stars, twisted so that however they were flung down, at least one tip was always upright to pierce an unwary foot. Bucket-loads had been flung into the eastern and northern ditches.

Titus Attius came over to inspect the works. He walked up the steps and stamped heavily on the platform, as he always did, "to test it", before looking out at the hillside. The tree-stumps stuck up like splintered, broken teeth now that the bracken had been cut back.

"Well done Boxer, a fine job and I've seen plenty of them. Take a walk with me, will you?"

They went up onto the western wall and leaned on the parapet. At this height, they could still feel the dying warmth of the day on their faces.

"Probably rain tomorrow, "Titus offered. "I can smell it in the air." He fell silent for a minute then began to speak once more. "Remember Centurion Lentus? A brave man and a fine soldier but he was beginning to lose his way. I had a word with him before he left us, like I'm having one with you now. We all know you're upset about Otto buggering-off on this mission of his without telling you. I understand that, but it shows me you're losing your way, a bit like Lentus did. Get this into your head. There is a man in this legion who has the right to be consulted and he is The Noble Legate Publius Quadratus; only him, not me, not you, not anybody else. You have no right to know what was said between Otto and the legate and you have no right to fear for your friend. You are a soldier. Comrades we loved like brothers are gone but we soldier on. That's part of what makes us what we are. Pray for his success, grieve for him if he is lost but soldier on; that is what we are here to do and so long as everyone does, all will be as the Gods will it. Fancy a flask of wine? You've had a long, hard day…."

The centurion commanding the guard at the western gate did not believe his eyes. An unmounted cavalry horse, caked in mud up to the withers, stood outside, pawing the ground with one front hoof. He shouted for the officer of the watch. Soranus had drawn that duty and hurried over.

"Take a look at that, sir."

Soranus leaned over. The horse lifted its head and looked back at him in irritation at being shut out of its stable.

"Better open the gate quick and get him in," the tribune ordered.

"Your heard the officer, lads, open up and get that nag in here before the Germans roast 'im."

They were still dragging the two leaves of the gate apart when the weary animal pushed through of its own accord. They heaved them back and dropped the locking bar back into position with a dull thud.

"Decurion Otto was riding it," one of the cavalrymen told Soranus and the centurion before he led it away.

This made sense of it coming in from the west. It had most likely got so muddy crossing Boxer's Canal. Once the news got out, the legion was split into two groups with conflicting opinions. Many believed it was a favourable omen; his horse had found its way home unharmed. That had to be good. The others thought it was the worst possible outcome. If Otto had made it into cover and then rode on, surely he would have taken it with him. It was a long way to headquarters and he would have need of a spare horse. No, he must have fallen. Argument and counterargument raged during every spare minute but there were not to be so many of those over the next few days.

Otto pounded up the track in the gathering gloom. At last he had to admit to himself that it was growing too dark to carry on. He noticed a game trail leading off to the right and followed it until it broke out into one of those small glades formed when a great tree fell. There was grazing but no water. He tethered his animals and sat with his back against a tree waiting out the long night. He dozed but sat forward, wide-eyed, and instantly awake at every rustle in the undergrowth. When the first birds began to twitter in the tree-tops and the world was no longer black but grey, he mounted up and retraced his steps to the track. "Giddup!" he yelled and drove his stolen horse forward as fast as its legs would take him.

When full daylight was spreading over the land, he came to a small stream. He let both horses drink, but only a little, before forcing them on, his heels drumming a constant rhythm on his mount's flanks. By noon, he could feel the horse under him beginning to fight for breath. The day was cooler; huge, black anvil shaped clouds were filling the sky downstream but for the moment he was racing ahead of them. He passed a bare hill with a seared top and recognised it as where Tertius Fuscus had ordered the bodies of the German ambushers to be cremated. On he rode without pause into the afternoon. He felt a tremor run through the horse beneath him. He gently slowed their frantic pace and felt its legs wobble when they had slowed to a walk. He halted and slipped out of the saddle. The animal was spent, soaked in sweat and so unsteady on its legs it could go no farther. He led it to some grazing under a sheltering tree near the river. He took off the saddle and bridle and set it free. With any luck, there would be enough nourishment in the grass to restore its strength and it certainly would not lack water; it had the whole of the Rhine to drink. He loped away holding Djinn's lead rope. The great stallion trotted beside him still relatively fresh; although he had kept up the pace, he had borne no weight on his back so far during their headlong dash.

Day came quicker to the Marcomanni camp than it did to Otto under the forest canopy. As he was mounting-up in the first dim dawn, Helmund and Hulderic had their people on the move in bright sunshine. They were going to be seriously damaged by missile-fire, they knew that but they had learned some lessons. Making the clan leaders and chieftains apply them had been a major battle in itself. Over ten thousand warriors were taking part in their first full-strength assault. Manoeuvring was going to take some time. The entire force had been divided into ten battalions of around one thousand men. Each man had been instructed to stand so that his spread arms did not quite touch his neighbour on either side and that there were two paces between each rank.

"If you close up too soon, their machines will kill you three at a time," Helmund warned.

They had reluctantly agreed but there was a sticking point. One of the chieftains had decided to ride his horse into the engagement. Hulderic told him that this was not a good idea.

"My warriors will look up and take heart at the sight of me in my battle finery and hear my words of encouragement."

"But you will make a bigger target for their bolt-throwing machines," Helmund told him hoping that stating the obvious would being him to his senses.

"Then these Romans will know I have no fear of them," he said jutting out an obstinate chin.

"Helmund and I will be on foot," Hulderic added.

The chieftain looked at him disdainfully.

"It is not for me to comment on the valour of others," he said.

As a result of his insistence, most of the rest felt they should also show the Romans they had no fear, which resulted in over two hundred mounted men forming up with the warriors on foot.

The Marcomanni knew they could move without fear of artillery fire as long as they were not within four hundred paces of the Roman walls. They walked across the open plain and fell into their ranks, spread out as instructed. The battalions began to separate from each other. Then half the force stepped out onto the farmlands and began to deploy to the west.

The Roman officers were watching from their northern parapet.

"Aye, aye, that's new," Attius said.

"I see a lot of men are carrying hurdles and ladders," Soranus remarked.

"And there are many warriors on horseback among them. Boxer, tell your artillerists to pay them special attention, if you will,"

Quadratus said, giving one of his polite suggestions which were, in fact, precise orders.

"Yes, sir," Lucius responded.

"Tell your lads to aim for the horses, not the riders. A big fat horse with a scorpion bolt up its arse can do a lot of damage before it drops dead," Attius added.

"Perhaps not as I would have put it but tactically sound as ever, Titus," the legate laughed before turning to Tertius Fuscus. "Senior tribune Fuscus, you will command the western wall for me. First Spear Centurion Titus Attius, take the northern side. We cannot neglect our other defences so let us have one cohort manning each of the south and east walls, we can bring them into the main fight if necessary. Tribune Lucius Longius, split Centurion Corvo's men between the two commanders. Tribune Rufus Soranus, I'm making you my permanent aide-de-camp. Find yourself twenty runners and an armful of wax-tablets. Titus, what are all these German axes doing propped up behind the parapets?"

"Took 'em off the enemy dead after their last performance. Handy for chopping through ropes they throw up and that sort of thing, sir."

Quadratus grunted his approval. "To our places gentlemen, Mars and Fortuna with us."

"Mars and Fortuna," the officers replied in unison and hurried away.

Helmund halted his division and waited while Hulderic marched the other half of the army into position. Horns blared and the orderly advance gradually speeded up until, within range of Lucius' scorpions and ballistas, it became a full charge. When the first missiles fell among them, they closed up instinctively and against all instructions. A horse was hit square in the chest and bowled over half a dozen warriors like skittles as it fell, thrashing in its death throes. Others followed in rapid succession. The proud riders now looked about them wild-eyed, wishing they had listened to Helmund but fearing the loss of face if they dismounted more than the threat of death swooping down from the sky. The thudding of artillery fire increased in rapidity as the mass of yelling men came ever closer and made it easier to pick out a target. They reached Boxer's Canal and flung down their hurdles using them as crude bridges, surging over in a mad dash to gain the shelter of the walls. Now javelins, arrows and sling bullets rained down on them. Men fell dead or with broken limbs, tripping their companions but still they came on. New levels of noise were reached as screams added to the cacophony when the caltrops in the northern ditch crippled feet.

But there had been over ten thousand of them at the outset. If hundreds were lost in the approach, there remained thousands to press the final assault on the walls. Ladders banged against the parapets, ropes and hooks were flung over them and the Marcomanni began to force the issue hand to hand. They had massed at the foot of the walls waiting their turn to climb. Arrows and sling bullets continued to crash into them but now they were no longer sprinting, they could hold up their shields for some protection. Still, Corvo's men took a fatal harvest.

The defenders snatched up the axes spread along the walkways and hacked through ropes If men were already climbing, they fell back among trampling feet or onto spear points in the ditch below. Shields and helmets rose up over the parapet, as the fiercest warriors scrambled up ladders or reached the top of their knotted ropes before they were slashed through. The first were quickly dealt with but as more and more followed, they began to gain footholds on the walkways. Knots of desperately struggling men fought to the death, the attackers trying to break out and give room for more of their comrades to join them, the defenders to hold them and force them back. Men fell to axes, to spears, to swords but the onslaught was unceasing. Walkways became slick with blood and faeces; bodies lay ready to trip a man and to fall was death. Additional centuries were sent up from the reserves. The hours passed but neither side could gain a decisive advantage. Then everything changed.

The rain which Titus had predicted fell in torrents from a black sky vivid with lightning and deafening with thunderclaps. It became impossible for the Marcomanni to grip their slippery ropes and ladder rungs. The pressure on the Romans gradually decreased until there was no living enemy left within their walls. They leaned forward and hurled stones and javelins down at the packed faces in the ditch.

A Marcomanni horn blew a call and they fell back, in tens and scores at first, then in hundreds as they raced each other out of missile range. The archers' wet bowstrings stretched and were useless but the weather made no difference to the slingers nor, in the short term, to the scorpions and ballistas. The enemy disappeared from sight into the grey sheets of rain.

The Romans had lost two hundred and thirty men, the Marcomanni nearly eight hundred but most significantly, only fifty mounted chieftains out of the over two hundred who had started out rode back to their lines. The mathematics could not be denied. Provided they had the will to keep coming, the attackers were going to win this war of attrition.

The corpses were dumped unceremoniously over the walls to lie sprawled and twisted in the ditch below waiting for the rain to wash them clean of their blood and filth. The legionaries who had not been in action were sent out with hooks on poles to drag the corpses out and pile them up in a hideous rampart thirty paces back from the base of the walls. The next time the Marcomanni attacked, and no-one doubted there would be a next time, they would have to advance over the rotting bodies of their own men. Every re-usable weapon and piece of ammunition was collected and brought back within the walls. Unceasing rain fell for the rest of the day. Both sides used the respite the weather had given them to lick their wounds and ponder their future tactics.

Chapter 9

Otto jogged or walked beside Djinn for the rest of the afternoon. He was saving his horse for tomorrow. As evening fell, with showers from the remains of the heavy storm downstream, he found a secure place with a rivulet running nearby to rest for the night. Man and beast both drank their fill. Otto remembered he had not eaten since before he set-out and instantly felt wolfishly hungry. He tore at his bread and dried meat, washed down with cups of water from the stream and fed Djinn a good half of the crushed grain he carried. He found a spot without too many protruding roots and lay down wrapped in his cloak. He intended to rest for a while and then be up and about before dawn but his exertions caught up with his weary body and he slept right through the night without stirring. He was woken by Djinn pushing him with his velvety muzzle and breathing his sweet breath into his face. The sun was well up. Otto came to his feet annoyed with himself. There were preparations to make and time was rushing past.

He pulled off his mail shirt, panicking for a moment when it jammed over his head but he struggled free and laid it to one side along with his shield and helmet. He ate the last of his dried meat and gave the remaining half-loaf to Djinn. He hoped that reducing the weight he must carry would help the stallion in the effort he was going to be asked to make over the next two days. He saddled and bridled him and mounted up with his grey cloak over his subarmalis and his leather skull cap on his head. He carried only the spear he had taken from the man he had killed on the road and the remaining two pounds of grain.

"You need to give me all the stamina and will that you have, my friend," he told Djinn and guided him into a mile-eating canter towards the north and east.

It was still raining heavily in the area of The Second Lucan camp. This was a relief to the Romans who felt confident that the Marcomanni would not make another attempt in these conditions. However, they kept a strong presence on the walkways.

"Helmund has come against us in two dawn raids on our northern and eastern walls and one daytime mass-assault. It seems we can do him severe damage only during his advance. Once at close quarters, our men are roughly handled. The question is, when and where he will come next time," Quadratus said.

"His strategy is to shift the point and scale of each attack to keep us unsettled," commented Tertius.

Quadratus nodded. "Correct, and he is succeeding more than we expected. Boxer, can you do something extra with the artillery to keep him at bay?"

"Sorry, sir," Lucius replied. "My men and I are maximising the effectiveness of our batteries. In the absence of additional ballistas and scorpions, we can do no more. The arrow supply is troubling, even with those we have been able to retrieve, though we have not reached a critical point."

"What about sling bullets?"

Lucius smiled smugly, "The pebbles we weighed and graded, sir; you may remember you remarked on it at the time? We have plenty of them to make up for any short-fall in lead bullets, sir."

"An "I told you so" attitude is inappropriate at the best of times, Boxer…and these are not the best of times," Quadratus responded with a brief smile.

"Below three thousand men we can no longer man our walls. We are not there yet but casualties are mounting…" Tertius said.

"If Otto…" Soranus began to interrupt but the legate rounded on him angrily.

"Tribune Rufus Soranus, let me hear no further talk along those lines. It is the men within these walls that must find answers to our predicament. We cannot allow ourselves merely to hang on in the vague hope of help and support; doing so will weaken our resolve. I will hear no more of it. Now Tertius, I take your earlier point but for the moment we can adequately defend ourselves. To that end, I want the walls and gates manned as at present but in addition, two cohorts fully armed on standby on the parade ground day and night. They can rotate every four hours."

"Permission to begin to train new men in the use of our artillery pieces, sir; in case of casualties among the experienced operators?" Lucius asked.

"See to it," Quadratus ordered. "And if the day comes when we can no longer man our walls…"

"Then we set fire to our camp and all its supplies and march down on the bastards. Even if we don't win, and I'm not saying we won't, we'll do 'em so much damage they wont be an army anymore, just a rabble of survivors," Titus Attius told them all with certainty.

Otto rode for an hour and jogged beside his trotting horse for fifteen minutes then remounted and rode again for another hour repeating the process until noon. He stopped, unsaddled Djinn, dried his back with his cloak as best he could and let him roll in the grass. Then, after a break to allow him to graze, drink and digest, he buckled on the saddle and off they went again. On they journeyed, hour after hour; ten miles for every hour Otto rode and half of that for every hour he jogged beside his horse. Spiteful showers of rain fell on them. The sun came out and dried them only for them to be soaked again. Late in the afternoon a cold north-easterly breeze began to blow in their faces, chilling if it had not been for the sweat of their running bodies. They splashed through steams and muddy puddles splattering themselves but barely slowing their onward rush.

Deep into the gloaming, Otto jumped down to rest Djinn again but staggered, his knees buckled under him and he sank to the ground.

His legs were too fatigued to bear his weight any longer. He stayed down for a few minutes then painfully got to his feet and dragged himself and Djinn into cover. He attended to the horse and laid down to sleep. All night long agonising cramps in his calf muscles jolted him awake. He was relieved to see the dawn.

The same drying breeze blew the storm away from the Roman camp. The temperature dropped and it grew even colder as night drew on. The stars shone dimly through the screen of the last of the dispersing hazy clouds overhead. There was no moon. Sentries re-wrapped their scarves about their necks and huddled deeper into their cloaks, stamping their chilly feet. The camp was at an uneasy rest. Two cohorts stood at the ready in the centre of the parade ground, their collective breath sending up wisps of white steam to vanish in the air above their heads. At midnight, shouted orders, stamping feet, the clash of weapons and jingling armour signalled the changeover. Two cohorts stood down and two replaced them. This was repeated at four in the morning by which time it was almost frosty. A heavy dew fell on helmets and armour and began to penetrate cloaks making them sodden and heavy.

Shortly after the changing of the guard, a sentry over the Porta Decumana reported he had heard an ox bellow to the south. Officers went up over the gate and listened but the sound was not repeated. A few weeks ago, he would have been told off for imagining things and been made the butt of his mates' jokes but now, anything at all out of the ordinary, no matter how trivial, was unsettling. Torches were thrown down but nothing could be seen. Tertius Fuscus was the officer of the watch. When he was informed, he came to the gate and looked out into the darkness. While he was making up his mind what action to take, the Marcomanni took the decision out of his hands.

A rumbling, growing louder, drumming over the bridge that crossed the stream signalled a big square mass hurtling towards the gate. It was one of the enemy's wagons which had become a feature of the landscape, parked down by the river for days on end. They had harnessed teams of oxen to it as soon as night fell and hauled it in a half circle to the south west. They unhitched the oxen, turned it and forty men had pushed it as fast as they could over the bridge to slam into the Porta Decumana. The tailgate had been removed. It was loaded with brush-wood faggots soaked in turpentine. The sharp smell rose up to the men standing over the gate.

"Alarm! Alarm! Tertius shouted, then. "Open up!"

As his voice rang out, the sound of men hurrying away was heard outside and the first fire arrow flared out of the night.

Tertius shouted down to his men standing by.

"Advance and form-up to cover the gate. You other men, rakes and buckets of water."

He ran down the steps from the walkway and drew his sword

More fire arrows followed and the wagon burst into flames. As both leaves of the gate were dragged aside, blazing, sizzling bundles of sticks fell off the back making an inferno in the open gateway. Tertius stood by watching and shouting encouragement as soldiers ran up, raked a bundle out of the fire and doused it with water. It was not quick but a better way of firefighting than trying to deal with the entire incendiary mass at one go. The wagon had left a narrow strip between it and the gateposts on one side. Thirty warriors erupted out of the stream and hurtled towards it.

They were all the sworn companions of chieftains who had ridden their horses into the last battle and died. Honour called on them for vengeance; they would be disgraced forever if they returned alive without it. They had crawled up in darkness and hidden in the frigid water under the bridge waiting for their chance. They had been prepared to endure until the gate burned down but the Romans had opened it. One of them saw, shouted to the others and they came. Screaming, faces distorted with hatred, beards and braids sending cascades of water into the air as they ran with only one aim in their hearts; bloody carnage.

The soldiers trying to extinguish the fire and the ranks standing by to defend the gap could not see beyond the brilliant flames. The heat had driven the sentries back along the wall on either side. One of them saw the enemy rush and shouted down but his voice was drowned by the crackle of the fire.

The first warrior ran through the gap straight at Tertius who had been trained in fencing by some of the best masters-at-arms in Rome.

However, their lessons had not included defence against a berserker in his battle-fury. The tribune raised his sword in the classical defensive parry but it had not been designed to stop a war-axe. His arm was forward of his body, slightly bent with the stubby sword hilt just above his head. He caught the full force of the axe handle on his blade. The shock ran down to his feet and his right arm jumped out of the shoulder joint. The axe continued on its trajectory but much of the impetus had been absorbed so that when it struck his helmet, it sheered off the crest and dented it but did not chop through the metal. Senior Tribune Tertius Fuscus hit the ground like a felled tree. His opponent stood over his unconscious body and raised his axe for the killing blow. It never came. He was pierced through by two javelins thrown from above and crashed down on top of him.

More had come through. They set about the legionaries who were holding rakes and buckets, hacking them down. One rake-man caught a burning faggot up and flipped it into an enemy face, setting fire to his beard before running behind the shield wall of the advancing defenders. But the Marcomanni could only get through the gap in twos and threes at the most. They were cut to pieces as they ran into the solid ranks of the legionaries. When the last one fell and no more appeared to be arriving, the senior centurion took decisive action.

"First four centuries out past that wagon and fall-in to defend the bridge. If those mad fuckers got in so can more of 'em."

They extinguished the fire within an hour. The four centuries guarding the bridge withdrew in tight formation into the camp and the Porta Decumana was closed. They dragged the wagon inside. The carpenters could take a look at it in the morning to see if it was salvageable. The enemy dead had been stripped of their ornaments and weapons before they were tossed over the walls. Tertius was in the care of the medical officer.

A ring of anxious faces surrounded him in the lamplight of his operating room. Tertius had been put on his side on the ground with two orderlies holding him tightly, although he was still unconscious. The medical officer had hold of his right arm which he had pulled out straight.

"You might want to look away gentlemen," he said and rotated the arm with a quick flick. There was a crunching sound. Tertius moaned and was silent again. "Better to get his arm back into its hole while he's still out, damn painful business," the doctor said, glancing with satisfaction at the horrified looks on the officers' faces. There was something about re-positioning a dislocation that made men wince, even if they were used to blood and skin all over the walls.

The orderlies lifted Tertius onto a cot and the medical officer felt the edges of the raised, black welt on the top of his head. He could feel no movement of bone under his fingers nor hear any crepitation, which signified the skull was not fractured.

"Rise him up," he ordered.

They lifted the wounded man so that he was half sitting and some feathers were burned under his nose.

He coughed and opened his eyes.

"Greeting senior tribune," the doctor said with a smile. "Who is that officer over there?" he asked pointing at Quadratus.

"Legate Puppilus Quaratus," came the mumbled reply.

"Near enough. Time to rest." He administered a weak dose of poppy juice. "Shave the area of the contusion on his head, very gently mind. Wash it with vinegar and apply some honey. If it oozes a little blood, so much the better. Stay with him until he wakes naturally and call me if he begins to snort as he's breathing or vomits," he told his assistants then turned to the legate. "It seems highly likely the Senior Tribune Fuscus will live. It will be two or three days before he is fully back to his senses and a month until his right arm is useable. He will require a sling and daily massage, sir."

"But he will make a full recovery, doctor?" Quadratus asked anxiously.

He shrugged. "Impossible to say with a head wound sir. I knew a man who seemed to be absolutely well except that he could no longer remember his family, otherwise, just fine…."

The brief incursion had cost eleven men's lives and temporarily disabled the legion's second in command; a result Helmund would have thought worth his own losses, had he known.

Otto welcomed the day after his uncomfortable night. He got gingerly to his feet and bent his knees to test his legs. The muscles felt tight but the rest had done him some good. He gave Djinn the last of the fodder and climbed into the saddle. Yesterday's routine was repeated; ride at the canter, then dismount, jog while his horse trotted then remount, again and again. At noon, they stopped by a wide stream running into the Rhine. Djinn grazed and rolled. Otto sat with his back against a tree and massaged his legs. When they were ready to continue, he manged to crawl up onto his horse's back. Too soon it was time for him to dismount and go on foot. After a few minutes he knew that he could no longer keep pace with the trotting horse. He pulled him to a halt and spoke into his ear.

"Djinn, my brave friend, I no longer have the strength to run. You must carry me all the way now, if you can."

He led him to a fallen tree and used it as a mounting block. They travelled through the afternoon at that same easy canter which suited Djinn so well. For hours he went on like some exquisite machine, the bellows of his lungs pumping air onto the inward fires of his strength and reserves of energy as if he would never tire. When the sun broke out after yet another cold, heavy shower, Otto could see their shadow dancing in front of his right shoulder, showing they were heading in the right direction. The shadow lengthened as the sun sank and evening began to draw on. Gradually, Djinn's head started to rise and fall like a rocking horse. He began to fight for each gasping breath. When Otto reckoned within an hour it would be too dark to go on, he felt that ominous tremor run through the great stallion's frame. Djinn had reached the end of his powers. Otto could force him on for perhaps, another ten or fifteen miles but that would destroy the animal. He pulled him to a halt, climbed out of the saddle and stroked Djinn's ears.

"What more can we do but our best, eh?" he asked.

The horse was so exhausted he could not raise his head. Otto looked around,. They were in a thicket of young trees. He decided to find somewhere to rest and walked at little forward. Djinn shuffled, his hooves scuffing the mud of the track. Otto could not straighten his back and felt like his knees had completely locked. They went on for a few yards and reached the edge of the copse. There before them, a mile away, was a five-legion camp; the headquarters of General Nero Claudius Drusus, stepson of Augustus and his recently appointed commander on the Rhine and Elba Rivers.

They picked their halting way down the slight slope to the nearest gate. It was just about to close as the last rays of the sun faded. There were two sentries; a stocky decanus and the other a tall thin legionary. They watched the man and horse coming towards them. Both thought Otto must be old at first with his bent back and slow pace. The horse looked equally decrepit, its head hanging as the pair wandered up to them.

"Greetings," Otto said. "I am Senior Decurion Otto Longius…"

"'Course you are, and that old nag's your charger, I s'pose," the decanus said, taking charge.

"Yes, but I must see the general…"

"No chance, on your way before you get yourself into trouble."

"You are not listening to me. I am a decurion of The Second Lucan and I demand to see your officer."

"Second Lucan? They're fucking miles away and you never got here from them on this lump of crowbait," the decanus said pointing at Djinn.

"Look, I order you to let me pass and to speak to an officer…"

"That's it mate, you've asked for it. You can have a night in the stockade for not pissing off when you're told to."

He lunged at Otto who tried to throw a punch but staggered slightly. The soldier dodged it easily and cracked him over the head with shaft of his javelin. Both of them dragged the half-conscious vagabond inside. Djinn shambled after them. Otto was thrown into a log cell. The decanus took his belt, dagger and purse.

"Here, you have these," he said to the legionary, stripping the silver arm-rings Otto had so recently looted himself.

"No, I don't want anything to do with this. We're supposed to report any goings-on…."

"Report it then, in the morning. He's just some German with beer scrambled brains."

"He spoke good Latin…"

"So do a few of them, don't make 'em cavalry officers, do it? If you're so worried, take that wreck of a horse of his over to the cavalry lines. I'll tell the optio where you are, it'll be alright."

Djinn ambled dispiritedly behind the soldier to the stables.

"A bloke just came in with him…." he began but the stable-orderly cut him short.

"Where is this bloke now?"

"In the stockade."

"Good, that's where he belongs, the bastard; this poor fellow's been nearly ridden to death. Come on, let's rub you down. Bucket of warmish water with a splash of wine and a bran mash and you'll forget all about it," he crooned to Djinn who allowed himself to be led into a strange stall without showing any resistance.

"Officers' assembly including Centurion Corvo," Quadratus told Soranus who sent his runners around the camp to convey the legate's orders. When they were gathered, the legate took Corvo outside.

"Am I correct in presuming that you are a commoner, centurion?" he asked.

Corvo hesitated. "I suppose I am."

"You have some doubt?"

"On my father's side, my grandfather was a provincial knight, sir but he drank…"

"I do not care if he drank half of Our Sea. That is a piece of luck and we need all we can find. Come on, back in."

"Report First Spear Centurion Attius," he ordered once they were sitting with the rest of the officers.

"Night attack by a force of thirty fanatics after their pals had shoved a burning wagon into the Porta Decumana. Gate undamaged, all intruders killed. We lost eleven of our good comrades. Senior Tribune Tertius Fuscus was wounded and will not be able to return to full duty for a month, according to the sawbones."

"Any comment on the action?" Quadratus asked.

"One legionary was firefighting when they broke in. He disabled one of them by using his rake to throw a bundle of burning faggots in his face. Initiative worth rewarding, sir?"

"Definitely, two gold pieces. Send him to me and I shall present them. Now, in view of the injury to Senior Tribune Fuscus, we shall have to reorganize our roles. Tribune Longius, you will take over the responsibilities of senior tribune until further notice. Centurion Corvo is appointed temporary acting prefect commanding all artillery and missile troops..." Shocked looks were furtively exchanged between the other officers. "...Centurion Corvo's paternal grandfather was a provincial knight. He is therefore of equestrian extract and entitled to serve in this capacity. Boxer, fill Corvo in on what he might need to know about the artillery situation. Someone send the legionary with the rake to me..."

Everyone went about their duties. The fact that they were under siege did not stop drills, kit inspections and weapons training.

Centurions and optios bellowed, vine-staffs bounced off helmets. Fatigue parties carried out maintenance and cooks provided sustenance for the legion. At noon, Lucius and Titus asked to speak with Quadratus.

"Sir," Titus began, "last night they chanced their arm at the Porta Decumana. I think it will be in our interest to take down the bridge over the stream to the south. They couldn't have got as far as they did without it."

"Point taken." The legate sighed. "Yet again we are reacting to the strategy of the enemy. We seem unable to make him dance to our tune."

"It's only a matter of time, sir. We'll have the bastards soon enough," Titus replied without hesitation.

"Permission to demonstrate something, sir?" Lucius asked.

The legate nodded. Lucius shouted and two soldiers came in carrying a thick, ten-foot pole with a blunt iron fork on one end.

"For their ladders sir. We can use these to push them over backwards."

"Excellent idea, Boxer…"

"Something else sir, you know the enemy's battering-ram housing…"

"Is there anything left of it?"

"Yes sir, the hurdles they used for the sides and the roof is more or less intact. It's covered with rawhide. If we could strip it off, we might be able to nail it to the outside of our gates… fireproofing, you see…"

"Anything and everything that can give us the slightest advantage, do it. If nothing else, it keeps the men busy and shows them their officers are being active on the legion's behalf."

Under a heavy guard commanded by Titus, Lucius supervised the demolition of the wooden bridge over the stream while inside the camp, the rawhides were being prised loose. Lucius made his team work carefully; stopping to examine how the bridge had been constructed at each stage so as to maximise what they could salvage. Every useful piece of timber was carried into the camp. Recent events had shown him how valuable reclaimed materials could be. So far, they had contributed to the new wall and the breastwork replacing the Porta Principalis Dexter. Who knows what these beams and support timbers might be used for in the coming days?

In the Marcomanni lines, they were building a structure out of heavy logs. Helmund was not about to let the Romans enjoy any respite. The attack the previous night had not been a serious attempt to take their camp. It was an honour raid which he had sanctioned, partly to show his warriors he understood their need for revenge but mostly because it meant another disturbed night for the Roman garrison; turning the screw just a little tighter on their morale.

"Wonder where Otto is now?" Felix said that night in their quarters that night, as Lucius spooned up one of the stews he invariably cooked.

"The legate says we are not to discuss that subject," Lucius told him.

"I know but it's only you and me."

"Felix, to tell the truth, I don't like to think of him out there alone…"

"Oh don't you worry about Otto. He's probably feasting with the general tonight…"

Chapter 10

The stable orderly looked over the half-door into Djinn's stall. "Well, a night in the warm and some grub have done you the world of good old lad," he said. The stallion was on his feet, head held high and looked back with bright eyes at this stranger. "Let's get you outside and give you a bit of a clean up, eh?"

Djinn consented to being led out and tied by his headstall to a ring in the wall. The orderly fetched a sponge and a bucket of warm water and began to wash off the caked ash, mud and sweat. As he worked, whistling and talking gently to calm the animal, his hands ran over Djinn's hide and felt the firm muscles underneath. He stepped back and looked at him from a distance.

"You're not old at all are you? You were only filthy and tired-out. Would you let me look at your teeth, I wonder?" He quickly found out that Djinn would not. "Aright, alright, not to worry. Let's dry you off and give you a bit of a brush, polish your hooves maybe…"

When he had finished and led him back inside. Djinn was unrecognisable as the nag that had shambled into the stall the night before. "You are something special, aren't you? I'm going to show you to a friend of mine. He'll know how old you are and what to do with you."

He ambled down the cavalry lines stopping to chat a couple of times and eventually entered a forge.

"Greetings, Passer," he said to the tall youth, all gangling limbs like a young colt, who was filing the back hoof of a charger into shape before a new shoe was fitted." Where's Decanus Flaccus?"

Passer grinned. "Uncle Martellus is still eating his breakfast. He'll be along just now."

The orderly sat down on a hay bale. "He'll kick your backside if he hears you calling him that."

"No, he won't," Passer told him. "He's used to it."

At the other end of the camp, a tall, thin legionary was standing to attention in front of his centurion.

"What?" the officer snapped before putting another piece of bread soaked in oil and garum into his mouth.

"Last night, sir, a German came up at sundown and asked to see the general, he said he was a cavalry officer, sir."

"What did he look like?"

"Bit of a derelict. He walked like a duck and his horse was half-dead."

"Drunk was he?"

"No sir. Said he was from The Second Lucan. Spoke good Latin."

Alarm bells rang in the centurion's head.

"Where's he now?"

"Stockade."

The officer crammed the last of his breakfast into his mouth, put on his helmet and stood up.

"Show me."

Otto was sitting at the back of his cage leaning against the bars, using his cloak as padding. For all he had taken a crack to the head, the long night's sleep and the hunk of soldier's bread and pannikin of water shoved under the gate had revived him. He still looked a disreputable specimen.

"Stand up!" the centurion ordered.

Otto climbed stiffly to his feet.

"Who are you and what are you doing here?"

"I am Principal Decurion Otto Longius. I am here to see the general and ask for urgent cavalry reinforcements because The Second Lucan are under attack by a force of around fifteen thousand Marcomanni."

"If you're an officer, where's your uniform and armour?"

"I discarded them to reduce the weight my horse had to carry. Where is he by the way?"

"Being looked after. Let this man out," the centurion told the legionary and gestured for both of them to follow him.. He repeated the story in front of his of his First Spear Centurion who took him to the Camp Prefect.

"Need to report this to the general's aide de camp," he said, "Follow me."

The two senior officers, with Otto, the centurion and the lanky legionary in tow, marched into the Praetorium.

"Wait there," the Camp Prefect ordered and walked through an inner door, closing it after him.

Ten minutes later it was re-opened. Otto and the others were beckoned inside. They stood in a line, Otto in the centre, in front of an ornate desk behind which a young man in exquisite armour was seated. He had large, expressive eyes, a long, straight nose and a well-shaped head with close-cropped hair. The others came to attention and bowed. Otto realised he must be the general and followed suit.

"What business do you have with the Noble Nero Claudius Drusus, Commander of the Army of Upper Germany?" an officer wearing a magnificently sculpted breastplate called out.

"This man has arrived in camp claiming to have a message from the Noble Legate Publius Quadratus of The Second Lucan, sir." The Camp Prefect responded and bowed again.

"Let him speak," the general said pleasantly.

"Sir, my legion is under attack by a force of fifteen thousand Marcomanni and requests urgent cavalry support," Otto told him.

"And you are?"

"I am Principal Decurion Otto Longius, sir."

The general studied Otto for a full minute.

"I am inclined to believe you Otto Longius. If you could provide us with some proofs of your story…"

"Sir, if my property was returned, I could show you my knight's ring…"

"Your what?" the Camp Prefect blurted out in astonishment.

"My knight's ring. The Emperor enrolled me in the Equestrian Order during my audience with him."

"You were made a knight on the express orders of my father?" the general asked, equally surprised at this turn of events.

"No sir, by the Emperor. He was very gracious to me. We had lunch together; he showed me his orchard."

"Did we not second Prefect Aldermar from The Second Lucan?" General Drusus asked.

"We did, sir," answered the Camp Prefect.

"Very well." Drusus continued. "Otto Longius, bathe, refresh yourself and report back to me in one hour, my orderly will find you some clean clothes.." Otto saluted and turned stiffly to leave. "What is wrong with your legs?"

"I have ridden or run beside my horse for four days sir."

"My masseur will attend you in the officer's bathhouse."

Uncle Martellus sauntered into the forge with a cup in one hand and a cold sausage wrapped in bread in the other. He handed them to Passer.

"Here's your second breakfast. The amount you eat you should be the size of a house."

"I stay thin because I work so hard," Passer answered with a grin and took the food.

Martellus grunted and noticed his visitor. "Greetings, to what do we owe the honour?"

"Greeting, Decanus Flaccus. There's a horse I want to show you. He was brought into me last night and looked ready for the knackers but this morning, what a recovery! I would like your opinion of him."

"If Passer hasn't made too much of a mess of this one's hoof," he said, slapping the charger on his rump, "I'll get his shoe on and take a look."

Twenty minutes later, all three walked over to the stables. Martellus looked into the stall and his jaw dropped open.

"Where's the man who brought him in?"

"A legionary told me he's in the stockade. Best place for him, riding a fine horse like that half to death…"

Martellus turned to Passer. "Find Prefect Aldermar and bring him to the forge now. Tell him it is urgent, vitally urgent."

Passer flew off without saying a word. He saw by the look on Martellus' face this was no time for questions.

"I know this horse," Martellus told the orderly. "I was there when he was bought with the Emperor's own gold. His name is Djinn and he belongs to Decurion Otto Longius. Don't tell me he's the one in the stockade?"

"I don't know but this sounds like big trouble."

"Let's get Djinn over to my forge to start with."

Martellus watched how the stallion was moving. He could detect a little stiffness, one of his shoes seemed loose, otherwise he appeared to be in good condition.

"What did you give him when he came in?" he asked the orderly.

"Bucket of warm water with a cup of wine and a bran mash. Hay bag in the stall. Cleaned him up this morning. Can't get over the difference in him."

By the time Aldermar strode in with Passer, Martellus had checked and tightened Djinns shoes, and was massaging his legs with liniment. Aldermar was astonished.

"Yes," Martellus told him. "It's Djinn alright and I think Otto is in the stockade."

Aldermar turned on his heel and marched rapidly away towards the guardhouse.

"Where's the prisoner who came in last night?"

"My centurion took him over to the First Spear Centurion's office. What's going on with that scarecrow, who the fuck is he?" the duty optio told him.

But the prefect had gone without replying. He retraced Otto's upward passage through the ranks of the legion until he found himself at the Praetorium where he asked for and was granted entry. He stood to attention and bowed to the general.

"Ah, Prefect Aldermar, how timely; can you confirm that this man is one of your officers?"

He looked across the room crowded with uniforms and saw Otto, dressed in a blue tunic and looked fresh, considering the fatigue he had so recently suffered. There was a bruise on the line of the blond fuzz where his hair was beginning to grow back on his shaved head. He smiled and nodded a greeting.

"This is Principal Decurion Otto Longius of The Second Lucan Legion, sir," he told the general.

"And what is his social status?"

"By decree of the Emperor, your father, he is a Roman Citizen and enrolled in the Equestrian Order."

"You are the son of Emperor Augustus?" the astonished Otto blurted out.

Drusus smiled. "A stepson but he is a good and kind father to me."

"I'm sorry that I did not know that. Please send him my kind remembrances when you next write, sir."

"I'm sure that will please him." Drusus replied dryly.

"If the Emperor can recall who you are!" a peevish voice called from the side of the room.

Many of the officers laughed.

"Since he wrote to me when I had returned to camp and sent me a box of figs from his own orchard, I believe he might," Otto answered sharply.

"Have a care gentlemen, this young man has the favour of our Emperor who would not wish him to be mocked," Drusus said with a smile on his face but an edge to his voice which brought instant silence. "Let us turn to the matter in hand. Bring in the prisoner!"

With clashing arms and stamping boots, the decanus who had robbed and struck Otto down was brought in between two Praetorian Guards. One of them laid Otto's belt, dagger and purse on the edge of the general's desk together with four silver arms rings.

"Is this your property?"

"Yes sir."

"What do you expect to find in this purse?"

"My knight's gold ring engraved with my initials on the inside, a marble finger mounted in gold and a few coins of little value."

The items were all there.

"You have offered violence to a Knight of Rome, stolen the emblem of his rank and other property. Do you have anything to say?" Drusus asked the prisoner whose face was the colour of cheese.

In spite of his obvious fear, he straightened and squared his shoulders. "It is true. I have nothing else to say."

"Then I have no choice but to pronounce your death sentence," the general told him.

"May I speak, sir?" Otto intervened and received permission. "I was in a dirty and poor condition when I arrived as was my horse. It does not surprise me that this man did not believe me when I told him who I was. I feel no anger towards him on that account. But by keeping me in the stockade overnight, he has delayed my mission. I find that criminal. However, he is a soldier and a decanus so I ask that he is granted the mercy of a soldier's death."

"Will you be my second?" the prisoner asked Otto.

"With the general's permission," Otto told him.

"Outside now and get it over with," Drusus said brusquely.

The guards, the prisoner and Otto bowed and marched out.

"That decanus is an impressive young man. No wonder the emperor raised him to his present position," said the general, voicing his thoughts aloud and then turned his attention to Aldermar. "The background to this, prefect, is that he has managed to escape from his legion camp and ride to us seeking help. He tells us they are besieged by around fifteen thousand Marcomanni."

Someone gave Aldermar a sheet of parchment and a piece of charcoal. He drew a rough map of The Second Lucan camp and its surroundings. The officers began to discuss the situation and possible responses.

Around the back of the Praetorium, the decanus stood stripped to his tunic. He was resigned and grateful to Otto. Without his intervention, death would have come both agonizingly and slowly; either under the lash of the scourge or by crucifixion. Cold steel was infinitely preferable. One of the praetorians handed Otto a sword which he put into the prisoner's hand. He placed the tip of the blade under the ribs on the left of his belly, tilted so that is would enter at an upward angle. He nodded to Otto who wrapped his hands around the pommel as well. They looked into each other's eyes.

"Go, knowing I wish you peace on the other side," Otto murmured.

"I am sorry, sir," the decanus replied, but whether for his crime or for his death sentence he did not say.

He smiled and pushed forward as both men slid the sword up into his heart. His head tilted forward, his legs went from under him and he fell, dead.

"We'll take over now sir," one of the guards advised.

Otto walked away without a backward glance. He was not allowed to return to the meeting and cooled his heels in the anteroom for half an hour before he was summoned. At attention in front of General Drusus' desk once more, he waited with some apprehension for the council of war's decision.

"Decurion Longius, tell me how you managed to leave your legion's camp undetected." Drusus demanded.

Otto described his successful ruse.

"That was your idea?"

"Yes sir, it was."

"And how long did to take you to reach us?"

"I left in the late afternoon, as I reported and arrived here on the fifth day,"

"A remarkable feat of horsemanship. I take it you were unopposed?"

"No sir, two Marcomanni warriors tried to stop me. I killed them both. These silver arm-rings are my spoils."

Drusus shook his head as if unable to take in anymore.

"You have heard, gentlemen? I believe that this confirms our decision in respect of this officer." He addressed Otto directly. "For the rest of today you will liaise with Prefect Aldermar amongst others. They will want every piece of useful information you can give them. Tomorrow at first light, a force of twelve hundred mixed Roman and Auxiliary cavalry will ride to the relief of The Second Lucan. You will be with them. Arms and equipment in keeping with your rank will be provided. The Second Lucan were over-supplied in cavalry but in hindsight, that unfailing source of wisdom, we should not have restricted them to a single turma. An ala of one hundred and twenty cavalry will remain at your camp once order has been restored. They will need a commander. In spite of your youth, the feeling of this officers' conference is that they are in agreement with my decision. You are hereby promoted to Prefect of Cavalry. What is the current salary?..."

"Thirteen thousand one hundred and fifty denarii, sir," a secretary advised.

"I take it you heard that? Off you go then Prefect Longius."

Otto bowed again and began to walk towards the door.

"Prefect," the general called. "I will pass along your good wishes to the Emperor. He will be interested to know we have met."

Otto spent two hours with the other cavalry officers. He added detail to Aldermar's drawing, showing the diagonal wall at the north-east corner and Boxer's canal. The steep eastern slope with its tree-stumps was their greatest concern. They would have preferred to engage from that direction but both Aldermar and Otto insisted that this was impossible. Eventually it was decided that one group would charge between the wagons and the Rhine while a larger group rode across the enemy front to join them on their western flank. From there, they would have room to manoeuvre as a combined force over the abandoned farmland.

"I told the legate to march out when he heard every horn in the relief force sound the order to mount up in unison," Otto explained.

Because he knew the layout of the area from personal experience, Aldermar had been given tactical command. He shook his head.

"That alone won't do. We shall need to get a message into the camp."

"Very well," Otto said. "If I go on ahead…"

"Out of the question," the general's Master of Horse who was overseeing the meeting told him. "You are a prefect of cavalry now, not a mounted spy."

"We have men so skilled in moving through enemy lines we call them ghosts. We can get a message over the wall. It will be useful if you write it with me. We shall speak of this later," Aldermar told him.

Otto received a rapturous greeting from Passer at the forge.

"How tall you've grown." Otto said. "And are you happy with the choice you made?"

"Oh yes sir, that I am."

Martellus was his usual amiable, plain-spoken self.

"Djinn is up to the return journey. You won't be hammering him into the ground like you did on the way up, I take it?" he asked reproachfully.

"I know, I know, Uncle Martellus. I ran or walked beside him as far as I could but my strength gave out on the last day. I even threw away my weapons and armour to save him the weight."

"I'm giving you a flask of liniment to rub on his legs every evening and morning, I'll make it two and you can do the same."

They kitted him out from quartermaster's stores and contributions from well-disposed officers under the watchful eye of the Master of Horse. Aldermar had told him what Otto had done to earn the Emperor's favour Once he knew the details, the most senior officer in the army's cavalry took a personal interest.

"We do not have a cuirass for you, it must be chainmail for the moment…"

"I prefer a mail shirt, sir," Otto told him.

"Your preferences are neither here nor there. A Roman cavalry prefect wears a cuirass. Perhaps you did not fully take in the general's words. You are a regular army officer commanding Roman cavalrymen now, no longer an auxiliary. I have a red cloak for you that I have no use for, it is not overly threadbare…"

Mounted on Djinn who was curvetting and showing off, his coat shining, his mane and tail combed through and flowing free, Otto was presented to his new command.

"Greet your new prefect the equestrian Otto Longius," the Master of Horse thundered to make his voice heard to the one hundred and twenty mounted men lined up in front of him. They took one look and saw an enormous young man who clearly was not a native Roman. They were. Lips pursed. Side-long glances of disapproval were passed between comrades. "Your prefect was raised to the Equestrian Order by Emperor Augustus himself in recognition of his gallantry when saving the life of his legate in battle. Prefect Longius rode here alone from the camp of The Second Lucan to request reinforcements, killing two renowned Marcomanni chieftains single-handed on the way. Respect him. Deserve him.."

"I don't think they were renowned chieftains, sir," Otto said as the two of them rode away.

"Do you know who they were?"

"One of them was called Audo of the Bright Axe…"

"There you are then; famous chap, old Audo. Listen to me now, your men will not be happy that their officer is not a Roman born and bred. But if you are good enough for our Emperor, you are good enough for me and most certainly for the likes of them. They'll soon come around after you've been in battle together."

Fifteen-hundred horses were assembled in the drizzle of the next dawn. If twelve hundred were riding to war, they needed packhorses with food and spare equipment, saddle-makers to make running repairs, scouts on light, fast mounts and all the support necessary to bring them to battle in good order. Wearing the uniform of a Roman officer, Otto rode at the head of his men for the first time.

The horns called, the flags caught the breeze and the column walked past the saluting rostrum and out though the gate. They fell into the standard routine of trotting for half an hour, cantering for half an hour and walking at the head of their mounts for a quarter of an hour in rotation. To Otto, it seemed they were travelling at a snail's pace but the miles were disappearing under their hooves at a steady rate and, more importantly, one they could keep up almost indefinitely. It was a relief for Otto to be sleeping beside bivouac fires, secure behind a picket line and no longer, cold, hungry and alone in the wilderness.

While Otto was sleeping among his new comrades to the north, the night was disturbed at The Second Lucan camp. The sounds of axes thumping into wood, picks striking the ground and ripping, tearing noises were heard on the eastern slope above Boxer's breastwork. The night was black, a faint drizzle fell and nothing could be seen from the camp. Fire-arrows were loosed to try to illuminate what was going on. They flared briefly in the wet vegetation, revealing a few of the enemy busy on the slope before they were stamped out. After an hour or so, the Romans began to hear heavy objects bring rolled down towards the ditch. They flung torches over. On the lower slope and in the ditch they could see the tree-stumps, chopped through and ragged, lying uprooted.

"The bastards are clearing the hillside," a sentry said.

"Looks like it. We'll see more by morning," his optio told him and reported the new development to Lucius who was officer of the watch.

He was still in conversation with the optio when a cry of alarm went up from the Porta Principalis Sinistra.

"What is it?" demanded Lucius when he arrived, breathless on the walkway over the gate.

"I can hear oxen, listen, sir!" a legionary told him.

They both stared out into the impenetrable gloom to the west. The could hear animals lowing and more, the squeak of wheels and water splashing in Boxer's canal.

"Think they're going to try that stunt with the burning wagon again, sir?"

"I don't know. Send for First Spear Centurion Attius and sound the general alarm."

After the clamour and turmoil of the troops tumbling out of their billets and standing-to, there was silence. Time passed. No wagon loaded with brushwood hurtled towards them. Torch after torch was thrown from the walls; nothing, no-one.

Immediately before daybreak there is a short period when the eye becomes uncertain. The brain is unable to decide if there is enough light to distinguish whether there is shape, motion and colour to be seen. That is when they heard the buzzing of giant bees below them, a rhythmic thrumming and then a clank as the first grapnel hook struck the parapet and bit home. Others followed almost instantly, ten, twenty; some caught the parapet, some the top edge of the gate, others missed and fell to the ground. The flames of the thrown torches showed warriors racing back towards Boxer's Canal. The sentries hurled javelins but none found their targets in the dim light. Men grabbed up the axes left behind the parapet for the purpose and leaned out to slash through the ropes attached to the grapnel hooks. The axes rebounded with metallic clangs. There were no ropes. They were attached to lengths of chain.

A tremendous yell accompanied by snapping whips and bellowing oxen was followed by a movement in the walkway under their feet, like a wave passing over. The timbers groaned. A plank in the gate split its full length. The walkway moved again, this time, swaying outwards.

"Get off!" Lucius shouted and dashed to the side with the guard party.

With popping and cracking sounds and a final rending crash, the entire length of the parapet and one leaf of the gate fell to the ground. The locking bar jammed and the second leaf was ripped off its hinges, tottered and toppled over. With a roar, Marcomanni warriors threw down their hurdles to cross the Canal and launch their furious onslaught.

Attius had anticipated an assault. He had his men in his favoured three rank open box formation but he had learned after the enemy's first incursion. His right and left flanks were five men deep to prevent them cutting their way through between the end of his ranks and the camp walls.

The Marcomanni had learned as well. They checked their run twenty paces out and threw their spears in a volley. They did not aim at the line of shields facing them but upwards so that the second and third Roman ranks were caught in a plunging fire. Fifteen men fell. It was enough. When the full force of the charge hit them, the front rank could not hold their position without the support of the fallen men behind them. The line bowed inwards, crumpled and broke. The yelling warriors were among them on all sides, hacking with axes and thrusting with lances. Attius yelled his orders and a second cohort stepped forward behind the melee, linking up with his left and right flanks. The legionaries of the broken ranks were forced to fight for their lives without their comrades being able to intervene for fear of cutting their own men down. The experienced and the lucky filtered through to the sides and reformed.

By now it was almost full light. The Marcomanni chieftain saw the Roman reformed defensive line. He lifted the horn he carried and blew a long, wailing note. His warriors turned as a man and ran back the way they had come A few were brought down with javelins as they retreated. In the distance, two teams of oxen lumbered across the ground still dragging pieces of gate and palisade on stout cables behind them. As they raced away, the enemy spread out wide across what had been the cornfields. Corvo decided not to waste artillery ammunition on doubtful individual targets.

The engagement cost the lives of forty Romans and one hundred Marcomanni. The figures were troubling. Previously, the enemy casualties had been much higher in proportion.

"This Helmund has a fine tactical grasp of the situation. I believe he will come at us in smaller numbers, inflict as many casualties as he can and then withdraw once he sees we are gaining the upper hand. He intends to cut our numbers down little by little. We can do nothing but oppose him tooth and nail. Boxer, can you make me a new gate?" Quadratus asked, his calm manner as unruffled as ever although his eyes seemed a little more sunken and his face thinner with each day that passed as the strain of command told on him.

"No sir. It will have to be another breastwork. I can use the wagon we took off them as the base but I need to fill it with ballast and we must keep all the stones we have for ammunition."

"Take the tiles off the barrack roofs." Titus Attius told him.

"Do you intend for the men to sleep in their tents, Titus?" the legate asked.

"Nowhere to pitch them sir. We need to be able to move freely across the parade ground and Via Praetoria day or night without tripping over guy-ropes. No, I propose to divide the day up into four six -hour watches. Half the men on duty, half off. We won't need to take the roofs off all the barrack blocks. Soldiers' personal possessions can be labelled and placed in the custody of the priests."

"Very well, let us make our preparations and be ready for their next assault."

The breastwork was a gimcrack affair when compared with the first one. The bridge over the ditch was dismantled and brought inside.

They shoved the wagon sideways-on in the gap and took the wheels off before filling it with roof tiles. When they were finished, it was so heavy that nothing was going to shift it. They built up hurdles sandwiched between horizontal timbers as high as they could go and constructed a fighting platform and access ladders. They nailed as much of the rawhide as they could find on the outside. When Titus Attius jumped up and down on it, the platform gave slightly under his bulk. He looked accusingly at Lucius.

"It's supposed to be springy, First Spear Centurion," Lucius told him.

"You are many things Boxer but a good liar is not one of them," he growled in reply.

That night, the enemy cleared a twenty-five feet wide swathe of the eastern slope. The sentries on the breastwork listened to them toiling through dark and rain. One of them was unnerved by the sounds.

"What are they up to now?" he kept asking his mates.

He irritated the optio. "You know they're ripping out the tree-stumps don't you?"

"Yes, optio."

"Can you do fuck-all about it?"

"No, optio."

"Well then, keep your trap shut like a good lad, eh?"

When day came, they heard saws and watched the tops of trees slew sideways as they were felled..

Senior Tribune Tertius Fuscus, in uniform with his right arm strapped across his chest staggered out onto the Via Praetoria. He was pale and a little shaky but he was on his feet. Lucius walked over and greeted him.

"Glad to see you up but should you be walking about?"

"I thought I would show the men that I'm getting better. Do you think it might help morale?" he asked suddenly feeling ridiculous.

Before Lucius could reply, an optio marched over with two legionaries, one of them holding an axe. The optio came to attention and saluted.

"These men ask permission to address Senior Tribune Tertius Fuscus, sir.," he said in a clipped voice.

"By all means," Tertius responded.

The two legionaries looked at each other sheepishly.

"Come on then. This was your idea, spit it out," the optio told them shortly.

"Well, sir," one of them said, "the lads was impressed with you taking on that big German all on your own like…"

"So we got his axe and the blacksmith polished it up…" the other one gabbled.

"And the carpenter smoothed and oiled the handle. Thought you might like it, sir, the lads thought…"

"…Sort of a souvenir, like," his mate finished.

Tertius took the axe in his left hand and swung it gently, admiring the mirror finish on the blade and at the same time, appalled at the idea of its weight crashing into his skull.

"Thank you very much soldier and all the others who were involved. I'm very grateful and when we have finished off the rest of these Marcomanni pests, I shall show my appreciation with some decent wine."

That night in his billet, Tertius looked across at the axe blade reflecting the light of his oil lamp. He had a sudden moment of self-awareness. The Tertius Fuscus of two years ago held an unspoken and barely concealed contempt for the common soldiers; ignorant oafs and not to be trusted. But today he had been proud to have earned their approval. Did that mean he now had different ways of judging his fellowmen or had the rough army life coarsened his sensibilities? He pondered the question while his eyes grew heavy. He slept.

Chapter 11

The wind strengthened out of the east overnight blowing away the clouds. The day was dry and bright. Bowstring weather. The annoying soldier who wanted to know what the enemy was up to found out. A trimmed, fifteen-foot log rolled down on the breastwork out of cover at the top of the hill. It bounced and deflected a little, gained speed then fell into the ditch. It was followed by another and another. The men who were launching them stayed well back. The Romans could not see them, let alone take a shot. But the Marcomanni archers took advantage of their elevation and sent scores of black arrows at the sentries or beyond them over the walls. They caused few casualties but they made the men keep their heads down. The level of frustration increased as the day went on under an irregular but persistent scatter of arrows and the thuds of yet more logs dropping into position on top of the others.

"They're filling it in," Titus said. "Better stand by lads, I'll send you some reinforcements and beef up the numbers on your side of the wall.

At two in the afternoon, the Marcomanni advanced in numbers. There were no horsemen among them this time. They spread across the ground, well spaced and out of artillery range before beginning their run in. There was no sophistication to this attack. They carried ladders, knotted ropes and their weapons but no hurdles. So many bloated bodies and wreckage had been left in Boxer's Canal after previous actions, it no longer functioned as an obstacle. Provided men were prepared to stamp over the stinking corpses of their fallen comrades, it barely hindered them.

They formed up and walked forward with the faintest hint of a swagger. They knew that many of them would die in the course of the next few hours but they had a growing confidence in their ultimate victory. The camp was not what it had been. They had torn down one corner and destroyed two gates. The Romans had been forced to demolish their own access bridges. They had burst through the defences and killed soldiers inside on their own ground. It could only be a matter of time and will.

The leisurely walk became a steady lope as the artillery pieces twanged and sent stones and bolts out of the sky onto them. Men were hit; they screamed where they lay or died but the remainder did not falter. The ballistas and scorpions no longer inspired the terror they once had. The warriors had become fatalistic. Either an iron spike pinned you to the ground or it did not. The best thing to do was to have faith and keep running.

They crossed the Canal and sprinted under the falling javelins, slingshot and arrows to the base of the walls. Ladders were heaved up, ropes snaked out and they began to climb. The Romans resisted them with all their might. Men fell into the ditch dead or injured, some to be ripped open when they landed on a hardened wooden spike. Some made it over the wall and fought man to man with their enemies on the narrow walkways. Blades and axes sliced through flesh and bone and brains. On both sides, men were consumed by battle-fury, laying about them with no regard to their own lives, shearing off hands, arms and hacking into necks. The north wall was transformed into a frenzied abattoir where each was both the slaughter-man and his victim.

A horn sounded, and a thousand men ran out of the eastern forest under a protective rain of arrows. They swarmed over the logs which had now filled the ditch to form a ramp over halfway up the front of the breastwork. A bitter fight, as bloody and merciless as that raging on the north wall, saw Marcomanni reeling backwards over the logs taking the legs from their companions behind and Romans disappearing from their defensive positions to lie dead or wounded inside their camp. Another horn sounded, repeating its minor key, an unearthly wail. The attackers on both fronts withdrew as quickly as they had come.

The conflict had lasted two hours costing three hundred Roman casualties, dead or wounded and eight hundred Marcomanni. Helmund was less worried about the losses than Quadratus; he was beginning to receive reinforcements. News of his prolonged campaign against the legion had spread along the river. Small groups of warriors, smelling victory and spoils on the wind, were joining him. Not in great numbers and not enough to replace his losses but any warrior with the desire to fight was welcome. Helmund knew more would come.

The next day, Felix took his place on the eastern breastwork with a siege spear in his hands. Some of the legionaries took that as the worst possible omen; a cripple the only extra man the legion could find. Others said it was a good sign. With Felix under arms their luck was bound to change. It became as contentious as the interpretation of the return of Otto's horse had been, but it kept them animated.

Day followed day. Raid followed raid. The Marcomanni seemed content to chip way at the Roman defences believing that time was their ally. Some incursions were successful, some were not. Felix in action was a revelation. He parried and thrust with his siege spear all the time keeping up a commentary as if he was chiding a badly-behaved child, not repelling a deadly enemy; "None of that now! Behave! Oh come off it!" The men fighting beside him found his voice reassuring in the middle of the mayhem. It was Felix who came up with the good idea.

"I've had a good idea," he said. "Someone run over to the kitchen and bring back three jars of oil."

Because he was an evocati, he had status beyond his rank and his order was obeyed, after the centurion assented with a nod of the head. The jars were lined up behind the parapet until the next time the enemy rushed out of the forest.

"Right lads, drop 'em over. No need to chuck 'em far."

They landed on the enemy's crude ramp and cracked apart. Viscous olive oil flowed out and spread down, coating several logs. Proud warriors in their war-panoply leaped to death or glory in front of the Roman defensive wall only to find their feet shooting out from under them. They flailed their arms trying to keep their balance only to be grabbed by a comrade, also skating perilously on oil-coated soles. The Romans hooted with laughter and shouted witty comments as they speared the helpless men or pushed them over the edge to fall into the spiked ditch on either side.

The pro-Felix party saw their belief that he brought good luck vindicated. "Good Idea Felix" was adopted as the password at the changing of the guard.

One night, there was an alarming noise of splintering wood at the base of the other breastwork. By torchlight, the sentries could see a group of the enemy holding overlapping shields above their heads. They were protecting a hidden man who was chopping into their outer wall which was the side of the wagon. If he made a big enough hole, they could drag the roof tiles out and destabilize the entire structure. Arrows and javelins had no visible effect in deterring them under their improvised defensive roof. Tribune Soranus shouted for the wagon-wheels to be brought up. The legionaries manhandled the first into position and tilted it over the parapet so that it dropped vertically onto the warriors below. The iron rim of the heavy wheel smashed through their shields and they scattered leaving the axeman dead. It had struck him on the back of his neck, breaking it.

"Good Idea Soranus" became the new password.

The ninth day came but it brought no cavalry, nor did the tenth. The legion did not lose its discipline nor did it give way to despair. The realisation that they had arrived at the end of their hopes created a calm resignation. They had three thousand four hundred fully fit men and an additional one hundred and thirty walking wounded. If the Marcomanni attacked on all fronts simultaneously, they no longer had sufficient numbers to defend their walls. The Second Lucan would not let their camp fall. They must shortly march out, burning it behind them and advance towards the enemy and their certain destruction. The sun set and a pitch-black night without sight of moon or stars followed, adding to the sense of impending doom.

Five miles away, three of Aldermar's "ghosts" slipped off their light horses' backs in a thicket. One stripped naked and stood with his arms outstretched.. His companions smeared the thick mixture of soot and mud they had carried with them all over his body while he rotated slowly in front of them. As his skin was coated he seemed to melt from sight until only his teeth and the whites of his eyes showed in the darkness. He tied a small leather bag around his waist, pulled on some doeskin shoes and walked away, instantly lost in the undergrowth. The other two sat on the ground holding the horses' reins waiting patiently for his return.

Two hours later, a naked wraith peered out of the edge of the forest at the camp below. The first part of his approach was relatively easy because the bracken hid him. It had been scythed lower down but there were still the sheltering tree-stumps; he slithered between them stopping for several seconds after every move to listen. He heard nothing; no breathing, no click of a weapon against armour or shield, no sound of furtive pursuit. He climbed gingerly down into the ditch, squatted and felt carefully around him for caltrops. He did not find any and crawled towards the side of the Marcomanni log-ramp fifty paces away. He swept the ground in front of him with alternate hands as he progressed for traps and spikes. After forty paces, he touched the first body. He crept on over the dead piled three and four high. His probing fingers found the end of a log and clambered up, nearly falling once when his hand could not grip the oily wood. Eventually, he balanced at one side of the breastwork with his head only two feet below the top if the parapet. He untied the string around his waist.

"Otto. Friend. Not Kill." He hissed. There was no response. "Otto. Friend. Not Kill." He repeated.

"Did you hear that?" one of the sentries asked his mate.

"No, what was it?"

"Someone outside whispering."

"Don't be daft...."

A small leather bag on the end of a string flipped over the parapet to land at their feet.

"What the fuck...Torches!"

They threw them down. The "ghost" lay motionless on top of a dead man and neither winced nor made a sound when flying sparks burned the back of his thighs. The flames spluttered out and he was gone, back to his friends, unseen and unheard; unless he chose to be.

Everyone packed into the office was silently intent as the legate held up a thong from which a marble finger dangled by its gold mount.

"We have received a message, gentlemen, thrown over the wall half an hour ago. I shall read it to you."

"To the Noble Legate Publius Quadratus, Greetings. I am come with twelve hundred cavalry. Leave your camp and advance on the enemy one hour after sunrise. So that you may have confidence in these words, Otto Longius sends this token and asks, do you remember how good the figs were, sir? And does Boxer remember when he wrestled Ursus?"

Prefect Aldermar."

"Do we believe it?" asked.

A roar of "Yes!" resounded off the walls.

"Well, I certainly remember the Emperor's figs, what's this about wrestling, Tribune Longius?"

"Otto took on our Molossian guard dog barehanded for the fun of it. Frightened the ladies of my family witless."

"To which I say that is just the sort of thing he would do and I expect it was a terrifying spectacle so no shame on your mother etc.

Now, I understand we all want this message to be genuine but there is always the possibility it is an enemy ruse. Senior Tribune Fuscus, your opinion please."

Tertius Fuscus had recovered from the knock on the head but still had his right arm strapped across his chest while his shoulder joint healed.

"I believe it is, sir but even if it is not, that makes no difference. Our numbers are so depleted that we shall have to march out and face the Marcomanni in open battle within the next three days in any case. May I suggest that sufficient men remain behind on watch ready to set fire to the camp if things do not go as we would wish?"

Quadratus nodded his agreement. "First Spear Centurion Attius?"

Titus Attius jumped to his feet.

"I'm with the tribune except there's no need to leave anyone in camp because we are going to stuff 'em. What are we going to do boys?"

"Stuff 'em!" the officers yelled at the top of their voices. To the legate's surprise, the refined Tertius joined in.

"In the face of such enthusiasm, I am bound to concur. Prefect Corvo, we recently mounted scorpions on mule carts to bring them in range. Can this be done again?"

"Yes sir, how many?"

"As many as you can manage. I will give you our remaining cavalry to form a protective screen but I have no doubt that they will be unable to resist joining their comrades once the action begins. Very well gentlemen, let us make our preparations."

There was no further sleep for anyone; in three hours time the legion would be facing the full Marcomanni force. They would be heavily outnumbered and with many comrades missing from the ranks but the general mood was cheerful. They had taken blow after blow and now they were going to do what they did best; join battle in open country.

"You cannot hold a sword, Tertius. It would be advisable for you to remain in camp. It is possible that a well-mounted man could escape to the south if all is lost…" Quadratus suggested.

Tertius Fuscus shook his head.

"I will ride out with the men, if you will allow it sir. I cannot fight, that is true but my presence may be of some use, although I cannot think what that might be."

The legate's orders to Felix were precise.

"Evocati Felix, we both know you cannot take your place in the line of battle. I am giving you a crucial role here in camp. You and fifty men will be left to destroy our artillery and fire the buildings and stores. You will stand over the Porta Praetoria during the action. If it is possible, I shall send you a runner with orders to destroy the camp. If I cannot, you must use your own judgement. You will all be free to attempt an escape once the fires have been lit."

The pale blue above him was striated with high white cloud; a mackerel sky indicating a change in the weather, as Legate Publius Quadratus in full armour stood on the rostrum to address his troops.

"Men of The Second Lucan, I can make speeches telling you we fight for the Emperor, for Rome; you have heard many such speeches and they are true. Today, I will only repeat the words of our First Spear Centurion Titus Attius. "We are going to stuff them!" Are you with me?"

"Yes!" roared out from thousands of throats.

"Then I can ask no more. Second Lucan advance!"

The Porta Praetoria swung open and the rhythmic stamping of booted feet echoed off the walls as they marched out. Once across Boxer's stinking, three-quarters full Canal, they began to manoeuvre on a wide front. The First Cohort took a central position. The right flank was bolstered by Corvo's units, including ten scorpions on mule-carts and the remaining cavalry. Within minutes, a solid line of legionaries four ranks deep spread from the base of the eastern hill across the farmlands to the west. Behind them five hundred men stood in reserve surrounding the legate and Titus Fuscus. The flags and eagles of the legion waved and gleamed above their heads. Titus Attius led the centre, Lucius the right flank and Soranus the left. They rolled forward without breaking step and halted two hundred yards from the

Marcomanni lines. The sound of their swords beating on their shields in challenge rolled like thunder and then there was silence.

The sun shone feebly, birds sang and a hare raced for shelter across the Roman front.

Helmund and Hulderic embraced. This was the day they had been waiting for. Helmund was elated. He had won. His tactics had weakened them so much they had been forced to come out. That was an act of desperation on their part. Yes, there was still a battle to fight and it would be bitter but his numbers assured him of the victory. He surveyed the Roman formation. He would roll up their left flank on the western side and force them all back against the steep hill where they could not manoeuvre. He had no fear that they would rush him; the remaining wagons would divide the Roman shield wall if they tried and he knew how much they dreaded that. It was time to arm, briskly but without rushing. This was a morning to savour.

"Lords and chieftains, today go into battle on your horses, like the noble warriors you are!" he yelled.

Fifty auxiliary cavalry led by Aldermar trotted down the forest trail to where Otto had first encountered Audo of the Bright Axe. His men were all German, flowing red or blond braids and beards, arms thick with silver rings. A score or so of yards before they would be out of the treeline, they were spotted by a dozen warriors. They saw no cause for alarm in the approaching horsemen who looked as if they could be remote kinsmen. As their leader put up his hand to stop them, two of the riders darted past him and spun their mounts to face back up the track. They were there to prevent any of the guards Aldermar and their comrades had now commenced to slaughter from escaping to warn Helmund's army below.

A horn was blown and a further three hundred and fifty auxiliaries joined the advance party. They trotted on in a compact body and emerged from the trees. Again the horns blew, urgently this time. The riders settled deeper into their saddles, took a firmer grip on their lances and launched themselves down the short incline onto the Marcomanni lines. They took the planned route between the wagons and the river. Ten abreast, they tore through the encampment riding down anything and everything in their path; fire circles, tents, shelters, half-armed men, women, children were pulped under hooves or pierced by lances. A great communal shriek of agony rose into the air. Helmund and his army forming up in the face of the Romans looked back in bewilderment. By the time the first division of cavalry had ridden to the end of their lines the Roman squadrons, twice as large in number, smashed the far edge of Helmund's left flank and then cantered arrogantly across his front, joining the auxiliaries who were now gathered in a body on the west of the battlefield.

The Roman infantry remained ominously still and silent. A whistle shrilled in the centre of their lines immediately followed by others to left and right. They took their first step forward and as they did so, the thunder roll of swords on shields filled the ears of

Helmund's army with dread. The combined cavalry spurred close to the Marcomanni formation and threw their lances before wheeling away. The result was carnage. Confused by the drumming of the advancing infantry, terrified by the sudden arrival of killers on horseback, they bunched up, edging away from the threat of the cavalry. They began to get in each other's way. Cohesion was being lost.

On the far side, the scorpions began to cut down the massed men, sometimes two at a time with a lucky shot. This had a similar effect, pushing the Marcomanni into their own centre. The pressure from both flanks, bulged their line outwards into the Roman advance. They were now less than one hundred yards apart. Arrows and slingshot rained down on them dropping men at random. Still the Roman line came on. Twenty-five paces away, the Romans halted and the centre threw their javelins, one, two, three volleys. Three thousand wicked, weighted blades plunging into the enemy. It was as if they had waited for Helmund's army to ripen like corn and were bringing in the sheaves. The whole front speeded up and smashed into the directionless mob the enemy force had become. It reeled back but reformed. The Roman advance was checked and they fought shield to shield. The cavalry hammered into Helmund's flank again, their long swords rising and falling while their chargers ripped men's faces with their teeth or broke their bones with heavy hooves.

Helmund looked around and saw defeat on the faces of everyone around him. Half his force had been pushed onto their own wagons and now fought with them at their backs. Out of his sight, women, children and some of his men were jumping into boats and paddling frantically across the river, the current dragging them downstream as they tried to get away. The bridge was a struggling chaos of people seeking refuge across the Rhine.

A body of warriors tried to burst through the Roman right flank and either attack the artillery or make their way up into the forest and safety. Their presence stopped the advance of Lucius' troops and the Roman line skewed as the centre and left continued to carve its way deeper into the enemy. From his vantage point on horseback, Tertius saw the danger and shouted the information to Quadratus.

"Take three hundred of the reserve and bolster Boxer's troops. We must keep going forward," the legate commanded.

Tertius trotted forward and filtered the extra troops past Lucius and into the line before returning to his original position.

"There you are, Tertius, you were of some use after all," Quadratus said with a grim smile.

Aldermar ordered Otto and his men to repeat the charge between the wagons and the river again in the opposite direction. Otto's heart was hammering, Djinn was dancing on the spot, eager to be let loose.

"On me! On me!" he shouted and felt the thrill of so many horsemen riding at his command. They galloped through the panicked crowd, hacking and stabbing. There was more resistance this time. Many of the warriors leaving the battle were still fully armed and holding weapons. They fought back but could do little against half a ton of horse and its merciless rider. The cavalry reached the end of the line. They were now behind the main Marcomanni force on their eastern side. Otto had no further orders. Hoping that the Roman artillery would notice them, and re-direct their fire, he shouted for his men to attack the enemy in front of them. They raced in and threw their last lances. As they were wheeling away, Otto saw Helmund. He had been riding his bay stallion all over his front yelling encouragement to his failing men. Helmund recognised Otto.

It was as if they met in the tranquil eye of a hurricane. The sounds and sights of battle no longer existed for them. Both saw in front of him one man who personified all the hatred, anguish and pain of the last days and weeks. They charged recklessly at each other, scattering anyone in their way, oblivious to the danger they might represent. An open space opened up around them as men scrambled out of the way. The Roman infantry frontline was now so close, the legionaries could see everything. Fighting ceased in the immediate area and everyone held their collective breath, awaiting the collision of Otto and Helmund as if it had been pre-ordained.

They passed each other so closely that their knees clashed painfully but neither regarded that. Helmund's sword took a big slice out of Otto's shield as he slashed downwards. Otto's blow to his opponent's head missed. They wheeled their horses and ran at each other again. Helmund split Otto's shield completely. Most of it fell to the ground leaving him only a half moon of painted wood with which to defend himself. Again, Otto's head strike found only empty air. They turned and charged for the third time. Helmund's head was bent to the right and his shield held high to avoid the anticipated third blow but Otto altered his attack. He leaned forward in the saddle and quickly extended his arm, his long cavalry sword pointed at Helmund's chest. The Marcomanni king saw too late he had been outfoxed. He could not avoid the inevitable. With the weight of horse and man and the impact speed of the two opponents racing towards each other, nothing could stop the blade bursting through his armour and ribs, splitting his heart in two. Helmund stayed in the saddle for a few more paces and fell forward, slumping to the ground. The Marcomanni who had witnessed the duel groaned. The Romans cheered. The spell was broken.

The warriors who had been standing by as witnesses a moment before rushed on Otto. Djinn lashed out with hooves and teeth Otto slashed to his right and left, drops of blood flying off his sword but the legionaries burst through and drove his attackers off. His own men came up and pushed further into the centre. The legionaries moved on and Otto was now in a quiet space behind the fighting, littered with the dead and dying. He detailed two of his men to stand guard over the body of the king and made his way back to the rest of the cavalry.

Aldermar had been blocking the bridgehead but withdrew when the left flank under Soranus wrapped around the remaining Marcomanni who were now in turn besieged; the legion advancing in a curved line in front and the Rhine at their backs. The last boats had gone and the inaccessible bridge was empty of refugees. They fought on singly or in small groups but the Roman mincing machine swallowed them up and spat them out as dead meat. The last die-hards fought up to their knees in the river. And then then were none.

"Seen Helmund?" Aldermar asked.

"He's dead," Otto told him.

"Yes, sir. Killed in single combat by our prefect," one of Otto's men told him.

Aldermar's eyebrows shot up in surprise but he noted the Roman cavalryman had said "our prefect" referring to Otto. "Everyone loves a winner," he thought.

"Well then, to the victor the spoils," he said. "Show me."

They sat on their horses looking down on the livid faced body of the king. One of Otto's men held the bay stallion he had ridden into battle by the reins. The legionaries had been ordered back into their cohort formations and awaited further commands. Under the eagles, the headquarters party rode down, joined by Lucius and Soranus.

"How did he die?" Quadratus asked. They repeated the story to him. "You have killed a king, Prefect Otto Longius, what once was his is now yours, take it" he said, loud enough to be heard several yards away. Everyone in earshot grinned. Otto dismounted.

Helmund had thirty silver arm rings in total and round his neck had worn a thick gold torque crafted to look like a rope with a snarling wolf's head on each end. Otto took it and put it on. He removed the arm rings and the dead man's sword belt, scabbard and sword. He walked over and ritually placed his hand on the bay stallion's flank to symbolise his ownership. The onlookers saluted him, "Hail Prefect Otto Longius!" He bowed to Quadratus and Aldermar in acknowledgement.

The legate issued a stream of orders. There would be no individual plundering of the enemy bodies. All items of value were to be collected into two heaps for general distribution to the legion and cavalry. Provosts were set to guard the wagons which were found to hold a quantity of grain, oil, smoked meat and ale. The body of Hulderic who had died an undistinguished death when a sling bullet hit him in one eye, was retrieved. He and his king were crucified at the far end of the bridge facing German territory. Several oxen had survived. They were hitched to the wagons and driven into the Roman camp. Their contents were loaded into the legion's stores and they were sent back to gather up the loot. The pathetic, naked bodies of their so recently fearsome enemies were pitched into the Rhine. They floated away, bobbing in the current.

It was noon. Felix, in gleaming armour and wearing his gold chain, had formed his invalids into a guard of honour through which Quadratus rode at the head of the legion.

"Wish you joy of your victory, sir," he called as the legate passed by.

"The victory belongs to us all, Evocati Felix, my thanks to you."

The cavalry were to bed down at the edge of the battlefield. Aldermar took over the signal station for himself and his officers.

"Prefect Otto, you are now once more of The Second Lucan, I suggest you return to your camp."

"Very well, but first I have a request to make. Can you find me the "ghost" who threw the message over the wall?"

After a short wait the man was brought forward. He was tall but very lean and his hair still bore traces of sooty mud. Otto shook his hand and slid one of the king's arm-rings on each of his arms. The honour that had been done to him was immense.

"I need scouts Aldermar, can you give me some?"

"I shall ask. If any want to serve with you, they'll be at the camp tomorrow."

"Thank you," Otto said and walked away coming back a few minutes later leading Helmund's stallion. He put the reins in Aldermar's hands, "My thank-offering to you. If you had not come, all our comrades would be dead."

"As they would have been if you had not made it through to headquarters but I accept your princely gift with gratitude."

The evening was drawing on, half of the oxen had been sent down to the cavalry lines, the other half had been roasted.

"Gentlemen, we bow our heads in remembrance of fallen comrades and drink to their shades," called Quadratus from the head of the table. After a pause he spoke again. "And now we feast our victory, or should I call it escape?"

"Victory! Victory!" the officers on all sides shouted.

Hunks of beef, fresh bread and wine covered the three tables pushed end to end around which they sat. After an hour of gorging and drinking, Otto slipped away. He returned with Helmund's sword in its decorated scabbard and tooled leather belt together with a number of arm rings. He banged on the table with his wine cup.

"With your permission, sir?" he called to Quadratus.

"Proceed, prefect, proceed,"

Otto gave a ring to Lucius and Soranus, much to his surprise, and to each of his decurions. He walked up to Tertius Fuscus.

"Senior Tribune Tertius Fuscus, would you do me the honour of accepting one of these rings as a token of our shared success?"

"The honour is mine," Tertius replied, slipped it on his arm and admired it in the lamplight.

Finally Otto approached Quadratus.

"Noble Legate Publius Quadratus, you have steered us safely through a great peril. I wish to offer you the sword of King Helmund in recognition of your leadership."

"Hear! Hear!" resounded around the room and the officers stood as one to lift their wine cups in salute to their legate.

Chapter 12

The atmosphere was a little subdued the following day. The release of the pent-up resentment the men had felt against their enemies and the aftermath of the adrenalin rush in combat left them feeling flat. Another fifty Romans had lost their lives in the final battle, among them a burly, one-eared legionary. Thirty were wounded, several of whom would either die or never be able to serve again even if they managed to hang on to life. Five horses had been killed or had to be destroyed. The German auxiliaries skinned and jointed them to add to their rations. Otto's auxiliaries who had been in the camp throughout the siege returned to the relieving force which would be leaving the next day.

Otto sat in what had been Aldermar's cubby-hole office in the stables and looked up at the sky. He had been shocked at the state of the camp when he rode in; makeshift defences and half of the roofs gone, debris everywhere. It was difficult to picture it as it had been when he had first arrived and marvelled at anything so huge, so populous. He shook his head and laughed at how little he had known then. But he had no time to spare for musings. He had one hundred and twenty men and one hundred and forty horses to settle-in and no roof.

Crucial repairs were already under way. Men were in the forest cutting trees for lumber in addition to the fifty useful logs the

Marcomanni had conveniently rolled in the ditch where the Porta Principalis Dextra had once stood. They had been dragged free, with some difficulty since half of them were slippery with olive oil. The carpenters were now sawing the best of them into planks. The air was full of the scent of pine and sawdust but underlying it was a cloying stink of burning bodies being carried on the breeze off the funeral pyres. Legionaries with scarves tied across their noses were clearing Boxer's Canal. The broken hurdles both sides had used to cross it were slung onto the fires where the rotting corpses were being consumed until only clean ash remained.

The bellowing of Titus Attius occasionally burst on Otto's eardrums as some unfortunate legionary met with his disapproval. Lucius was busy with the repair fatigue parties, Soranus was closeted with the quartermaster running through manifests and Tertius resting; his shoulder joint was still painful. Of Quadratus nothing was to be seen. He had shut himself in his office with his clerks to write up his report and despatches. His guards had been told to admit no-one to the Praetorium until further notice; no matter who, no matter what their business.

"Does that include First Spear Centurion Attius, sir?" his guard commander asked.

"Of course it does, I said no-one is to disturb me," the legate replied shortly.

His men smirked at the thought of their commander telling Titus Attius to go away and come back later, "Rather him than me," they all thought.

The first raindrops fell on Otto where he sat. He sighed and went over to Lucius.

"Greetings Boxer, can we have a roof please?"

Lucius looked at him blankly for a moment, then understood.

"Of course you can."

"When?"

"Ah now, that's a different question. Most of the roof tiles are ballasting the breastwork where the Porta Principalis Sinistra used to be. If the carpenters can make a new gate on this side today and we can remove the breastwork and hang it, and if we can…."

"So, sometime soon is the best you can say?"

"Exactly."

Otto turned on his heel and marched away. If there was no prospect of being under cover today, he must arrange for the saddlery, harness and fodder to be protected from the weather. The men and horses would have to suffer in silence. He was making the arrangements when a legionary doubled up to him and saluted.

"Some Germans at the Porta Praetoria, sir; asking for you, we think. Keep saying "Otto", sir."

Six men on light horses, each leading a spare mount, waited patiently for him oblivious to the cold rain.

"We have decided to scout for you,. You are the one who killed King Helmund?" their leader said in his Suevian dialect.

Otto thought he had better start as he meant to go on.

"You will not be scouting for me but for Rome, if you are accepted," Otto replied in the same language. "Dismount and let us talk things over."

They sat on some new-cut logs. Each man recited his ancestry and a history of his experience in war. Otto listened gravely and without comment.

"The cavalry I command are all Romans. None of them speak our language. You will be able to talk with me alone. If this is not acceptable to you, you may leave now with no ill-feeling. If you stay, you must take an oath to serve Rome," he explained.

Without saying another word, two of them stood up, mounted their horses and rode away. The remaining four looked at Otto impassively.

"Wait here," he said and went to find an aquilifer.

Their oath was administered under the eagle. When they had finished, Otto greeted them again as comrades and brothers and led them to the stable block. He called his decurions over.

"We now have four good scouts recommended by Prefect Aldermar. They speak no Latin at present but are properly sworn in. Now understand this. I shall not tolerate any disrespect, so called "jokes" or any behaviour which might offend them. They are vital to the success of our operations in this area so repeat my words to the men. I'll fall on anyone who disobeys like the wrath of the gods."

The rain faded away during the late afternoon. Otto was summoned to the legate's office. Lucius was already there.

"Prefect Longius, I am going to ride down to Aldermar's encampment to bid him farewell and give him my despatches for the general. You will escort me with a party of ten. He will be leaving at dawn tomorrow. Boxer will be travelling with him…." Otto's face fell. The legate could not avoid noting the look of distress on his face. "… You have perhaps forgotten that Tribune Longius is summoned to the Engineer General's staff at headquarters. We must be happy that he has the opportunity for advancement."

Otto made his expression blank. "Of course sir, you are correct; it had slipped my mind."

"In addition, I shall need a middling sized cart with six mules so that the cavalry can carry off their share of the spoils. Please be ready to depart in one hour," the legate said dismissing both of them.

Lucius and Otto sat with the table on which they had shared so many of Felix's dinners between them. They had come to a fork in their road and must part without knowing when, or if, they would meet again. They both had much to say to each other. Lucius owed his life to Otto and that life had been transformed as a result of a hand clasp from a skinny Suevian lad not so many years ago. It had set a chain of events into motion leading him to Rome, an interview with the

Emperor and his promotion prospects. Equally, everything Otto had become could never have been achieved if Lucius had spurned his offered hands in that burning village far across the Rhine.

The wise woman had told Otto his fate would be determined by a man bearing black plumes and so it had. She had not said that Lucius' future was guided by the same meeting but in truth it had been.

They were both bursting to say what they felt; a sense almost like mourning the death of a loved one but neither could. They did not dare to show their feelings in case they wept, which would have been shameful. Instead they grinned awkwardly and made jokes, recalling some of their happier times. They laughed but their eyes remained haunted.

"Time to mount up, sir!" a voice called from outside.

They stood up, clasped arms looking intently into each other's eyes as if trying to fix the face in front of them in their memories for ever and walked out into a chilly late afternoon.

The honour-guard followed by a cavalryman driving a mule-cart and towing his horse behind for the return journey, made its way down to the river. Otto was resplendent in his parade armour; the legate and Lucius had also dressed formally for the occasion. Aldermar took the leather satchel of despatches and was grateful for the cart to carry the heap of silver, weapons and ornaments that were his share of the victor's bounty.

"May I speak with Prefect Longius, sir?" he asked Quadratus who assented. Aldermar put one arm over his shoulder and led him to one side. "Listen my young friend, you have risen very high in a short time on your own merits. Don't think I believe your success is undeserved because that isn't so. You are an example of what we people the Romans call "Germans" can accomplish. Remember that you represent us. Be true to yourself always and may the Gods be with you. Now, I've got something for you." He grinned and beckoned to one of his men who ran up carrying a steel cuirass and back plate. The cuirass was modelled to represent an idealized muscular chest and belly. The centre had been beaten out into the shape of the Goddess Minerva's head. "Took it off a dead Marcomanni chief. He must have nicked it from a Roman officer years ago but I know the Master of Horse likes to see his officers properly dressed so take it with my best wishes."

Felix was in raptures. The cuirass was a fine piece of metal-working but it was dull and scratched in places. "Needs a right good polish does that," he said and sighed with satisfaction at the thought of the hours of restoration work ahead. He had been assigned to act as Lucius' soldier servant but his actions during the siege had made him a talisman for The Second Lucan. The legion wanted him to remain so Lucius had raised no objection.

Otto dined that evening with Quadratus, Fuscus and Attius. It was his induction into his new role as one of the four senior officers of the legion. He found it uncomfortable at first. They talked generally of the condition to which The Second Lucan had been reduced.

"There can be no question of leave, for anyone," the legate said.

No-one disagreed, not only because he was their commanding officer but it was obvious that their reduced numbers made it impossible. Tertius winced as he leaned over the table to pick up his wine cup.

"Shoulder still troubling you?" Titus asked.

Otto who had been silent up to then spoke.

"Did you know Martellus Flaccus, sir?" he asked the senior tribune.

"When we are alone it's first name-terms, Otto, unless we are addressing our legate," Titus pointed out.

"Yes Otto, you are now a senior officer and you must conduct yourself like one." Quadratus said, not unkindly.

"Become a "gentleman" sir? You often begin meetings by saying "Gentlemen". I shall have to take lessons."

"I suppose I do often say that, now you mention it. You have natural good manners, although you do tend to speak out of turn at times; not always a bad thing. Cultivate yourself, Otto. Who is the most accomplished Roman officer you have come across?"

"Say "the Noble Legate Publius Quadratus" if you've got any sense," Titus growled.

They all laughed.

"That goes without saying, Titus," Otto replied, growing a little pink in the face at calling the First Spear Centurion by his given name for the first time.

"See?" said Titus. "He's a born flatterer; half the battle!"

"Uncle Martellus!" Quadratus said, taking the conversation back round to its beginning. "He was a character; a decanus and master farrier, Tertius. He went off with Aldermar. Why do you mention his name Otto?"

"When I arrived at headquarters, I was in a poor state; could hardly straighten my knees and back. Anyway, Martellus gave me a flask of liniment for the joints. It did wonders for me and I've got half of it left. I wondered if it might help your shoulder, Tertius," again he reddened.

"Thank you for thinking of me. I shall try it if I may."

"I'll bring it over in the morning…"

"No you won't Otto. You will send Felix over with it," Tertius told him.

"I see I have much to learn, although I am better than I was," Otto said and told them the story of how he had eaten the entire bowl of sausages the first time he sat down to dinner in Boxer's home. He recounted his tale well, impersonating the various family members and spinning it out, rather like the bards he had heard as a boy. It was the highlight of the evening.

When dinner was over, he left with Titus Attius who gave him the benefit of his experience.

"When the legate advises you to get some airs and graces he's doing you a big favour. Remember all your decurions are Romans born and bred. Right now, they think you're marvellous because they saw you kill that wicked old king on the battlefield. But if you show yourself up at dinner, they'll decide you're nothing but another fucking German who just happened to be tougher than Helmund was. They're all young men of good family; spend some time with them and pick up some of their ways. Don't get too friendly, mind; you might have to order one of them to do something that'll get him killed tomorrow or the day after."

"What about you, Titus, where do you fit in with all of this?" Otto asked.

"I'm a commoner and that's what I'll die; either in the army or in the inn I'm going to buy when they chuck me out. None of it matters to me but then, the Emperor's never heard of me. Think on that, goodnight."

In the morning, the Romans saw that the bodies of Helmund and Hulderic had been taken down off their crosses in the darkness and removed by unseen hands.

Repairs went on at the same rate even though Boxer had left. Otto reflected that it demonstrated the nature of an army. One man made no difference, duty and discipline were all. Within a week, the camp had two new gates, the bridges and parapets had been replaced and Boxer's Canal cleared. If it had not been for the missing corner and the peculiar diagonal wall replacing it, the camp looked exactly as it had before the siege. The stables and barracks had watertight roofs and all was returning to normal. The signal fort was refurbished; it had suffered almost no damage during the conflict. Because there fewer mouths to feed, the quartermaster's stores did not need to be restocked for winter; the grain they had taken in the enemy wagons helped considerably.

The reduction in numbers meant that a greater burden was put on the cavalry; if the walls were to be manned, there were less infantry available to operate outside the camp. Otto's men patrolled more often and further afield but never below thirty men and one scout in strength, led by their decurion. Otto went on one in three of these missions which were an important show of force. The local tribes knew the Romans had been badly mauled by Helmund. Quadratus wanted to let them know the legion was still a potent and self-confident force. There was no major demonstration of opposition; it seemed that they understood.

Otto took Titus's advice and ate dinner regularly with his officers. At first they had been awkward affairs. The decurions were wary of their prefect; not only because he was their superior officer but he was thirty pounds heavier and half a head taller than the biggest of them. He seemed to loom over the table and dominate the small room in which they ate, perched on chairs and stools; there was no room for couches. They did not like to speak first and Otto had never practiced the art of polite conversation. There was also the issue of the food. Felix had not lied when he had told Otto and Boxer he could make a good stew and bake soldiers' bread but he had not told them that was the extent of his culinary range. After the third dinner, Otto began to pay one of the cooks to cater for them. It was not fine dining but there was some variation in the dishes on offer. The talk improved with the menu. At first it was centred on the business of the day then expanded to include horses, horsemanship and the races in Rome. Otto mentioned that he had never been to one. That set them off, each one describing great events he had seen, multi-chariot collisions and why the team he favoured was undoubtedly the best and anyone who thought differently knew nothing. Once the ice was broken, conversation flowed freely during subsequent shared meals. Otto contributed freely but listened to them carefully, picking up on their ways of expressing themselves, their nuances of speech and manner, together with their prejudices, spoken and unspoken; all those social interactions which typified Romans of their class.

Although he was only a temporary acting prefect responsible for artillery, Corvo became infected with the strange fascination of the deadly machines. He was often to be seen hard at work dismantling one of them, greasing trigger releases, adjusting tensions and all the other constant tasks required to keep them in optimal condition. He borrowed a scroll on geometry from Tertius and studied it nightly until he had the required mathematics off by heart. His dedication did not go unnoticed by the legate.

"Admirable as his efforts are, I cannot help feel that Corvo is developing an unhealthy obsession with his scorpions and ballistas. In fact he is becoming quite a bore; they are all he talks about," Quadratus remarked to Titus Attius.

"Cannot disagree, sir; very odd lot artillerymen…"

Winter was biting harder every day when Otto was called into the legate's office. This was an official meeting with a clerk present so military courtesies were observed. Otto stood at attention and bowed to Quadratus who acknowledged him with a salute but did not offer a seat.

"Prefect Otto Longius, you are summoned to our general's headquarters., I shudder to imagine what disreputable state you were in the last time you were there. Take an escort and a cart with your best uniform in it. We do not want to make an impression that reflects discredit on The Second Lucan, now do we? Dismissed."

Last year, Otto would have asked when he was to leave and why the general wanted to see him. Now he knew better; the time to go was right now and the reasons were none of his business until he got there.

He left the next morning accompanied by ten troopers, his most junior decurion, one scout and Felix driving a cart with a waterproof cover pulled by four mules. The scout had sniffed at the cart and said he could take a day and a half off the journey if they left it behind but Otto refused. The rain blew into their faces but was less troublesome once they had gained the cover of the trees. Though most of the oaks and birches were now bare of leaves, there were plenty of pines to break the force of the wind. Otto tried to find the tree he had hidden behind to ambush Audo of the Bright Axe and his comrade but was not sure of its exact location. He told the story that night when they were bivouacked. That brought up other tales of subterfuge and sudden deadly encounters.

Considering that they were cold and wet most of the time, his men were cheerful enough. They complained in the ritually humorous way soldiers do, each one finding a story of misery and discomfort to top anything that had gone before until they became so exaggerated, they were ridiculous.

"So what happened next?" one naive youngster asked.

"We all died of course!" the storyteller told him, to gales of laughter.

Their progress was uneventful apart from the streams they were forced to cross. A few weeks ago, they had been knee-deep at most when Otto and Djinn had made their journey along this route. Now they were brown, foaming torrents, only forded with extreme care. They nearly lost the mule-cart more than once. When headquarters was an hour away, Otto stopped the column while he changed into his cuirass. Felix was outraged. He had polished it to perfection, a saddler had replaced the leather straps, the buckles had been recast in bronze and now Otto was going to put it on outside, in the rain.

"It'll get water spots on it," he complained.

"Yes," Otto replied.

"If you know, why don't you wait until we're under cover, sir?"

"Don't want to," Otto told him, unwilling to be bullied into explaining about the Master of Horse and his standards for cavalry officers' uniforms.

As it turned out, he had done well to put it on. They were led straight to the most senior cavalry officer in the army. The first thing he said was, "Greetings Prefect Longius, properly dressed this time I see…"

Otto's instructions were simple. He was to attend the general at noon the next day for a formal meeting. Further orders would be given at the end of it. If the Master of Horse knew more, he was not saying anything. Otto saw his horses and mules fed and stabled and only afterwards found billets for himself and his men. He had hoped to see Lucius but he was up-country with the engineers involved in some bridge project on the River Elbe. Aldermar was on patrol and not due back until the morning. Disappointed, he sat alone in his room wondering why he had been summoned.

The reason he was called to headquarters lay with Legate Publius Quadratus' official report. He had given Lucius a glowing recommendation to the Engineer General in view of the way the tribune had reacted to problems thrown up during the siege but he had done nothing other than make a flat statement of Otto's actions and added a list of witnesses. Opinion among the general's aides was divided.

"He has received his reward, sir. You promoted him to a rank beyond his age and experience," said one.

"And he demonstrated how fitted he is to fulfil that role in his very first battle. If he had been a Roman citizen when he saved his legate's life he would have been awarded a Civic Crown..." the general said.

The aides began to argue among themselves.

"But he was not. I must say how unlike our Emperor it was to confirm citizenship on him..."

"The Divine Julius did so frequently..."

"Yes, but Emperor Augustus has always said he does not want the value of Roman Citizenship to be diminished ...

"Our Emperor saw something remarkable in Otto Longius, and events have proved his judgement to be correct," the general told them. "The facts are that Prefect Longius led Roman cavalry into a battle in which witnesses confirm he killed the enemy leader in single combat. By tradition, this merits at the very least a gold crown if not much more."

"Why did you give him Roman cavalry in the first place?" one of them asked the Master of Horse.

"Because it was a mistake to strip Quadratus of his cavalry and he needed replacements. German Auxiliaries are more use to me in the situation in which we find ourselves than Roman cavalry so he was given command of an ala I could spare," he replied with some irritation.

"Roman troops are the best in the world...."

"Infantry yes, cavalry no; that's why we need the German Auxiliaries." The Master of Horse replied with finality.

General Drusus had listened to enough bickering.

"It occurs to me that, without anyone saying so directly, we are discussing how "Roman" Prefect Otto Longius truly is. Some of you seem to doubt his commitment to Rome and the Emperor but what more could the young man do to prove himself? I am not prepared to continue this discussion. I shall write to the Emperor with my recommendation and request his confirmation. Thank you for your comments on the matter," he told them.

Augustus had received his stepson's letter with a copy of Quadratus' report attached and had responded so Otto was ordered to headquarters.

Felix had brushed, cleaned and polished Otto to dazzling perfection. He stood back and admired his handiwork. "Very nice, sir, if I may say so," he commented then added in a worried tone, "you will try not to get anything dirty walking across camp, won't you sir?"

"Thank you, Evocati Felix," Otto replied with a smile. "I shall be careful not to spoil all your hard work. You have done me proud. "

Standing in front of the general and his senior officers, he certainly looked the part; from his gleaming boots to the carefully brushed crest on the burnished helmet in the crook of his left arm. He came to attention and bowed.

"Greetings Prefect Otto Longius," General Drusus said looking keenly at the young officer. He saw that something had changed; a certain naivety had gone from those pale eyes and had been replaced with a new assurance. "You are called to this assembly of the general staff in view of your recorded exploits in the service of Rome. Alone and at great personal risk, you made your way to us from your besieged camp to request assistance, killing two of the enemy on your way. You fought the leader of the Marcomanni besiegers of The Second Lucan, the so-called "King", Helmund and bested him in single combat, stretching his lifeless body on the battlefield. By bringing down the enemy leader, you contributed to shortening the conflict and saving the lives of many of our officers and soldiers. The Emperor has been made aware of your latest services to Rome and personally approves of the awards I now make you in the presence of my general staff and others. Prefect Otto Longius, step forward and receive this Gold Military Crown I now place on your head. Accept my personal gift, this golden cup. We honour you."

The officers bowed and hailed hm. Otto bowed to them.

"I am overwhelmed by these magnificent rewards and thank you most sincerely. I hope to continue to be worthy of the approval of my Emperor, my general and this army."

They were simple words, well-chosen to set the required tone and spoken in faultless and barely accentless Latin. They came as a surprise to many who heard them; they had expected a stumbling reply; ungrammatical and barely comprehensible. In truth, that is what they wanted. Otto and his like were troubling to many Romans. Peace and prosperity after the recent Civil War had led to old assumptions being challenged. Commoners acquired wealth and education and showed themselves to be at least the equal of the sons of the nobility. If barbarians were to be made citizens and then succeed even excel, in the army, where did that leave the old guard? Otto did not fit in with their preconceptions, they feared what he represented in a deep, unspoken way.

"How did you manage to seek out this Helmund on the battlefield, prefect?" called an officer in a drawling, superior voice.

Drusus looked around to see who had spoken, barely able to hide his irritation. The implication of the question was that Otto was a glory hunter, less concerned with his duty than with drawing attention to himself.

"I did not seek him out, sir. I was ordered to make a charge in a certain direction. Once I had completed the manoeuvre, Helmund and I saw each other. What followed seemed inevitable," Otto replied.

"Inevitable? Are you saying that it was the will of the Gods?" came the mocking response.

Otto smiled. "Are not all things decided according to the will of the Gods, sir?"

His questioner laughed and changed his tone. "Well argued, prefect. I see you are a young man to be reckoned with on or off the battlefield!"

Everyone indicated their approval calling out, "Well said!" and "Hear! Hear!" or slapping their hands down on the table. Drusus smiled. He was pleased that Otto had not fallen into the verbal trap that had been set for him. Had he seen it and deliberately chosen his replies to avoid it or was he simply speaking the truth as he saw it? The general could not decide.

"You will dine with me this evening, informally, a small party. Dismissed Prefect Otto Longius," he said.

Otto came to attention, turned on his heel and marched out to be greeted by an honour guard of the general's praetorians and his own men who gave him three cheers as he passed through the double line they had made to receive him.

He wore his striped knight's tunic and soft boots under his military red cloak to dinner. He had left the military crown with Felix but had brought along his gold cup.

"No crown?" Drusus asked.

"A gold crown at an informal dinner, sir?" Otto replied. "But here is the cup you kindly gave me. I thought it would be appropriate if it was filled for the first time at your table."

Otto reclined on his left elbow on a couch while he ate. He found it a peculiar custom to eat half lying down but managed to do justice to all the dishes with the exception of the bowl of Garum.

The conversation was light at first, not dissimilar to the talk around his own table when he invited his decurions to eat with him so Otto found it no strain to take part. Gradually, it turned to the recently lifted siege and became more serious. Otto repeated his assessment of Helmund as a dangerous enemy detailing his tactical innovations, unheard of in a German warlord. At the end of the evening, the general's steward took Otto's cup, washed it and gave it back wrapped in a brocade napkin.

When he had gone, Drusus lay back and stared up into the darkness above the glow of the ornate, gilded oil-lamps.

"Something troubles you sir?" asked his aide-de-camp.

"I was thinking that if the Marcomanni had ten Helmunds and one hundred Ottos our position here would be untenable," he answered.

"I think you will find that Otto Longius is almost unique, sir."

"Let us most sincerely wish you are right," the general said with an emphatic nod of his head.

Aldermar came to see him off the next morning.

"Congratulations Otto, I wish I could have been there to see the award ceremony," he said warmly shaking the young prefect's hand.

"So do I. The general was very gracious to me..."

Aldermar's face clouded over with worry. "Listen," he said without letting go of Otto's right hand, "you are getting a reputation as a favourite of the Emperor, perhaps of the general as well. Be very careful."

"Why?" Otto asked, pulling his hand free.

"Envy, simple envy. You have what many want and are not able to get; fame, rewards, promotion. I say again; be careful. There are a lot of men who cannot rise to your heights so they'll try to pull you down to theirs. You like these wise quotations, here's one from Aeschylus, some old Greek or other, "Few men have the moral force to honour another without envy." Think about that one and have a safe journey, my greetings to Publius and Titus."

Chapter 13

"So where's this gold crown, then?" Titus demanded on Otto's return.

"I can hardly wander around the camp with it on my head, now can I?" Otto replied.

"Why not? I would if I had one."

"It looks like I'm bragging if I wear it, that's why."

"Wouldn't stop me. Seriously though, the men would like to see it. It's a rare thing, a Military Crown for killing an enemy leader man to man."

"I could show it to everyone, I suppose."

"Good idea, we could display it outside the Praetorium. I'll borrow two of the legate's guards to keep an eye on it; big temptation to the lads, they'll nick anything given the chance…."

"Surely not!"

"Oh yes. They're very fond of you but even fonder of a dirty great lump of gold. They'd have it bashed flat and cut up before you could blink. Leave it to me. You will be giving a feast and buying wine?"

"Of course; you've told me, "It is the custom", often enough."

The crown and its owner were a sensation for a few days then everything returned to normal. Drills, patrols, fatigues, arms-training;

the hard routine of the legion. They paraded in front of their legate in a biting cold wind reddening cheeks and producing dewdrops on the end of noses.

"Evocati Felix stand forward," Titus bellowed.

Felix hobbled up and was presented with a bronze medal and ten gold pieces in recognition of his contribution to the defence of the eastern breastwork. He had his medal welded onto his armour and placed his money in the legion bank. Corvo was called up and similarly rewarded but received twenty gold pieces. Tertius Fuscus was called to the front of the rostrum and cheered by the men as Quadratus read out his citation for outstanding conduct. The parade was dismissed, formally closing the episode of the siege and the pitched battle following it.

Once more a champion was put up to contest the javelin-throwing prize with Otto. Yet again, he lost; like all the others before him. This pleased Titus Attius who capitalized on it mercilessly.

"Call yourselves legionaries? Call yourselves heavy infantry? You lot can't even chuck a javelin as far as a fucking cavalryman can. We'll have to do better than that; double practice every day this week…"

At the beginning of November, an unexpected event occurred that threw the legion into a cauldron of gossip. An Imperial Messenger arrived at the start of that season when only the most important despatches would normally be carried. He brought a summons for

Publius Quadratus to return with him to Rome where the Emperor awaited him as soon as matters could be arranged. He left the day after with his praetorians and a turma of cavalry led by the most senior of Otto's decurions. It began to snow feathery, wet flakes before the party cleared the camp gate.

Augustus was wearing two tunics under his toga, thick socks, soft boots and fingerless, woollen mittens, yet still he complained of the cold to Publius Quadratus who sat opposite him at a small table in the room where he had received Otto and Lucius. They sipped hot spiced wine, very heavily watered, and broke off pieces of bread and cheese to eat as they talked.

"Cold all the time. Unbearable. How do you manage Publius? Used to it in Germany no doubt. How are you, old friend? You look tired and drawn. Bad journey?" the Emperor asked.

"Not too severe for the time of year, sir. The weather improved once we arrived in Gaul."

"Glad to hear it. Now then, Second Lucan. Badly mauled. How many men have you lost?"

"Over sixteen hundred. I expect the figure to be nearer seventeen hundred by springtime. Some of the wounded will never leave the infirmary, some will recover but be unfit for service and we always lose a few to disease in the cold, wet months."

"How long have you been a soldier?

"Twenty-three years sir, twelve of them in Belgic lands or on the Rhine, ten as one of your legates."

"Never understood the military mind" Augustus told him. "There was Alexander the Great and then there was the Divine Julius. No-one will ever be a finer general than either of them. So why do it, eh? Why do it?"

"To serve Rome, sir."

"Well yes there is that, but it's mostly because it gets into a lot of young men's blood. They despise civilians, don't deny it..." Quadratus had no intention of doing so. "...I'm bringing your legion back to Italy. Two reasons. First, that complete shit Marcus Antonius lost the first Lucan and I'm not joining his company by losing the second. Do you know why Pompey the Great was beaten by Caesar? Shouldn't have been. He had more legions. But they were not the battle-hardened men that my adoptive father led. Not going to repeat Pompey's error of judgement. Big mistake. Easy to always look at far-off borders and forget what's next door. I want good, experienced troops in Italy. The Second Lucan can provide me with over three thousand of them. Map, Menities," he called to his secretary who spread out a parchment roll on the table, holding down the edges with wine cups. Augustus placed his forefinger on it. "I am establishing a permanent garrison here, inland of the rough line made by Spedia, Luca and Pisae. You will take over an existing fortress in disrepair and make it fit for purpose. It will be fifteen years before the last of your legion's veterans is given honourable discharge. So I can call on them for some years yet to protect the approaches to Cisalpine Gaul, the coast or indeed Rome, if need be."

"In which case, sir. I ask you to accept my resignation."

"Offended Publius? Surely not?"

"By no means, sir and if you need me at any time, I am yours. But, as we previously discussed, twenty- three years a soldier, twelve…"

"…up north and ten a legate. Very well. At least bring them home for me in the spring."

"That will be my honour sir."

"Replacement?"

"Senior Tribune Tertius Fuscus. You sent him to me as an able military administrator. He wanted to see border service. He has avoided an ambush in the field and turned the tables on the enemy, he has withstood a siege and taken part in a pitched battle. I doubt if he will complain at garrison duty near the Adriatic sir."

"Don't suppose he will. What about you?"

"I should like to retire to my estates, with your permission. I have a fancy to live out my days as a private citizen or perhaps as a minor provincial official. I have been too long away from Rome to enter politics…"

"Very wise. Dirty and dangerous business. Rome is a bear-pit of ambitious and double-dealing backstabbers. No place for an honest soldier. Stay in with us until all preparations are made then you can tell your legion the good news."

Twice when Otto was on patrol with his men, they were ambushed. On both occasions, the attackers went straight for him. He fought them off and killed two more warriors who were renowned fighters judging by the arm-rings he stripped off their bodies.

"It is clear that they want to defeat the man who killed Helmund. Perhaps you should avoid patrolling with the cavalry," Tertius Fuscus suggested.

"If I did that, wouldn't it be giving in to the enemies of Rome? "

"Yes, but are they your enemies or Rome's?"

"I am a Roman officer, there is no difference."

"Of course but you are putting Roman lives at risk, your men's lives each time you lead them...."

"And there it is," Otto thought, remembering Aldermar's words. "The worm of resentment working away without its host even realising he has been infected."

"If you order me not to leave the camp, I shall obey, Senior Tribune Tertius Fuscus," he said coldly.

Tertius looked embarrassed but quickly composed his features. "I do not believe we need go to that extreme..."

"Thank you, sir," Otto told him, turned on his heel and walked briskly away.

It grew colder, the snow deepened so the issue did not come up again. Otto was always perfectly correct in his dealing with Tertius but their relationship, never that friendly, had been soured. Saturnalia came around, a subdued affair that year in the absence of the camp-followers' wine-shops and brothels. Otto shut himself away in his quarters emerging only when it was over. That pushed him a little further out of the circle of his brother officers with the exception of Titus Attius who was a great believer in the saying, "Once bitten, twice shy," and understood Otto's reason for keeping out of the way.

It was a dreary time. Too many familiar faces were missing from the ranks for the old esprit de corps to be re-established. The legate was away and no-one knew why. If any officer speculated about the possible reasons, Tertius Fuscus slapped them down.

But time inevitably passed, February came and then March bringing Publius Quadratus back but accompanied only by his escort; no new recruits and no supply wagons. He called an immediate general assembly of all legionaries and officers, no exceptions even for the walking wounded, of whom there were still twenty or so. Travel-stained he mounted the rostrum. He looked over his legion for a full minute with a half-smile on his face. They did not know it but he wanted to fix their image in his mind for the last time he would call them together in this place.

"Men of The Second Lucan, you are aware that I was called to Rome. Emperor Augustus knows of your sacrifices and courage during your long tour of duty on the Rhine. He commends you. He has decided that The Second Lucan is to return to Italy. I am informed that your replacement legion is one week away. As we march out of the Porta Decumana for the last time, they will enter through the Porta Praetoria…..."

The legion erupted into a frenzy of cheering, men slapped their comrades on the back, helmets were taken off and waved in the air, swords beat against shields in a spontaneous display of joy. It took a full five minutes to restore sufficient order for the legate to continue. He stood patiently waiting during this time; he had expected this demonstration.

"Men… Men…" They began to pay full attention. "We are to be permanently garrisoned between Luca and Pisae in a camp yet to be constructed. For those of you approaching honourable discharge, the Emperor has graciously agreed to found a new veterans' colony in the immediate area. Land will be allocated between Spedia, Luca and Pisae, the exact locations to be determined. So that is it, comrades; we are going home with honour, undefeated; having held-fast to our soldiers' oaths through every difficulty in the face of a ferocious enemy. I salute you, my soldiers."

He stepped down and walked away, fighting to avoid a tear and preserve his Roman dignity. He held individual consultations with his senior officers. Tertius Fuscus was first.

"I shall be retiring from the army when we reach Italy. The Emperor has accepted my resignation and offers you command of the legion, Senior Tribune Tertius Fuscus. Will you accept?"

Tertius did not hesitate for one second.

"Gladly, sir although it will be a wrench to see you go."

"Decent of you to say so, Tertius, even if you can't wait to take command. We shall speak further but in the meantime, do not mention my departure and your promotion to the other officers. I naturally wish to tell them myself."

Titus Attius was quiet for some while after he heard the legate's news.

"I have served under you…" he began at last.

"… with me, Titus," Quadratus interrupted.

".. served with you, sir for over twenty years. I cannot imagine a new commander. No, it is time for me to say goodbye to the legion as well. I shall stay on for a year or so to see the lads properly established in their new camp before I go."

"I am relieved to hear it. What will you do then?"

"I'll buy an inn and sit back in the Spanish sunshine and grow soft and fat."

"Why Spain? Do you have family there?"

"No, no-one that I know of but I did have long ago. Because it's warm, sir and a bloody long way from the Rhine."

Corvo's interview was more complicated.

"Temporary Acting Prefect Corvo, what is your first name by the way? I never asked, how rude of me."

"It is Marcus sir,"

"Well then Marcus Corvo, with the active assistance of the Emperor's secretariat we have established that you are entitled to equestrian status. I can therefore confirm your commission as prefect of artillery and drop the "temporary acting". But, there is always a "but" in these matters, to have your name enrolled in the Equestrian Order, you will have to show sufficient wealth. I take it that you are unable to do so at present?"

"No sir."

"Not even with your officer's share of the Marcomanni loot?"

"That might take me half-way sir."

"That's a start. Thinking that this would probably be the case, the Emperor has confirmed your status and commission and deferred enrolment until the end of your military service, unless you find yourself in the financial position to act before that arrives."

"Thank you, sir."

"You should thank your Emperor."

"I am grateful to him sir, but I am also sure you had a lot to do with this."

"That's as maybe. Now, under your particular circumstances, you have a choice. If you return to Italy with the legion, you will lose command of your century. It will return to purely infantry duties.

Cretan archers and Balearic slingers will be recruited to take over their special function. You will command the auxiliaries and your artillery. If you wish, you can transfer to headquarters as an artillery prefect. You still lose your archers and slingers but you can take any specialised artillerymen who want to go with you."

"And their equipment sir?"

"…Along with their equipment. The new legion has their own and it will save dragging a lot of heavy artillery pieces all the way home."

"May I have a word with my men before giving you my decision, sir?"

"Of course; if you decide to go to headquarters, it will be with my recommendation. If you decide to stay with The Second Lucan, you will be welcome."

Otto looked stricken.

"Without you, sir? I've already lost Boxer and now you?"

"Otto, the life of a soldier is one of farewells. Comrades fall, they are transferred or they leave the service. It is as natural as the turning of the seasons. You have friends in Luca, your estates are there, this could be ideal for you. Know that I am in your debt and shall never cease to answer if you call on me. As long as I live, you will never lose the friendship of Publius Quadratus."

Two days later, Prefect Marcus Corvo, with thirty artillerymen and their weapons, headed north to join the army of General Drusus.

The jubilation the soldiers were feeling did not long survive First Spear Centurion Titus Attius.

"No-one is going to able to say The Second Lucan did not leave its camp in spotless order," he told the men. "Right then, get busy."

They swept, scrubbed, re-arranged, cleaned until they were dropping with fatigue. When they had dealt with the buildings, walls, walkways and parade ground, he said how pleased he was at their efforts but that they all looked damnably scruffy. The next days were a frenzy of polishing, sharpening, combing out crests and parade after parade where he managed to find some fault and make them do it all again. He had new latrine pits dug and the earth used to fill in the old ones. The new facilities were off-limits.

"What am I supposed to do, first spear centurion?" one of them dared to complain.

"You can shit in your helmet for all I care but make sure you polish it afterwards," was the unhelpful response.

The changeover was more complicated than Quadratus had said but he was fundamentally correct; as one legion left the other would take up occupation. The new legion was coming up the Rhine from the west. Five thousand men and officers with their horses, transport animals artillery train and stores carried in ox wagons arrived over a period of two days on what had been the farmers' fields before the Marcomanni had either chased them off or slaughtered them. Some of the officers were invited in to inspect their new home and plan how they would occupy the camp. All seemed satisfactory other than the diagonal wall across the northeast corner. Titus Attius explained why it was there.

"Fine bit of military initiative," he told Titus. "First thing I'll do is get my lads to square it off again. Keep the idle sods busy and it'll help to make the place their own…."

The day of departure dawned with high, white clouds flying on a stiff easterly breeze. The fleeting sun had minimal warmth but at least it neither rained nor snowed. The gates were flung open and The Second Lucan marched out, eagles glittering and flags snapping in the wind. Quadratus took up the rear, behind his cavalry which was screening the priests carrying their statues of the Gods, altars and the legion treasure in a stout wagon. Horns blew and the column rumbled over the remade bridge across the stream to the south. As Legate Publius Quadratus passed through the Porta Decumana, his replacement entered through the Porta Praetoria. The fortification that had cost so many of their comrades' lives to defend, was given up in military pomp and without a backward glance.

Their progress was slow. They made fifteen miles on a good day but less than ten if the weather was against them or the terrain difficult, or both. Ten days and one hundred and twelve miles south-west of their starting off point, the German scouts were released from their service. The legion was well clear of the Rhine and the dangerous tribes alongside it so the scouts no longer had a useful role to play.

They would return to Prefect Aldermar but not empty-handed. Quadratus presented each of them with a gold piece and their spare horses were loaded with sacks of provisions for their journey north. When they were mounted and ready to leave, Otto took off four of his many arm-rings and gave one to each of the scouts. They raised their lances in the air and chanted in their own language before wheeling their mounts and trotting away.

"What did they say?" Quadratus asked.

"Oh, just a farewell," Otto mumbled, clearly uncomfortable.

"Prefect Otto Longius, I order you to repeat to me in good Latin what was said to you a moment ago," the legate ordered.

"They said goodbye to the killer of kings and mighty warriors until we meet again in the next life, sir. Nonsense really…"

"No, it is not "nonsense"; it is a measure of the high regard they have for you."

After weary weeks on the road, they crossed the border into Italy. The spring air was balmy, almond and fruit trees were in blossom. There were fat farms and villages on either side of the paved road on which they marched. They had almost forgotten how different Italy was from the dark, cold and menacing forested landscape in which they had lived and fought for so long. It lifted their spirits simply to look around and breathe in the sweet-scented warmth. They changed their route of march to the west approaching the Tyrrhenian Sea coast and that is where Quadratus left the column. He headed south towards Rome and was gone. Tertius Fuscus was now the commanding officer of The Second Lucan. It had happened so quickly and with so little ceremony that it was impossible to believe such a major change had occurred in the life of the legion. For days afterwards when anyone referred to the legate, Publius Quadratus came to mind but gradually, the new order was established.

Their garrison fortress was impressive on first view. A great rectangle of high stone walls stood near the head of a gently sloping valley fanning out towards the distant sea. A small river ran close by. It was spanned by a good stone bridge over which lay the road leading to another bridge some miles away which crossed the River Arno. It was twelve miles from Pisae and ten from Luca. Spedia was twenty miles away and the sea eight as the crow flies. Inland, the ground rose to wooded slopes with naked rocky mountains rearing above them. There were no villages or farmsteads in the valley although stock grazed on the free grass and drank in the river shallows. There had been a battle in this place during the Civil War during which the locals had been indiscriminately slaughtered by both sides. They had never re-settled the immediate area. At first glance, it was idyllic. Then they marched closer.

There were no gates, the ditch was choked with brambles out of which well-grown saplings raised spindly arms to the heavens. The walls to the north and west were covered in moss and ivy. When Tertius Fuscus and his officers rode in, they were met with a rich aroma of goat. Dried sheep and cattle dung crumbled to powder under their horses' hooves. The interior buildings constructed of pink, thin bricks, lacked roofs, doors and windows. Weeds grew in every crack in the parade ground.

"Seen and smelled worse," Titus Attius commented. "Marching-camp, sir?" he asked Tertius.

"Definitely, Titus," the legate replied. "It will be some while before we can move in."

Even in peaceful Italy, they were not about to take any chances; with practised efficiency, the ditch and rampart were dug and the palisade erected in less than two hours.

The legionaries began to scrape, sweep and weed under the ever-watchful eyes of their centurions who were in turn aware that First Spear Centurion Attius was always lurking, ready to bellow at them, even when they thought he was somewhere else. The first logging party was sent up to the hillside to collect the timber they would need. A helmeted optio in full armour led a century of soldiers in tunics to the lower edge of the treeline accompanied by two ox-drawn heavy wagons.

They stopped by a fine, straight tree. The optio slapped the trunk and shouted to his men.

"Right lads, this 'un will do to make a start with…."

But he fell silent when he heard shouting and saw two figures hurrying up on a footpath. One was a sturdy man with a broad, sunburned face. The other was very old; a few strands of white hair barely covered his head. His skinny legs and back were bent and he hobbled leaning on a stick.

"What's your game? You can't just come along of us and cut down our trees. Go on, bugger off!" he shouted in a quavering voice.

Half of the legionaries sniggered but the other half looked worried. Their optio was quite capable of sending his sword plunging into the old man's guts.

"I don't think you understand citizen…" the optio tried to explain.

"I understands all right. You're one of they soldiers. We 'ad enough of you lot last time; having battles and killing folk," he shouted then burst out coughing and sat down with his back to the tree-trunk.

"Grandad don't mean to cause no offence, sir," the younger man said. "But that there tree is a chestnut and it's a wicked shame to chop 'im down. Us collects the nuts, see, in autumn, like."

The optio sighed; there was always an added difficulty.

"No need to get off on the wrong foot," he told the pair of them. "You show me what trees my lads can have and we'll leave the ones you need alone. How's that?"

"Better. What you doin' 'ere anyway?" the old man asked

"We're moving into the fortress down there and we need wood to rebuild it, granddad."

"I ain't your granddad," he replied.

"Well you could be; I never knew my granny," the optio told him and this time the men felt safe to laugh aloud.

On his return with two wagonloads of freshly cut timber, the optio reported the encounter and what he had done to his centurion. The centurion reported it to Titus Attius who approved.

"Tell him he did the right thing; no need to antagonize the locals," he said and issued a general order to all logging parties; oak, ash and birch only.

Otto and his men had nothing practical to do during the period of reconstruction once they had scrubbed out their stables. Stalls and doors would be fitted when the carpenters got round to them; the priority was replacing the gates and re-roofing the praetorium and barracks. Legate Fuscus sent for him.

"I have a task for you, Otto," he said. "We want recruits and if we can get them locally so much the better. I want to you ride to Spedia, in the first instance, and deliver a message to the magistrate. We need eighteen hundred men to bring us up to full strength, including as many fit veterans as we can get. Of course, Spedia cannot supply all our needs so I'm asking for six hundred. The magistrate is to proclaim this in the city square and we shall return in two weeks time on market day to inspect any volunteers who have come forward."

"What day is the market held, sir?"

"No idea; you can find that out for me and also, have a good look at the condition of the roads and make a note of anything which might be useful to the legion. You know the sort of thing; bridges, fords, and all that. I want you to go with your entire force, flags, best armour; make a show. A bit of military finery always encourages farm-boys to sign up."

The round trip to Spedia took a full day after an early start. The subsequent mission to Pisae and back was accomplished in a few hours. Otto came back with formal greetings from both cities, a note of the market days and a detailed sketch map of his route in each case.

"I believe you have connections in Luca?" Tertius enquired.

"I do, sir. It is the home of Tribune Lucius Longius."

"Very well, send my greetings to his family and take three days to renew your acquaintance with the city."

"Thank you, sir. I think I should send my men back more or less straight away and keep a small escort with me. No sense in straining relationships by expecting the authorities to feed and stable an entire ala for longer than necessary."

"They should feel honoured to accommodate the Emperor's troopers. After all who else keeps them safe from the barbarian hordes on our borders?"

"Exactly, sir; I completely agree. But in practice, it would be an awful lot of fodder to find without prior notice."

"You may be right," Tertius grudgingly conceded.

Centurion Massus had seen the cavalry column approaching when they were two miles away. He had plenty of time to form an honour-guard of his men so that Otto rode through the city gate between two rows of legionaries who snapped to attention as he passed. Massus threw a salute which Otto acknowledged with a smile and a nod of his head. The square resonated with the click of iron-shod hooves on paving stones, the clink of armour and weapons, the jingling of bits and the snorting of horses. One hundred and twenty cavalrymen and their officers and a two-mule cart filled the square as they formed ranks and came to a halt facing the city courthouse. Their arrival had caused so much noise and excitement that people hurried out to see what was going on. The court waiting room emptied. One of the clerks ran in to say an army had come. The magistrate snorted his disbelief but strode out of his office and pushed through the onlookers at the top of his steps. He found himself at eyelevel with a glittering officer mounted on a black charger which pawed the ground with his front feet sending sparks flying.

"Greetings sir, on behalf of Legate Tertius Fuscus of The Second Lucan. You will be aware that the legion is occupying the previously derelict fortress on the Pisae road. I have the honour to serve our Emperor as prefect of the legion's cavalry." All this was said in a loud enough voice for most of the onlookers to hear. Otto stepped down from the saddle and walked up to stand beside the magistrate, towering over him; the difference in their heights exaggerated by the high-crested parade helmet he wore. Otto handed the official the scroll confirming his orders and half-turned to make sure as many as possible could catch his next words. "The legion seeks to recruit six hundred sound young men of Luca. On market day two weeks from now, officers will be here to inspect and enrol suitable volunteers. We hope you will make this known throughout the city and surrounding villages, sir."

"I know, you don't I?" the magistrate asked. "Aren't you that friend of Lucius Longius?"

"Yes, I am; pleasure to meet you again, sir. Now if you would excuse me?"

He remounted Djinn and walked him over to Massus, still by the open gate. He leaned down and shook hands.

"Can you put me and half a dozen of my men up for three days?"

"My pleasure, sir," Massus replied.

Otto turned Djinn so that he was standing beside the centurion looking over at his troopers.

"Men, this is Centurion Massus. He was awarded a silver spear for his actions in saving an entire Roman army in Africa. You may never see another soldier so highly decorated in the rest of your careers. Salute Centurion Massus!"

As one, they raised their lances and shouted their acclamation. Massus squared his shoulders and stood a little taller. He bowed in acceptance.

"Decurion," Otto shouted, "lead the men back to camp. Those six I have already spoken to fall out."

Within a few minutes they had all clattered away leaving Otto, his escort and Evocati Felix on his mule cart.

"Thank you for the public commendation, sir," Massus told him. "It wasn't necessary."

"Yes it was centurion. People should not be allowed to forget."

As it fell out, few of the citizens knew that their garrison commander was a celebrated soldier who was still spoken of with pride in the army. When the news spread around town, he did not have to buy himself a flask of wine in any tavern for a month.

When the men, horses and mules had been settled, Otto sat down with Felix and Massus in the guardroom office.

"I need to visit Boxer's family," Otto said, "but I don't have any gifts for the ladies."

"Course you do," Felix told him. "You've got half a ton of silver rings on each arm. Get a jeweller to polish a couple of them up. They'll just love that; genuine barbaric spoils of battle, just the job, sir."

Otto selected three and one of Massus' men carried them over to the nearest jeweller who promised to have them ready by mid-afternoon. An urchin was sent to Vitius Longius with a message asking if Otto might visit the next day. He came back in a short while with a scrap of vellum on which was written an invitation to spend the day and dine with the family.

That evening, Massus, Otto and Felix sat around the barrack-room table with Otto's troopers and ten of the off-duty legionaries eating and drinking. It had been uncomfortable at first; the cavalrymen were not inclined to say much in the presence of their prefect and the garrison soldiers did not know what to make of this glittering, senior officer.

"Remember that night when you carried Lucius Longus in, half-dead and covered in blood?" Massus asked.

"Was that you, sir?" one of the legionaries said.

"No, it was that big German who was a pal of the tribune's," one of his comrades answered.

"That was me alright," Otto told him. "Some night!"

"I should say," Massus added. "Killed three very naughty boys did Prefect Otto Longius; two with a pugio and one he just bashed to bits."

"Did you really, sir?" one of the troopers put in, not sure whether to believe it.

"Oh yes, he really did for three armed robbers and him just a lad. Bloody enormous lad mind!"

The banter flowed after that. Old stories were retold. Felix recounted how he was awarded his medal.

"They were coming in over this pile of logs so I got the lads to pour some olive oil over them. You should have seen it boys! They was slipping and sliding all over the place. Could hardly spear 'em for laughing."

"What happened with the leg?" Massus asked him.

"German axe. What happened with the eye?"

"African arrow. Here's to the horrible bastards who tried their best to put us down!"

They clinked wine cups. It was as pleasant a night of light-hearted comradeship as Otto had enjoyed for a long while.

Chapter 14

"This is ridiculous. I'm not doing it," Otto protested.

"You've got to, sir. They'll expect it," Felix insisted.

"Oh, you're an expert on high-born ladies now are you?"

"Lads, who thinks they would want to see the prefect in his poshest armour?"

"We all do," the assembled legionaries and cavalrymen shouted as they sat around the garrison mess-hall finishing their breakfasts.

"I cannot stay all day long in the home of Boxer's family wearing full armour. Out of the question," Otto said decisively.

"Ah, I'm ahead of you there, sir. I go with you on the mule-cart with a change of clothes. They have a good old squint at you for half and hour then you can take it off and I'll fetch it back to the billet," Felix told him with a smug grin.

"Centurion Massus, tell them all that this is stupid," Otto pleaded.

Massus shook his head. "Felix and the boys are right. Nothing the ladies love more than to see a soldier in his glory, all polished up and manly."

"I'll give in if one of you will run along to the butcher's and get me an ox's knee-joint; a fresh bloody one with a foot of bone either side."

"Who's that for?"

"My hostess, of course," Otto said, deadpan.

Otto knocked sharply on the stout gate which led into the garden of the Longius' family home. A hatch opened and the face of Janus the guardian peered up.

"Greetings, Janus, I have come to visit….."

"Oh Master Otto, is that you sir? Come in, oh do come in," he said beaming.

Otto stepped through. "Can you direct this soldier to the stable gate, please?" he asked indicating Felix on the seat of the cart.

"Of course, of course. The family are waiting for you, sir."

Pinerus the major-domo bustled down the path and bowed before greeting him. "If you would follow me, sir" he said and gestured towards the front entrance of the neat villa.

Four figures stood with happy smiles on their faces watching him but as he came nearer, the smiles gave way to looks of surprise. Otto had grown two inches in height and put on nearly twenty pounds of hard muscle since they had last seen him. He strode towards them now, seven and a half feet tall from the top of his helmet crest to the soles of his boots. The width of his shoulders was emphasized by the harness he wore under his cuirass. His red military cloak swirled about him as he walked with one hand rested on the hilt of his cavalry sword in its decorated scabbard. He reached the top of the steps up to the house and smiled broadly.

"Greetings noble sir, ladies. How happy I am to see you again."

They all looked up at him in silence with something like awe.

The smile left his face. "Is anything wrong?" he asked.

Aelia, his friend's grandmother, answered for them.

"Nothing is wrong, Otto. It is just that, well, you are so huge in all your wonderful armour, you look like a statue of Mars in a temple that has come to life."

Otto blushed. "Everyone said it would be a good idea to wear my parade armour. I told them it was stupid. Here, is this better?" he asked removing his helmet.

"Oh, you've cut off all your lovely golden hair," Poppaea, the daughter of the house said and blushed in turn.

"You are as welcome as ever," her mother Sabina put in to cover Poppaea's embarrassment, ever the gracious hostess.

"We thought we might sit in the garden. It's a lovely day and all the blossom has come out to scent the air," his host, Vitius, suggested.

They sat around a marble table in the dappled shade of the flowering creeper growing up and over the wooden loggia. As soon as they were seated, Pinerus appeared carrying a tray loaded with jugs of fruit juice, wine, water and precious glass goblets. He set his tray down and clapped. Two women came around the side of the house, each carrying a tray of snacks; bread, biscuits, honey-cakes, cheeses, cold meats and the inevitable bowl of garum. Otto recognised one of them as the family's cook and Passer's mother.

"May I speak with your cook, lady?" he asked Sabina who nodded puzzled assent.

He rose and stood in front of her. Her head barely came up to the embossed image of Minerva in the centre of his breastplate.

"Woman," he said in a soft, kindly voice, "late last year I saw your son, Passer at army headquarters in Upper Germany. He has grown tall and is in good health. He has a natural talent for working with horses and is learning his trade well. Everyone has a high opinion of him".

Tears filled her eyes. She took one of his hands and kissed it.

"The Gods' blessings on you sir," she sobbed then caught her mistress' disapproving glance and scurried away.

"That was kind of you, Otto," Aelia said, looking askance at her daughter in law. "Did you see our Lucius when you were last there?" she asked with a mischievous light in her eyes.

"No, madam. He was away on a bridge-building mission."

"And why were you summoned by your general?"

"Oh, army administration," he mumbled, avoiding her gaze.

"Liar, Otto, wicked liar! We know you went to receive your golden crown of honour! Lucius wrote and told us how disappointed he was not to be there."

"How is he?" Otto asked eagerly.

"He is well and happy…"

"And writes a lot of boring stuff about foundations and spans and engineering," Poppaea interrupted her grandmother.

"Indeed he does, but never mind "Boxer" as we know you all call him. Tell us about the golden crown…"

"And why aren't you wearing it?" Poppaea added.

With a lot of coaxing, they extracted the story and sat back thrilled once they had heard it. He went on to speak about Lucius and all he had accomplished during the siege. His mother and sister listened bright-eyed and his father was clearly proud to learn how vital their son's expertise had been to his comrades during that dangerous time.

"One of my men is in your stable yard. I need to speak with him if you will excuse me," Otto told them.

The mules were contentedly munching out of their nosebags but there was no sign of Felix. Otto found him in the kitchen in front of an empty plate with crumbs of bread and cheese and some scraps of meat on it, He was regaling the wide-eyed female servants with terrible, bloody tales of the German borderlands. Even Pinerus looked impressed.

"Want to give me a hand with this armour?" Otto asked.

"Of course, sir," Felix replied and walked over to the stable block with him.

"You were laying it on a bit thick weren't you?"

Felix chuckled. "Just telling the civilians what they want to hear sir; plenty of blood and guts with the brave Roman lads coming out on top every time."

He helped Otto out of his armour and boots and into a striped, Equestrian tunic. Soft boots and his belt with its scabbarded pugio finished his "casual" look.

"Give me those presents, please and come back for me at the ninth hour. Better bring four of the men along with you; even round here it can be hairy after dark."

Otto came back and shouted in his parade ground voice for Janus to release Ursus the guard dog. His voice echoed off the garden walls and Sabina winced slightly at the assault on her delicate ears. The huge Molossian hound bounded out of his pen barking but stopped short when he recognized Otto. He lowered his head on his extended front paws and wagged his enormous tail; he was showing the first hint of grey around the muzzle but was still a powerful animal. Otto produced the ox bone from behind his back, red with strips of meat and rich with marrow. Ursus eyed it. Twin strings of silvery slaver flowed down each side of his jowls. He came forward slowly, one step at a time. Otto thrust at him with the bone. Ursus leaped and clamped onto one end. They played a furious game of tug of war. The dog growled and ground his teeth further up his side of the bone, Otto laughed and pulled back on his side. At last Ursus' fangs gripped into the cartilage and tore it out of Otto's grasp. He tossed it into the air, reared up on his back legs and caught it nimbly. Still wagging his tail, he trotted in triumph back into his pen to gnaw at his prize.

The family applauded. Pinerus re-appeared with a bowl of water and a towel for Otto's greasy hands.

"He remembered you," Vitius said.

"I brought that bone in case he didn't!" Otto laughed.

He produced three doeskin bags out of his tunic. "The warriors of the northern lands have a tradition of wearing silver arm-rings. If one is defeated, the victor takes them...."

"You had them right up each arm before," Poppaea interrupted but Otto carried on without directly responding.

"... I have a gift for each of you ladies from Upper Germany." He passed the first bag across to Poppaea. "This was taken off a great warrior of the Chatti who tried to ambush me." She opened it and her eyes widened at the sight of the thick silver ring inside. She slipped it over her wrist but her arm was so slender it fell back. "This was worn by Audo of the Bright Axe, a chieftain of the Marcomanni," he said giving his gift to Sabina. "Finally, my lady Aelia, this one belonged to King Helmund, again of the Marcomanni, who led his army against us when your grandson did such great works to save the camp and the legion."

"Each one of these comes from a man you have killed in battle?" Aelia asked.

"They were all thoroughly cleaned and polished by a jeweller, there's no blood or anything…" Otto began but Aelia silenced him by cupping his face in both her hands and laughing.

"Famous hero, cavalry officer, fierce warrior, under it all you remain our dear, dear Otto, earnest and without guile. Thank you very much," she said and kissed his cheek. It was Sabina's turn to look askance at Aelia.

The afternoon was taken up with business. Vitius had asked his estate steward and his son, who acted as Otto's local man of business, to attend with the accounts. The son was nervous. He had never met Otto before and did not know what to expect. In the event, he was pleasantly surprised. His employer listened carefully, asked relevant questions and showed a quick grasp of matters relevant to his land and tenants.

"After taxes and my salary as agreed of twelve-hundred denarii per annum, you have so far made a profit of sixteen thousand denarii. By the end of this year, that sum should rise to twenty-two thousand, if all goes well," the young man said and sat back looking nervously at his patron.

"Where is this money?" Otto asked.

"In your bank, sir. All of it…"

"You have started well. To reward your honest efforts, I want you to take a bonus payment of three hundred denarii for yourself."

"Oh, thank you master…"

"Do not call me "master"; Otto or Otto Longius will do."

He wrote an order on his bankers which Vitius witnessed.

After they had gone, the ladies returned.

"You made that young man a generous gift Otto," Vitius told him. "He is about to be married so it has come at a particularly useful time for him."

"Who is getting married?" Sabina asked.

"The steward's son."

"Oh him," she remarked, with no further interest.

"Otto will have to find a wife shortly," Poppaea giggled.

"I have no thoughts of that," he responded with a smile.

"It is not entirely your choice to marry or not. Emperor Augustus is very keen on promoting public morals. The Julian Laws put all sorts of restrictions on who can marry whom but underlying them is a requirement to find a partner and be fruitful," Vitius told him.

"Yes, and he is even keener that the Senatorial and Equestrian classes find spouses and produce children, preferably sons," Sabina added.

"May be I should marry Poppaea," Otto laughed.

"No, you can't," Sabina said in a rush, then realising her mistake smiled sweetly. "She is already betrothed... or practically betrothed."

But the speed with which she had forbidden him to think of marrying her daughter was not lost on Otto. He was usually modest but

Sabina had wounded him. His remark had been meant as a joke. Her reaction showed her fear that it was to be taken seriously.

"That is a shame my lady. I am a Roman Knight and Prefect who can offer a bride my estate, a fortune of over one hundred thousand denarii, a gold cup, the gift of General Drusus, and a Military Gold Crown. I hope the lady Poppaea's chosen one could provide as much, when she is more than "practically" betrothed."

Sabina's eye's went wide and she reddened to the roots of her hair. The mood had changed. Conversation became desultory and forced. After an uncomfortable half hour, Otto said that he had remembered things he must do and took his leave. He walked down the hill to the barracks feeling humiliated and sad in equal measure. One look at his face told Massus and Felix to ask no questions.

"It isn't my fault," Sabina told her disapproving family. "It just slipped out. I mean, marrying Poppaea! How ridiculous and anyway he can't possibly have that sort of money."

"He has over thirty thousand in the bank to my certain knowledge, plus his accumulated army pay, I doubt if he spends much, together with an officer's share of his legion's campaign loot. I think one hundred thousand might be an understatement, my dear" Vitius told her drily.

"It's not merely about money, Vitius," she shot back.

"What is it about then, dear?" Aelia asked in an infuriatingly reasonable tone.

"Oh, you know perfectly well!" Sabina retorted as she slammed out of the room.

"That was unfortunate," Aelia said, summing up the mood.

"No denying that. I shall go to the barracks tomorrow and make my peace with Otto on behalf of the family," Vitius told his mother.

"That would be the right thing to do. Mind you, Sabina is quite right, you know. A union between Poppaea and Otto would be a disaster."

"It was never being seriously considered," Vitius snapped.

"Indeed not; just so long as you realise your wife was not wrong in what she said, only how she said it."

Otto and his men had left by the time that Vitius arrived. He sat on a bench beside Massus and sighed.

"I take it the visit was not a success," Massus remarked.

"No," Vitius replied with a shake of his head. "It was going splendidly then the subject of marriage came up. Otto made a joke and my wife …"

"…Took exception to it. Of course she did. Marriage is too serious for women to make jokes about. They marry and their husbands turn out to be drunken brutes or they die having children or bring six into this world and attend the funerals of all of 'em. No, nothing funny about it for women."

"You are undeniably right but the fact is, Otto is gong to have to find himself a wife and soon. The Emperor proscribes marriage for the nobility and the equestrian class."

"Well, good luck to him, is all I say," Massus snorted.

"Why? He is a citizen and a knight surely many families would like their daughters to be united with him …"

"Not a chance. Two reasons; firstly he was born the wrong side of the Rhine. How can I put the second reason to you without being crude? I can't. Would you have your fine-boned trotting pony covered by a war-horse stallion? Of course you wouldn't. The poor little mare could never carry his foal to term and give birth to it. Now think of the average young lady round here and the size of Otto. Same difficulty."

"Massus, we are not mere animals."

"We are when it comes down to it. Mating and producing the next generation is what it's all about and the same rules apply. If he seriously wants a wife, let me know."

"He says he doesn't.

"Clever boy!"

As a legate, Tertius Fuscus had the final say in the choice of his officers. He found himself extremely popular all of a sudden. He received letters daily from the parents of acquaintances in Rome asking to be remembered to him with fondness and wanting to know if he was aware that their youngest son yearned to join the military tribunate? He replied politely without committing himself. Rome worked on favours exchanged. Even if he had no interest in giving a particular youngster an appointment, it did not do to offend his family. Who knew what could arise in future to make their friendship essential?

Then the letter from his father was delivered. Fuscus senior was seeking a higher elected position in Rome. He needed financial support and he needed votes. The father of Nonius Priscus would offer both if his son was commissioned as the new Broad Stripe Tribune of The Second Lucan. Nonius was twenty-three. He had spent two years as a tribune in a legion settled in Italy. He was too young and inexperienced to be acceptable in the second-in-command position on the Rhine but the legion was no longer in Germany. Men may rise or fall in Rome as a result of their networking skills or lack of them but family overrode any other consideration. Tertius' father had spoken and his son would obey. He replied saying how delighted he would be to accept young Priscus but covered himself by saying his decision was subject to the Emperor's final approval.

The Noble Nonius Priscus arrived shortly after the troops were able to move into their renovated fortress. He was followed by a train of four carts. One carried his furniture, another his staff; a cook, a barber, a masseur, two body servants and a clerk. A third held his stock of wine and delicacies and the last his carpets and ornaments. He rode a white horse with a decorated saddle and bridle. On one hip he wore an ivory handled sword in a gold-embossed scabbard. He was of middle height, and handsome with chestnut hair and perfect teeth.

After he had been sworn in under the eagle standing on the parade ground rostrum beside Tertius Fuscus, he gave his introductory speech to the legion gathered to greet their new senior tribune.

"Men of The Second Lucan, you do not know me yet. You will come to do so over the next few days. You will find me hard; hard but fair. I will not stand for sloppiness of any sort. Uniforms will be spotless, armour will be polished, swords will be sharp, drill will be perfect. Do your best to please me and all will be well, fail me and you will be punished."

Tertius stared over the men's heads at some undefined point in the distance while Priscus spoke. The men looked at him expressionlessly.

The legate called a meeting of the senior officers to introduce them to Priscus individually.

Titus Attius bowed and took the tribune's hand to shake it. It was very soft and white; each evening Priscus rubbed scented ointment into his hands to keep them that way.

"A centurion, marvellous, backbone of the army," he said.

"Not "a centurion" sir; I am "the" centurion, Titus Attius First Spear Centurion of The Second Lucan."

"But still, a centurion as I said, eh?" Priscus responded, irked at being corrected as he saw it.

A look of distaste flickered over his face when he met Soranus and saw the tribune's maimed left hand. Soranus noticed and went slightly pink.

Priscus did not offer to shake Otto's hand.

"You'll be one of the auxiliary chappies," he said.

"I am Otto Longius, Prefect of Cavalry, sir," Otto told him.

"Yes, but auxiliary cavalry."

"No, regular Roman cavalry, sir."

"I do not understand",… Priscus began.

Tertius Fuscus came to his aid. "Prefect Otto Longius was made a Roman citizen and enrolled in the Equestrian Order by the Emperor himself," he explained.

Priscus gave a short chuckle. "How eccentric our dear Emperor can be at times."

The first problem arose after the meeting. Soranus showed the new Senior Tribune to his quarters. He found them unacceptable. As he told Tertius, there was no accommodation for his suite of servants.

"You have a bedroom, a reception room and an office, the same as all the senior officers," the legate told him.

"But I need somewhere to put my people. I'm sure two of the other officers could share so that I could take over one of their quarters…"

"Ask Roman officers to double up to make room for your servants? No, Nonius, it won't do. It will not do at all!"

Eventually the quartermaster found a storeroom that they could use.

"Have it swept out and whitewash the walls," Priscus ordered him.

"Who by, sir"

"Soldiers; there seems to be plenty of them with nothing better to do."

"You expect the men to clean up the place for your servants?" asked the astounded quartermaster.

"I expect you and the legionaries to obey the orders of their senior tribune," Priscus told him coldly.

A surly fatigue party cleaned out the room while an angry optio snapped at them. He thought the duty beneath a soldier of Rome as much as his men did.

The recruits came in. Not the sixteen-hundred Legate Fuscus had wanted but after the initial weeding out, there remained nearly fifteen-hundred willing young men. There were divided into groups of eight, the basic number who shared a tent on campaign, and then combined into centuries of eighty. Among them were thirty old sweats still fit enough to serve and twenty-two who had been corporals or optios. Titus Attius would not confirm any man in his former rank until they had been through basic training once more and he could assess their qualities of leadership. They drilled and marched endlessly, or so it seemed to the new recruits. Their lives were punctuated by the yelled abuse of their officers and the thwack of a vine-staff across the shoulders or the back of their legs. By the end of the first month, forty who were not up to the rigours of army life had been discharged and the remainder were beginning to get to grips with the grinding routine.

"Javelin drill tomorrow, Otto, fancy coming along to let new lads see how it should be done?" Titus asked.

A practice range had been set up on level ground outside the walls. The targets were three straw dummies on poles. The men lined up twenty paces away and threw the heavy javelins for the first time. An appreciable number hit the targets or plunged into the ground either side or beyond them. This was not a bad result. These weapons were generally used against a massed enemy so, in practice, a close miss would kill or wound the man standing next to the enemy at whom they had aimed. After three attempts, the throwing line was moved back five paces. There were still a good number of strikes. At thirty paces, the number fell dramatically. Otto strolled up bare-headed and wearing only his boots and a belted tunic. He saluted Titus Attius.

"Greetings First Spear Centurion Attius, what are you doing?" he asked loudly enough for the trainees to hear.

"We are learning how to cast a javelin today, Prefect Longius. Would you like to have a try?" Titus replied, in a voice also designed to carry.

"Show me how to hold it, then," Otto responded, acting out the usual pantomime with Titus.

Titus played his part and Otto grasped the javelin.

"Which target?" he asked innocently.

"Try the one on the left," Titus replied.

"I'll do my best," Otto said.

The target wobbled; transfixed dead-centre.

"A chance shot, prefect. I bet you couldn't do it again; the one on the right, this time."

The right-hand dummy exploded at the impact; wisps of its straw stuffing blowing away on the slight breeze.

"Oh my, what luck you have Prefect Longius. Let's make it a little more difficult shall we?"

With Otto beside him carrying his remaining javelin, Titus loudly counted out fifteen paces back. and scratched a line in the turf. They were now forty-five paces away from the final target. Otto spat on his hands and grinned at Titus. This was the final act. It was to show what could be done. The watching recruits would almost certainly never be able to match the power and skill Otto displayed.

"What do you think you are doing?" a voice behind them asked.

Senior Tribune Nonius Priscus stood in immaculate full uniform looking at them with feigned surprise.

"I'm helping Titus Attius train the new men," Otto replied.

"And do you think it appropriate for a cavalry officer to be performing arms drill with common infantrymen? Eh? Improperly dressed and behaving in such a way as to lose the respect of the men for their officers?"

"Prefect Longius is…" Titus began but Priscus interrupted him.

"I was not addressing you," Priscus snapped at the First Spear Centurion. "Longius, what have you to say for yourself?"

Otto said nothing but spun and launched his missile. The central straw man burst apart and was knocked to the ground. The javelin, thrown with the additional force of his anger, destroyed it. The recruits gave a cheer. Priscus reddened.

"Would you care to have a go, Senior Tribune Priscus?" Otto asked

The tribune turned on his heel and stalked back inside the fortress.

He did not let the matter rest there. That night was an officers' mess evening. Titus Attius sat hunched over his food in hostile silence. Otto was equally withdrawn.

"How is the training coming along, Titus?" Tertius Fuscus enquired.

Before he could answer, Priscus jumped in.

"On that subject, legate, I am still waiting for Prefect Longius' answer to my question. Why was he practising javelin throwing out of uniform with the other ranks?"

"It assists First Spear Centurion Attius to turn recruits into effective soldiers."

"But is it appropriate? That is the question."

"No it isn't" Titus growled. "But anything that anyone, officer or ranker, can do to help these new lads learn their trade is the right thing to do. About that, there's no question."

"I practice sword drill on the posts three times a week under the training officer," Soranus said, trying to lighten the mood.

"No-one asked you to speak, Soranus," Priscus told him.

"Since when does an officer have to be granted permission to speak on mess-nights?" he demanded indignantly.

"Junior officers should be silent," Priscus retorted.

"Prefect Longius is the best javelin thrower I have ever seen in my long service. His expertise gives the men something to strive for. In fact, there is a standing reward of one gold piece for any man who can best him. It's a tradition of The Second Lucan," Titus growled, speaking for the first time that evening.

"And when did this so-called tradition start, centurion?"

"Up on the Rhine a few years ago, tribune."

"I think you meant to say, "Senior Tribune Priscus" did you not?"

"As much as you meant to address me as First Spear Centurion Attius."

"In Germany a few years ago? Not what one might call an "ancient" tradition, then. In any case, behaviour and indeed personnel suited to the barbaric wastes of the borderlands will not necessarily do in a legion garrisoned in Italy," Priscus told him.

Titus, Otto and Soranus looked at Legate Tertius Fuscus for some supporting comment but none came. Tertius was a troubled man. During his service in Upper Germany, he had come to see the legion camp as an island of security in the perilous wilderness surrounding it. The interdependence of officers and men was an unstated pact necessary for mutual survival; this had altered some of his long-term attitudes because they were irrelevant if not harmful in the hostile situation in which he had found himself. But now, things were different. The legion, officers and men, no longer needed to stick together through thick and thin simply to ensure that most of them would be alive the next day. As the fear of imminent danger diminished, he found he was slipping back to his previous ways of thought.

Officers were noble, soldiers were commoners, centurions could become Equestrians if they lived long enough and accumulated sufficient money. Nobles disdained commoners as uncouth beings. If one of them managed to gain wealth or rise in the political world, he could never truly become one of Tertius Fuscus' class. In Germany Tertius would have scoffed at the idea that Otto Longius was letting the side down by joining in weapons drill. Here, close to three Roman cities with nothing but peaceful countryside in between them, he was no longer sure who was in the right. So he said nothing. Nonius Priscus took his silence for assent.

New tribunes arrived, the privileged sons of the Fuscus tribe's political allies. They contributed the minimum they could and spent much of their time hunting in the hills. As the longest serving tribune below Priscus, Soranus should have been next in rank and privilege but he found himself over-worked because he was ordered to perform the duties the young huntsmen avoided. Protesting got him nowhere and alienated his superior officer. It all came to a head one mess-night.

"Tribune Soranus, could you do us all the favour of keeping your crippled hand below the table out of sight? It puts me off my dinner to have to see it," Priscus called down the table.

One of the new tribunes giggled.

"I lost my thumb to a German spear," the humiliated Soranus explained

"Some while ago, you told me you regularly attend sword drill under the training officer. Can't be much use at it if some hairy barbarian can do you that amount of damage. Please keep it in your tunic or something. Your left hand is quite repulsive; reminds me of a chicken's foot."

The colour drained from Soranus' face. Livid and red-eyed with outrage he stood and stared at the senior tribune, murder written all over him. The next day he resigned his commission; the day after he was gone.

"I am sorry for this," Otto told him.

"Not as sorry as I am. I once behaved badly towards you, Otto but I have always counted you as a friend. We have been through a lot together, unlike the fashionable newcomers. I could write to you when I am settled in Rome."

"I would like that, my friend."

The upheaval of Soranus' sudden departure emboldened Priscus. One day several weeks later, Felix limped past him on the parade ground, whistling as usual. He fell silent and saluted the officer without breaking stride.

"You, man," the senior tribune shouted. "Stand still." He walked around Felix examining him. "Don't you come to attention when addressed by an officer?" he demanded.

"Doing my best, sir," Felix replied.

"Don't speak until given permission. Here," he called to a nearby optio, "lend me your stick thing."

He reluctantly handed over his vine-staff. Priscus took it and rapped Felix on his bent leg.

"Come to attention in a proper, soldiery manner," he ordered. Felix hissed with pain but the offending leg could never be straightened again. Priscus hit him again, much harder. Tears welled up in Felix's eyes and he bit his lip against the wave of agony in his knee. The tribune raised the vine-staff high to strike him a third time but the optio's plea made him stop before the blow fell.

"Sir, don't do that I beg you. This is Evocati Felix, his knee was smashed by a German axe," he said.

"In which case, why is the useless cripple still wearing the uniform?"

The centurion was horrified. "Evocati Felix was awarded a gold chain for gallantry during an ambush and received a commendation and medal for his conduct when we were besieged. You mustn't abuse him like this sir, you really mustn't."

"Mustn't? Mustn't! Who do you think you're talking to? When Attius hears of this you will be reduced to the ranks and flogged. I shall see to it personally," Priscus roared and flung the vine-staff back at the optio. He caught one end but the other flipped up and struck his left eyebrow. A few drops of blood welled up.

Felix and the optio looked at each other in shock.. They were both left speechless by the criminal disrespect that had been shown to the centurionate and feared the consequences.

A delegation of junior officers told Titus Attius the story. He did not explode in foul-mouthed rage as they had expected. He nodded grimly and marched away to request an urgent meeting with the legate and the senior tribune.

"When Senior Tribune Nonius Priscus threw the optio's vine-staff at him he committed an outrage. The situation can still be recovered if he will apologise to the man concerned," he told them calmly but in a tone of voice shaking with repressed outrage.

"I will not," Priscus replied with a sneer.

"I was not addressing you, sir," Attius told him. "My remarks were for my legate."

"Impossible, Titus. I cannot countenance a senior officer humiliating himself in front of the men as you suggest," Tertius told him.

"I did not mean a public apology, sir, I know that would be out of the question. I suggest in private, to the optio who was insulted. That will do."

"I will not order Senior Tribune Nonius Fuscus to demean himself in such a manner. That is my final word."

"Demean himself? He has shown contempt for your centurionate in front of the men, on the parade ground and in broad daylight. He has demeaned us all!"

"You have heard my final word," Tertius said through pinched lips.

"In which case I request my discharge from The Second Lucan."

"Come, come, Titus. You speak in haste, I'm sure. Will you not sleep on it at least?"

"I request my discharge from The Second Lucan," First Spear Centurion Titus Attius repeated blankly.

Within three days, he too was gone.

"Everything is changing around us. Be careful which side you choose in such times," was his parting advice to Otto.

That night as he lay in bed, Otto recalled the words of Lucretius, *"Time changes the nature of the world. Everything passes from one state to another and nothing stays as it is."*

Chapter 15

After Titus Attius took his discharge, he was followed by a steady stream of men and junior officers who had either served their full terms of engagement or requested transfers. Naturally, they were the experienced legionaries, corporals and centurions. Replacements were found easily enough but the make-up of the legion had altered. Of the nearly five thousand who had endured the siege of their camp on the Rhine, less than two thousand remained. Otto looked around the table one mess-night and realised with a shock that only he and Tertius Fuscus shared the experiences of that time. The talk around the table was different as well. Most of it was gossip about Rome and the latest scandals. Otto could play no part in these conversations and he became increasingly withdrawn. He was not a member of the inner circle, therefore he was ignored and excluded. This increased his sense of isolation. He turned further inward and was consequently more disregarded.

Spring changed to summer but brought no joy to Otto who now performed his duties conscientiously but avoided the other officers as much as possible. He spent most of his free time riding or with Felix in their quarters. A letter from Rome brought some cheering news.

"To Prefect Otto Longius, Greetings,

I trust all is well with my friends of The Second Lucan and especially with you, Otto. It was a happy day for me when circumstances forced me to resign my commission, although it did not feel like it at the time. Our Emperor has reorganized and increased the number of the Urban Cohorts and I am now tribune of one of them. I command five hundred men. We form up and look menacing if there is unrest on the streets, sometimes we break up riots and combat armed gangs. Hardly the danger and excitement of legion life on the Rhine but at least I often get to sleep in my own bed at night.

My mother wept with relief when I came home and is busy trying to find me a suitable wife. My injured hand is an obstacle to her efforts but she is undaunted. She describes my missing thumb as "a badge of honourable service to Rome". I just call it bad luck.

I have made the acquaintance of a Praetorian officer called Cassius Plancus. He says he met you when you were presented to the Emperor. Cassius asks to be remembered to you and if you recall the night of the Trojan pig? He would not tell me what he meant by that. I hope it is not insulting.

Enough for now. Please reply and tell me how you are getting along under Tertius Fuscus. Do you ever hear from Boxer? How is the awesome Titus Attius?

Rufus Vulso Soranus."

In his loneliness Otto took huge pleasure in reading and re-reading the friendly, candid letter from his former comrade. He wrote back, circumspectly, unwilling to say too much in case his words were intercepted and used against him. This was the start of an infrequent but warm correspondence and of something else. It made Otto decide to reach out to Vitius Longius in Luca. He had clutched his resentment of Sabina's reaction to his joke about marrying Poppaea to him all this time but it had brought him no happiness. He sent a note to the city asking if Vitius would meet him at Massus' barracks the next day at noon then applied for a day's leave. No-one showed any interest in where he was going or why and the permission was granted without comment.

Centurion Massus was a friend to both and was ready to act as referee if needed over a flask of the best wine taken in his private office. In fact, it was difficult to see who was more delighted at the reconciliation, Otto or Vitius.

"I had no right to speak to the lady Sabina as I did. I ask your forgiveness."

"As I ask yours, once again you were offended when a guest in my home."

Otto smiled wryly. "It seems that I have a knack of alarming your wife. At least she no longer thinks I am waiting for the chance to murder her in her bed!"

They laughed and clinked wine cups.

"All over finding a wife, eh? I told Vitius you should have asked me," Massus said.

"It seems too hazardous an undertaking," Otto replied and went on to relate the story of Soranus' injured hand and his mother's effort to obtain a suitable match for him.

"Don't worry, when the time's right I'll sort you out a good 'un," Massus told him

A few days after his return to camp, Otto received a note from Aelia saying how glad she was that the rift had been mended. *"The ties of mutual respect and friendship between us are too strong to be discarded over a foolish quarrel,"* she wrote.

One mess-night, Priscus was well gone in wine when he shouted down the table to where Otto sat alone at the far end.

"Hey, Otto, why don't you get this fabled gold crown out to show your brother officers? Come on, it will be fun., We can all try it on."

"I think not, sir." Otto told him calmly.

Priscus flushed. "I order you to fetch it, now!"

"I respectfully decline," Otto replied.

"Oh, do you? Then I shall send out and have it brought to this table. How do you like that?"

"The Tesserarius guards the legion treasure…"

"I know perfectly well who the Tesserarius is and what he does…"

"Then you will know he would not accept an order to remove any man's personal belongings from it and if pressed, would refer the order to the priests."

"Not much of a feat anyway," said one of the new tribunes. "Everyone knows the Germans are always drunk. Probably find that old king was slightly drunker than Otto and fell of his horse!"

A roar of laughter broke around the table. Otto said nothing and finished his dinner in silence. But that was not the end of the matter. An anonymous wit caused Otto irreparable harm by scrawling a piece of doggerel on a wall where everyone could read it.

"How do I get a crown asks Nonius,

Simple, kill a king like Longius."

From the instant it was read and repeated among the men, Otto's days were numbered.

Priscus never failed to take the opportunity of belittling him to Tertius Fuscus. Otto's morose behaviour played into his hands.

"The man's clearly out of his depth, Tertius. Anyone can see how unhappy he is. It has a bad effect on morale…"

"I cannot simply dismiss him. He was promoted Prefect of cavalry by General Drusus…"

A disastrous event with long-term consequences for the whole of the Roman world sealed Otto's fate. Drusus broke his leg in a riding accident. Infection set in and he died. Some whispered he had been poisoned on orders from Rome but whose orders no-one could, or would, say. His elder brother Tiberius was grief-stricken. Always a bitter man, the death of Drusus snuffed out the last spark of human feeling in him but nevertheless, he walked in front of his brother's funeral cortege all the way from Germany to Rome.

There was no longer any obstacle to the removal of Otto Longius from The Second Lucan. Even if Tertius Fuscus did not take on board all of the poisonous things Nonius Priscus had to say, Fuscus had a cousin who was a senior decurion down south near Brundisium. He had complained that it was too hot and the mosquitoes bothered him. If a vacancy arose nearer to Rome he would be delighted to fill it.

The legate and the senior tribune called Otto into a private meeting.

"Prefect Otto Longius," Tertius began, "As your commanding officer I am reluctantly forced tell you that I am unhappy with your continued presence in my legion. Your surly manner has been noticed and the way you hold yourself aloof from the other officers damages morale. I urge you to do the right thing and resign your commission."

"I took an oath under the eagle. I cannot break it," Otto told him.

"Officers have the right to leave the army if circumstances require it. Nowhere and by no-one is that regarded as oath breaking. You took an oath to serve Rome and Rome thanks you for your service which has now come to an end. You do nothing but harm The Second Lucan if you remain. Go now with honour for the benefit of your legion."

Otto was devasted but made a Herculean effort to remain composed and in control.

"Do it the easy way, Longius," Priscus added. "Otherwise you could be accused of a military crime or even have an unfortunate accident one night…."

Otto looked at him in disgust then turned to the legate.

"Do you intend to let what this man has said pass?"

Tertius Fuscus shrugged but made no further remark.

A crowd of off-duty old sweats stood around the mule-cart while the Tesserarius under the supervision of the chief priest loaded it with Otto's treasure. After talking things over with Otto, Felix, had taken his own discharge; they had agreed to face whatever came next together. He sat immobile on the seat looking straight ahead, studiously avoiding Priscus who was also standing by. Chest after chest filled with small leather bags of gold coins were counted out. The Tesserarius kept the tally with an abacus and the priest nodded his assent as the beads clicked over the wires and the amount grew.

"That must be far too much. Count it again," Priscus complained.

"It is correct. I have supervised the filling of the chests and I am satisfied that all is exactly as it should be," the priest told him.

"What about all those looted silver arm-rings he wears. Surely the legion is entitled to a share of them?" Priscus demanded.

"They were all won in single combat, sir. Personal property of Otto Longius," he was informed.

"Why don't you fight him for 'em, Tribune Prickus?" a voice shouted out of the crowd of legionaries.

A burst of laughter followed but when Priscus spun around, he could see nothing but straight faces. He strode away without looking back. The laughter rose again and followed him across the parade ground. Otto was handed a final sack, this one containing silver; his past month's pay less deductions. The priest asked him to acknowledge a receipt for eighty-two thousand six hundred and thirty-five denarii. He reached down from the back of Djinn, signed and took back the priest's copy of his will in favour of Lucius. His connection with The Second Lucan was now severed and he was no longer an army officer. The cart rattled out of the fortress with his grey gelding tied behind. Otto followed without a backward glance.

He was half a mile on his way when he heard approaching hoofbeats. The decurion ordered his turma to halt.

"Routine patrol, sir," he told Otto. "Happened to be out this way so thought we might as well accompany you into Luca. Could be bandits around, you never know."

"You will be in trouble with the senior tribune if he finds out," Otto replied.

"But he won't, will he men?"

"No sir!" the troopers shouted in unison.

At the city gate they turned back with a final salute. Otto and Felix entered alone. Massus took one look at the contents of the cart and detailed six of his men to escort Otto around to the bank.

"I am no longer an officer. I have resigned my commission..."

"Makes no difference to me," Massus told him. "I don't want citizens robbed and murdered in the streets in broad daylight, let alone Equestrians. Look very bad on my monthly report, that would."

The chests were deposited. Otto rented a private box in which he placed his gold crown and cup. His business was done. They stamped back over the paving stones to Massus' headquarters.

"I need a favour of you," Otto said.

"Ask away," the centurion replied

"Can you store my weapons and armour for me? I'm going to be staying at the Wayfarer's Inn and I think they might be too much of a temptation for some of the other guests."

"Oi, you two," Massus shouted to a pair of his men idly eavesdropping, "Get this kit into the armoury where it stays untouched, mind, untouched until further notice."

Otto gave the centurion twenty denarii to reward his temporary guards and pay for storage before making his way over to the inn. As soon as he was out of sight, Massus sent a runner to Vitius Longius with the news.

Otto and Felix had barely put their belongings into their rooms and seen to the stabling of their two horses and mules when Vitius burst in, followed more sedately by Massus.

"My dear Otto, whatever has happened?" Vitius demanded.

All four of them sat at a quiet table in the dining room with bread and wine in front of them while Otto told his story. Felix added his own experiences.

"This is appalling, unheard of!" Vitus exclaimed once the tale was told.

Massus snorted and raised his eyebrows. "Unheard of? Why do you think I am serving here as city garrison centurion? I was the famed "Cyclops Massus", saviour of the army and holder of a silver spear. For six months I was on my way to being First Spear Centurion of my legion and then it began. Innuendo, belittlement, always given the worst duties, why? Envy; but not from the centurionate, no, from senior officers. I am common and they are noble. They resented that my commoner name was known and their noble ones were not. So I took this appointment and I am not discontented with it. If anyone outside of Rome's privileged circle of influence rises up, be sure he will be cut down. Otto's golden crown has cost him his commission as surely as my silver spear cost me my promotion prospects. That's how it is, cheers," he finished and threw back a cup of wine.

After a long silence while they all contemplated the injustices of this wicked world, Vitius spoke up.

"What now, Otto? What will you do?"

He shrugged. "The army does not want me. My life would not last many days among the Suevi over the Rhine. I have land here…

"And friends," Massus said.

"Good friend," Vitius added.

In an uncharacteristic gesture of affection, Otto placed a hand on both of their shoulders.

"I have land and friends," he continued. "I shall stay here and lead the life of a farmer."

Massus and Vitius passed a quick grin between them, noticed by Felix who smirked as well. The thought of Otto chewing a straw while he leaned over a gate admiring his sheep was hilarious.

"You'll need a house then. Can't live in an inn forever," Massus remarked.

"Have a word with your banker," Vitius suggested. "He will know someone who is desperate to sell but doesn't want to advertise the fact. You'll find a bargain. I'll go with you if you like..."

Otto frowned. "It seems like taking advantage of another man's bad luck to get the best price," he said.

"Which is what farmers do all the time so get used to it!" Massus told him.

There was a small villa for sale half a mile outside of the city overlooking the river. It had a perimeter wall, garden and orchard, stables, bathhouse and outbuildings. It was built of brick under a tile roof. The mosaic floors were not of the highest artistry but were in good condition. It was close enough to Luca to be secure against bandit raids but far enough off to be private. Otto bought it for twenty-two thousand denarii because the owner was up to his eyes in debt due to his faith that it was only a matter of time before the dice ran in his favour. They never did.

Vitius brought his family to inspect it. Felix led them from room to room explaining the special features of each one.

"Catches the morning sun, ladies. Opposite the main gate so a good view of whoever might be coming or going..."

"You will need furniture and household slaves," Sabina told him, as if there was no difference between buying a chair or a human being.

"And a wife, perhaps?" Aelia added mischievously.

Sabina flushed. "Otto, I am sorry..." she began but he cut her off.

"No need, there is nothing to be said. I think we should accept the fact that we will fall out from time to time but let's always forgive each other and remain friends."

"I don't want any slaves," Otto told Felix once the visitors had gone.

"Well you can't expect me to do everything. What am I for here anyway? Do I stay or what?"

"You stay and your position is second in command. You get your keep and a hundred denarii a month. That suit you?"

"It'll do. Now, about these slaves…"

The slave-dealer sized Otto up by his equestrian's tunic, soldiers' boots, belt and sword.

"Greetings general," he said with a gap-toothed smile. "What can I do for you today, noble sir?"

Otto remained silent, unable to bring himself to say he was there to buy people.

"House slaves, good strong 'uns. None of your runaway farm-hands lashed half to death," Felix called from his seat high on the cart.

"Nothing much in at the moment, new shipment coming in at the end of the month. I could let you have a gander at the leftovers but they won't do for a refined gent like yourself, sir…"

"Show me," Otto told him brusquely.

He walked into a walled courtyard with iron cages on three sides. The stench of unwashed flesh and faeces made his eyes water. He gagged. The slave-dealer no longer noticed. As he had said, most of the cages were empty but a few on the far wall were still occupied. He stopped and turned to Otto.

"Look, there's nothing here for you. This lot will go to the farms or the mines next auction. Do yourself a favour and come back at the end of the month when the good stuff comes in."

"Show me," Otto repeated.

"Alright, a cook, then, I suppose" he unlocked a cage and flung the gate back. "You, out," he ordered.

A ragged woman in her late twenties slunk out hunching her shoulders against a possible whiplash. The skin of her right arm and half of one cheek were red and puckered.

"She was a cook. The oil spilled on the fire, blazed up and left her like that. Her owners didn't want her ugly mug around the place. Said you wouldn't be interested."

"Get back in," he snapped but Otto stopped him from pushing the her inside.

"What is your name, woman?" he asked.

"Tullia," she mumbled.

"Tullia, sir," the dealer said and slapped the back of her head. "Tell you what, she has a son in there with her. Wizened little bugger like a sick monkey, only a few months old. I'll chuck him in with her if we can come to a price. No guarantee mind, he's on his way out in my opinion."

The next cage was opened. A barely half-covered pubescent girl was dragged out.

"There you are, almost a virgin."

"What does that mean?" Otto asked.

"Lightly fucked. Her master got on top of her so her mistress threw her out. No two for one with her though. She's bled since she's been here. One for the brothel, probably. Do you want to see more?"

Out of the last cage walked a tall, well-proportioned man. He looked like he might have been in his early thirties but it was difficult to tell because his face was a mass of new and old bruises; bright purple and fading through green to yellow. He had boot-stud injuries on his legs.

"Caught a fever and went deaf a year or so ago," the slave dealer told Otto.

"What are all the marks on him?"

"Oh, kicks and punches when he didn't catch on what was wanted quick enough. Can make you very impatient, a deaf man can…"

"Five hundred for all you have shown me," Otto said.

"Oh come off it, a thousand at least!"

Otto turned on his heel and walked away.

"Alright then, alright but it's stealing off an honest tradesman that's what it is!"

They left the city seated on the back of the cart, ragged and stinking. Felix drove them down to the river where Otto ordered them to strip and wash. Felix was sent back and returned with some clean, second-hand clothes; ill-fitting and unsuitable but at least covering their modesty. They stood in a line looking terrified. Otto found that Tullia's son was called Pollux; a famished mite with the sharp face of starvation. The girl was Didia. He smoothed the riverbank sand with the toe of his boot and wrote "Name?" with a stick before handing it to the deaf man. He looked at Otto with something approaching a smile, bent and wrote "Libius".

Back on the cart he had them driven to the magistrate's office where he formally gave each one their freedom. They looked at him in confused amazement.

"Now you can go where you want. You can come and work for me as free people. You will be fed, clothed and given wages, not much in the way of money but something." He wrote his words on a borrowed wax tablet for Libius.

They decided to entrust their futures to this strange, blond giant who looked like a barbarian but spoke good Latin. They settled into his new villa and began to perform their duties under the watchful eye of Felix. Sabina was horrified when she visited and saw his "staff".

"Who would want to live surrounded by oddities and cripples?" she asked. Felix walked past her ostentatiously hobbling. "I exclude our brave legionaries injured fighting for Rome against the barbarians…" she gabbled then saw Otto grinning at her. "Oh just be silent, before you even say it," she snapped.

Otto tried to take an interest in his farmlands but his heart was not in it. He walked around his grounds, he hunted, he had long written conversations with Libius who turned out to be a well-educated and interesting man. He had an encyclopaedic knowledge of plants and trees and when his master did not recognise them by the names he wrote down, he drew them for him. He drew so well that Otto put him to redecorating the inside walls of the house with imaginary gardens of flowers, birds and animals. The results were spectacular, if the perspective was a little skewed.

Saturnalia came around. Felix ordered the household not to involve Otto on pain of dismissal. Winter gripped, released and spring arrived over the hilltops with milder winds and a green flush on trees and meadows.

Otto rode for hours into the hills and woodlands or fished in the river. He had given up his pretence of studying agriculture. It was a mystery to him and he accepted it would always be so. He roamed about his estate or the villa, increasingly lost and alone. Then Massus came.

"Ride with me tomorrow. I'm going up into the hills to visit an old friend. You might like him."

"Who is he?"

"I'll tell you as we go; it'll pass the time. It's a good hour or so's ride. If we're lucky, we might be asked to stay for a bite to eat. Still got your mail shirt and a lance?" Otto nodded. "Wear 'em. From a distance you could still pass as a warrior."

Otto went in to ask where his equipment was.

"In here," Felix told him.

His chain mail hung on a rack. It was shining under the lightest coat of oil. His helmet and best sword were propped up beside it. His army boots and belt had been newly polished and his leather subarmalis waxed and rubbed to a dull gleam.

"Why have you cleaned all this up?"

"I always keep your kit like this," Felix told him.

"How did the helmet get here? I left it at the barracks."

"Fetched it the other day when I went into the city. Massus mentioned you might be needing it for your trip…"

At that moment, Libius walked in carrying a newly cleaned oval shield and a sharpened lance. He smiled and nodded to Otto as he passed them to Felix.

"What's going on here?"

"Nothing," Felix replied with an attempt at wide-eyed innocence. "Look, you rattle round in this house like a pea on a drum or go out on your own looking miserable and come back hours later looking just as miserable. Take this little trip with Massus, do you good to have some company. I'll give your arm-rings a clean up…"

He mounted Djinn, groomed to perfection, under the smiling gaze of his people. They were unrecognisable as the wretched rejects he had first encountered. Tullia felt secure and valued. It showed in her relaxed posture and calm eyes. Little Pollux was taking his first steps on chubby legs. Didia had grown and filled out; Tullia had become a mother to her. Libius' handsome face was unmarked.

Felix waved, and Otto and Massus were off early on a sunny, April morning full of greenery and birdsong.

They rode along the riverbank for half an hour then turned off along a valley leading inland to the east. They travelled in silence for a few minutes until Massus began to speak.

"Right then, I'll tell you all about my friend Julius Albus. Long story; goes back to the Divine Julius early on in his wars in Gaul. He was short of men, you see, so he offered citizenship to a tribe in Cisalpine Gaul in exchange for them taking the soldier's oath. He ended up with a whole legion full of these big, blond "Romans" who didn't speak a word of Latin to start with. Anyways, there was a huge stink about it in Rome but they fought well and the rest of Caesar's army took to them, eventually. The legion still marches; they call it The Alaudae, which is to say "The Skylarks"; no idea why. As it happens, a few of them got knocked on the head and they needed replacements among which was my friend Julius Albus. Of course, that wasn't his real name, that would have been something peculiar ending in "ix" but it's how I've always known him. He was good at his trade and rose to be the second centurion of his legion. When their Tesserarius was killed, he took on the duties on a temporary basis but the men and officers trusted him so much, he retained the position as their banker and guard commander. He retired with a spotless reputation, medals welded all over his harness and a shedload of money; Caesar's lads were never short of loot. That's the man you're going to meet."

"Sounds interesting."

They altered their course again, heading a little north, down a defile and into a pleasant valley with a broad stream running through it. It was lightly wooded with ploughed fields. Lines of beech-wood posts with grapevines strung between them climbed up into the south-facing hillside. There were fenced pastures in which cattle and horses were penned, Sheep roamed freely cropping the abundant grass. A fine villa stood in the middle. Massus reined in.

"This is the next part of Julius Albus's story. There he is, a likely, youngish man with more money than he knows what to do with and here is his late father-in-law's estate; senatorial family, lost nearly everything in the Civil War except this land. Julius bails them out, marries the daughter, Clodia, and is enrolled in the Equestrian Order. He has one son who's a decurion up north and a daughter. Come, on we might be on for lunch."

They cantered into a yard where a tall man in his fifties stood with his hands on his hips watching them ride in. He was dressed in a plain tunic with a broad leather belt and soldiers' boots. A blade somewhere in between a short sword and a long knife in size hung scabbarded by his side. His grizzled hair was cropped close and he was beardless but sported long, Gallic moustaches falling below his chin on either side of a wide mouth. His eyes were almost as pale as Otto's.

"Greetings Centurion Massus," he called.

"And greetings to you Julius. Let me introduce my friend the Equestrian Otto Longius, former Prefect of Cavalry and holder of a gold military crown. Otto, this is former Centurion and Tesserarius, the Equestrian Julius Albus."

Otto bowed in his saddle and Julius returned the salute.

"Dismount and take some refreshment," their host told them.

His groom saw to their horses and a few minutes later they sat at a stone table under a shady tree drinking good wine. Otto had removed his helmet which he placed on the table with his lance and shield leaning against it.

"It seems I'm honoured by the company of famous warriors; Massus with his silver spear and you, Otto Longius, with a gold crown. How did you come by it?"

"I killed a Marcomanni warlord in battle. He called himself King Helmund."

"If he said he was a king and his men agreed, then a king he was. Don't do yourself down by calling him a mere warlord, young man," Julius told him with a smile. "I believe you have an estate near Luca, also as a result of killing this king, or maybe some other one?"

"No, sir, it was for saving my legate's life in an ambush. In his generosity, the Emperor granted me citizenship, elevated me to the Equestrian order and awarded me the money to support my rank."

"And that magnificent black horse?"

"The Emperor's gold paid for him."

"But not the arm-rings stretching from both of your wrists up past your elbows. Those you earned yourself, I take it."

Otto grinned. "Their former owners didn't hand them over willingly."

They all laughed briefly, more as an indication that they were comfortable in each other's company than at Otto's attempt at wit.

"What do you think of my farmlands?" Julius asked.

"To be honest, sir, my opinion is worth little. I have tried but I am no farmer. I rely on my steward who is an honest man."

Julius raised his eyebrows. "What makes you think he is honest?"

"He is too terrified of me not to be."

Both Massus and Julius roared with laughter this time.

"Now that is a damn good reason. In any case, who ever heard of a German farmer?" his host asked.

They laughed again and more wine was drunk. Julius went silent for a moment and then seemed to come to a decision. With a slight nod to Massus, he rose to his feet.

"Come and meet my family," he said and strode off without waiting to see if they were following. They walked under wide eaves into a tile floored chamber with plain white walls. Two women were sitting over a pile of sewing; repairing tunic hems and adding ribbon to necks and sleeves. They looked up when the visitors entered.

"My wife, Clodia," Julius said.

"You are welcome here, sir," she told Otto graciously with a bend of her neck. "And you of course, our good friend Massus."

The other woman stood up and looked directly at Otto. He saw a young woman, dark-haired, the cornflower blue of her eyes accentuated by her olive skin, tall; close to six feet in her sandals, broad-shouldered with an athletic length of arm and leg nearly visible through the light material of her blue dress. She smiled. Otto felt like he had been punched, hard. His senses swam momentarily and he found himself unable to say anything in his confusion. She noticed his embarrassment and smiled, a hint of rose mounting in her face before she lowered her head and turned away.

"I forget my manners," Julius went on. "Clodia, this is the equestrian and former cavalry officer Otto Longius. Otto, my wife and my daughter Lollia."

"Ladies," Otto mumbled in reply and felt too big and clumsy to be in this room in his heavy mail shirt.

The lunch that followed flew by in a haze for Otto. He wanted to look at Lollia but thought it would be rude to stare so he avoided her gaze, subtly as he thought. Finesse was not a strong part of his social skills so it was obvious to everyone, including Lollia who tried not to show her pleasure at her conquest. That too was plain to see.

"My daughter is a great admirer of horses, Otto. Perhaps you would show her your charger if I had him brought round to the front of the villa?" Julius suggested.

The two young people would be alone, it was true but they would be outside in broad daylight and plain sight so the decencies would be upheld.

"Well?" Massus enquired once they had left the room.

"Blessings on you, Massus," Clodia said and kissed his cheek. "It seems as you were right. They are taken with each other."

No-one gave down to earth Centurion Massus credit for social manoeuvring but he had said he would help his friends find a husband for their daughter and perhaps he had succeeded.

Lollia was eighteen, a little old to be unmarried and unattached. This had begun to cause her mother a great deal of worry. The young men of their acquaintance were intimidated by the girl; they did not want to be half a head shorter than their betrothed. In addition, although brought up by her mother as a proper young Roman lady should be, she had inherited a Gallic freedom of spirit and action from her father. She was a strong young woman and it was clear she would not be forced to play a submissive role. But Otto now, a proven warrior, towering above her, accustomed to women of independent mind; he was a distinct possibility as a suitor.

"Still, a German, a bloody-handed Suevian…" Julius mused with lingering doubts.

"You both know the Longius family in Luca, don't you?" Massus asked. They signalled that they did. "Visit them. They have a strong connection with Otto, in fact, he took their name as a mark of his respect for them. They can tell you what sort of a man he is."

Chapter 16

"To be honest, he terrified me when my son first brought him home," Sabina told Clodia as they sat in the garden of her home with Aelia; Poppaea and Lollia had been sent out of hearing to look at the flowers. "I still get a shiver down my spine when he looks at me with those wintry eyes," she shuddered, "like chips of ice. But he saved my son Lucius' life when he was set upon by thieves in the city one night. What greater service could he do us?"

"I think I heard about that. Didn't young Servius run away and leave Lucius to his fate?" Clodia asked.

"He went to find help," Sabina told her firmly, keeping up the diplomatic fiction.

"I will be frank, ladies," Clodia said. "Do you think he would make a good husband?"

"He has the income of a sound estate. He is a decorated former officer and an equestrian. He does not drink excessively nor is he addicted to the dice box. He has instinctive good manners although he is socially awkward. Altogether, I think he would make an excellent match...."

"But not for your Poppaea," Clodia said drily.

"Look at the girls," Aelia told her. They were a good way away standing with their backs to the ladies. Poppaea was the average five feet and maybe half an inch; Lollia was the same half an inch under six feet. Poppaea's head came to the level of Lollia's shoulder. "Otto is around six inches taller than Lollia, the same difference in height between my late husband and me. After marriage the babies are sure to come along. I will say no more out of decency."

"No need," Clodia said. "Your point is made." She sighed. "If only Lollia had not grown so immensely tall, there would have been no problem but as it is…"

"Nevertheless she is beautiful. That counts for nearly everything with men."

They all nodded their weary agreement.

"Are you going to marry him if they let you?" Poppaea was asking Lollia while they supposedly examined the flower beds.

"Don't know; what's he like, really?"

"Well, he's killed loads of people and he wrestled our guard dog just for the fun of it. But he's kind and likes to laugh. I would marry him if were allowed but I'm not."

"Why not?"

"They're frightened he'd split me up the middle. You know, on our wedding night! Do you think he's that much bigger than other men all over?"

They burst into giggles then howls of laughter which floated down the paths of the garden to where the older ladies were discussing delicate matters unfitted for the ears of their virginal daughters.

Julius cross-examined Vitius on Otto's financial standing.

"Julius Albus, normally, I would answer by referring you to Otto himself but I appreciate the seriousness of your interest. Although he is no blood-relative of mine, we have the strongest ties of mutual regard so I believe I may speak as if I were his uncle. His lands return an income more than adequate to support Lollia in a manner appropriate to her rank. His house is well-situated and in good repair. He can lay his hands on nearly one hundred thousand denarii lodged with his bankers and he is without vice, to the best of my knowledge, so there is no danger of his fortune being frittered away on whores or in gaming houses. I cannot say more than that I am proud that he has chosen to adopt our family name."

Clodia Albus had decided it would be a good thing if Lollia were to marry Otto and enlisted the tactical and logistical support of Sabina. They began their campaign to make it happen without enquiring if the potential bride and groom would be happy with each other. In truth, they had no need to do so. The looks passing between the young pair said enough. Vitius and Sabina hosted a dinner to which the Albus family and Otto were invited. For reasons neither mother could understand, Poppaea and Lollia insisted on going to look at Ursus, the Molossian hound, before they entered the dining room. Like well-mannered Roman girls, they sat at the foot of their parent's couches throughout the meal, not speaking unless spoken to.

"It seems from all I hear, Otto Longius, that you are a young man without fault, a very paragon…" Clodia said.

"True, if you do not count his eccentric taste in household slaves." Sabina responded. "They are really, shall we say, an "unusual" sight?."

"How so, Otto Longius?" Clodia asked, suddenly wary. Was his household composed of tattooed barbarians or dancing girls and ex-gladiators?

"My people were unwanted; unfortunates who needed only an opportunity to live with dignity," Otto responded, uncomfortable at the direction the conversation was taking.

"Noble, I am sure but why were they unwanted in the first place? Surely there must have been something unpleasantly wrong with them?" Clodia asked.

She and Sabina shared a complicit smile at the undoubted naivety of this young man in taking on wiser people's discards. Otto bridled and flashed an irritated look at her. For the first time, Clodia saw the stare that Sabina had mentioned. She shivered.

"I have an excellent cook called Tullia. She was burnt on part of her face and one arm when hot oil flared up on her. She was sold by her owners because they no longer liked the look of her. She has a little son, Pollux. When I bought her he was dying. Now he chatters and toddles about the place. Didia my housemaid was raped by a cruel master and flung onto the slave market by an even crueller mistress.

Libius, an educated, thoughtful man, fell deaf after an illness three years ago. He was beaten about the head and face for not being able to respond to orders quickly enough. He is my gardener and decorates the walls of my home. Oh, and my major-domo is an ex-legionary called Felix who limps because a German battle-axe smashed his left leg. After he was discharged as medically unfit, he became attached to me and my dearest friend Lucius Longius. Felix was awarded a gold chain for courage by acclamation of his comrades and a medal for his part in the defence of our besieged camp. These are the folk of my household. None of them are slaves, I freed them all. I will not support slavery where I can avoid it."

"But if everyone did as you, the whole system would fall apart; it would be dreadful," Clodia exclaimed.

"It would not," Otto replied. "It would be better. My people can leave my service if they are unhappy or if I do not treat them fairly. This makes me try to be a better man. And I am not the one who is frightened of having my throat cut in the night by some desperate slave abused or flogged into madness."

"How could society function without slaves, Otto? What a ridiculous idea!," Sabina suggested.

"The wealthy would be poorer by the wages they had to pay the people who worked for them and richer in humanity because they would no longer be free to act viciously and cruelly on a whim."

Lollia's eyes were shining in admiration. Aelia caught her glance and nodded at her in approval.

"I didn't know we had a philosopher in our company," Julius said, trying to change the subject before things became even more controversial.

"I am no philosopher, sir. I see the world as it is but I do not have to accept everything upon it."

Otto decided he would return the hospitality he had received and ask Julius Albus, Clodia and Lollia to attend as well.

"We shall have to find a catering company who can bring the food in for the feast…." he began.

"Bring food in? What am I, then, a scullery maid? Tell me how many guests and the date you want to hold the party and I'll cook your feast in a proper manner, not like some greasy caterer with rats and roaches all over his kitchen!" Tullia scolded him.

"Alright, alright, you shall cook but I don't know what to do about having ladies here if they need to…"

"You put a table with a mirror and a basin of clean water on it in a side room. You provide a chamber pot or two behind a screen and some towels That's how it's done, sir." Didia told him.

"Why can't they just go to the jakes like the rest of us?" Felix asked.

"Oh yes," Tullia said. "In the middle of dinner one of them is going to stand up and ask, "Where's the jakes then? I need a piss." That's very polite that is, I don't think."

"Well I didn't know," Felix grumbled.

"No, you didn't, so perhaps you and the master should leave it to them as does."

They scrubbed and polished the villa until it shone. They hired couches and a flautist. They garlanded the dining room with flowers. Tullia cooked roasted capons and quail in honey. She stewed a brace of hares in red wine with pine nuts. There was fruit, cheese, freshly baked bread, steamed vegetables, bowls of garum and Falernian wine. A side room was tastefully decorated with vases of blooms, a table and chair set against one wall and the modesty screen placed across a corner.

When everything was laid out and the visitors due to arrive, Otto thanked his small staff with a beaming face. He had not completely believed it was possible that they could transform his house as they had done. He was delighted and it showed. They glowed under the appreciation and it was a happy home that greeted the first to arrive. Didia led the ladies away to refresh themselves leaving Otto, Vitius and Julius waiting their return before going in to dine.

Otto took a deep breath, went red, then pale and spoke in an unnaturally loud voice.

"Julius Albus, sir, I admire your daughter Lollia Albus and I would like to offer her marriage."

"Otto Longius, that strikes me as a very good plan. I accept your offer."

"You do?" Otto asked in genuine surprise. He had prepared complicated arguments, sure that Julius would be reluctant.

"Of course I do. You're a grand match for her and her mother will be very pleased."

"But what about Lollia?"

"What about her? She'll do as she's told."

At that moment, the ladies returned, escorted by Didia who would leave them at the dining room door but be ready to attend to any needs they might have later.

"Wife, daughter," Julius said, without any preamble. "The Equestrian Otto Longius has asked for Lollia in marriage. I have consented."

Clodia took Lollia's hand and brought her forward. "Kiss Otto Longius, my dear," she instructed. Lollia kissed him, briefly and blushed. "There, now you are betrothed. We shall get the contract drawn up as soon as possible."

Otto was elated. As far as he was concerned, Felix and Libius preformed the duties of butler and waiter to perfection, the food Tullia presented was the Ambrosia of the Gods, and the flute music better than anything he had ever heard. Now he could look at Lollia openly, he could talk with her, he could show her around his home, soon to be hers, accompanied by her mother for the sake of propriety. Lollia told

Tullia her dinner had been superb and that she hoped she would want to cook for them after she and her master were married. She asked Didia to be sure to stay on as she was such an excellent lady's maid. She made herself pleasant to Libius, as best she could, and to Felix.

The Albus family left first. Otto handed Clodia and Lollia into their carriage, was kissed again, by both of them and watched them rattle off into the distance. Sabina cried and kissed him, Poppaea blushed and pecked his cheek. Aelia took his hand and looked up into his eyes.

"You have chosen well, Otto. Lollia Albus will prove to be the wife you need to complete your life. Cherish her. She thinks she loves you because she is young and full of dreams; make sure she has reason to love you truly when you are one. To have an advantageous marriage where, in addition, the young couple have warm feelings for each other is a true blessing."

The contract was written and signed. Lollia came with five thousand denarii, her jewels, her clothes and a set of bedroom furniture suitable for a lady's boudoir. Otto had consulted Aelia about suitable gifts for her mother and father. For his bride he had something special; the gold cup given to him by the late General Drusus now called Germanicus. On the Ides of May, the priest cut the white kid's throat and examined its guts. The omens were favourable; the priest always said when they were at a wedding. Why disappoint people and lose a generous tip? Most of them would only marry anyway and live to regret it or otherwise. Lollia came to him wearing a saffron coloured veil and matching shoes over a white dress. He carried her over the threshold and they feasted with her family and his friends. Their wedding night was satisfactory. Both of them were virgins but neither had any inhibitions about sex or any other bodily functions. They came together naturally, explored each other and enjoyed their mutual pleasure without guilt.

For a week or two, Otto treated Lollia as if she was fragile and might easily break. Then he came to realise she was strong, bold and quite capable of looking after herself. She told him she could ride but had been forbidden to do so. Her mother had been afraid she would break her hymen. That was no longer of any concern. Her legs were long enough for her to ride Otto's grey gelding. Wearing boots and a tunic with her hair tied back under a straw hat, Lollia roamed the estate lands and hillsides for miles around with Otto beside her riding Djinn. She asked him to teach her how to use a sword and a lance and he was happy to indulge her. Otto found he had two wives. The demure Lollia with her face and hair covered by a veil when they went into the city to call on their friends or her mother visited. The other was the free spirit galloping her horse and laughing beside him or sweating as she thrust and parried with a short sword in the privacy of their walled courtyard. She was like the Roman ladies he saw all around him in public; when alone, she was like one of the powerful, confident women of the northlands he had known as a boy.

She was happy to have a husband who was strong enough to allow her to be herself but respected the conventions in public for both their sakes. The only cloud on her horizon was quickly blown away. Her mother and Sabina had spoken to her about the household staff.

"A deaf man? A scarred cook and that limping old soldier? You must make your husband find you some more suitable slaves. It won't do to be talked about you know," Clodia told her.

"Be clever, though; don't come straight out with it, my dear," Sabina added. "Men are easily manipulated but confrontation seldom achieves anything with them."

"Tullia is an excellent cook, her little boy is lovely. Didia is a skilful hairdresser and Libius, the "deaf man", is teaching me how to draw and paint flowers. Limping Felix is a war hero. No, I like things as they are but thank you both for the advice."

"For your own good, you really must make some changes...."

"Mother, Lady Sabina, I believe I am the mistress of this house. It will be run as I choose..."

They said no more to her on the subject. Lollia did not repeat the conversation to Otto but did speak to Aelia about it.

"You were right to stand up to them, Lollia. You must let them know you are in charge. In any case, I agree with Otto; it must be better to be served by free people than slaves."

Their idyll lasted the summer. Long days of spending each moment together; riding in the cool morning air, swimming in the green depths of the river and drying in the warm air of secluded glades; dozing, limbs intertwined, under the arbour on hot afternoons hearing the crickets chirruping all around them. Then there were their nights. It was as near to perfection as possible but it came to an end one day in September.

An Imperial Courier, cantered into their courtyard on a foam-flecked horse.

"You are the Prefect Otto Longius?" he demanded.

"Former prefect," Otto replied.

The courier made no remark but handed a leather scroll case out of his satchel. The wax was sealed with the Sphinx of Augustus. Otto signed the receipt and began to offer rest and water but the horseman shook his head and rode off as quickly as he had arrived. Otto opened the scroll.

"To the Prefect Otto Longius. You are to attend the Emperor in Rome. Leave Luca as soon as you receive this. Your permit to use the Imperial Relay Stations is enclosed.

Menities"

No greetings, no friendly aside; an order and one clearly to be obeyed without the slightest hesitation. Otto passed it over to Lollia.

"What can it mean? It's very cold; have you done something wrong?" She was picking up the same impression as he had. "It doesn't say the "former" or "ex" prefect. Do you think he knows you have resigned?"

"The Emperor gets to know everything, sooner or later. Lollia, you understand I must leave straight-away? You had better go back to your father's house…"

"No."

"For your security, please?"

"No. I'm closer to the city here. I have Felix and Libius on hand. I'll be safe enough."

"As a Roman husband I can insist that you obey me."

"You can but I'll never forgive you."

Felix drove Otto into Luca where he stopped at the barracks to pick up a post-horse.

"I'll keep an eye on your house while you're away. Good luck," Massus said.

The Emperor kept his head down examining a document in the same room where Otto been given his first audience.

"Why aren't you in uniform, Prefect Longius?" Augustus growled after letting Otto wait a long time, becoming more nervous by the minute.

"I am no longer a prefect, sir. I resigned," he replied.

"Resigned? Who gave you the right to resign? Eh? Did I say you could, eh?" Augustus almost shouted. Otto was so shocked he could not speak. "Come on, answer. You look as scared as a man giving an elephant a penny bun for the first time. I'll answer for you. No-one.

No-one said you could walk away from your duty and your emperor on a whim…"

"But, sir… Otto began, piqued at the unfair direction this interview was taking.

"Don't dare interrupt. Listen. You are a prefect until I say otherwise. Spoken with Rufus Vulso Soranus, know what went on. It enrages me. Battle-hardened legion where I want it for home defence and in a year, officers and best part of the men who served on the frontier are gone. Who replaced them? Cousins, brothers-in-law, political allies. Disgraceful. I dream of restoring the old Republic of Rome but I am thwarted. Intrigue, petty corruption everywhere. You are an Imperial Military Prefect appointed by your Emperor. You have responsibility for the city garrisons of Pisae, Luca and Spedia. Salary twenty, no eighteen thousand denarii, permanent mounted escort of six. Second 'em out of The Second Lucan cavalry to be maintained at the legion's expense. I require your commission read out to the assembled officers and men before you pick who you want. That's it, off with you."

Otto saluted and marched towards the door. Augustus called after him.

"You are my man, Otto Longius, not the army's. I will have work for you in the future. Best wishes on your marriage. Menities has my gift to your bride as well as your paperwork."

Otto thanked him, but the Emperor waved him away and returned to his scroll.

Massus stood at the head of a guard of honour as Otto rode back into Luca. They came to attention and saluted as he stepped down off his tired horse.

"Greetings Imperial Military Prefect Longius," the centurion said with a broad smile.

"How did you know?"

"Courier. Will you be wanting to inspect the men and the barracks now?"

"Very funny; I just want to get home. Oh, one thing, I am to have an escort. Can you accommodate six troopers and their mounts?"

"Yes, no problems with the men, the horses will be a tight fit but we'll manage, no doubt, sir."

"Centurion Massus, is the "siring" going to be necessary?"

"In front of the men, absolutely necessary, sir!"

Lollia opened the package Otto had brought her all the way from Rome. She unrolled the scroll inside and read.

"To the Lady Lollia Longius. Greetings.

Best wishes on your marriage to my esteemed Imperial Military Prefect Otto Longius. May good health and prosperity be yours and your children's.

Augustus.

She held it up and showed it to Otto, wide-eyed. "It's from the Emperor. I've got a letter from Emperor Augustus!"

"Yes, what has he given you for your wedding present?"

She prised open the lid of a carved onyx box sitting among the wrappings. It contained a pair of earrings. Each one was a delicate cage of gold filigree holding a pearl as large as her little fingernail. She held them up and was about to put them on when Otto asked her to wait and called in their servants.

They looked a little apprehensive as they lined up but Lollia's radiant face reassured them.

"You all know I was called away to Rome; well, I have come back with good news. Our Emperor has appointed me to his staff. I am a military officer once more. He has also sent a marriage gift to Lady Lollia. Didia, help your mistress," Otto ordered. Didia came forward and threaded the gold wires through the piercings in Lollia's earlobes. "In view of the good fortune that has come to this house, I am increasing your salaries by one quarter as of today. If we perform our duties as best we can, we will give the Gods reason to continue to favour us."

Lollia scribbled the gist on a wax tablet for Libius so that he could understand why everyone was celebrating.

"I'm coming with you to the fortress," Felix said in a voice that showed he was not going to be denied.

"Of course you are. We'll need the cart to carry the escort's kit and personal gear."

"I'm going to be in my uniform," Felix told Otto, again daring him to refuse.

"Good, make sure to wear your gold chain as well."

There was an unfamiliar face commanding the guard as Otto rode up. Djinn's black hide gleamed as he pranced up to the glowering walls. Otto wore his parade armour polished to blinding perfection. Felix sat arrow straight on the seat of his mule-cart.

"Imperial Military Prefect Otto Longius to see Legate Tertius Fuscus. Open the gate, now!" he demanded.

He dismounted at the steps of the Praetorium and handed Djinn's reins to a passing legionary. They recognised each other from the old days.

"Pleasure to see you sir, coming back to us?" the soldier asked.

"Thank you but no, other business. I'm glad to see you looking well and not shivering in the cold like we all used to eh?"

The guard admitted him to the secretaries' office.

"If you would care to wait, sir," one of them said, "I'll tell the legate you are here."

"No," Otto replied. "Just announce me."

Tertius Fuscus and Nonius Priscus looked as if their worst nightmare had walked through the doorway in broad daylight. Otto saluted. "The Emperor requests that I make you aware of my presence in the area," he said, handing his commission over to Tertius.

Priscus leaned around to read it over the legate's shoulder. "Not you tribune," Otto snapped. "The Emperor's words are for the commander of The Second Lucan alone. You can order the First Spear Centurion to call a general assembly right away." Priscus looked at his legate who nodded to show he should do it.

"Put your best uniform on, and your armour; you know, dress up as if you were a soldier," Otto called at his retreating back.

"Well, Otto, an unexpected turn of events. Will you take wine with me?" Tertius asked trying to make the best of what was, for him, a desperately awkward situation.

"No," Otto responded brusquely. "I'll wait outside."

The first of the men were hurrying into position to the calls of the horns. Some of them saw Felix on his mule-cart.

"Good idea Felix! Give 'em some oil!" a wit yelled to general laughter and shouts of "Watcher Felix!" from the old sweats and to the bafflement of the recruits.

"Silence in the ranks, there!" the centurions bellowed but the older ones had smiles on their faces.

Otto mounted the rostrum with Priscus and Fuscus. He looked around him for a moment waiting for silence and the full attention of the parade.

"Soldiers of The Second Lucan, it makes me glad to see you once more; comrades I served with and new faces who will bring as much honour to the legion as those they replace. I am here at the order of Emperor Augustus. Your Senior Tribune Nonius Priscus will now read you the Emperor's letter," he declaimed and handed the scroll to Priscus.

The tribune unrolled it, saw the contents, immediately paled and began to mumble. Otto stood forward and held up one hand.

"Can you hear him, lads?"

"No!" the massed ranks shouted.

"Better speak up, Nonius," he said to the tribune who glared at him but began to read again in a ringing voice.

"To My Loyal Officers and Soldiers of The Second Lucan, Greetings.

Know that the Equestrian Otto Longius is commissioned as a Military Prefect under my direct orders. Prefect Longius is a member of my Imperial staff reporting to my secretariat in Rome and no other.

As the resident legion in his area of operations, you will comply with any and all of his requests for support and assistance without hesitation, as if they came from me. Failure to do so in fact or in spirit will be regarded as treason.

Augustus Imp."

"You made me do that to humiliate me. I'll pay you out for it," Nonius hissed and handed back the scroll.

With a smile on his face, Otto turned to Tertius Fuscus. "You have heard this man threaten an Imperial Staff Officer. Do you think it's a good idea to keep him on the strength?"

Priscus looked at Fuscus' expression and his heart sank. He had gone too far; his outburst had finished his career, connections or not.

Otto strode to the centre of the rostrum again. "Mars and Fortuna with you boys; your First Spear Centurion will now dismiss you all except the Tesserarius and the cavalry." Within two minutes the parade ground was largely clear. "Come closer," he shouted. "I want six men to act as my escort....."

"I say," the cavalry commander bleated, "I say, you can't simply take my chaps without permission. It isn't done ..."

"Are you hard of hearing?"

"No, since you ask."

"Are you a person of slow understanding?"

"I say that's rude you know...."

"What did you fail to hear or understand of, "comply with his requests" when Nonius read it out?"

"Still, you mean, it isn't on..." he grumbled but no-one was listening.

"I need six volunteers. You will escort me on the roads in between Luca, Pisae and Spedia. There may be some action involving bandits or local citizens causing trouble. You will be billeted in Luca and earn your standard pay. Step forward anyone who is interested."

Over fifty men took a pace towards him. "I'm grateful to you but you've made things a bit difficult. Tell you what, another pace forward anyone who saw action in Germany." This time there were twenty of them. "Any man who saw action in Germany under General Drusus Germanicus…" The final count was ten. "I can only take six, we'll have to draw straws."

Once his six successful candidates were lined up in front of him, Otto called on the Tesserarius to make a record of their names and told him that the troopers remained on The Second Lucan payroll.

"Right, men, he said, "get your kit on the mule-cart and we're off."

Otto carried out his duties conscientiously. They frequently travelled the dusty roads between the three cities. Otto inspected each garrison, but deliberately avoided forming a pattern. None of the centurions knew when he would appear. But he was fair and knew what he was talking about so the commanders at Spedia and Pisae respected him and were amenable to any suggestions he might make. With Massus, it was a different story. Otto knew that the one-eyed centurion was an exceptionally capable soldier and leader so his "inspections" of the Luca garrison were more like social events.

He now had less time for Lollia but as her belly was rounding out and her breasts growing heavy, riding the countryside was no longer advisable for her. She was content to be comfortably at home, waiting for the baby developing inside her to be ready to enter the world. She was also happy at the difference in her husband. Having a part to play on the big stage gave him a sense of purpose and structure.

Massus had been right about the garrison stables being too small for an extra six horses. Otto built a new block with billets for the troopers above and their own bathhouse and latrine at the back of his villa. This caused a problem for Tullia. Otto drew on legion funds for their rations but feeding six hungry new mouths was too much for her. She and Otto went into Luca and found her an assistant. Tullia had blenched and clamped her mouth tightly closed when they entered the slave dealer's yard. The tears that came to her eyes were as much a result of her agonising memories of her own humiliation in that place as the stench. They settled on Plotina, a tall, stick-thin woman of around thirty. She had been a slave in a cookhouse that had gone bankrupt who was being auctioned off with the other assets to meet the demands of the former owner's creditors. Otto bought her, took her to the river to wash then dress and freed her. She was in a daze for three days until the fact that she was now a free woman registered with her. She followed Otto with adoring, doe eyes every time he passed.

Winter came and went and with the spring came a new source of trouble. Bandits were stopping parties of travellers on the open roads and kidnapping them to sell as slaves to big estates or mines. They operated mostly around Spedia and were ruining commerce; fewer people were prepared to run the risk of bringing goods in and out unless in armed convoys which put up all the prices. Cavalry patrols from the fortress were useless. The criminals simply lay low until the troopers had shifted their area of patrol to a different location and then came out of hiding to strike again.

Otto came up with a plan. Felix drove the mule-cart carrying three soldiers of the Spedia garrison dressed in tunics but with their swords and shields out of sight down on the floor. They hired two prostitutes to go with them to give the effect of a couple of families of tradespeople. The girls were happy to be paid to be driven around the countryside and have a picnic. Otto and his escort rode parallel with Felix in the cover of the woods. On the fourth day, a dozen men took the bait. They burst out of the undergrowth and surrounded the cart. The girls screamed. The bandits laughed; they were bully boys with cudgels and knives, wearing leather jackets and caps for protection. They might terrify an unarmed carter and his mate but they were out classed by the professional killers suddenly racing at them as Otto's men attacked with lances levelled. It was all over in less than five minutes. The cavalry drove them close enough to Felix and the soldiers for a swift sword thrust in the back while they tried to fight off the troopers. The girls stood up and yelled encouragement once they saw their side getting the best of the encounter.

They left one alive who took them to their hide-out; a cave in the side of a steep defile. There were eight beaten and half-starved victims roped together inside. The soldiers released and fed them with what was to hand. They cried and kissed the legionaries rough hands as they helped them to a freedom they thought was lost forever. The property they identified as their own was returned to them.

"What about this one?" Felix asked pointing at the battered but surviving bandit.

"Crucify him," Otto said.

"No, no wait," the abject prisoner shouted, "I'll show you something."

He did. There was a hollow under the hearthstone where his gang had hidden the money they earned by selling their fellow citizens into slavery. It contained over six thousand denarii.

"Thank you," Otto told him and turned to his troopers. "Now crucify him."

He shouted, swore and cursed until a blow from the butt of a lance broke his jaw and knocked most of his teeth out. After that, he just moaned and sobbed.

The prostitutes demanded a share of the loot.

"You didn't do any of the fighting," a trooper reminded them.

"Yeah but we was there and we could've been killed or worse…" one of them told him.

"It was risky for us an' all…" her friend cajoled.

Otto decided they had a point so awarded them each a half share. The rest was split evenly between all who had taken part, himself included. Five hundred and nine denarii was a rich reward for four days driving or riding and less than the same number of minutes fighting. It took them an hour and a half to get back to the road, walking or on the cart. One of the troopers rode ahead to Spedia and transport arrived to pick them up when they were ten miles out of the city.

"Remember your centurion chose you for this duty, lads. See him right, fifty denarii each should do it. Let me know if there's a problem," Otto told the garrison soldiers.

There was no problem.

The city council of Spedia hosted a dinner for Otto. The trade guilds clubbed together and awarded him a commemorative silver tray. They were so glad that the roads were secure once more, they wrote to Rome extolling Otto and his men. A very civil acknowledgement signed by the Emperor in person arrived in due course. It was framed and hung in the city court room where it was a source of continuing civic pride.

Chapter 17

Quintus Mucius sat nervously on the edge of the chair Augustus had offered him. He was twenty-nine years old, under the minimum age to be elected to the office of quaestor but exceptions were not unusual for members of senatorial families. He was short and a fraction overweight. His dark hair was naturally curly and fell over his forehead in a fringe which he brushed aside in a nervous gesture with the back of one of his long-fingered, artistic hands. He had a thorough understanding of the duties of a quaestor; supervising public finances in the city. What he did not understand was why the Emperor had summoned him. He had taken up his duties less than three months ago and had made no major errors that he could recall. He had even refused a substantial bribe to ignore a shortfall in the road-repairs budget. But here he was in the Emperor's private office on a sunny first of June.

"Do you know what Britain is?" Augustus asked him.

"It is a large island off the coast of…"

"Not what I meant. Don't be dense. Supposed to be bright, that's why you're here. Annoyance, Britain is an annoyance. The Divine Julius said he conquered the place forty odd years ago but what I say is, poor show. Won battles, nearly got himself marooned, ships wrecked on the beach by a storm, and then home he comes. So you see, young Quintus, it is a problem."

"If you say so sir, but I do not quite understand…"

"Course you don't. Thing is, Britain is an Imperial Province. Can't simply ignore it. Most of the dreadful natives violently hostile but we have a few friends. Need to develop them, the friends. Need to let them know we value them. The other lot, the hostile ones, are forever fomenting trouble in Gaul and the Belgic lands. Must, "demonstrate our presence with boots on the ground." as good old General Agrippa always used to say. Keep our allies on side, that's the order of the day and where you come in."

"I do not quite see how I can be of use to you in this matter, sir,"

"Because I have not told you yet. Menities, bring it in!" he called.

The secretary entered the room carrying a sandalwood box which he placed on the side table.

Augustus opened it to reveal a large portrait of himself in the form of a cameo exquisitely cut in Sardonyx. His highly detailed profile was creamy white with his hair and laurel wreath a golden yellow fading into a warm, brown background. The carving was framed in chased gold and rested on the purple silk padding of the box.

"The king of the Cantiaci is a client and ally. You are going to Britain where you will present him with this cameo. Ideal gift. It shows Romans are technically skilled, rich and generous. It also has my face on it. Remind him who is the king and who is the emperor, eh?"

"Why me, sir?"

"Why not? If you don't want to go, say so. I am no despot. Find someone else, not a problem."

"Not a problem if I am happy to say goodbye to any hope of rising up the political ladder," Quintus thought but said "It will be my honour to undertake this task for you, sir. I was merely questioning why I had been chosen."

"Never question emperors young man, not likely to lead to a long and happy life. You will not be going alone. However, military aspect problematical. If I send a cohort, looks like the advance party of an invasion. Natives up in arms. Cohort wiped out. Then there will be have to be a real invasion! Ha ha!" Point is to show the advantages of being friends with Rome but not leave you defenceless. Send a squad of shiny troops to make you look important, which of course you are, to me, your Emperor. I'll give you Otto Longius to commend them. Just the man for you."

"Otto doesn't sound very Roman sir…"

"Equestrian, Imperial Military Prefect, Gold Military Crown, Otto Longius. All-round good chap. You'll like him…."

After he had left the office, Menities hovered about not saying anything but obviously curious.

"Out with it, Menities, what do you want to ask me?" Augustus said.

"Since I wish to live a happy life, sir, I am unwilling to question an emperor," he replied.

Augustus laughed briefly. "You wish to know why I have chosen young Mucius?"

The secretary nodded. "Understanding your way of thought helps me to serve you better, sir."

"Oh what a diplomatic creature you are! Very well. Quintus Mucius has intelligence. He is honest; refused that bribe in the road-repairs fraud. But how far is he prepared to go in the service of his Emperor? To Britain clearly, but how much more than that? I want to tie him tight to me at the outset of his career. If he is successful in this mission he will be rewarded and ready for the next…."

"And Otto Longius?"

"Is he not a living example of the benefits of alliance with Rome? Born a barbarian, he is a decorated officer and an equestrian. Let the courtiers of our Cantiari king see what rewards can come to any man who is diligent in our service."

"Otto Longius is not merely "any" man, sir."

"You and I know that, my Menities, but they do not."

Lollia was very heavy now. In spite of her height, her belly was full and round. Her navel had stretched and was protruding and her back never ceased to ache, day or night. Didia tended her constantly, fanning her and fetching her cool drinks against the growing summer heat. Tullia and Plotina plied her with specially prepared meals to tempt her appetite and nourish the baby curled in her womb. Once a week a doctor came to examine her.

"All is well, lady. All is as it should be. Your child will be born in the second half of July," he promised. She no longer slept in the same bed as Otto. The heat of his body was too much to bear and she constantly woke to urinate, clambering out of her bed alone but needing Didia's help to get back in again. The maid slept on a cot in the corner of her mistress' room. Lollia's moods passed from elation, through quiet contentment to impatience and sometimes fear, but at least Otto was with her. He held her hand and spoke gently to her when she was very uncomfortable or afraid. His reassuring presence was the solid foundation on which she relied. When he rode out, she counted the anxious hours until she heard his boots on the tiled floor and felt his hand brushing the damp hair off her face. He smelled of horse and sweat, leather and metal polish but it was welcome to her. She always inhaled deeply, drawing his essence into her before pushing him away and telling him to bathe. As long as Otto was there, huge, powerful and gentle, all would be well. But another Imperial messenger cantered into the yard; as ever, in a cloud of dust on a lathered mount.

She scanned her husband's face as he read his dispatches and her heart fluttered within her. Before he told her, she knew he was being sent away at this time when she felt her life depended on him being with her. She did not consider asking him to stay. His duty was to his Emperor in his world of men. Her duty was to give him a child in her world of women. That was what he was bound to do and what her primary function was.

"I am ordered to the port of Gesoriacum in Belgica with eight soldiers. I must liaise with the Noble Quaestor Quintus Mucius and take ship to Britannia. We go to the lands of the Cantiari, clients of the Emperor. There is a map…."

"When?" she asked, trying to keep the tremble out of her voice.

His wry smile was her answer; now, it was always now.

Otto seconded eight legionaries out of the Luca garrison selected by Centurion Massus.

"All volunteers sir. I know as I volunteered on their behalf; they were too shy to do it themselves. They're all good lads, they won't let you down."

"And if anyone arrives from The Second Lucan wanting my troopers back?"

"I shall respectfully tell them to piss off until they can show me an order signed by the Emperor," Massus replied.

"Thank you," Otto told him. "I'm going to put them under your orders but let the garrison commanders in Pisae and Spedia know in case they need them."

On the twelfth day of June, Otto said goodbye to Lollia. She waved him out of sight with a smile on her face and then sobbed as if her heart would break once he was gone. Felix looked almost as sorrowful. He had been told he was needed to help manage and defend the household. At least he could console himself with the thought that he was still of some use, in spite of his damaged leg.

Otto rode north at the head of his column with a hired four-mule wagon carrying all their kit and supplies to travel the seven hundred miles to Gesoriacum. He rode his grey gelding as he was not going to war. On the paved Roman roads with the cart, they might make thirty miles in a day, less once they were on rough tracks. Massus' troops were not as fit as both he and they had believed. He let them take turns on the cart part of the way each day for the first few days until their feet hardened up. They soon shook down into the mile-eating pace of Roman infantry and marched all the hours of daylight with only brief breaks.

They reached their destination on the seventh day of July. Wooden buildings at crazy angles and thatched huts sprawled beside a river estuary. A featureless strand of sand and green mudflats, smelling of stale fish and rotting algae stretched to the horizon, raucous gulls swooped overhead. At low tide, the sea ended a mile offshore so the tilted and rickety jetties with boats squatting in the mud below them seemed out of place. Most of the boats were coastal traders or fishing smacks but one stood out. It was higher, fully decked and three times the length of the other craft. It hunched down on the tidal flats, kept upright by three stout wooden posts on either side. Its single mast towered to the sky, a Gallic boat; heavily built to sail the German Sea. A plank led across to the foredeck on which Otto could see a figure staring at the arrival of the legionaries. His white tunic bore a wide red stripe demonstrating that he was a Roman nobleman.

"That'll be him," Otto thought.

"Prefect Longius?" the stranger called. "Come aboard!" Otto clambered onto the gunwale and jumped down making the boat shake as he landed. "Greetings Prefect Longius, I am Quaestor Quintus Mucius. I am pleased to see you are here in good time. Everyone in this smelly hellhole seems to understand me but I cannot make out a word they say. Perhaps you will do better…."

At that moment a hatch in the foredeck flew back. The skipper and boat owner emerged into the daylight. He was a thickly bearded man with immense arms and hands tanned by a lifetime of salt spray, wind and sun. He nodded and looked over at the legionaries unloading and stacking their gear. He watched them keenly for a while, turned to the two Romans and began to speak. Otto thought the quaestor was right, this man was incomprehensible but as he listened, straining to make sense of what he was hearing, he began to pick out that it was a form of Latin. A Latin spoken in a guttural accent with little attention to grammar, full of idiom and the seafarers' patois. Otto replied in his German dialect. It was close enough to the local Belgic for the skipper to understand. He smiled broadly showing unexpectedly good teeth and answered Otto in his native tongue. Otto translated for Quintus.

"He says he's happy to have you aboard but needs to know what baggage and how many men and animals you have."

"Oh, is that what he was trying to say? This voyage was booked by shipping agents so he should have been told. However, I have four mules and my horse, a secretary, a clerk, two servants and my valet. The usual chests of clothes and effects, a portable desk and chair, saddlery, tack...."

Otto explained to the skipper who seemed troubled and responded with a long speech.

"He says he cannot carry both our parties. His vessel isn't big enough. His brother has the twin of this one and can bring it up on the next high tide. He suggests that you and your people go with one of them and I and my men set out with the other. He told me if we leave together, we should be able to keep in sight all the way; the boats are the same size and carry the same amount of sail."

"Sounds like a neat way of doubling his charter fee to me," "Quintus said eyeing the skipper suspiciously.

"I know nothing about sea voyages so I'm prepared to take him on his word," Otto told him.

After a pause, Quintus sighed and gave in. "Tell him to find his brother and fetch his boat over for us. I still think this is sharp practice, mind."

They walked up to the inn together, the file of legionaries behind them. Their kit had been loaded on deck under a tarpaulin in the skipper's care. Otto had paid off the carter who was not happy. It was one thing to spend twenty-five days on the road with eight soldiers and a mounted officer, quite another to return alone. He asked if they would pay him a retainer to stay in Gesoriacum and wait for them but he was told that was not possible. He glumly began to enquire around the town for a convoy leaving within the next few days he could join, hopefully with a load of freight.

"I hope you enjoy eating fish, prefect, because you are going to be very hungry if you don't. It is all they seem to serve. Fish, bread, brick-hard cheese and ghastly vinegar they have the nerve to call wine." Quintus warned.

That is all there may have been for him but there was sausage and stewed pork for Otto, simply because he could ask for them in a language their waitress understood. He shared with Quintus. They sized each other up, sitting at opposite sides of the table over dinner.

Quaestor Quintus Mucius could not keep up his pose as a haughty nobleman for long. His fussy, bureaucratic but fundamentally good nature showed through very quickly. Otto liked him. He seemed a decent, straight-dealing sort of man. As for the praetor, he had been a little patronising towards Otto at first, mostly because he was intimidated by him. He had done a little discreet research into his companion on this mission to Britain. Otto had the reputation of a brutal killer, largely as a result of gossip inflating some of his exploits on the Rhine border. He had anticipated a sort of grunting Germanic gladiator and had been pleasantly surprised. By the end of their meal, they were beginning to forge a friendship.

"Why do you complain about the smell of fish when you drench all your food in Garum?" Otto teased.

"Garum is piquant."

"Well that's one word for it."

"What has shocked me in the short time I've been here is the tides," Quintus remarked. "Thirty, forty feet! Why can't they go just a little up and down like in Our Sea?"

Otto could not tell him, but the walls of water that built and receded twice daily were impressive on this flat coast. At first, when the tide began to make, a low, white line of surf moved sedately inland. Soon it built to a rush of grey-brown water that rocked the beached boats and finally lifted them free of the grip of the land. Within three hours, they were floating level with the jetty in twenty-five feet of water. For two hours, all was calm until the ocean at first sneaked away then rushed back into the deeps carrying its water with it and the keels stuck in the gluey silt once more.

The skipper's brother brought his craft alongside the jetty using four long sweeps which could be used to manoeuvre the craft in harbour or if the wind died. Not only was his boat the twin of the first one, the brothers bore a very strong resemblance to each other. Unlike their boats, they were not twins; Otto had asked.

They explained the loading procedure to Otto. The first one would carry the praetor, his people and baggage plus his horse and two of the mules. The second was for Otto and his solders, his horse and the other mules. With the additional weight of the men's lorica segmentata armour, weapons and Otto's parade armour, the weight would be roughly equal. They would load just before the highest point of the tide and sail on the ebb which would help them out into the deeper waters. Of course, this could only be done on a day when the wind was in the right quarter. Gallic sea-boats were true sailing-craft, not equipped with banks of oars like Roman galleys.

They waited for three days. A sailor had been detailed to tell them each day if they would be embarking. Once he had told them they would not, they had time to fill. Quintus told Otto the full details of their mission and showed him the Emperor's gift. They walked around the town. They rode a little in the countryside. They talked and their friendship grew.

On the fourth day as they sat over breakfast, their sailor put his head around the door. "We're going now," he called over to them and hurried down to the waterside.

Both vessels had a crew of four in addition to the master. They were practised in the art of stowing cargo, acting as one and needing no orders. "Like a well drilled legion," Otto thought. They put bags over the horses' and mules' heads and passed a broad band under their bellies to support them while they were hoisted by a winch. With dangling heads and legs, the animals were lowered through a midship hatch into the dark maw of the hold. The passengers could stand or sit near the steering oar, one half on the port side, the other half to starboard. If they got in the way, they would be sent below with the livestock and the baggage, whether they liked it or not. Otto relayed these instructions.

"How long will the crossing take?" he enquired.

"Depends on the wind," the master answered.

"If the wind is favourable?"

"Depends on the currents."

Otto realized that superstition forbade the man to say more, so he went to the side, spat into the sea and made the sign against bad luck. The skipper nodded his approval. The sailors loosed the mooring ropes and pushed away from the jetty with the sweeps. For a few moments they drifted until the sail was rattled up and made fast. The boom swung over, the sail filled and they felt the chuckle of the seat under them as they gained speed. In a surprisingly short time, the jetties were far-off spidery black lines and soon lost to sight. The distance between Gesoriacum and Dubrae on the Cantiari coast is twenty-three miles in a straight line. But boats do not sail in straight lines. They zig-zag across the face of the ocean, tacking and falling off, always responding to the often-competing thrust of wind and current. The ebbtide had helped them leave the Gallic shore but now it was pushing them south and west down the channel while the sails and steering oar were fighting the vessel a little north of west. After an hour, no land could be seen either behind or in front. The skipper had made this voyage in both directions countless times and so had his brother. They now relied on the colour of the sea, the play of the forces on their hull and the strength of the wind on their cheeks to find their safe haven.

The dirty brown of the silt laden estuary water had given way to a deep green with indigo highlights. Small waves peaked out of the surface to fall back in a hiss of white bubbles. The fat-bellied sail was taut. Their vessel slid along with almost no pitching or rolling under a sky mottled with small white clouds like the hide of a grey seal. The skipper stood at the steering oar with his feet braced apart on flexed legs glancing from the rigging to the sea, making constant, fine adjustments to their course. The boats were within hailing distance but not so close that they might accidently collide side-on if a high wave caught one of them. A school of porpoises arced out of the water and fell back, heading fast down channel. The two helmsmen saw them at the same time and shouted across, waving and pointing them out; they did not like what they saw. A quick look behind showed that no gulls were following them. There were none to be seen under the whole inverted bowl of the sky; another ominous sight. The steady wind, a point or two south of east dwindled to the softest breeze. The boat began to wallow in the gathering procession of waves bearing down out of the north with a rising current of air following after them. Black and yellow clouds mounted in the north-eastern sky. It grew darker and deathly cold. The inky line of a squall tore towards them with flashes of lightning and the roll of thunder heralding its arrival.

Everyone was ordered below. The sailors closed the hatch over the heads of the frightened legionaries in the stygian hold lit only by the feeble glimmer of an oil lamp resting in a metal bowl to contain spills. On deck, the sail was furled until only a scrap was left to give them steerageway. The crew huddled under the forepeak gunwale hanging on to the shrouds. The helmsman lashed himself to one of the steering oar supports. He brought his vessel about until her stern was against the rollers. As the frigid northern wind mingled with the warm summer air, rain cascaded down destroying visibility.

The main force of the storm hit like a sledgehammer, sending the first of its mighty waves to smash across the deck. They could do no more than to run before it. Behind them lightning flickered but now they were hurtling blindly over the sea with no way of knowing how far they were from the land with its ship-killing cliffs and reefs.

In the hold, men and animals were thrown from side to side. Otto ordered the legionaries into the wooden stalls to brace their shoulders between the timbers and the animals. The horse and mules risked being battered to death or their legs broken if they fell in the narrow space. The men were terrified. Not a single one of them had been on the ocean before. Few Romans were good sailors. They eyed the unpredictable waters with suspicion and employed Greeks to man their war-fleets. Now the soldiers stood, shoving into a beast to hold it upright in the gloom with the drumbeat of the waves smashing against the hull and the wind howling outside so loudly they could not think, let alone speak to each other. The lamp tipped over in its basin and went out. Hour after hour they rushed onwards in a version of lightless Hell; unseen demons shrieking and crashing all around them in seemingly never-ending torment.

Otto woke with his head resting on his gelding's flank. He had fallen asleep on his feet but something different had roused him. He did not know what it was and then he realised. The noise had dropped. He was no longer aware of the boat juddering as the waves tried to destroy it in its headlong flight. He heard bare feet slapping on the deck overhead. The hatch was lifted and a grinning face lit by a lamp leaned in.

"Do you want to come up or are you happy where you are?" one of the seamen shouted down.

Otto and the soldiers scrambled up the short ladder and stood under a starry sky with a half moon shining down on them. The sea was calm. A gentle warm, breeze began lift the chill from their cramped limbs.

"What happened to the storm?" he asked.

"A sudden blow will soon go is what we sailormen says, general," the man replied flashing a grin.

"Greetings to you," the skipper called from his position at the steering oar. "Alive alive-oh?"

"I believe so," Otto replied. "Where are we?"

"See those lights ahead? That's a little Belgic port. We're making our way in. If my brother's not there already, he'll be along by and by."

"So we are back where we started…" Otto said.

The skipper laughed and repeated what Otto had said for the benefit of his crew. They all guffawed.

"No, sir, not that you'd know, being a landsman as you are. The Isle of Vectis is behind you over your left shoulder and we're coasting into the Belgic part of Britain. Dubrae is to the north and east of us; we overshot it in the storm. But at least we've made landfall with no loss or damage," he explained cheerfully.

"You seem to have taken it very calmly; we were nearly shipwrecked and…" Otto told him

"Hear that boys? Nearly shipwrecked the gentleman tells us!" he shouted to the crew then spoke to Otto once more. "Such things happen to men who make their lives on the face of the sea. No point getting upset about it. Won't be the last time, of that I'm sure. But here we are, safe and sound."

The crew edged the boat carefully towards the port. The sea was choppy with low, short waves, the result of the storm in the channel. They would subside in a day or two, provided the weather stayed fair. They moored against the jetty with a gentle bump in the early hours of the morning after fourteen hours at sea, twelve of them in the hold. The passengers gratefully shared the seamen's rations of hard bread and smoked fish before lying on the deck wrapped in their cloaks. The fresh air was sweet and the stars above a blessing but a greater blessing was the gentle rocking of the deck; no longer leaping and plunging like a mad horse.

Otto slept a long and peaceful sleep to be woken when the sun was high by the sounds of the busy port. He opened his eyes to see a herring gull roosting on the gunwale above him. It stared down at him with a speculative expression. Otto moved his head, the bird decided he was not edible, shrieked and took to the air. Rowing boats bustled to and fro about their mysterious maritime affairs, fishing smacks that had been kept in port by the bad weather set sail. Men busied themselves alongshore with ropes and nets, others loafed, calling down to their mates afloat, enjoying a warm and cloudless morning ashore for a change. A few lounged in shadowy places, purposefully watching the activity but with no apparent reason to be there.

The landsmen were ravenous and disembarked under Otto's guidance to find an inn, preferably with fresh bread, bacon and cheese. They succeeded and ate until they were forced to let their belts out a notch. Stuffed full, they made their way back to the quayside followed by a boy carrying a basket of provisions to repay the crew for their smoked fish. The mules and Otto's horse were heaved out of the hold. He enquired and found a stable quite near where they were fed and rubbed down; exhausted but otherwise none the worse for their night at sea. The legionaries hauled their kit on deck and began to dry and lightly oil it against the saltwater.

Late on in the morning, a sailor hallooed the skipper and pointed out to sea. A vessel was skimming over the sparkling blue water towards them.

"My brother," he exclaimed with a broad smile in which relief could be detected.

Quintus Mucius bounced onto dryland with his pale and green-tinged staff behind him.

"What a storm!" he exclaimed. "The lightning! Our vessel flew across the wild ocean like a champion racehorse at the circus. Did you see it, Otto?"

"I was in the hold."

"Were you? I had myself tied to the mast and missed nothing. The waves were like snow-capped mountains just about to fall and crush us when our gallant craft rose up and defied them to do their worse as we clawed up their slopes! It was a wonder."

The master of his boat had found a sheltered bay under the lee of the Isle of Vectis and ridden out part of the storm there before crossing over to the mainland that morning.

Quintus and Otto entertained the two skippers to dinner that night; partly to celebrate a safe landfall but also to discuss what they would do next. Otto had to translate for Quintus which slowed up the discussions. There were two possibilities. The first was to wait for a favourable wind and sail up to Dubrae. It was a deep- water port like the one in which they were moored, accessible at low tide. If they left at dawn the voyage could be made in one long day, perhaps a day and a half. Otto asked when the wind would be in the right quarter but received only shrugs in reply. The alternative was to go overland. One of the brothers drew a map in gravy on the table. They were deep in the arms of a long bay divided by a river a little to the north. Beyond the river, the land bulged outwards. They would have to find a reliable guide to lead them to a river crossing and then on through the hinterland unknown to either of the brothers. They estimated it would take at least two weeks if all went well; probably double that time. Quintus was not convinced.

"Of course they want us to hang about and go by sea. It's in their interest. Otherwise, I would end their charter and pay them off, hiring another vessel in Dubrae to carry us back to Gesoriacum."

The brothers could not understand Quintus but it was clear he was expressing doubt.

"There is a Roman trading post here, ask them if you aren't happy with what we've told you," one of them said.

"Where is it?" Otto asked.

"Up past the stables. You can't miss it; there's a damn great wooden eagle nailed to the gable-end."

Wearing his best tunic and toga, accompanied by one of his servants, the Noble Quaestor Quintus Mucius made his way through the town. He had dressed to make sure any Roman in the trading post would instantly understand the status of this visitor. The locals gazed after him. It was not every day a Roman nobleman walked the streets of their port in his formal clothes. Some had never seen such a sight before; they nudged their mates and pointed. Others followed after him, commenting in their own language. Otto had gone with him as far as the stables. He wanted to check on the horses to make sure they were being fed properly; he was paying for grain and did not want to find out it was being adulterated with chaff.

"I'll see you there in ten minutes," he said and watched Quintus striding uphill along the cluttered street before he ducked into the dim interior of the stables.

The horses were in good condition; well recovered from their ordeal. The mules were their usual phlegmatic selves; placidly eating and content that no-one was whipping them on, for the moment. Otto went back into the open air. He walked up the hill towards the weather-beaten wooden building with the carved head of a nondescript hook-beaked bird nailed high up on the end wall. He passed the mouth of an alley at the end of which two dogs growled and snarled at each other over a pile of refuse. He reached the trading post and went in. The ground floor was one large room. Bales and sacks were stacked around the floor and on wide shelves. It smelled musty with an underlying odour of fish. A solitary clerk sat behind a counter.

"How may I help you sir?" he asked. "Oysters perhaps, finest native British oysters, salted herrings…."

"I'm looking for my friend who came in a few minutes ago," Otto told him.

"No-one has called during the last hour…"

"A Roman nobleman, Quaestor Mucius, he was wearing his toga. You can't have missed him. Where's your master?"

"Sir, nobody at all has been here in the last hour. I have not left this room and my master is down in the port…"

Otto felt the onrushing nausea of shock then took a deep breath and collected himself. He turned on his feel and hurried away. The two dogs in the alley were still contesting their prize. He saw what it was now that they had dragged it half-free of the rubbish. A human foot, gnawed and torn but still attached to its leg lay draggled in the muck. He kicked the dogs aside, ignoring their raised hackles and dripping jaws. He pulled the body free. The sightless eyes of Quintus' servant stared up at him. The man's throat had been cut.

Otto ran for the boat. He struggled into his chain mail and buckled his cavalry sword around his waist as he shouted orders. The boat skippers were to search around the town asking for a Roman nobleman taking with them an escort of legionaries armoured and helmeted but carrying swords only, no shields or javelins.

"Worst you'll face is a couple of bully boys with knives, nothing you can't handle," he told them.

With the help of a sailor the servants were to sent to fetch the dead man's body back.

"Watch out for the dogs and take a scrap of canvas to wrap him in. Don't being him onboard; the crew might think that's bad luck. I'm going to ride out and see if I can spot anything on the road. Quintus Mucius can't have been gone more than twenty minutes."

Otto cantered his gelding through the streets yelling for everyone to get out of his way and receiving shouted curses and shaken fists as he went. Beyond the last house there was a single dirt track leading up to the headland. The slopes were lightly wooded with low trees sculpted into fantastical shapes by the salt-laden sea breezes. The summit was bare of trees but thickly blanketed in gorse bushes, brambles and heather in a dense tangle. He pulled up his blowing mount, high above the roofs of the port with a view over the ocean to Vectis with its white cliffs topped with green and the waters around and between dotted with mustard-coloured and faded-red sails.

Chapter 18

Otto examined the track. It was dry and dusty, rutted by wheels, scuffed with foot marks and hoofprints both coming from and heading towards the port. There was nothing to indicate that Quintus had recently passed this way. He could see far ahead from his elevated position on the gelding's back. Nothing was moving; not a horse, not a human figure. But the gorse bushes on either side were taller than they first appeared. It could be that they were high enough to conceal a man on foot. He rode on for a mile until the road forked. One branch led north towards the river of which he had been told, the other inland down a gentle incline to sparse woods three or four miles away. He took the northern fork since there was nothing to choose between them. After half a mile, it broke into narrow, sandy paths not wide enough for two horses to pass each other that divided again and again into a maze between the clumps of spiny gorse. The mass of bushes blocked the breeze, intensifying the heat of the day. There was no sound other than the shuffling of his horse's hooves in the sand and the droning of insects. He began to sweat. The flies settled on his face and the corners of the gelding's eyes. At the point when he had decided he was wasting his time, two men stepped out in front of him.

They stood side by side to block his path. Wild-haired and bearded, they were dressed in a motley assortment of rags and skins.

They grinned up at him exposing a few brown, rotting stumps of teeth. One carried a hatchet and the other a cudgel which he repeatedly slapped against the palm of his free hand. They had come across a lone horseman in a place where he had no room to manoeuvre and the pickings were going to be good. Otto kept his eyes fixed on the pair of them wishing he had been riding Djinn. His charger would have reared on command, snapping at them with his teeth and battering them to the ground with his front hooves. But he was on his riding horse which was not trained for combat. One of the men's eyes flicked past his mount's right side. Otto instantly understood the significance of the glance. He jabbed his knee into the horse's flank; it stepped to the left. Simultaneously, he drew his long sword, twisted from the waist and leaned backwards in the saddle, sweeping it down. The blade caught the sun and then the flat of it smashed onto the head of the third man who had been stealing up behind him.

The man stood stock still for an instant as if made of stone. Then he raised both hands to his head feeling around in his matted hair. His mouth formed a perfect circle. "Oh," he said softly, then "Oh," again. His hands dropped to his sides and he began to shake and spasm, hopping from one foot to the other, spinning and spinning on his heel until he fell backwards, thrashed awhile and lay quiet. "Oh," he whispered once more and died. The sword blow on the crown of his head had driven a piece of bone deep into his brain without breaking the skin of his scalp. His nervous system had short-circuited leaving his body uncontrollable until it received no more scrambled signals and shut itself down, permanently. Otto turned to face the two men in front of him. They looked from him to their dead comrade in horror. Yelling and screaming spells against witchcraft, they ran off.

Otto worked his way through the tangle of sandy paths among the islands of scrub and back to the road. He made his way down to the port. At the quayside, he learned that enquiries and a search of alleyways and outbuildings had revealed nothing. Quintus Mucius had vanished off the face of the earth. The dead body of his servant witnessed to the fact that a crime had been committed but what crime; abduction or another murder?

"What are we going to do now, sir?" Mucius' secretary asked.

"Arrange the funeral rites for your unfortunate companion and then think," Otto replied.

He withdrew to the stern of the boat making it obvious he did not want to be disturbed while he considered the possibilities thrown up by the disappearance of the quaestor. Otto was in a quandary. He did not want to abandon Quintus but he could not stay in this port forever. He knew the objective of their mission and he could present the Emperor's gift to the King of the Cantiari himself, if necessary. How long should he search for his new friend? Where should he search? He slept badly that night, dozing and waking again as his thoughts ran on. Dawn brought relief and a stranger. A dark-headed man stood on the quayside looking silently at their boat. He was short and muscular with powerful, bandy legs. He wore a plain, light-brown tunic over doeskin breeches and soft shoes, like those Otto had worn as a child; not much use for hard roads but ideal for fields and forests.

"What're you after, man?" one of the crew called over to him.

"I am looking for the big Roman with the grey horse," he replied.

The sailor pointed at Otto who saw the gesture and walked along the deck until he was level with the newcomer. The unexplained disappearance of Quintus had made him extra cautious.

"What do you want with me?" he asked in Latin.

"My master says you if come to him you will find your lost sheep," the man told him in the same language but stumbling to express himself, unfamiliar with that tongue.

"What is this nonsense?"

"My master's words," he told Otto and closed his lips firmly as if to indicate there would be no explanation.

"What is your master's name?" There was no reply. "What is your name?" Again, silence. Otto sighed. "I am the Imperial Military Prefect called Otto Longius."

"My name is Tud," the messenger told him and bowed.

"Greetings Tud, is your master in this town?"

"No. You ride.

"And how long will the journey take?

"Days, weeks, cannot say."

"Won't say you mean.," Otto remarked. "Wait there."

He called the skippers, his soldiers and the secretary to him. They huddled around him and he spoke quietly so as not to be overheard. He translated what Tud had said for the legionaries then asked everyone what they thought. The consensus was that it was a trap of some kind but no-one could say why it was being set. Otto walked once around the deck and came back to them all.

"How long is your charter?" he asked the brothers.

"Open-ended but we haven't seen any money yet, just a promise on parchment. Can't pay our way with that." one of them told him.

Otto unstrung his purse and counted out one hundred denarii to each of them.

"This is good-faith money. If I don't come back by the end of next month, take my people to Gesoriacum. The Roman authorities will settle with you there."

All three spat on the palm of their hands and shook on the bargain.

"Right lads", he said to his men, "which one of you is going to be temporary acting decanus?" they shuffled about and mumbled then one came to the front. "Right decanus, guard these boats and the quaestor's servants. I don't expect you to stay on board every hour of every day but employ proper military discipline. Here's ten denarii each for the lads and twenty for you. Don't get pissed and start any fights." He fished the little marble finger on a chain out of the front of his tunic. He had worn it as a souvenir ever since it had been given to him by a sculptor on his first visit to Rome. "If any man arrives and says he has come with a message from me but cannot show you this, he is a liar. Kill him and set sail." He repeated these instructions in Belgic for the skippers. Finally he spoke to the secretary. "Fetch writing materials," he said and dictated an account of events to date. "This will exonerate you if it all ends badly."

"Thank you, sir, oh thank, you," the secretary told him with tears glinting in his eyes. A missing presumed-dead master would mean certain torture and probable execution for him and all the other servants without proof of their innocence.

In chain mail, helmeted, carrying his oval shield and a lance, Otto rode steadily along the same route he had followed the previous morning. Tud scurried by his side. When they came to the fork in the road, they carried on inland to the woods that Otto had seen in the distance. They travelled in silence, the sun shone on them, larks hung in the sky overhead and piped their songs. Butterflies were everywhere. More than once they flushed a covey of partridges out of the undergrowth which made the gelding start and snort. After three-quarters of an hour, Otto dismounted and walked for quarter of an hour before getting back into the saddle. He always adopted this method of saving a horse's strength on a long journey. After three hours, they were deep under the canopy of the woodland. Otto stopped, unsaddled his gelding and let it roll in the soft grass. He had not spoken to Tud nor asked him a single question all the time they had been on the road. Tud broke the silence.

"You take great care horse," he remarked.

"Yes," Otto replied but said no more.

Shortly after he was back in the saddle with Tud trotting beside him on his strong, untiring legs. They turned onto a narrow path under the trees and enjoyed the cool, dappled shade before crossing a brook where Otto let his mount drink. Onwards they went, Tud leading him through the woods without hesitation. At last he stopped and pointed ahead to where the trees grew closer together.

"We are close," he said and walked briskly forwards.

Otto was forced to duck his head and sway in the saddle to avoid over-hanging branches for a few minutes and then they were out, into brilliant afternoon sunshine. Ahead was a small lake, perhaps, two hundred yards across. There was an island in the middle, reached by a wooden causeway. Otto followed Tud across. The centre of the island was hidden by a hedge of holly and yew. The hairs on Otto's neck prickled. He knew he was entering a sacred place and felt the power emanating from it.

"Lead your horse," Tud instructed.

They walked together through an archway into the centre of the grove. There was a well between two wooden huts with thatched roofs. A stable stood at the far side. There was no sound, no sign of life, even the noise of his horse's hooves was muffled as they fell on springy turf underfoot. Tud took the reins out of Otto's hand. He smiled reassuringly for him to go on. Otto approached the huts. A figure stepped through the entrance of the larger one into the golden sunlight. A slender man of above average height, his long, unplaited hair and his beard were snow white. He wore a long white robe falling to his feet tied about his waist with a cord decorated with silver acorns at each end. Around his neck was a silver torque. In spite of the warmth of the day, he had a cloak over his shoulders. Otto stopped dead. His senses began to swim. He blinked rapidly and looked again. The cloak reflected iridescent glimmers of purple and metallic light as the sun caught it but it was black; made of ravens' feathers sewn onto fine cloth.

Otto felt dizzy. He staggered and tripped over, bouncing his head off the ground and knocking the air out of his lungs himself when he landed flat on his back. In his mind, he flew back through time and space and was again in the cave staring at the wise woman, smelling the Frankincense, hearing her words in his head somehow screaming and whispering at the same time, "*A man is entering your life. He wears black plumes; black as the deepest night; black as death within the grave. Your spirit already knows him. Wherever he finds you, whenever he finds you, whatever you must sacrifice, go with him and he will set you on the path of your life's journey. This is the way the gods have chosen for you.*"

"Drink," a voice told him in Latin and he felt the edge of a wooden bowl pressed against his lips. Cold water filled his mouth, he swallowed. He opened his eyes, the world looked as it he was seeing it under water but it cleared in a few seconds. He drank again. Someone had removed his helmet. He was lying with Tud supporting his head and shoulders. The black-cloaked man knelt over him holding the bowl. He smiled. His lips were very red, his teeth white and sharp and his eyes green, flecked with yellow. He was much younger than the white hair had made him appear at first glance. Suddenly all was calm, all was clear. But as he regained complete consciousness, for one fleeting moment he saw his father sitting on a log contentedly watching a small river. *"Take care, my son,"* he called, waved one hand and faded.

"Father!" Otto cried out involuntarily and struggled to a sitting position.

"You saw your father?"

"I did," Otto said with a regretful sigh.

"He is far away?"

"He is dead".

They helped him to his feet. He pushed them away and took a couple of wavering steps. His full strength returned and with it shame at the weakness he had shown.

"Your father's shade came to you in this holy place, young man. It is not unknown. The dead may pass between the worlds and here the veil separating them is very thin. After you fell, you were half here and half in the other realm. Now you have wholly come back to us," he explained. "But these experiences are exhausting; you must rest a little and have something to eat and drink to restore your forces."

They sat on a bench eating the soft bread and thick soup Tud had brought them.

"Why did you invite me here?" Otto asked after a while.

"Introductions first; I am Cynan, a humble priest in the service of the Gods," Cynan answered in his perfect, cultured Latin.

"I am Otto Longius, an Imperial Military Prefect in the service of Emperor Augustus."

"You do not look much like a soldier of Rome to me."

"Nevertheless, I am a Roman citizen, an Equestrian and an officer."

"You wear the arm rings of a German warrior."

"I took them off the bodies of enemies of Rome who fell to me. It is the custom. It honours them because they are not forgotten as long as I wear these trophies. Now that we know each other's names, why am I here?"

"You are here of your own free will because you want to be. I asked you to come for two reasons. I wished to meet a mighty Roman who owns a magic sword. If he strikes a man with it, no blood flows but the one who received the blow will dance until he falls dead…"

Otto snorted. "Some men tried to rob me. I hit one of them on the head with the flat of my sword and he twitched and convulsed before he died. I have seen this before on the battlefield. What is your second reason?"

"You are looking for someone, a Roman. I know where he is…"

"He is alive?"

"Yes."

Otto said no more. After a few minutes silence, Cynan spoke again.

"You have no further questions?"

"You know where to find my friend and that he is alive. You want something from me. You will let me know in your own time."

"He is your friend?"

"I have not known him long but I believe we shall become good friends."

"You are confident that you will see him again?"

"Is that not your purpose, to take me to him?"

Cynan laughed. "I can see you are more than a commonplace killer of your fellowmen. You have a glimmer of intelligence, Otto Longius." The priest stood up. "I have affairs to which I must attend. Tud will look after you. We shall speak again."

Tud helped to tether the horse in the stable which contained three mules, one of them white. Once the gelding's back had been rubbed dry with wisps of straw and his feet checked, Otto was led over to the smaller of the two huts. It held a bed and a pitcher of water. Tud brought him bread and cheese and then left him. Otto sat outside for a while musing as the gloaming deepened. When the dew began to fall, he lay down in the hut wearing his mail shirt, his sword near at hand and his lance and shield propped at the side of his bed. He had disciplined himself to act normally in Cynan's company but he had been shaken to the soul and needed to clear his mind.

He saw himself again as a youth facing armed legionaries with only an axe in his hands, his world ending in blood and fire all around him and Tribune Lucius Longius, nimbly stepping down off his horse and the smoke clearing to show his youthful, broken-nosed face under a glittering helmet topped with black plumes. *"He wears black plumes; black as the deepest night; black as death within the grave."* He had followed Lucius because he had believed that was what the prophecy demanded of him. The result had been honour, promotion and wealth, although he cared little for that, comradeship, friendship, his wife and by now, perhaps his son or daughter, had followed. The wise woman had called him "Killer of Kings". He had cut down King Helmund. Surely all this must mean that he had been treading his destined path and yet...

Cynan the priest wore a cloak of raven feathers. Cynan had intervened in his life. Could it be that he had been misguided and that the priest was the one to lead him to his destiny? But as he pondered, he recollected the priest's green eyes and sharp teeth; a forest-cat of a man. He was instinctively wary of him and he did not feel that "his spirit already knew him". Another train of thought occurred to Otto. Had Cynan been sent by the Gods to test him? Had he been put in his path so they could see whether he was to true to the oaths he had given, first to Lucius and then to Rome? He had heard the Immortals played such games with men. His last thought before sleep overtook him was of his father's warning.

The dawn chorus awoke him. He stepped from the hut onto the damp grass and struggled out of his mail shirt and subarmalis. He stripped naked and poured buckets of icy well-water over his head and body. Gasping but cleaner, he jogged around the enclosure in the growing warmth of the sun to dry his skin. He had dressed in his loin cloth and tunic when Tud appeared and beckoned him to the bench where Cynan waited. He served them a breakfast of cracked-wheat porridge, cheese, warm fresh bread and milk but Otto had seen no oven, no cow.

"Is he an important man, this possible good friend of yours?" Cynan asked.

Otto considered before replying. "Not important yet not unimportant. He is young and in ten, or fifteen year's time he may be one of the chief men of Rome."

"He is of a noble family then?"

"He is."

"And you are not. Can you hope to be more than you are now?"

"Who knows?"

"Who knows indeed, but we do, you will never rise to the highest rank. Your lowly birth condemns you to be a servant, even if your service is prestigious and well rewarded."

"Are you not a humble servant of the Gods, as I believe you told me?"

Cynan laughed and slapped his knee.

"A telling shot. Otto; your friend now, is he an official?"

"He is a quaestor."

"And what were you and the quaestor about that you ended up where you did?"

"We were caught in a sudden storm off Gesoriacum and ran before it until we reached a safe haven."

"And if the storm had not driven you off course?"

"We would have made our rendezvous with a Roman naval ship off the mouth of the Sequanae river in Gallia Lugdunensis," he lied without the slightest hesitation.

"I do not believe you."

"Then there is no point in questioning me further. If you think I lie, how can you be sure if anything I say in the future will be true?"

Cynan's green eyes flared with sparks of irritation but he took a deep breath and controlled himself. "Otto Longius, if you do not tell me the complete truth I cannot assist you in finding your friend," he said with a note of finality in his voice.

"I did not come to you begging for your help. If you have none to offer, I shall be on my way, thanking you for your hospitality." Otto told him and stood up.

Before he could take one pace, Cynan put a restraining hand on his forearm.

"We leave now to go to him. You will not need your armour when you are in my company. I am sure that will be more comfortable for you. It will take us ten days to reach him."

Cynan led the way on his white mule. Otto rode behind him, wearing his subarmalis under his tunic with his sword at his side. Tud brought up the rear on foot, leading the two other mules, their packsaddles loaded with Cynan's baggage and Otto's mail shirt and equipment. Once they were beyond the woods, the land rolled in front of them rich with pastureland, fields of ripening grain and orchards. Small hamlets with rickety protective fences and half-filled ditches were dotted about always near the numerous brooks and streams. It was a fatter, kinder land than the Germany Otto had known as a boy. Here, the forests were long gone but belts and groves of beech, oak and ash covered the hilly ground where it would be difficult to plough. Cattle and sheep grazed or dozed as much as the flies would let them in the heat of the day. The farmers and their families did not rush to grab weapons or find themselves somewhere to hide as Cynan and his party rode by. They watched respectfully and then carried on with their work once he was out of sight. Otto insisted on keeping to his alternate riding and walking routine even though they were not travelling faster than a walking pace. Cynan never dismounted to rest his mule during the entire day. Towards sunset, they stopped at a palisade encircling twenty huts so low that the thatch of their roofs touched the ground. Cynan called out and after a short wait, two frightened, dirty-faced women came out holding a water skin and a sack. Tud took them.

"Will we sleep here tonight?" he asked his master.

The priest shook his head. "I am not interested in sharing their lice as well as their food," he said then made complex gestures with his hands and called out what Otto took to be a blessing in a tongue unknown to him. They camped in an oak grove. Tud pegged down a low-growing branch and cut others to lay over it like a pitched roof. Cynan slept in its shelter on a thin mattress stuffed with fragrant herbs that Tud had unrolled for him. Otto lay down on the bare ground wrapped in his cloak. It was a long time since he had slept in the open. The stars were brilliant through the trembling leaves overhead. The air carried a rich scent like mushrooms. The branches of the oak sighed and creaked gently in the night breeze. Otto drifted away. In the morning, one shoulder and hip were aching. "Getting soft," he reproached himself.

It began to rain later in the day. That night they slept undercover in a barn. There was little hay or straw left at that time of year but enough for Otto and Tud to make themselves more comfortable than the night before. The farmer's wife came in with bread and a bowl of vegetable soup. She knelt and whispered to Cynan. He touched her breasts and sang in a high, nasal register. When he had finished she kissed his hands and left with a light step. Otto looked at him enquiringly.

"She wants a child," Cynan explained. "She thinks she'll get pregnant now."

"And will she?"

Cynan shrugged. "Who knows? But at least she's happy. If she approaches her husband tonight, her enthusiasm may spur him on to greater efforts and her prayer will be granted."

They finished the soup. Tud had not been allowed to share it with them but now he used the breadcrusts to wipe the bowl clean.

"Tell me, why not carry on with your mission? You still have the boats." Cynan asked.

"You know I cannot abandon the quaestor. In any case, I don't know the details of what we are supposed to be doing. I am only the captain of the bodyguard."

The priest shook his head. "I seriously doubt that, Otto. In their arrogance the Romans may think of you as a weapon they keep at the ready but we both know you are worth more than that. Tell me, would the man we seek search for you if you were lost?"

"The question does not arise," Otto told him. "He is neither trained nor equipped for a rescue attempt."

"I still ask whether a noble Roman would go out of his way to help someone like you. They regard everyone else as dispensable."

The next day they descended into a valley with a broad sluggish river running through it. A ferryman took them over in three trips. When they were assembled on the far bank, Cynan mounted his mule and blessed the man. He did not seem to be overwhelmed with gratitude. Otto winked at him and flipped a silver coin out of his purse. He caught it in mid-air with a broad smile and a nod.

"You undermined my authority by doing that," Cynan complained.

"Not at all," Otto told him. "He ferried both of us over; you paid him your way, I paid him in mine."

The priest thumped his heels into his mule's sides and hurried on, his lips pursed into a thin line of disapproval.

"You understand that if this quaestor is not safely returned to them, the Romans will punish you?" he asked Otto that night as they sat beside a small fire in a hazel coppice.

"I don't believe so," Otto replied.

"Oh they will! They are a vengeful people. Someone must always answer and in this instance it will be you."

"Considering that you hold Rome in such contempt you seem to know a lot about it. You even speak the language."

"My Order is centred far to the west on the holy island of Ynys Mon. There you may find men of deep learning. I speak the language of Rome, Belgic and the Brythonic of this land. My peers know Greek also and some can interpret the symbolic writings of the Egyptians. It is our knowledge that enables us to guide the people and help them...."

"By eating their food without paying for it," Otto retorted.

"Not so," Cynan protested. "They receive a blessing and the additional spiritual reward of offering their hunger as a sacrifice to the Gods. They are well compensated for a little bread and a few vegetables."

After three days, they made a second river crossing. This time the channel was narrower and the current ran swiftly over a gravel bed. Where they forded, the water came up to Otto's knees but the mules were not as tall as his gelding. He grinned to see Cynan's robe soaked nearly to his waist. On the far side, Cynan took it off and spread it on some branches to dry by a fire Tud had made.

The priest's body carried no spare flesh and was hairless but what caught Otto's attention were his tattoos. His belly up to his throat, half-hidden under his beard, and his back were covered in fantastic writhing beasts, suns, moons, trees and birds. They were picked out in blues and greens, some had red eyes. They seemed to move independently as his muscles played under his skin. He saw Otto staring.

"Each one records a study completed and a higher degree of lore attained. They are to me what your arm rings are to you; symbols of victory," he said with pride in his voice.

They rode on. The land began to rise until they reached a high plateau. It was almost treeless and empty of signs of human habitation other than the rough, drystone shelters shepherds built against being caught in the open by sudden storms There were circles and lines of lofty standing-stones put there by forgotten people who were long gone. Small flocks of bleating sheep scattered at their approach but soon returned to nibbling the heath once they had passed by. When the sun was low, Tud collected dried dung and heather and lit a small fire outside a shepherd's crude hut. A coil of grey smoke rose into the sky. Half an hour later, a figure loped towards them over the moor. He was shaggy-haired and dressed in equally unkempt, greasy sheepskins. He knelt at Cynan's feet and held out a loaf, a block of white cheese wrapped in green leaves and a dozen wild plums. He received his blessing and made off. Otto watched carefully. He must have travelled over two miles before he was lost to sight in a fold in the ground.

The plums were small and bitter. Tud boiled them in a pot until they burst their skins. He picked the stones out and mixed in a little honey out of the jar he carried in his packsaddle. With sheep's cheese, the sweetened fruit and the good bread, they ate well.

"See how far that humble shepherd came to make his offering? He knows that a blessing is a thing of immeasurable value," Cynan crowed.

"Or he fears a curse if he ignores you," countered Otto.

But the priest's complacency would not be shaken. "In either case, he acknowledges my power." he said.

The descended to lower ground among the woods and fields once more. As it grew dark on the evening of the ninth day since they had set out, Cynan made an announcement.

"Tomorrow we shall reach our destination. Your friend is held captive there and he will be alive, although in what condition I cannot say. You are to make yourself as inconspicuous as possible. Give your sword and subarmalis to Tud who will put them out of sight with the rest of your arms. I shall ride your horse, Tud will ride my mule and you will lead the others…"

"You seriously expect me to give up my horse and sword?" Otto demanded incredulously.

"I do."

"Cynan, I can think of three men I would trust so far and you are not one of them."

The priest stared angrily at Otto with his sly, green eyes; they seemed to glow with a yellow flame. Otto thought again of a wild cat backed up on a rock, hissing and glaring defiance.

"I have not brought you here on a whim. I have not brought you to some country market fair. We are going to enter a place where death is already waiting. Whether yours or another's is beyond my knowing. Make no mistake, Imperial Prefect Otto Longius, if you do not obey me in every detail, your friend will not see two more sunsets. Sleep on it and tell me in the morning that you agree."

The sun rose blood-red behind a low bank of cloud.

"Priest, I will do as you say but I will not make myself helpless for any man who lives. I will keep my pugio dagger behind my back under my cloak.

"Agreed," Cynan told him and they set out.

Chapter 19

They set out with Cynan in the lead mounted on the gelding, Tud on the white mule and Otto trudging after them, sweating already in the grey travelling cloak Tud had dug out of the packsaddle for him. It was too short but it did have a hood and he could cover most of his body with it. The horse was nervous with a new rider on his back. He danced across the track and tossed his head. Cynan jagged the bit into his mouth to bring him to obedience. Otto dropped the mules' lead reins and ran up. He grabbed Cynan's arm and shook him.

"No more of that, he said. "Let the beast get used to you…"

"Fool," the priest hissed at him. "Go back to your mules. Suppose we are being watched…"

The travelled into the early afternoon when they entered a broad valley. It was rich with fields of ripening grain and orchards full of green apples beginning to blush the faintest red. Much of the hay had been taken in and was stooked for drying. It would be stacked under cover before the persistent rains arrived. Herds of cattle were penned in wide pastures beside the two streams that ran through the valley. It was dominated by a hillock on which a high stockade had been built which enclosed an area large enough to house several thousand people. It was by far the largest settlement Otto had seen in this country. They passed along tracks between fields where ragged slaves worked in a lethargic way, scarcely bothering to lift their heads to watch the cavalcade pass by. As they moved closer to the towering wooden walls, Otto could see a deep ditch had been dug around them. Sharpened stakes spiked the rampart to deter attackers. It reminded him of a legion marching-camp on a grander scale. They clattered over a wooden bridge and through the open gates. Armed guards looked at them with barely veiled hostility but did not hinder their passage.

Each low, thatched house stood in its own garden, enclosed behind a straggling fence. Scrawny fowls scratched in the dust, goats or milk-ewes were tethered under apple or pear trees. The earth had been dug into strips which were now green with the top leaves of planted vegetables. Faces stared at them from dark doorways. Men and women sat on benches against their wooden or wattle and daub walls or busied themselves with the day's tasks. Some glanced up, most ignored them. Children squatted in groups absorbed in their games or ran shrieking along the roads. The whole place stank of faeces, animals, unwashed clothes and wood smoke.

The party walked up the incline along the twisting roads nearer to the centre. The gardens grew smaller. There were more workshops and traders' booths to be seen the deeper into the city they went. Cynan ordered them to halt outside a substantial inn. The owner was leaning against his doorjamb. He looked at them with a jaundiced eye. Cynan dismounted.

"Food, shelter," he demanded brusquely.

The innkeeper looked him up and down and spat. "Full up, priest. Find somewhere else," he responded. Cynan nodded and smiled. Then he raised both his arms in the air and began to chant. "No, no," the panicked man shouted, suddenly frightened that he was being cursed. "There are no rooms left, truly. I can let you have the stables…"

"Food?" Cynan repeated.

"It will be brought to you sir, please, this way..." He ushered them round the side, through a yard and into a clean and airy stable.

They unsaddled and watered the animals. A fat boy arrived straining, carrying a tray heavy with food and a flagon of ale. As he put it down, Cynan scraped up a handful of dust behind his back. When he was leaving, the priest called him to stop and watch. He muttered and sprinkled the dust across the stable entrance. It scintillated in the sunbeams as it slowly fell back to earth.

"I have called up a guardian spirit. If anyone crosses the mystic line I have drawn without my permission, he will sicken and slowly die. Tell your master. Now go," he told the awestruck boy who turned and wobbled away as fast as his legs would let him.

They stayed in the stable uninterrupted for the rest of the afternoon. The sun sank, the cloudless sky grew purple. Venus, the evening star, rose as the purple faded to black. Infinite sparks of light showed themselves in their constellations. The moon began to rise, full and yellow, a harvest moon. Cynan looked at it once or twice, waited for it climb nearer to its zenith, then he called Otto.

"You will accompany me now. Whatever you see or hear, say nothing; do not react and draw no attention to yourself. Tud will wait here. Guardian spirit or not, I do not want anyone ferreting about in our belongings."

The street they walked was so well-lit by the moon they could have been in daylight but for the lack of colour. Cynan preferred the shadowed side. Other hurrying figures passed them, all going uphill. Their street opened into the main square of the city, filled by a crowd of thousands. The timber buildings overlooking it were high, with window openings and balconies on their upper floors. People jostled for a place at every vantage point. Some had climbed up onto the roof ridges where they perched like crows. Cynan pushed his way up onto a cart at the side of the square. Otto was tall enough to see everything by standing on the wagon tree. He noted the reluctance with which people had moved aside for the priest.

An unlit log fire had been laid in the middle of the square with a wide space left free all around it. With a rumbling sound, two men trundled a huge bronze cauldron in and hoisted it up on the logs to the cheers of the onlookers. Otto saw that the front rows of the spectators were made up of women sitting cross-legged or squatting on the ground. A group of men began to shove people back to make a lane on one side. He heard the drumming of hoofbeats. A wild roar broke out from thousands of throats. The women's ululations rose above the tumult and echoed off the surrounding walls. A man riding bareback on a white horse burst into the circle. The entry lane disappeared as the crowd pushed forward and filled it once more.

The horseman cantered around the ring made by the spectators. He was heavy-set with massive shoulders and a pelt of red hair growing on his body to match his beard. His head was shaven and he was naked other than for a knife in a sheath carried on a string around his waist. He directed the horse with a jaw- rope, jerking it mercilessly as he drummed his heels into the heaving flanks, forcing it round and round in frantic circles. Otto noticed that it was a mare. A small one and young; scarcely more than a filly. She was far to fragile to carry the weight of her rider. She showed the whites of her eyes in her terror, bloody froth flying from her open mouth. She began to falter but the sawing jaw-rope, thumping heels and baying crowd would not let her rest. Finally, she came to a halt, shaking, her hide twitching; driven to the limit of her strength. She was beaten.

The man slipped off her back and raised both his arms to accept the plaudits from all sides. He strutted to the edge of the crowd and walked slowly past the women Some giggled and reached up to caress his growing erection as he brushed past them. Others cried out their willingness and offered themselves. He went right around the square and stood in the centre again, turning on the spot so all could admire his engorged, rigid penis.

The mare was breathing hard, her head hanging low, too exhausted to move from where he had left her,. He stepped behind her, raised her tail and thrust deep inside her. Once, twice, three times he thrust then his body arched and quivered as he ejaculated with a great roar, like a wild beast; a bear, a bison. He withdrew to silence from the men but cries of admiration and more wild shouts from the women. He went to the mare's head jerked it to one side with the jaw-rope and withdrew the knife from its sheath. He held it aloft; a thin sickle shining in the moonlight. He cut her throat. She collapsed without a sound.

The women rushed forward with basins to catch as much of the gushing blood as they could. The horse rider, abuser, killer climbed into the cauldron where he stood with his arms held out from his sides. They began to empty the blood over his head to the sound of chanting. The dead horse was butchered where it lay. Oozing lumps and dripping joints of meat were flung into the cauldron around the nightmare figure standing in it, his face and body black with congealing blood and his eyes glittering. They lit the fire and poured pitchers of water over him. He was helped out when the first steam swirled up and strode away through the silent crowd bowing to him as he passed.

No-one left the square. The women threw beans and cracked barley into the cauldron, they added wood to the fire beneath until it blazed. They danced around the flames in long lines singing and clapping to the rhythmic stamping of their feet; a drum sounded, shrilling pipes joined the ritual music. A smell of stewing meat began to steal across the square. Old women with long-handled ladles dipped the broth out of the pot and let it fall back until at last they were satisfied and called out to the others. The song changed. A high-backed chair was carried into the square and torches were lit.

The previously naked rider entered, dressed in a red tunic and cloak. He sat on the chair. A bowl of broth was reverently brought over to him. He put a hand in and withdrew a lump of meat which he sucked into his mouth, chewed then tipped the remaining contents of the bowl down his throat. An immense cheer blasted Otto's eardrums. He felt someone plucking at his arm. It was Cynan. He had climbed down and was hurrying away in quick purposeful strides gesturing to Otto to follow him.

He said not one word until they were back in the stable when he exploded with rage.

"You saw that abomination? You saw that sacrilege? The insult to our Goddess Epona? Does our Lady of the White Horses wish to see her symbol, humiliated, raped and slaughtered while a gang of ignorant oafs look on, whistling and cheering. They are feasting on her flesh as I speak. It is disgusting, depraved. And that man, that despicable creature now calls himself the Horse King. He did all that was done and cut her throat to make himself the Horse King, above all other men, above even the High Priests of Ynys Mon. Oh what pride, what folly! My Order will not tolerate that ceremony being performed anywhere on this island. He will not hold himself exempt from our rule! Tomorrow, Otto Longius, you will kill him!"

Otto's mouth fell open in surprise. "Why would I do that?"

"Because if you do not, the Horse King will kill your friend."

"Why…"

"Why, why, why, can you say nothing else? He is going to prove to his assembled people that he fears nothing, not even Rome, by defeating a Roman in single combat…."

"But Quintus Mucius is no warrior…"

"I take it that is the quaestor's name? It doesn't matter. No-one will care, Otto. The Horse King will have cut down a Roman; by the time the tale is told half a dozen times, Quintus Mucius will have become a giant. Now, can you kill that man?"

Otto reflected for a moment. "I do not know. It is to be seen. But I will fight him."

"Good, then let us rest."

Otto spread the cloak he had been given over a truss of straw and lay down. He wriggled around to find a comfortable position, eventually turning onto his back, gazing up at the few, faint moonbeams filtering through the stable roof. Cynan's words had given him much to think about. He recollected what the priest had said to him and things he had noticed on their journey. He smiled; he was close to composing a full picture. Tomorrow would see it finished. The combat he faced did not cause him undue worry. There had been so many of them, one more made little difference. The result would be decided as the Gods wished. He had only to fight and let them concern themselves with the outcome.

In the morning, Tud woke him with a dish of hot porridge and bacon, the first meat he had eaten since he had left the coast. He ate it greedily then went to straight to the privy.

"A man does well to empty his bowels before a fight," he explained cheerfully on his return. "Makes him lighter on his feet and stink less if his tripes are ripped out."

He walked over to the horse trough, stripped and washed himself from head to foot. Wrapped in a cloak to dry, he sat with Cynan who was in a nervous frenzy; unable to sit still without one of his knees jiggling up and down or constantly pulling at one of his earlobes or scratching his neck. Otto was as calm and unmoving as one of the standing stones on the high heathlands.

"If a man defeated the Horse King, he could rule over these people. Call himself a king if he wanted," Cynan told him. "This is a fine, populous city. Using it as a base, such a man could rule from the coast where you landed right across the country to the estuary of the great river to the west of us. Think, Otto Longius, a kingdom of your own the full breadth of the land. Of course, my Order would need to be present to advise and see to the spiritual welfare of the people. What does Rome offer in comparison? Scraps off the tables of the nobility that all the rest must fight over like the dogs they are. You will never have real power while you serve them. Think what is being held out to you here."

And with his words, the last few details dropped into place for Otto. He smiled broadly.

"Later today, I shall choose," he told the priest.

The sacrifice had been made in the full of the moon, the affirmation by force of arms would be at noon. Tud worked on the links of Otto's mail with a stiff brush and rubbed them over with an oily rag to make everything shine. He helped him dress in subarmalis, mail shirt and polished boots, then handed him his sword-belt, shield and lance. Otto settled his helmet in the crook of his left arm and smiled at the priest and his servant.

"Shall we go?"

He found it difficult not to stride ahead of Cynan who carried a peeled hazel-wood staff in his hand and wore a wreath of fresh ivy. Tud, who was with them this time, had also prepared his master for the conflict. The square was filled as it had been the night before. The cauldron had been taken away and all that remained of the fire was a patch of black ash. This time, the front rows were composed of armed men, sitting on low stools or leaning on their spears. Each of them dressed for war to a greater or lesser extent. Otto estimated that there were over five hundred of them. As Cynan had said, the core of a powerful force. The sense of anticipation among the onlookers waiting for the combatants grew to a point where the tension was almost tangible. A ripple of movement as men moved aside, and the Horse King stepped into the arena to the welcoming shouts of his followers. His small eyes under his bushy red brows flicking across the crowd judging the extent of their approval.

Otto drew in a surprised breath. The man was armoured exactly as he himself was, even to the oval cavalry shield. If he had served as a Roman auxiliary, it would make a great difference and not in Otto's favour.

A flurry opposite him marked the arrival of his opponent. There was a world of difference in the appearance of today's Quaestor Quintus Mucius from the dapper Roman nobleman Otto had met for the first time only a few weeks ago. His hair stuck out in tufts at odd angles, an uneven growth of beard covered his lower face, one side of which was swollen and discoloured. Blood encrusted one nostril and raw wheals encircled both his wrists where he had been tied up. He was thin, dirty and seemed smaller than Otto remembered. A short infantry sword was thrust into his right hand; a battered legion shield flung down at his feet. Quintus looked at the menacing figure he was to fight. He picked up the shield and slipped his left hand through the loop and took a firm hold on the grip. Trying his best to put Roman hauteur and contempt for his adversary into his expression, he stared over at the Horse King who thumped the shaft of his lance against his shield. In response, Quintus shuffled a few paces forward. Advancing his left leg, he brought his own shield up and held his sword level with the edge as he had been trained to do. His year as a junior tribune in a legion stationed at Regium in which he saw no action, meant that he knew the basic drill even if he had never used it. He looked fearlessly over at the man who would soon cut him down and tear him apart. Quintus defiantly stood his ground.

Before Otto could move, Cynan threw off his cloak and barged forward through the throng of spectators. He stood n the ring and pointed his staff at the Horse King, leaned forward resting his hands on his thighs and roared, bellowed, with laugher. When he was sure he had caught everyone's attention, he stood upright. He spoke in the Belgic tongue using the rich, full voice of a trained orator. Everyone in that square could hear every word, every syllable.

"Is it this man's blood you will spill to confirm your pretended kingship?" he called out and walked over to stand beside Quintus who understood nothing of what was going on. He tore the sword from his hand and flung it to the ground. "Why give him a sword, every man here can see his is no match for you? Why not simply kill him while he is unarmed? Because that would be murder? What else is it, sword or no? If you would fight a Roman to assert your right to your false kingship, find an opponent of your own size and strength. Measure yourself against a man like the Roman Prefect Otto Longius," he gestured to Otto who settled his helmet on his head and stepped forward.

He stood with his legs slightly apart, his lance grounded and his shield held loosely at his side. The Horse King looked from Cynan to Otto and back. He was angry. He had intended to toy with Quintus for a few minutes before ending it but now he had a serious fight on his hands. He could not back down in front of the assembled warriors he aspired to lead. He studied Otto, he took in his size but also noticed that he was twenty pounds lighter and ten years younger. A hard contest but one he was likely to win, he decided. The Horse King pulled himself up to his full height and shouted, not in Belgic but in heavily accented Latin; a second surprise for Otto.

"I am Farval, son of Berinhard. I fought for Rome as a cavalryman. Then I discovered that all Romans are weak and corrupt. Now I kill them."

"I am Otto son of Badurad, now called Otto Longius. I too fought as a Roman cavalryman but I did not break my sacred oath taken under the eagle."

Apart from Cynan and Quintus, hardly anyone understood a word of what was bring said. It did not really matter to them. They had heard the recitation of pedigree and the ritual exchange of insults before single combat many times.

"At first I thought you wore many arm rings, Otto son of Badurad. Now I see they are the bangles rich Romans buy for their sweethearts. Are you the plaything of a rich old Roman?"

"Your own arm rings are scanty but I will enjoy adding them to mine when I have killed you, Farval son of Berinhard."

"Not an easy matter to kill a king, boy," Farval snarled.

"If fucking a horse made a man into a king, every braggart with no self-respect would be one," Otto told him.

It was enough to goad him into action. Farval ran a few steps forward and hurled his lance. Otto deflected it and cast his own. It was lighter than the legionary javelin he was used to which spoiled his aim. It flew out of his hand so fast that the watching warrior saw only a dark blur in the air. It hit Farval on the boss of his helmet crest, a poor shot for Otto. The force of the strike snapped Farval's neck back and raised a grunt of appreciation from the assembled warriors. Farval heard it and was further enraged. The two men ran at each other drawing their swords and striking almost simultaneously, blade to blade. The steel rang, sparks flew. The combatants stepped back and crouched. Each had felt the force of the other's right arm. Otto knew that Farval was too strong for him; his extra weight in the chest and shoulder tipped the balance in his favour. He must move and probe and think, seeking a way to wipe out the other's advantage.

They circled, launching attack after attack, defending with shield and sword, parrying the other's blade aside, blocking and side-stepping. They had been tight-lipped to start with but now their mouths hung open in the effort to drag oxygen into their burning lungs. Sweat beaded on their eyebrows and rolled down their faces. Their feet kicked up clouds of dust around their legs. If Farval was stronger, Otto was faster; quick enough to keep him out of danger. They fought on, five minutes, ten minutes, muscles screaming, chests heaving then Otto spotted his enemy's weakness. Farval used his weapon in overhand cuts. He rarely thrust and when he did, he kept his sword arm locked and lunged forward on his right leg. It was a cavalryman's thrust, relying on the speed of his horse and leaning forward in the saddle to send it home. It was highly effective; except that now, they were fighting on foot. Otto had spent years training with infantry legionaries. He had learned their method; whipping the blade out with the strength of his right arm from the shoulder with a snap of the elbow and a twist of the wrist. It was the lightning thrust from the side of a shield that had made Rome victorious from Parthia to the German Ocean. He had to find the opportunity to perform it.

They fought on, hacking crudely at each other now as fatigue took its toll. The onlookers shuffled on their stools or leaned forward on their spears, knowing the crisis was imminent. Farval aimed a blow at the side of Otto's neck. It was a fraction slow and gave Otto his chance. He took it on his shield but instead of counter cutting, he cocked his elbow and launched a straight thrust at Farval's face. The blade entered under his left cheekbone and as Otto twisted his wrist to withdraw, it smashed Farval's upper-jaw and destroyed his hearing on that side. Blood welled out and he began to go into shock. Unconsciously he let his shield drop and a second thrust burst through his chain mail into his chest below the collarbone. Blood bubbled at the corners of his lips and he fell. Silence followed the clatter of his armoured body crashing into the ground.

Otto knew that he had to act swiftly now or all would be lost. He did not know how well supported Farval had been among the people of this city. He raised his dripping sword and walked to the edge of the crowd. He drew a deep breath, feeling his heart pound as adrenalin still flooded his bloodstream,

"What do you call the man who kills the Horse King?" he shouted in Belgic, to Cynan's combined astonishment and fury. There was no response so he answered his own question. "You call him the King! Does any man wish to dispute my right? What do you call the man who kills the Horse King?" This time a few voices shouted, "The King!" back at him. He went round the circle yelling his challenge and demanding their response until the whole square resounded with voices chanting, "The King! The King! The King!".

He drummed his sword against his shield for silence.

"Let no man enter this circle unless he is called," he proclaimed then switched to Latin. "Greetings Quintus Mucius, would you care to join me?" With a foolish smile on his face, still not quite sure if he was dreaming, Quintus limped over. "Just hold on to your courage for a little longer and we shall be out of here, he muttered. He placed one hand on the quaestor's shoulder and reverted to Belgic. "This Roman is the grandson of the great general Julius Caesar. The priest Cynan and I must return him to his own people before a Roman army comes to massacre every man, woman and child in this city. They will slaughter all your livestock and burn your homes and barns to the ground. You know they have done such things elsewhere. It was a grave error to bring him here but if he is returned unharmed, I will obtain mercy for you."

The name of the Divine Julius still had enough force to strike fear, even though so much time had passed since his death. A low mumble of approval rose from the crowd.

"One of you fetch me Farval's two best horses, saddled and bridled, now!" Otto barked.

A young man stood up at the back of the crowd and jogged through one of the entrances of the square. Otto stripped the dead man of his ornaments and picked up his sword.

"Who is the wisest among you? Which man among you is best fitted to lead this city? I will wait while you decide."

A concentrated discussion broke out and went on for several minutes but Otto could see most eyes and pointing fingers were aimed at one older man, dignified in appearance, well dressed and armed, obviously of high rank. At the insistence of the crowd he stood up.

"Stand forward," Otto commanded him.

He walked over, boldly but without swaggering. Two horses were led in. A heavily muscled bay charger, snorting and stamping his hooves and a leggy, mouse-coloured mare, a riding horse. Otto put the late Horse King's sword in the man's hand and helped him up onto the back of the charger.

"You have elected this man to govern your city. I share my spoils with him to show he had the authority of the new King. Obey his lawful commands. Now I must leave for a short while to take the Roman back to his people."

Half an hour later, Otto had paid the incredulous innkeeper for what they and their animals had already eaten. He handed over something extra for provisions loaded onto one of the pack-mules for their journey and they left through the gate by which they had first entered the city.

Quintus, mounted on Farval's riding horse, was too stunned to talk. Cynan was in a sullen, bitter rage. Otto was cheerful, singing and whistling as they rode along, Tud trotted behind with a broad smile on his face.

That night they made camp beside a pool in a babbling steam. Quintus stripped and washed himself while Tud scrubbed his tunic and loin cloth. Tud boiled up some water and shaved him before applying an ointment to his battered face. Wearing almost clean fire-dried clothes, Quintus began to look like his previous self although his hollow cheeks showed that he had lost a lot of weight. Bread soaked in warmed, honeyed wine revived him even more. He could tell next to nothing of his kidnap. He was walking towards the trading post when a sack was thrown over his head, he was hit in the face and passed out.

He came to, still hooded, lashed onto the back of a horse. Wrists tied, lying in a dirty shed, kicks, mouldy bread and foul water. Punches, cold porridge and then being marched into the centre of a throng of fierce barbarians. The rest they all knew.

"How long will it take to get back to the port?" he asked.

"Three days at most," Otto told him.

Cynan glared. Otto laughed.

"Let me tell you my tale, Quintus…"

"Wait a little before you do," Quintus said and wandered off among the trees. He returned a few minutes later. He had made a wreath of freshly picked oak laves. He placed it on Otto's head.

"Imperial Prefect Otto Longius, you have saved my life today. I, Quaestor Quintus Mucius proclaim your courage and present you with this civic crown. The Emperor will hear of this and you have my undying gratitude, my dear friend. Now, tell me your story…"

"This man, Cynan the Priest led me to you. But before you express your thanks, you might like to know it was for his own reasons. You and I were supposed to be the means by which he re-established the dominance of his priestly order. He spun the journey out over ten days so that we would arrive on the night of the full moon and the ceremony. The warrior I fought had been proclaimed the Horse King and he needed to kill a Roman to show how brave he was. You happened to be in the wrong place at the wrong time; it was nothing personal. Did you think I didn't know what you were doing Cynan?

What really gave away your ruse is when we crossed the same river twice in different directions. That's all there is to say…"

"Except, Otto Longius, in your stupidity you have turned your back on a kingdom…." Cynan snarled.

"Oh yes; I nearly forgot," Otto continued, talking to Quintus once more, "I am now the king of that city where you were held captive. Our friend the priest wanted me to rule as his puppet but I prefer to stick to my oath."

He turned to Cynan. "You insinuated and flattered and finally asked me to choose. So hear my choice. It is Rome. You are a clever man Cynan but like a lot of intelligent people, you underestimate the rest of us. Did you ask if I could speak Belgic? No. Did you not consider that I might be able to find my direction by the sun and the stars? No. You have partially succeeded; the Horse King is dead. Be content with that."

At the coast, eight days of careful grooming by his body-servant and regular meals restored Quintus to his former elegance. They sailed on sparkling sapphire seas to where the land rose presenting them with soaring white cliffs. Dubrae was in an inlet and from there they were conveyed to the court of the Cantiari King. Praetor Quintus Mucius was the picture of Roman nobility as he stood in front of the king in his capital and presented the gold-framed cameo portrait of Augustus. The king was delighted and gave a gigantic pure-white wolf pelt in return.

"My king knows that the Emperor has given him a fabulous treasure but we believe the wolf is the totem animal of all Romans and he humbly offers this skin with that in mind," the translator told Quintus who replied that there could be nothing more thoughtful or that would please the Emperor more.

The quaestor with his translator and his secretary spent a day in talks ostensibly aimed at cementing the mutual ties between Rome and the Cantiari but really to make the tribesmen feel more important to the Emperor than they truly were. Otto was left at a at a loose end. The nobles of the king's court were curious about him. The younger warriors in particular had envied his fine parade armour, his medals and trophies. They plucked up the courage to ask questions.

"How can you be a Roman? You don't look like the rest of them?" one asked by means of another translator.

"I was born in Upper Germany but the Emperor himself made me a Roman."

"And an officer?"

"I commanded over five hundred cavalrymen with lower-rank officers under me."

"Were these men also Romans? "

"Indeed they were," Otto replied. "But I am nothing special. Any man in the Empire can rise as high in the service of Rome if he is loyal and steadfast…."

As he said these words, Otto saw with a flash of clarity why he had been chosen to accompany Quintus. He made sure that he sang the praises of Rome and the Emperor every time he could from then on.

Their duty done, they took ship again, waved off from the quay by a group of young Cantiari nobles.

At Gesoriacum, after a voyage of less than a day under fair skies, they set foot on the mainland once more. The boats were paid off with a little extra for the skippers by way of thanks for accommodating Farval's riding horse.

Despatches were sent ahead to Rome. It was arranged that the legionaries would escort the servants and baggage as far as Luca by road. They would return to barracks; the quaestor would organise his people's onward transport from Luca to Rome. Otto lined up his men on the quayside and presented everyone with an arm ring taken from the Horse King.

"In token of service overseas," he told them. "Literally overseas; storms and all!"

He and Quintus used the Imperial Courier Service to hasten their own journey to Rome, the others would catch up, eventually. The news of their success had preceded them and by the time they arrived the city was buzzing with the story.

This time, Otto not was received by the Emperor in the intimate room leading on to the garden terrace but in a grand audience chamber, pillared in marble and floored with mosaics of the triumphal Gods.

Some old friends and fifty of Rome's influential men stood along the walls at either side of the chair of state occupied by Augustus. Otto was pleased to notice his first commanding officer, Publius Quadratus, among the throng standing beside his old comrade Soranus with his maimed hand and the exquisitely uniformed and turned-out Praetorian, Cassius Plancus. He halted, came to attention and bowed to the Emperor. Quaestor Quintus Mucius was already there with a scroll in his hand. He bowed his head and began to read an abbreviated but florid account of their adventure in Britain. When he finished, he rolled up the parchment and bowed again.

"Do you have anything to add, Imperial Prefect Otto Longius?" the Emperor asked.

"Yes sir, I do. Quaestor Quintus Mucius is the bravest man I have ever seen. He looked without fear at Farval the Horse King, a bear of a man, sir. Without disrespect to the noble Quintus Mucius, he had no chance of surviving the combat, let alone winning. But there he stood, sword and shield in the ready position, defying his enemy to do his worst. You would have been proud to see it sir, I am sure."

Quintus squared his shoulders and his father who was, unknown to Otto, standing next to Cassius Plancus, beamed with paternal pride.

"And yet you killed this fearsome Horse King. In the habit of killing kings, Otto Longius, are you?" Augustus enquired, his expressive eyes suddenly cold and piercing.

"Kings are of no account in Rome, sir, where we are guided by The Father of the People," Otto replied, holding the Emperor's gaze.

Of all the honours and titles awarded to Augustus, the one he held dearest was that; "The Father of the People". He smiled broadly and wagged a finger at Otto as if to say, "Don't flatter me!" but he was delighted all the same. He stood up and held out his right hand. An official placed a golden oak leaf wreath in it.

"Imperial Prefect Otto Longius take this civic crown awarded to you for saving the life of a fellow citizen. Although it is passed to you by my hand, the family of Quintus Mucius had it made at their expense to thank you for what you have done."

He leaned forward and as he did so he whispered, "Well done again, lad," before passing the wreath over to Otto who put it on his head to general applause. Friends crowded round and congratulated him while the Emperor looked benignly on. After a few minutes a steward called them to order. Formal silence was restored.

"Gentlemen, this is how affairs of state should be carried out; with mutual support, with courage and seen through to the end. I commend them both. Otto Longius, return to your duties as Imperial Prefect stationed in Luca. Your Emperor's personal reward awaits you outside. Menities will explain."

A few days later as the afternoon sun slanted across the garden and into the house, Lollia lay back in her reclining chair. The filet of gold oak leaves on her head had slipped forward over her left eyebrow.

She looked at the open chest of gold coins placed at her feet and over at Otto with a contented smile on her lips. He was leaning over a cot staring down in wonder at his first child.

The End

I hope that you have enjoyed reading this book.. Please mention it on social media or leave an Amazon review. I have suggested more of my fiction which you may like on the following page.

Thank you for your support.

Regards,

Malcolm Davies

(Contact me at: malcolmdav46@outlook.com.

Best Books by Malcolm Davies on Facebook.

My website is www.malcolm-davies.com.)

The Butterfly Fool Part One

Being an account of the Remarkable Early Life of Mr. Augustus Reynolds of Split Water City, Montana Territory. How he came to leave the Country Of His Birth to travel to the Frontier of the United States of America. His Thrilling Voyages by Steamboat up the great Mississippi and Missouri Rivers. His Dangerous Encounter with a Savage and Fearsome Blackfoot Chief. How he Comported himself in Mortal Combats with Ferocious Wild Beasts and Brigands. And the Many, Remarkable and Diverse Characters he met on his journeys. Also the History of Miss Charlotte Reynolds, Sister of the Above who Heroically accompanied Her Brother on his Adventure. How an English Gentlewoman fared in the Wilderness with neither Cook nor Maid. Her Primitive Domestic Economy. A Romantic Attachment which would have distressed the Many Friends she had left at Home. In Addition, how the Thriving Metropolis of Split Water City rose from the Plains. Its Rude Beginnings and First Development.

The Butterfly Fool Part Two

The Second and Final Volume Depicting the Exploits and Times of Mr. Augustus Reynolds the Celebrated Frontiersman, his Family and Friends. A Theft and Pursuit across the Vastness of the American Prairies. Retribution upon the Felons. Confrontations with Fierce Natives. A Hunt for the Indigenous Bison. A Violent Death followed by Remorse. The Moral Repugnance of Mrs. Reynolds at developments in Split Water City, Metropolis of the Plains. The Arrival of the Mechanical Wonders of our Age in the Remote Wilderness. Celebration of the American Public Holiday known as "The Fourth of July". Wonder at the Resilience of The Inhabitants of The Far Western Territories. Thrill to the Dangers Faced and Overcome by Them with Undaunted Steadfastness

Willy Maddox Went To Texas

Coming off a cattle drive from Split Water City to St. Louis, young Willy Maddox has a bitter quarrel with his cousin Ed which changes the course of his life. Willy is in the wrong of it but for all he cares, Ed can go home on his own; he would rather ride off south with his two new friends, heading for Texas. At twenty years old Willy believes he can handle anything that life throws at him. He has already learned the ranching trade up in Montana, endured the rigours of a long cattle-drive and fended off stock-thieves. What could Texas show him he had not seen before? So, what did Texas show Willy Maddox? Only outlaws, deserts, blizzards blowing up out of nowhere, renegade Comanche and worse but also great opportunity, transforming new technologies and finally, his journey's end. (Willy Maddox first appears in "The Butterfly Fool Part Two", the sequel to "The Butterfly Fool Part One".)

Printed in Great Britain
by Amazon